Pirates

&

Privateers

The Intelligencers ⚓ Book One

By

Jane Glatt

Other books by Jane Glatt:

The Conjurers Series:
The Bookbinder's Daughter
The Shaman's Son

The Mage Guild Series:
Unguilded
Unmagic
The Unmage

The Intelligencers Series:
Pirates & Privateers
Traits & Traitors (January 2019)

PIRATES & PRIVATEERS

The Intelligencers ⚓ Book One

By

Jane Glatt

TYCHE BOOKS LTD.

Published by Tyche Books Ltd.
Calgary, Alberta, Canada
www.TycheBooks.com

Cover Art & Design by Indigo Chick Designs
Interior Layout by Ryah Deines
Editorial by Karley Hauser

First Tyche Books Ltd Edition 2018
Print ISBN: 978-1-928025-97-9
Ebook ISBN: 978-1-928025-98-6

Author photograph: Eugene Choi
Echo1 Photography

This book was funded in part by a grant from the Alberta Media Fund.

For Mirella and Elizabeth, the girls next door who inspired
me to write about twins and the many ways they are - and are
not – alike.

CHAPTER 1

"Debrief, my office."

Dagrun turned to see Joosep Sepp, her boss, standing in the corridor.

"I'll be there in a moment," Dagrun said. "I just need to let Inger know I'm back." Dag's first assignment as an Intelligencer had meant she'd been away for almost a month. She and Inger, her twin, had never been separated for so long.

"Now, Dagrun!" Joosep's normally expressionless features twisted into a scowl, and Dag suppressed a frown.

Something wasn't right; she itched between her shoulder blades as though her Trait had been triggered. Had *Joosep* done something that he didn't want her to know about? She resisted the urge to roll her shoulders—Joosep would know what that meant.

"Sure," Dag said. She turned away from the hallway that led to her and Inger's suite of rooms and fell in step beside Joosep.

Silently, he shepherded her to his office, a space she always thought of as the centre of the spider web: partly because of the way the corridors that led to it circled around, but mostly because it was the office of the spymaster for the Fair Seas Treaty Alliance.

She stepped into his office and sat down while he settled into his familiar chair behind the desk. Dag plucked at the rough fabric of the domestic servant disguise she still wore, the light grey fabric washing out her pale skin. This was her first debrief, but didn't Joosep usually allow Intelligencers a chance to clean up and change first? Why was he making her debrief immediately after returning to the Hall? Especially since her news was so inconsequential she doubted anyone other than Joosep would hear it.

"Report," Joosep said. He centred a sheaf of paper in front of him and picked up a quill and dipped it into a bottle of ink.

"I can confirm that Clan Freeholder Timonis believes that he will become the next Grand Freeholder," Dag said.

Joosep wrote a few things down before looking up at her. "Did your Trait uncover any opposition?"

"No one I came into contact with believed differently," she replied. "They all expect Timonis to win. But I was only a maid. I did take the coats of a few people who were hiding something from Timonis, but it wasn't about his election to Grand Freeholder."

"And you know what they were hiding?"

"Of course." Dagrun's Trait—Unseen—meant that anything being hidden was soon exposed to her. Most of the time she didn't have to do anything other than note the clues. Like Joosep stopping her from seeing Inger. "One woman was having an affair with Timonis' brother, and a couple of his business partners are cheating him."

"Very good," Joosep said. He dipped the quill into the ink again and wrote a few more sentences. He looked up. "You can include their names when you write your report. It's due by the end of the day tomorrow. You can go."

Dagrun didn't move. Something was going on and she wasn't leaving until Joosep told her what it was. Eventually he looked up at her, and she could feel the defeat coming off of him.

"Something's happened to Inger," Dag said. "What."

"I can't hide anything from you," Joosep said and sighed.

"Why would you need to?" She was shocked: because he knew how strong her Trait was, Joosep had never before tried to hide anything from her. "What about Inger?"

"She's gone," Joosep said. "She's left the Hall and she didn't go home. I've had people out looking all over North Tarklee, but no one knows where she went."

"When!?" Her sister wouldn't go *home*, even Joosep knew

that. Their mother had remarried and moved to her new husband's farm near Falkis. Dagrun didn't bother hiding her anger just as she didn't bother asking why her sister had left. Her Trait meant she'd learn why. She *already* knew Joosep was somehow behind her sister's disappearance.

"A week ago."

Dagrun's heart sank and her anger rose. "You're saying that my sister has been missing for a week and no one bothered to inform me?" She stood up, her hands balled into fists at her side. "And it wasn't the first thing you mentioned to me when I got home." She wasn't sure why Joosep had done that. What was he hoping to gain? And Inger!

"You know how vulnerable she is!" Dag continued. "And that I'm the best person to find her." As twins, she and Inger had opposite Traits. Just as Dagrun was Unseen and nothing could hide from her, Inger was Seen. Not only was she *always* noticed, but she took people at face value. She wasn't stupid, not by any stretch, but she couldn't see underlying motives. That made her susceptible to believing every lie she was told.

"You were on assignment," Joosep said calmly. Too calmly. What was he still trying to hide? "And Inger isn't my responsibility. You and the rest of the Intelligencers are."

"Who was the last person to see her?" Dag asked. Responsible for Inger or not, her Trait was telling her that Joosep had played a part in her disappearance. The way he was acting made her suspect that he might even be the cause. For him to be so calm meant that he either didn't think Dagrun would figure out what part he'd played, or he thought she wouldn't act on the knowledge of his involvement.

He was wrong on both accounts. She would do *anything* for Inger, including making an enemy of the Master Intelligencer. And if Inger was hurt—or worse—then no one even partly responsible for her disappearance would be safe from her anger.

"She was last seen in the Hall by one of the younger students," Joosep said. "As soon as I heard that you were back, I sent word for him to meet you outside your rooms."

"All right." It was unusual for Joosep to have her speak to a student from a different training group; the students were usually kept separate so that only Joosep knew them all. And what their Traits were.

Except Dagrun already knew them all because of her Trait. She kept her anger in check as she left Joosep's office, but as soon as the door was closed, she broke into a run.

The younger student, Vilis, a boy of about sixteen, was waiting outside of her door, and Dagrun practically pushed him into the apartment's main living area.

"Tell me everything," Dag said as she rushed into her bedroom. She rummaged through her clothes, pulling out a pair of dark trousers and matching dark shirt. "I can't hear you!" she called out as she changed. "How do you know it was Inger?"

"I've seen her before," he replied, and Dag grunted. Inger's Trait made her hard to miss.

"When did you see her? I need details."

"She was crying," Vilis said. "But she didn't want help, when I asked her."

"Where was this?" Dag asked. She grabbed her pack from the hook beside the door and shoved a few things in it: a coin purse, a change of clothes, and some fresh socks. She pulled on her boots and headed back into the main room. Vilis was staring at the floor, and Dag stopped.

"Where was this?" Dag asked again, quietly.

Vilis looked up and met her gaze.

"And I want the truth, not whatever lie you were told to tell me." Dag crossed her arms over her chest, ignoring the itch between her shoulders. Her Trait had been triggered; most likely because Joosep had asked Vilis to lie to her. She didn't know *why*. Not yet.

"What do you mean?" Vilis asked but he flushed, and Dag didn't think it was from anger . . . it seemed like it was more from embarrassment at being caught out so easily.

"You won't get past my Trait," Dag said. "So, don't bother trying. My Trait is as strong as any can be." Only a triplet could have a stronger Trait than a twin, and even then, it was only if both of the other siblings had the opposite Trait.

"I already know Joosep told you to tell me a lie," she continued, "although I don't understand why he'd ever think you could fool me. Unless . . ." *Unless he wants me to believe the second thing that Vilis tells me.* "Where did you see my sister; when she was crying, where was she?" What was Vilis's Trait? Joosep would only have sent the boy if his Trait meant that even *she* should believe him.

"She was coming out of your training team's dining hall," Vilis said. "At least that's what Joosep asked me to tell you."

Dag sighed. Even without her Trait she would have known this was false. Inger wasn't an Intelligencer; she would never feel comfortable eating in the dining hall without Dag. "And the truth?"

"She was coming from the hallway that leads to where one of the older training teams live," Vilis said, hanging his head. "Older than mine, I mean. I think she must have had a fight with one of them."

"How do you know who lives there?" she asked. Students knew there were other students, but for the most part they didn't actually know each other. Unless their Trait revealed them the way hers had.

"I've seen a few of them," Vilis said. "In Joosep's office."

Dag stared at the boy. It sounded reasonable: Joosep obviously trusted Vilis for some things, perhaps he had been in his office.

Vilis looked up and met Dag's eyes, looking a little defeated, a little like he'd known that somehow this would get him into trouble but that he felt compelled to tell Dag the truth.

"Who was it?" Dag asked. "Which student was she fighting with?" She could feel that there was *some* truth to this, a truth that Vilis didn't even realize he was telling her.

Someone had upset her sister, but she didn't think it was a student. She also didn't think Vilis was lying about everything. He really *had* seen Inger; Joosep knew she would have immediately recognized that as a lie.

"She didn't say," Vilis said.

Dag stared at him. A student's Trait was their secret to tell or not tell, even to their training team. Only Joosep knew everyone's trait, or so he thought—so they *all* thought. But Dag's Trait meant that she'd figured them all out ages ago.

And now she remembered what Vilis's Trait was: Trust.

"Right," Dag said. "Now tell me where she really was." She crossed the floor until she stood eye to eye with the youth. "I know you're lying."

Vilis looked up in confusion.

"I know you're lying," Dag repeated. "Despite your

Trustworthiness." She wanted—*needed*—to get going so she could find Inger, but looking in the wrong place would consume even more time than she was spending on this. "Where was she really?" *And why doesn't Joosep want me to know?*

"How do you know about my Trait?" Vilis asked. He was pale now and looked worried.

"I know everyone's Trait," Dag replied, "the same way I know most things. Because of *my* Trait. Now tell me where she was!"

Dag thought she might have to resort to force—never the best way to get information—but she would do it for Inger. After a moment, Vilis swallowed and looked away.

"I was running an errand for Joosep," he said. "I did see her and she was upset and she was in a hallway." He turned to face her. "But she was coming out of Tarmo Holt's office."

"Holt!" Dag shut her mouth. She didn't want Vilis to tell Joosep how shocked she was by this, but Holt? He was the head of Nordmere's Freeholders and currently the Grand Freeholder for the three Fair Seas Treaty countries. And Joosep's boss. What was Inger doing there?

"Yes, Holt," Vilis said. "Can I go now?"

"Sure, go ahead and report to Joosep." Concern flitted across Vilis's face. "Don't worry," Dag continued. "I won't tell him you told me the actual truth. And it will be a good chance to put your Trait to the test, don't you think? To see if your Trustworthiness convinces the Master Intelligencer?"

Vilis's eyes narrowed, but he turned and left the room. The door closed quietly behind him.

Tarmo Holt. What did he want from Inger?

Dag spun on her heels and headed to her sister's room. She'd check to see if Inger had left a clue to where she'd gone, but Dag didn't hold out much hope. Her sister didn't have the ability to leave a subtle clue, so anything overtly out of place would have already been seen by anyone Joosep had sent after her.

The bed was neatly made and her sister's clothes were stacked and hung in the cupboards and closets. Nothing looked like it didn't belong.

It didn't seem like Inger had left in a rush, at least not from here, which made Dag believe she'd left on her own and with a plan.

She sat down on the bed and took a deep breath. Ok, Inger had a plan and because of her Trait, it would be an obvious one. Obvious to Dag if she knew *why* she'd gone.

But she did know it involved both Tarmo Holt and Joosep. Holt wanted something from Inger, and Joosep had tried to help him get it.

But what? Sex? That seemed too obvious. Inger was always being approached by men—and a few women—because they thought she was beautiful, which always made Dag shake her head. They were twins, identical twins, so if Inger was beautiful, then so was she. But because of her Trait, Inger was noticed. Always. It also meant that she'd had plenty of practice turning down unwanted advances. So maybe Tarmo Holt didn't want to take no for an answer. What part did Joosep play?

Skit! Joosep was her boss: he had power over her. He must have threatened to do something to *her* if Inger didn't do what Holt wanted. And because of her Trait, Inger would never be able to pretend to cooperate long enough for Dag to return.

Inger's choice—the most obvious choice—would be to leave. She would also know that Dag would follow her.

Dag scanned the room. What was missing? What had Inger taken with her?

She opened a closet. Her sister's weatherproof gear was gone, as were her boots, trousers, and plain shirts. She flipped through the dresses: every single dress was here.

She slammed the cupboard door shut and headed out to the living area. She knew where to start, at least: the docks. Inger had taken clothing suitable for wearing at sea.

JOOSEP EYED VILIS as he stood in front of his desk.

"She believed that you saw her sister outside a student's room," he said. Vilis nodded. "Good." He didn't want Dagrun to be angry with him: she and her Trait were far too valuable. Especially now that she'd finally reached the end of her ten-year training period. He sighed and waved Vilis away, and the boy quietly left his office.

He rubbed a hand over his close-cropped hair. Dagrun's value was the reason for this mess in the first place. He never should have told Tarmo Holt about Dagrun's Trait and how strong it was. All he'd wanted was for Holt to have confidence in his ability to find out more about the Freeholder Swyford would choose as the next Grand Freeholder. He'd told himself that Holt's position meant he deserved to know a few secrets. Not only was Holt Nordmere's Clan Freeholder, he was also the Grand Freeholder. At least until the election in the fall.

But once the man had learned of Dagrun's Trait, Holt had been trying to convince Joosep that Dagrun should report directly to him. That could not be allowed: Intelligencers could not become the personal spies for any single Freeholder, no matter how powerful they might be.

Joosep had finally persuaded Holt that Dagrun would see through him anyway; that it wouldn't take her more than a few days to uncover all of his secrets. That's when the man had started to focus on Inger. Not that he wanted her specific skills: he'd ridiculously spoken about having her bear children with useful Traits. Even Joosep's weak Unseen Trait could see that Holt was hoping for children with Traits that *he* would control.

Joosep had finally agreed to help him: to have Inger talk to him, but only because any children with Traits would be his to train no matter who fathered them.

Apparently, he'd made a terrible miscalculation. Inger had run away, and worse, Holt had finally admitted to him that he'd threatened to have Dagrun sent on dangerous missions if Inger didn't do what he wanted. Holt didn't have the power to do that, but Inger wouldn't realize that. Because of her Trait, she *couldn't* realize it.

Joosep blew out a breath and started tidying his desk. He put the notes he'd written from Dagrun's report in a pile to be filed. He'd talk to her tomorrow, when she'd calmed down a little. Maybe she would even have found her sister by then and things could get back to normal.

Because Dagrun was right about that; she was the one who would be able to find Inger.

DAG TURNED A corner, staying in the shadow of a warehouse. She paused to survey the dark hulks of barges that were tied up at the docks. Barges ferried goods that arrived on ships up the Dareveth River to the warehouses that lined both sides of the river. The two cities, North and South Tarklee, straddled the Dareveth, each one the capital of a different country.

Beyond the barges, the sea going ships huddled in the

harbour, their dark shapes contrasting with the light grey of the Pale Sea. Glacier run-off and silt from chalky cliffs gave the sea its name although beyond the shoreline the water was differing shades of blue, depending on the season. Right now, in summer, the sea farther out would be dark.

A few lanterns shone along the dock, and every once in a while, the low rumble of voices from a tavern or card game drifted to her.

Movement on one of the unlit docks caught her eye: a glint of moonlight on a shiny belt buckle, maybe. Was it her Trait showing her where to look?

Someone in a long coat stepped off the dock that paralleled the shoreline onto a smaller pier that jutted out into the sea. A small dinghy bobbed in the water and a second person crouched beside it. The coated figure stopped and leaned over something behind them on the dock. That's when Dag saw two smaller figures hanging onto the coat. The person on the dock stooped and one by one, placed the children—it could only be children—into the dinghy. Once they'd stepped in and settled in the middle of the boat, the second person threw something—a rope, she thought—into the boat and shoved it out from the dock, jumping in as it glided away.

Dag was trying to decide if she had time to run down the dock and jump into the dinghy when she heard a cough. Someone stepped out of a shadow and slowly walked to shore.

Dag took one last look at the dinghy: one of the occupants had found some oars and it was silently being rowed out to sea. She tracked its path to a ship that was out beyond the rest that sheltered in the harbour. Then she stepped out of the shadows to follow the person still on land.

She was beside the person—an older woman—before she was even noticed.

"Heya," the woman said. "What are you doing, sneaking around like that?"

"I was about to ask you the same thing," Dag said. She stepped forward and pulled her patch from her pocket. It was just a small piece of fabric with the emblem of the Fair Seas Treaty Alliance on it. She didn't expect the woman to recoil the way she did.

"I don't want trouble," the woman said. "I didn't do nothing wrong."

"I just need information," Dag replied. She didn't actually have any authority on the docks; at least she didn't think she did, but this woman didn't have to know that. "Who were those children and where are they going?"

The woman stared at her for a moment and then she sighed. She was younger than Dag had first thought, but she was thin and her face was lined with old despair.

"Something this city places no value on," the woman said. "Children with no homes or families. Mostly girls, left to starve in the street, or suffer abuse unless someone with a kind heart takes them." She spat towards the city.

"Takes them where?" Dag asked. Had Inger been taken like this? Is this what her Trait was showing her?

"To where they can't be used by people who don't care whether they live or die as long as coin can be made off them," the woman said. "Poor little innocents deserve better than that, and I help them get it."

"Where do you send them?" Dag asked quietly. "And who takes them from you?"

"The privateers take them and they give them good lives. Better than they'd have here, leastways."

"Privateers," Dag repeated. They liked to call themselves that, but her instructors said they were pirates who robbed ships that travelled through the Frozen Pass. She didn't know much about them. "How do you know? That they have better lives?"

"'Cause they come back to thank me," the woman said. "Three of 'em have come back to thank me: and to take any new little ones away with 'em."

"Like tonight," Dag said. "How often? How often do they come?"

"When they can," the woman said. "I find the children and keep 'em fed and safe until the privateers show up. They pay me for my trouble, which helps since the little ones are so hungry when I find 'em."

Wrong question, Dag thought. That wasn't going to help her find Inger. "Do they take older people?" she asked. "My age?"

The woman peered at her as though she was seeing her for the first time.

"Might be," she said. "Why?"

"My sister is missing and I need to find her," Dag said,

wondering if anyone Joosep sent had even talked to anyone in the harbour. He'd said he had people looking for Inger but who? And where had they actually looked? "A week ago, so I've been told. I was away." She wasn't sure she'd ever forgive Joosep for that.

The woman stared at her for a moment before she nodded. "There was a young woman," she said. "Could be a week ago."

"She went with the pir . . . privateers?"

"Yeah, though she weren't in the same circumstances as most people who go. She was prepared. Had a warm coat and all."

"The same privateers who are on that ship out there?" Dag asked, pointing to the ship. There were a couple of more lights on it now; was it getting ready to set sail?

"The same."

"Thank you." Dag had already started to run before she finished speaking. She couldn't afford to miss boarding this ship, not when it might be her only chance to follow Inger to wherever she was. She headed right toward a small dinghy that was tied up nearby, and in moments she was awkwardly rowing towards the ship.

She wasn't an experienced rower, and keeping the dinghy pointed in the right direction took all of her concentration. Every time she paused to look over her shoulder, the boat drifted off track and she had to pull on one oar to get back on course. Eventually, she made it into the shadow of the ship's prow.

She stared up at the ship, trying to determine the best way to board it. She heard shouts and saw figures scrambling up the masts in response. White sails dropped and billowed in the faint breeze. But no one looked down, or if they did, they didn't see Dag in her small boat. Her Trait at work, she assumed.

She managed to maneuver the dinghy close enough to grab a rope that looped over the side of the prow. Standing precariously on the seat, she hauled herself up, wrapping her legs around the rope and shimmying up it. She slipped over the gunwale and dropped to the deck of the ship. Unnoticed, she made her way to an upturned dinghy. She slid under it while the activity of setting sail went on around her.

Eventually, the shouted orders came less frequently, and the sounds that reached Dag quieted to creaking wood and flapping sails. She lay down and stared at the deck just beyond the dinghy but no feet appeared and no faces peeked under to find her. She wasn't surprised that she hadn't been seen, but that didn't mean she wasn't relieved.

CHAPTER 2

JOOSEP REACHED FOR his office door and paused. The door was ajar; someone was here. He gently pushed the door open a few inches wider and leaned into the room. A familiar head of hair caused him to sigh, and he opened the door completely.

"This is a private office, you know," Joosep said.

Tarmo Holt, seated in front of Joosep's desk, turned and scowled at him.

"And this is a conversation that needs privacy," Holt said. "Where have you been, Master Intelligencer? Gathering intelligence for me, I hope?"

"I was here late into the night," Joosep said as he skirted both the desk and Tarmo Holt, to sit in his chair. He scanned the desktop and relaxed; there was nothing out in the open that the Grand Freeholder shouldn't be privy to, but it didn't mean that from now on he wouldn't lock up all his paperwork, along with his office. "Dealing with the report of one of my Intelligencers."

"Yes, yes," Holt said. "The Lund girl. That's why I'm here. Has she found her sister?"

"If she has I haven't been told," Joosep said, wondering why that was Holt's first concern. Had he already looked through the report on Clan Freeholder Timonis? "It's only mid-morning; surely you aren't expecting her to work quite so quickly?"

"But isn't that her Trait? To find the Unseen?"

"To see the Unseen," Joosep corrected. "Seeing Unseen clues that point to where her sister can be found is very different from *finding* her. It could take time." Again, Joosep regretted telling Holt about the Lund sisters' Traits. "And you agreed that if Inger Lund declined your proposal that you would give up this plan."

"She didn't decline me," Holt replied.

"She ran away. I think that is a very definite no. You must drop this."

"Why should I?" Holt asked.

"What use is it? The soonest you can be named Grand Freeholder again is in another six years. Even if Inger Lund had agreed to have a child, it would barely be old enough to know what Trait, if any, it had. There is no way that could help you."

"I suppose you're right," Holt said and stood up. "I am sorry for taking up your time. Please let me know when the Lund girl is found."

Joosep stared at the door for a long time after Holt had left. What was the man planning? He hadn't even asked about Swyford's choice of Grand Freeholder: the whole reason for Dagrun's mission. And it seemed he hadn't given up on Inger Lund. Or . . . had he set his sights on Dagrun?

He leaned back in his chair and frowned. He almost wished he'd let Tarmo Holt try to recruit Dagrun because she would have quickly discovered what his true goal was, and that was something Joosep dearly wanted to know. He cursed his Unseen Trait for being so weak: his Trait was the main reason why he'd always felt he was such a good Master Intelligencer, but it seemed it was not strong enough to help him uncover Tarmo Holt's intentions.

In the meantime, he needed to see what information Dagrun had found about Inger's whereabouts. She must have found something by now. He'd also remind her to write her report. In his opinion the discipline of reporting was one of the fundamentals of spying; no matter what his people were dealing with, the records had to be kept current.

Mid-afternoon, hours after he'd sent Arnor to find Dagrun, his assistant burst into his office.

"She's gone," Arnor said, panting. "Dagrun hasn't been seen by anyone since she talked to Vilis."

"Calm down," Joosep said. "She's just not been noticed, that's all." Her Trait meant that she was rarely noticed; that had to be the explanation. "Where have you looked?"

As Arnor went through an exhaustive list of places he'd looked and people he'd spoken to, Joosep started to get an uneasy feeling. First Inger and now Dagrun. Was Dagrun simply following her sister, or was something more sinister going on? And did this have anything to do with Tarmo Holt's earlier visit?

"Mobilize all of the instructors," Joosep interrupted Arnor mid-sentence. "Have them start looking for both sisters. And see if any other Intelligencers have returned to the Hall."

Arnor nodded and rushed out, leaving Joosep wishing he'd involved the instructors in the search for Inger initially, instead of just having the few available Intelligencers look for her. But Inger wasn't his responsibility and he'd assumed that Dagrun would quickly find her when she returned. But what if Dagrun *had* found her sister and had now met the same—perhaps terrible—fate?

Joosep needed to put all of his resources into finding Dagrun—so many of his plans depended on her. And her Trait.

SOMEONE SHOUTED NEARBY and Dag woke up, her heart pounding. She blew out a breath. She was still under the dinghy and she hadn't been discovered. She hadn't meant to—it went against all of her training to sleep when in a dangerous place—but she'd fallen asleep. At least the shout hadn't been about her.

Daylight edged under the overturned dinghy and bare feet scampered past. Someone shouted again and the reply came from nearby.

"Drop them sails quick, now," a rough, male voice called out. "Unless you wanta end up on the Teeth."

He has to mean the Serpent's Teeth, Dag thought, surprised. What were they doing here? It was a notoriously dangerous expanse of sea that paralleled the eastern shore of Ostland Island in the north all the way south to the Blighted Woods. The Teeth were jagged pieces of rock that punched up through the waves, barring any southern route around Ostland that could lead out of the Pale Sea. To Dag's knowledge, no one had been able to map all of the Teeth. There were rumours that they actually shifted, but her instructors had explained that wind and waves never revealed them the same way twice.

Was the ship heading to Lavais and the shipbuilders? The island was part of Swyford, one of the three Fair Seas Treaty Alliance countries, but it was possible the pirates had business there. Perhaps they had to get their ships repaired at Lavais: it was the only ship building facility in the Pale Sea.

She was more interested in finding out if that was where Inger had been taken. And what about the children she'd followed on board? Would they be left on Lavais? And would it be with pirates or with honest Swyfordians? She had her patch so she'd be safe enough if she was discovered, but that wouldn't help her find Inger.

An hour passed and she heard more activity: calls for jibs and mainsails to be trimmed and other orders she didn't understand. Then the boat stilled, and she heard sailors calling from all over the ship. *To starboard five feet: hard to port and hold the wheel for a count of eight* then *hard starboard* again.

It took a few moments to realize that they were sailing through the Teeth. But she'd been told that it was impossible!

Did the pirates have a map or were they navigating solely based on sight? The constant calls that came from across the ship sounded practiced, like they'd done this before. She had to wonder if there was a Trait involved, maybe even an Unseen Trait.

In the next hour, the calls came faster and faster and the ship barely seemed to move. Wood groaned and every once in a while, the ship dipped slightly. The air under the dinghy was hot and still. She wiped sweat from her forehead wondering when she'd feel a breeze again.

There was a long silence, and then someone shouted, "We're out!" and a cheer went up.

A few minutes later multiple, sets of bare feet ran past Dag, and someone called for the sails to be let out. The ship lurched and rolled as it gained speed across waves. Finally, a puff of wind made its way under the dinghy and she sighed.

DAG JERKED AWAKE, her heart pounding. Someone was handling the dinghy she was under! A pair of bare feet moved from one end to the other, and a rope coiled onto the deck near the bow.

"Bow's untied," a female voice said. "You get the stern."

Dag rolled away from the feet to the far edge of the dinghy. They were getting ready to put her dinghy into the water. How would they do it? She wished she knew more about the workings of sailing vessels, but no one had ever told her to expect to work on one, let alone stow away on one.

They'll lift it where it is, she thought. She crawled towards the bow: its slight curve left a foot of space between the deck and the gunwale of the dinghy. Hopefully, she'd be able to get out from underneath it without being noticed.

"Man the boat," someone called, and dozens of bare feet lined the side of the dinghy. Thinking that her boots would be noticed amongst all of the bare feet, Dag pulled hers off and awkwardly tucked them into her shirt.

Fingers lined the underside of the dinghy as people gripped it and someone shouted, "Hands on and up!"

The bow of the dinghy lifted, and Dag ducked out from under it, squeezing in beside the boat and the outside wall of a cabin, across from the sailors raising the boat. She was half standing with her hands on the gunwale by the time it reached her waist. A few sailors slid underneath the dinghy to join her, and together they lifted their side up until the boat evened out at waist height.

No one seemed to notice Dag; she assumed it was her Trait at work. She kept her head down as she walked forward, carrying the dinghy towards the ship's gunwale.

"Anchor's down," a large woman called as she strode past. "Get this dinghy into the water. We're home."

As soon as the woman passed, one of her neighbours leaned towards her. "We all know the Captain's real home is this ship," she said. "Strongrock's just a safe harbour."

Dag simply grunted in response, which seemed to satisfy the woman who'd spoken to her. Strongrock Island was just south of Ostland but the only way to get there—so she'd been taught—was to go north through the Frozen Pass. That journey took two or three days, depending on the weather, not the single night and day they'd just spent coming through the Serpent's Teeth from North Tarklee.

The group of them—about a dozen sailors, half men and half women—walked the dinghy towards the side of the ship.

"Overhead!" a woman called, and in unison they hoisted the dinghy above them.

"To the gunwale," the woman said. Dag almost stumbled and the bow dipped towards her as she fought to keep the boat aloft. The sailor beside her shifted over a step, taking some of the weight as a boy who looked to be about ten scampered around the dinghy, making sure that a rope that was tied to the bow was clear.

"Ready and flip!"

Everyone on Dag's side of the boat raised their arms and shoved the dinghy high into the air; at the same time the opposite side dipped low, allowing the boat to flip over and expose the ribs to the sky. Copying her neighbour, Dag crawled underneath, bracing her back against the keel of the dinghy.

Two more sailors joined them underneath the dinghy: they all walked towards the side of the ship before straightening their legs to lift the dinghy up and over the gunwale. Hands reached out as the rest of the sailors kept the dinghy clear. Once the dinghy was over the side, Dag stepped away to watch it be lowered to the water. After a quick check to make sure she hadn't been noticed, Dag slipped away from the crowd.

She needed to figure out how to get into the dinghy and ashore. She thought the small boat would hold about ten people. She guessed there were thirty or so sailors on board. How many of them needed to stay on the ship and how many would go ashore?

She looked towards the shore: there was a small community on Strongrock Island, but really all she knew about it was that it was not part of either Ostland or the three Fair Seas Treaty countries.

She wasn't a very strong swimmer, but the dock looked close. She might be able to make it that far, but then what? Haul herself out of the sea and wander around dripping wet until she found Inger? This was the only ship in this harbour: everyone would know she'd stowed away on it. Would they help her if they knew how she'd gotten here?

The dock led to a huddle of wooden buildings: most were small but there were a couple of larger two-storeyed structures. The whole settlement seemed to be wedged into a strip of land at the bottom of a steep hill that led up to a plateau of some kind. At least from here, it looked like it flattened out on top.

She'd be better off getting to Strongrock by boat, she decided, assuming that the dinghy would make more than one trip.

Sailors hauling crates arrived on deck, bringing goods up from the hold, and Dag walked past them with her head down. She found a shadow and settled into it as the goods were lowered over the gunwale to the dinghy below.

A few sailors without burdens climbed over the gunwales. One tossed a rope down and laughed at her mates. "I'll save some seats for ye at the Mast," she called before disappearing from Dag's view.

Dag relaxed: it seemed that more sailors were expected to go ashore, if that sailor was planning on seeing them later. Still, she was nervous until more crates were brought up from below indicating that they were making at least one more trip. A pair of sailors wandered past her, muttering about being forced to eat on board rather than joining others at the tavern.

The deck had cleared a little, and now only the sailors who were carrying crates remained. Dag made her way to the pile of goods, trying not to stare at the Fair Seas Treaty Alliance seal on a wine cask that was waiting to be taken ashore. It was possible that these goods had been purchased fairly, and anyway, that was not her business. She was here to find Inger, make sure she was safe, and take her home.

IT WAS DUSK by the time the dinghy was loaded for its second trip. Dag grabbed the edge of a wooden crate as a sailor hauled it to the side of the ship. Only a few sailors were still helping to load the small boat, and Dag assumed that this would be the last trip ashore tonight.

She helped hand the crate to a sailor who straddled the gunwale, and then she climbed over the side of the ship. The rope ladder swayed as she stepped down it. A hand steadied her as her bare foot hit the wood of the boat.

"Last oar's free," a man said to her. He held a lamp up and gestured to an empty seat.

Dag nodded and crab-walked over to it and sat down in front of the unmanned oar, shifting her boots, which were still tucked into her shirt.

A moment later, the sailor who'd spoken to her waved up at the ship.

"I'll have a drink for you," he called out, and the rest of the sailors in the dinghy laughed.

The sailor in charge turned to the rowers. "Sit up, now row!" As one, everyone leaned forward, reaching with their oars. Dag did her best to imitate them but she'd never rowed as part of a large crew before and her boots shifted every time she moved. Her oar stuck in the water, and she dragged at it, trying to get it out. Finally, she was able to raise it out of the water.

"New, are you?" the man in charge asked from her side. He'd hung the lamp from a pole and it swung wildly with each stroke of the oars.

"I guess it's obvious," Dag said. "Sorry, I really thought I could do this."

"You'll get the timing eventually but for now, hold it like this." He made fists and bent his arms so that his elbows were at his sides. "That'll keep your oar out of everyone else's way."

Dag copied him, concentrating on holding the oar steady and out of the water.

"We don't get many new ones your age," the man said. "What brought you?"

"My sister," Dag replied. "I'm here to see her." Joosep always said it was better to tell the truth—just not all of it. You never knew what Trait someone might have.

"There are other ways to get here."

"Not this fast," Dag said.

"True." He stood up and stared ahead. "You do look familiar. A young woman came in last week. I think she's at the Broken Mast."

"Thank you," Dag said. She looked up at him, trying to read him. The planes of his face came into and out of relief with every sway of the lamp. "Why are you helping me?"

"I don't think you mean harm," he said. "Heya!" he called out and waved to someone in the distance. "Toss us a line. Hold up," he said to the rowers.

The jerky movement of rowing stopped, and Dag chanced a glance behind her: a dock was lined with lamps and a couple of people stood at the edge. A rope flew through the air and the woman in the bow grabbed it.

The dinghy was towed in, and Dag followed orders as they shipped the oars and unloaded the goods. The sailor in charge waved her off when she bent to pick up a wooden cask from the dock.

"You go on," he said. "Find your sister. The Broken Mast is that way."

"Thank you," Dag said. She nodded and headed along the dock. The sailor had been nice: he hadn't reported her to anyone and had actually told her where to find Inger, but she didn't think he was only being nice. The pirates might not want her to know where they stored their goods, especially if they had been stolen. But she was fine with that. All she wanted was to find her sister.

The buildings closest to the dock lined a square but they were dark: the noise and lights were from the two larger buildings—the tavern and what looked like an inn—that each bore signs that said The Broken Mast.

Dag headed past the inn and pushed open the door to the tavern, pausing just outside to scan the smoky interior. She heard a familiar laugh and stepped in. This was the right place.

Inger stood beside a table full of rowdy drunks. She leaned over them and placed mugs on the table.

After setting the mugs down, her sister picked up some empty ones. What in all of Nyorden was Inger doing? Was she *working* in the tavern? Coins were handed to Inger, and she grabbed them before threading her way through the crowded tables to the bar.

Dag took a more direct route.

"Another three mugs of barley ale," Inger said to a woman who stood behind the bar.

"You're a barmaid," Dag said.

"Dagrun!" Inger squealed. She set her tray down on the bar and turned and hugged her. "I knew you'd come," she whispered. "I knew you would."

"But you're all right?" When Dag felt her nod, she squeezed Inger until she gasped. "Then why did I have to track you down?"

"Later," Inger said. She stepped back from Dagrun. "Ursa," Inger turned to the woman behind the bar. "This is my sister, Dagrun. Dag, meet Ursa Ozlinch, my employer. And friend, I hope."

"The one you've been expecting?" Ursa peered across the bar at Dag. "I see a likeness, but twins? That I don't see."

"Well, it's true," Inger said. She turned and winked at Dag, who nodded.

No one ever believed they were twins. That was one reason

why it had taken so long for Joosep to hear about them despite spending years looking for twins with Traits. Inger was Seen: everyone assumed that she was the older—and prettier—sister. And Dag was overlooked. Not that she minded: she always felt better not being the centre of attention. And if that was due to her Trait, she didn't care.

"If I'm a paying customer that means you have to serve me," Dag said. She heard Ursa snort with laughter.

"Of course!" Inger said. "Find a seat. I'll just bring you whatever I think you'll like, right?"

"No," Dag said. Now that she'd found Inger, she was going to make her pay for all the worry she'd caused. And the trouble she'd be in with Joosep for leaving without telling him. "I need to know what's on the menu." She paused and looked around the room. Most customers were drinking but a few had plates or bowls in front of them. "And what can be made special."

Ursa gave another snort. "Sisters for sure."

"All right," Inger pouted. "But you better leave me a big tip." She turned to pick up her tray, which Ursa had filled with brimming mugs.

"That will depend on the service," Dag said. She trailed Inger through the crowd until she spotted a table with only one other person at it. She sat down as far from her tablemate as possible. The woman had her head down; Dag wasn't sure but she thought she'd passed out from drink.

With one eye on her table companion, Dag surveyed the room. Like the crew on the ship there was an almost equal mix of men and women in the tavern. And there seemed to be all different skin tones, hair colours, and nationalities. She recognized a handful of languages: she'd had instruction in some but couldn't be considered fluent in any of them. Most of the customers had the look of sailors: weathered skin and bare feet, but there was the odd tradesperson or crafter mixed in.

The noise level was no different than any other tavern she'd been in, but there was something in the tone that was . . . different. She watched Inger banter with some customers who had clearly been drinking for a while. One of them made a comment and Inger, giggling, did a twirl, which made them all laugh. Patrons at nearby tables joined in even though Dag was pretty sure most of them hadn't heard any joke.

And that was it: that was what was different here. In most taverns, underneath the drunken chatter and laughter there was always an underlying menace: a threat of danger, a fight just about to boil over. And most serving girls spent their time dodging the unwanted hands of customers, not twirling in front of them.

What was it that made the customers in this tavern behave differently?

"Ah, Hanne's table, a wise choice," Inger said when she arrived. "She won't bother. What would you like?" Inger rattled off a few dishes.

"Fried fish," Dag said, stopping her. "As long as it's fresh."

"Shh," Inger leaned down. "Fish is brought in every few hours. Ursa would be offended if anyone accused her of serving anything but the freshest fish."

"And bread too, then," Dag said. "And cider."

"Cider's very dear, do you have enough money?"

"I still have Joosep's," Dag said. "From my assignment."

"Oh, right, how did that go?" Someone called to Inger from across the room. "We will talk, I promise." She turned away and then abruptly turned back and hugged her. "It will make sense, I promise that too."

In between serving other customers, Inger delivered her food and drink. The fish was indeed fresh and the pear cider was pleasantly tart. Dag ate and sipped her cider, watching the other customers. Whether she wanted to or not, by the end of the evening she would know many of their secrets. But which ones were worth knowing? That was always the trick.

JOOSEP LOOKED UP when he heard a knock on the half-open office door. Calder Rahmson poked his head in.

"I heard you were looking for help from anyone in the city," Calder said. He slipped through the door and took the seat in front of Joosep's desk. "I just got back in this afternoon."

"Lucky for me," Joosep said.

Calder groaned, leaned back in his chair, and put his boots—dirty boots—on Joosep's desk.

Joosep smiled. He deserved that, after his horrible joke. Calder's Trait was Luck, but he didn't always have a sense of humour about it, and for some reason, Joosep couldn't help needling him.

"I appreciate you coming in," Joosep continued. "I hope your mother is in good health?" Calder spent the rare weeks between assignments at his mother's home up north in Byholt, in the Woodlea Forest.

"She's well," Calder said. "Thank you for asking. That's more than my father ever does."

"Ah, right, you saw him on your last trip," Joosep replied. It had been in Calder's report but Rahm wasn't the target of their intelligence gathering. "In Pilalia."

Rahm was Pilalian and Calder took after him, with dark skin and hair, although he had the blue eyes of his mother's people. Joosep found Calder's background useful for gathering information in the Sapphire Sea. All Intelligencers were taught other languages but not all of them became fluent. And even fewer spoke like they were born to the language the way Calder spoke Pilalian.

"He has his uses," Calder said. "Although I'd never tell Mother that."

"He did leave her with three children to raise," Joosep said. "She's bound to be resentful."

"I was already here at the Hall," Calder reminded him. "So there were only two left at home. I think she kicked him out. He was gone more than half the year anyway, and when he came back, he assumed he was in charge." Calder shrugged. "He still sends coin home with me and she has no problem taking it. But that's not why I'm here."

"No, it's not." Joosep straightened the papers on his desk. Neither Inger nor Dagrun had been seen and his Trait was telling him that something had happened. "I'm missing a couple of Intelligencers . . . well, one's an Intelligencer and the other is her sister: her twin sister."

"Do you mean the Lund sisters?" Calder asked. "I've seen them: they're hard to miss. When did they go missing? And why?"

"Inger has been missing for over a week," Joosep said. "Dagrun was out on assignment and returned the day before yesterday. She debriefed and I told her Inger was gone. Dagrun hasn't been seen since."

"What's the hurry?" Calder asked. "Dagrun's only been gone a few days. Why not give her a chance to locate her sister and bring her back?"

"According to a Trait we need to find her—them—now," Joosep said. He didn't feel the need to mention that it was *his* Trait that was triggered. Besides, he wanted Dagrun back in the Hall more because of the value of her Trait.

"How much time do I get?" Calder asked.

"As much as you need," Joosep replied. He reached down and pulled his strongbox from the desk drawer. He unlocked it and pulled out some coins. "Let me know if you need more. This is urgent."

"All right," Calder replied.

"Do you need me to give you more details?"

"No, you know me; I come across what I need when I need it. Including information."

Joosep nodded. That was the thing about Calder's Luck. It couldn't be trained or enhanced—or forced—Calder just had to let it work.

Calder pulled his feet off his desk, rose and sauntered out. Joosep let out a sigh. He'd sent the best to find Dagrun; all he could do now was wait.

CHAPTER 3

CALDER JINGLED THE coins in his hand: there was a nice mix, mostly from the Fair Seas Treaty Alliance countries, but there were a few from beyond the Pale Sea including one from Pilalia—a baisa—which Joosep always gave him. But the value of the coins was far too high for what sounded like a babysitting job.

And he had to ask the same question he always asked: why him? Why was this task assigned to him? Oh, he knew why Joosep would want to send him, but what he wondered, what he *always* wondered: was he assigned this task because of his Trait? Because of Luck? And if so, what was the benefit to him, what was his Luck trying to give or show him?

He shoved the coins into his satchel and headed down the first corridor that caught his attention, not worrying about where it led. That was the thing about Luck, he'd found. Making plans and trying to be methodical about things didn't work: he had to let his Trait work the way it wanted to.

Joosep understood that. That's why he didn't bother giving him more information. But the little he had said? About the sisters needing to be found right away because of a Trait? If it was Joosep's Trait that had been triggered, why hadn't he just told him? Something was odd about that statement.

He shrugged and turned a corner. He was heading out of the

Hall now, away from the school and training grounds for Intelligencers and into the government district. Clan freeholders who represented North Tarklee, Nordmere, and the Fair Seas Treaty Alliance all had offices here, although to him it seemed that the different governing bodies had all the same people overseeing them.

At another intersection, he turned into yet another corridor. He was heading east, so he would be getting close to the most expensive residential apartments. Clan Freeholders were the landowners: some of them had enormous freeholds that were larger than countries like Pilalia, although the largest were mostly north, where his mother lived, and that land was only good for logging. But many wealthy Freeholders also had luxurious apartments in North Tarklee. It was the seat of power for the Fair Seas Treaty Alliance and where the decisions affecting trade and property rights were made.

He'd been wandering for almost an hour—not an incredibly long time for his Trait to take to show him something—but he wasn't in a part of the city he'd expected to be in. He didn't think the Lund sisters were staying in one of the luxury apartments these hallways led to, so his Luck was only showing him a clue. Which meant the truth was going to take time. The longer it took to get Lucky, the more deeply hidden something was. And the deeper something was hidden, the more dangerous the secret tended to be.

Calder turned another corner and stopped. The floor of the corridor ahead of him was punctuated by splashes of moonlight. He'd reached the outer wall of the building: beyond these stones was the Pale Sea and below were the working wharves and docks of the city's harbour. The stench of the city and docks would never penetrate this high up and bother the richest and most powerful people who lived here.

His focus narrowed on the hall in front of him, and he leaned against the wall, his dark skin and clothing helping to hide him in the shadows. It wouldn't be long now. This was the exact place and the exact time for him to learn what he needed to know.

There was a noise from down the hall. Light spilled out from an open door. A woman exited, followed by two small girls. One girl rubbed a tiny fist against her eye.

"Bring them back when they're six," said a male voice from

inside. "And don't tell me again that they already are."

"Yes, Freeholder," the woman said. There was fear in her voice. "Their mother said they were the right age, but I can see that you're right."

"Are there any more to come?" the man asked.

"Not in the city," the woman said. "Not on either side of the river."

"Then check outside the city. Surely the Three have more than a few sets of twins."

At the word twins, Calder felt his focus narrow again. That was it; that was what his Luck had led him to. Someone was looking for twins—someone other than the Master Intelligencer. They had to be looking for Traits, which meant it was someone who knew that twins with them were easier to identify: and had stronger Traits.

The woman towed the children along the corridor away from him, and the door closed, blocking the light that had spilled onto the flagstones.

Calder backed away without even bothering to try to find out who lived in that apartment. His Luck would show him when and if he needed that information. For now, he knew why Inger and Dagrun Lund were missing: someone was after twins with Traits—like them.

A few corridors later, he felt safe enough to break into a jog. It was late and he needed some sleep. He'd start his hunt again in the morning.

"Are you asleep?"

Dag blinked up at Inger, who stood beside her holding a lamp. She lifted her head off the table, and her cider, only half finished, almost tipped over.

"You *were* asleep!" Inger said with glee in her voice.

"Yeah," Dag replied. "It's not like I had anywhere else to go." When Inger had taken away her empty plate, she'd said she had a room and that they'd talk there later. That must have been hours ago. "What time is it?" She'd fallen asleep, again. Some Intelligencer she was turning out to be, sleeping all the time. Although, she knew that Inger would never let anything happen to her so she *was* safe.

"It's time to go," Inger said. "We've finally asked the last couple of customers to leave. Ursa never wants to make more than three leave; she feels like it's saying she doesn't want the business, which she always does. She never knows when the next ship will arrive."

Inger dragged a hand through her hair, and Dag realized that she was tired too. She got to her feet.

"Lead the way."

Inger nodded and, with a lamp in hand, headed to the back of the tavern. Dag followed her through a small door that led past the kitchen to a narrow set of stairs.

"It's not very big," Inger said as she led the way up to the next floor. "And it's nothing like our rooms in the Hall." Halfway down the hallway, she paused, pulled a key from her pocket, and unlocked the door.

"But it is private," Inger continued. She put the lamp on a table just inside the door and stepped aside to let Dag enter before she closed the door.

"I've never lived by myself before," Inger said. "At least not until you went on your assignment."

"I never have," Dag replied. "I had to share when I was away." She didn't go into more details. Inger didn't need to know about her assignment, and what she was—what she did—*was* secret.

The room was small, less than half the size of either bedroom at the Hall. Two narrow beds were pushed up against opposite walls and a carpet ran the length of the floor that separated the beds. Dag picked the one that didn't look slept in and flopped down on it.

"You should take your boots off," Inger said.

Dag sat up, dragged her boots off, and tossed them to the floor. Her feet were dirty from her time on the ship. She sighed.

"All right, let's talk," Dag said. "Why did you leave without telling me?"

Inger sat down on the other bed and stared across at Dag. "I knew you'd follow me," she said. "And I was afraid to wait for you to come back."

"Why?" Dag knew that Joosep was involved in some way, but she didn't want to unintentionally put ideas in Inger's head. It was better if she told her what she knew—what was on the surface—and then Dag could start figuring out what was really going on.

"Tarmo Holt," Inger said. "Joosep asked me to see him." Inger paused. "He is not a very nice man."

"Joosep or Holt?" Dag asked. She knew Inger had seen Holt: that's what Vilis had told her. But why had Joosep asked her to meet with him? And what did Holt want from Inger?

"Holt," Inger clarified. "But in this case, Joosep too. Tarmo Holt wanted me to have children."

"He wants to marry you? Lie with you? What?" Dag couldn't help her surprise. What in all of Nyorden was Holt after?

"Not with him," Inger said, "not his children. He was going to find someone for me to have children with. Tarmo Holt would pay me very generous living expenses for the rest of my life, and all I had to do was have children."

"You told him no." Dag hadn't expected *this*. Holt was buying children. Did Joosep even know what Holt had wanted with Inger? Was he a party to it? "That's why you left?"

"No," Inger replied. "I mean, of course I told him no, but I left because he threatened *you*. He said he'd make sure you were sent on dangerous missions—the most hazardous, unlikely to succeed missions."

"My assignments are determined by Joosep," Dag said. She didn't believe Joosep would put any of his Intelligencers in unnecessary danger because someone with more authority asked him to. Or would he? He'd already tried to conceal his part in Inger running away.

"I only know that he believes he can make it happen," Inger said. "He *is* the Grand Freeholder."

"Only for another few months," Dag replied. "But Joosep sent you to him?" She still couldn't believe that Joosep had played a part in *this*.

"Yes, Joosep Sepp, your boss, asked me to talk to Tarmo Holt." Inger sighed. "I didn't go right away, either. He had to ask me a few times."

"When did he first ask you?" Dag felt a pit forming in her gut.

"A few days after you left," Inger said. "I was able to postpone the meeting until the week before you were due home."

"You did the right thing," Dag said, hiding her fury. She'd only been gone a few days when Joosep started urging her sister to meet with Holt. What if her mission had been created to get her out of the way?

And what was Tarmo Holt's goal? He'd pay Inger to have children by some as yet unnamed man in what seemed like an effort to breed Traits. But why? Besides, if Holt had learned about Traits from Joosep he also would know that any children with Traits would be the Master Intelligencer's to train. Unless Joosep and Holt were working together. But if that was the case, Holt wouldn't need to find children with Traits: Joosep already did that.

She was left with the question of why Holt wanted people with Traits. And now she'd circled back to *what was Tarmo Holt's goal?*

Dag shook her head. "I'm not going to figure this out tonight," she said. "I need some sleep."

JOOSEP ENTERED HIS office early, hoping that it was too early for a man like Tarmo Holt to be up and around. He wasn't expecting any news from Calder: his Trait didn't work that quickly, and Calder never tried to force it. Luck worked in its own time, he always said.

He sat down at his desk and picked up the report he'd written when Dagrun had debriefed him. The only interesting intelligence she'd uncovered had to do with Clan Freeholder Timonis' business partners cheating him. Was this the type of information Holt was after?

He'd initially been uncomfortable when Tarmo Holt had asked him to send Dagrun to spy on Timonis. At the time, he'd thought it was because he'd told the Grand Freeholder about Dagrun's Trait but now, looking back, he wondered if it had been more than that. Since his Trait hadn't been triggered, he'd convinced himself that it really was a good idea to know more about the man everyone expected would be the next Grand Freeholder.

It was Swyford's turn to supply the Grand Freeholder; nothing would change that. It was up to Swyford to elect their choice, but information Dagrun might uncover could help Joosep navigate the transition.

Now he wondered about Tarmo Holt's motives. He hadn't asked about this mission yesterday, and unless he had read the report when he was in Joosep's office alone, he didn't seem to care. Had it been done in order to separate the Lund sisters? Had

Tarmo Holt tricked Joosep—and his Trait—into being complicit in some scheme?

Not for the first time, Joosep wished he had Dagrun's Trait strength. It would make him an unstoppable Master Intelligencer. He was hopeful that one day she would replace him, but she wasn't ready and wouldn't be for years. It was one thing to know people's secrets: it was another thing to know what to do with them.

He sighed. *He* wasn't sure what to do with Tarmo Holt's secret. Or if he even had to do anything. In three months, Holt would step down as Grand Freeholder, and Joosep would no longer be required to follow his direction. He could wait that long, couldn't he?

CALDER LOOKED OUT across the sea. It was calm this early, and wisps of fog drifted off the still, greyish-blue water. He took a bite of the bun he'd grabbed for breakfast and savoured the sharp tang of the cheese it was stuffed with.

His Luck hadn't necessarily brought him to the dock, but he hadn't had a destination in mind once he'd bought breakfast. The sisters could be hiding in the city on either side of the river, or they could have travelled inland. But inland travel was very difficult, especially in summer.

Most towns in the Fair Seas Treaty Alliance countries ringed the Pale Sea. The logging camps went further inland every year as they harvested the thick forests and the Dareveth River was navigable upstream for a fair distance, but eventually the Blighted Woods barred the way. Calder had met a few people who claimed to have gone up the Dareveth as far as a giant waterfall, but that had been in the winter, when the frozen river could be skimmed over with an ice boat and the Blighted Woods—and the creatures that lived in it—was covered in ice and snow.

He finished his bun and wiped the crumbs from his hands. So, the Lund sisters had most likely left by sea. But to what destination?

From farther along the pier, a woman stared at him and he nodded to her. She nodded back so he slowly ambled her way.

"It's a beautiful, still morning," he said softly when he reached her. "I love the sea at this time of day."

"Me too," the woman agreed. "Though I don't recall seeing you here before."

"I usually greet the morning from *on* the sea," Calder replied, "from the deck of a Merchant Adventurer ship."

"You must have seen some sights then," the woman said. She eyed him more closely. "And are from somewhere else?"

"My father is," Calder replied. "From the Sapphire Sea."

"Is it really so blue?"

"Yes," Calder said. "As blue as a Nordmerian's eyes." Including his, in truth.

Calder paused and stared out at the sea. He felt most at home there, but he assumed that was because he didn't really have a home. He'd left his family at six—just after Hakon died—and moved into the Hall. But the Hall had never really felt like a *home*.

"Did you see a young woman about a week ago?" he asked. "In her early twenties, blonde, blue eyes." He didn't know either sister well, but he knew what Inger looked like: she was pretty hard to miss. But when he thought of Dagrun all he could visualize was Inger. Were they that alike? They were twins, but were they identical? He'd never seen them together: did they look the same? Identical twins had stronger Traits, so they must.

"Lots of people asking things these days," the woman replied.

"I just want to make sure she's all right," Calder replied. "I heard someone was causing trouble for her."

"I try to stay out of other people's trouble," the woman replied. She looked over at Calder, nodded, and turned to leave.

"That's usually a good idea," Calder said. "Staying out of other people's trouble." He sighed and stared out across the harbour. Maybe this wasn't the person he was supposed to talk to. He wasn't even certain that his Luck had brought him here.

He checked the angle of the sun. Fishermen would be returning with the early catch soon and the pier would be too busy for confidential conversations. He was about to leave when someone bumped into him.

"Sorry," a boy said. He was about ten, with shoulder-length, dirty blond hair that he shoved out of his eyes.

"No worries," Calder said. He was about to move past the boy when his focus narrowed on him. This boy was why he was here this morning.

"Where would you go if you were to run away?" Calder asked

abruptly. "If you needed to get away from someone?"

The boy shrugged. "Strongrock," he said. "That's where everyone goes." Then the boy took off along the pier.

Calder watched him run up to a fishing boat that was docking, grab the painter, and tie the boat off before accepting a fish as payment and then hurrying to a second boat that was arriving.

"Strongrock," he said to himself. It made sense.

It had been years since he'd last been there, before Joosep began having him monitor the Merchant Adventurers. The small island was nominally under Ostland's control, although the people who lived on Strongrock claimed to be neutral. And they were, but they were also pirates.

He turned and headed back towards the Hall. He had his destination. He'd need to raid his old, clothes chest for something appropriate, he thought absently, his usual worn but good quality clothing would not get him on a pirate ship. He either needed to be down on his luck—he snorted at that—or well-off. He usually went with well-off: if he was forced into a card game he'd win, and it was hard to seem downtrodden when the cards always fell your way.

He entered the Hall. A guard stopped him, and he had to show his Intelligencer patch before he was allowed to pass.

He shoved the patch back into the waistband pocket. Should he take his patch with him to the pirate's stronghold? What would they do to someone with a patch if they found it? But if at any point he needed to prove who he was and he didn't have it with him, he really would have to depend on Luck.

When he finally entered his own apartment, he'd decided to trust his Trait and resolve the issue of taking his patch with a coin toss.

DAG DRAGGED A hand through her hair, wincing when she tugged it to untangle a few snarls. Her day spent on the ship hadn't done her hair any favours. She sat up and shoved the covers off her. Or her feet. The soles were dirty and one toenail was ripped. But they weren't as brown and calloused as a sailor's. If anyone had noticed her feet they would have known that she didn't normally go barefoot.

Inger had left about an hour ago and Dag had only half-woken up. Her sister hadn't said where she was going or when she'd be back, and now Dag needed to piss and she had no idea where to do that.

She lay back down and stared at the ceiling, trying not to think about her full bladder. She must have fallen back asleep because she woke up when Inger returned.

"Aren't you up yet?" Inger asked.

"To go where?" Dag sat up. At least Inger had a tray of . . . toast and what looked like pickled fish, and a pot that hopefully contained tea. "Where's the privy?"

After a quick visit down the hall, she re-entered the room to find that Inger had pulled the table from beside the door into the space between the beds. The tray was on the table along with two plates filled with toast and fish. Dag gratefully took a steaming mug from Inger and sat on the edge of her bed.

"Thanks for getting breakfast," Dag said as she sipped her tea. She closed her eyes and sighed.

"It's part of my wages," Inger said. "Room and board." She dropped a key onto the tray. "An extra one for the room. Ursa means my room and board to feed one, but I made the argument that the man who cleans the tavern eats more than twice what I do and I bring in more trade."

"You mean trade in the tavern?" Dag asked. She picked up the key. She didn't want to think that Inger was doing any "trade" other than serving although she knew prostitution was often expected of serving girls. She picked up a piece of toast and laid a slice of fish on it.

"Yes," Inger replied. As usual, her sister missed any insinuation that trade could be anything other than serving in the tavern. She picked up her own toast and fish. "It's real easy for me to get a customer to buy a bowl of stew or another beer." She grinned. "Or a cider instead of beer."

Dag nodded as she ate. "I can see how that would be appreciated by the owner," she said between bites.

"Oh, I get part of that," Inger said.

"From the customer?"

"Sometimes they leave a little extra," Inger agreed. "But Ursa, she tallies up each day's takings and gives everyone a percentage. We all get the same, no matter our job; because Ursa says one can't succeed without the others." She pulled out her purse and shook it and coins jangled. "That's where I was. Ursa does the accounts in the morning and gives us our shares at breakfast."

"That's a decent way to do things," Dag said. And it was, if it was true. Inger seemed so happy about it that Dag didn't voice her concerns. Besides, her Trait would show her whether it was true. And they'd be going back to the Hall anyway. Or they would once she figured out what to do about Joosep.

"I like it," Inger said. "Ursa is fair and the work is fun, although I'm on my feet a lot."

"What about the customers? Do they ever trouble you?"

"They wouldn't dare," Inger said. "Ursa owns pretty much every business on Strongrock. If she banned them they'd have nowhere to eat or drink other than their own ship or cabin."

"I thought Strongrock was Ostland territory," Dag asked. "Ursa didn't strike me as an Ostlander."

"She's not," Inger said. "At least she says she's not, but she's never told me what country she is from." Inger grabbed another piece of toast. "And when I started working here she told me that Strongrock—and especially her—are neutral. No country has a real hold on anything here."

"I guess that would be good for the pirates," Dag said. Someplace where no country had jurisdiction? That was exactly what they would want in order to sleep soundly at night without worrying about being raided and rounded up for their crimes.

"They're not pirates!" Inger stared at her. "They're privateers."

"So, they don't rob ships?"

"Well," Inger paused. "All right, they do, but only the ships they suspect are bringing in goods that are a danger to the Fair Seas Treaty Alliance countries."

"How do they know which ships to target?" Dag asked. Targeting specific shipments made her suspicious. And what happened to these dangerous goods? She'd never heard of any dangerous goods being handed over to the Fair Seas Treaty Alliance. Joosep would know that, wouldn't he? And because of her Trait, she would know it too.

She frowned. She liked it better when she thought they were simply pirates stealing valuables from *everyone.*

"Captain Margit Ansdottir finds out," Inger said. "She knows people who warn her which ships to look out for. The captain is a great friend of Ursa's; she's the one who brought me here."

"Captain Ansdottir brought you here," Dag repeated. "Why?"

She was itchy between her shoulder blades: her Trait letting her know that there was some hidden reason behind the Captain of the privateers being great friends with the woman who owned everything on the island.

"She found me by the docks." Inger gave a wry smile. "Because of course *someone* would find me. Anyway, she was picking up two children that she was bringing to Strongrock when she saw me." Inger shrugged. "I didn't know what I should do, and I must have looked a little lost. So, the Captain asked if I'd like to come here."

"Why?" Dag asked. "Why would she offer to bring you here?"

"It's what she does," Inger replied. "There's a woman who lives in one of the shanties by the port who takes in children who have no one. Captain Margit meets with her every few weeks and brings any children she's found here. Apparently, spring is the busiest time for foundlings. Things happen over the winter and children are left on their own."

"Who told you this?" Inger had just confirmed the story about unwanted children she'd heard from the woman she'd met on the pier.

"The two children who came here on the same ship," Inger said. "They were sisters and their parents were both dead. Their father died just this past winter, leaving them alone. They walked to North Tarklee from their cabin when they ran out of food. They were starving on the streets when the woman took them in. She fed them and kept them warm and safe until Captain Margit showed up."

"There are orphanages in the city," Dag said. "Why didn't the woman take the children there?" She wished she'd asked that woman this question, but she'd been too intent on finding Inger. She still didn't like the idea of children being taken—abducted— from Nordmere.

"I guess she gave them the choice," Inger said, but she didn't sound very confident. "If I was given the choice between an orphanage and the Fair Seas Seafarers, I know which one I'd choose."

"These are children," Dag said. "Of course, they're going to choose the Fair Seas Sea . . . whatever in Nyorden that is."

"It's what the privateers call themselves," Inger said. "The Fair Seas Seafarers, on account of—"

"I know what it's on account of," Dag said. "But why are they naming themselves after the Fair Seas Treaty Alliance? Especially when they have nothing to do with it?"

"I'm not sure," Inger said. "But they've helped me. Both Captain Margit and Ursa have helped me."

"They have," Dag agreed, still no closer to understanding *why* they had helped Inger. Or why they were bringing children here to Strongrock Island.

Inger put her dishes on the tray and stood up. "I have to wash up," she said. "I'll have some time off in the afternoon, but right now I have to get ready for the noon meal service." She grabbed a few things from the cupboard that was set into the wall near the small window. "There's a closet outside to wash up in," she said, "beside the door that leads here to the staff quarters. It's cold seawater, but it does the trick."

"All right," Dag said. She put her plate and mug on the tray. "Will most of the staff be busy during noon service?" At Inger's nod, she continued. "I'll wash up then. For now, I'll take the tray down and wander around for an hour or so." She shoved her feet into her boots, picked up the tray, and left with Inger.

Downstairs, Ursa pointed her to the kitchen, where she left the tray. A door leading outside was ajar and she stepped out to the rear of the tavern. A rocky slope rose up steeply and Dag peered up at the top. She didn't see any obvious trail leading up: was anything up there? It would be a very good place to view any approaching ships.

Inger waved at her from outside of a square, wooden closet-like structure built against the wall of the tavern. Water sluiced into it from a trough that led down from the roof. With a thunk a metal slat dropped, blocking the flow of water.

Dag waved back at Inger but didn't head her way, deciding to let her sister get ready for work in peace. Instead, she headed in the opposite direction.

CHAPTER 4

CALDER WAVED HIS hat—complete with snow white owl feathers—at the man standing by the dinghy. He was wearing his most flamboyant set of clothes: a ridiculous hat, a shirt with multiple bows and great billowy arms, a sharkskin vest that was the least gaudy yet the most expensive piece of clothing he wore, and a pair of shiny black trousers. His feet were bare—no one would hire on a sailor who wore anything on his feet, even if he was sensibly dressed.

"Is your ship taking on experienced sailors?" Calder shouted. "I'm looking for working passage to the Sapphire Sea." Once he reached the sailor, he flourished a bow. "I've had word that my father's father has taken ill."

"And you want to be there when the family goods are divvied up?" the sailor eyed him. "We're not heading that far. Just to Strongrock."

"That would do for me," Calder said. "I can likely get a ship from there to the Sapphire Sea."

"Captain's on shore," the sailor said. "We'll be leaving as soon as he gets back from his business."

"Then I shall wait and ask him when he returns if he has need of me," Calder said. "I'm Rahm," he said, using his father's name.

"Tepio," the sailor said. "And the Captain is Olmar, of the

Bright Breeze; as fine a ship as ever sailed any sea."

"How many seas has she sailed?" Calder asked. It wasn't a ship he was familiar with, so it was probably not a Merchant Adventurer. If it was a ship that only traded along the Pale Sea that would be Lucky: it meant no one would recognize him. "I remember one time in Arressa, when the waves were as tall as the mast . . ."

Calder kept Tepio entertained with story after story about real and imagined events. It was what was expected, from a sailor dressed like he was, but he made sure to sprinkle in enough truth for Tepio to believe he was what he said he was: a well-travelled, experienced sailor.

Captain Olmar wouldn't hire him without knowing he had some skills, and Calder was hoping that he'd trust Tepio to assess him. Not that he expected any great responsibilities onboard.

"There's the Captain now," Tepio said as he gestured to a barrel-chested man in a dark overcoat.

He looked more like a Freeholder than the captain of a ship, and Calder wondered what cargo they hauled. And if Strongrock was as far west as they ever went.

"Captain Olmar," Tepio said when he stopped in front of them. "This here's Rahm. He's looking to work as far as Strongrock, if you're taking on anyone else."

"Strongrock? What's your business there?" Olmar asked.

Calder bowed low, sweeping his hat along the dock. "I am Rahm, from Pilalia on the Sapphire Sea. I have no business in Strongrock other than the hope that I can find a ship heading to my home. I have family business that requires my presence."

"His father's father is ill," Tepio interjected.

"Is he?" Olmar asked. "In Pilalia?" He turned back to Calder. "What part of Pilalia?" Olmar asked in Pilalian. "I know the place very well."

"It's a small town along the northern coast," Calder answered in the same language. "Named Shiori." It wasn't unusual for the captain of a ship to speak Pilalian or any of the other half-dozen languages of sailors.

"Shiori, yes, I believe I've been there."

"I am surprised," Calder said. "It's not much more than a fishing village, which is why there are so many of us who take to the sea." Calder grinned. "But family is enough to take me back there," he said in Nordmerian.

The captain looked at Tepio, who nodded.

"All right," Olmar said. "You can crew with us as far as Strongrock. Tepio will introduce you to the First Mate and get you settled."

"Thank you, Captain Olmar," Calder said, but he was already speaking to the man's back. The captain stepped into the dinghy, followed by Tepio. Calder got in and with a wave at Tepio, seated himself at the oars.

Tepio pointed at a ship that looked capable of sailing to the Sapphire Sea, rather than a more squat log hauler that would be limited to the Pale Sea. That made him wonder at Captain Olmar's skills: the farther you travelled the more profitable trade was. He supposed he would learn why if it was important to finding the Lund sisters.

For now, Calder rowed them away from the dock toward the ship. He would only be on board for the few days it took to get to Strongrock, but friends were always good to have. By relieving Tepio of the chore of rowing, Calder hoped he'd made one of him.

First Mate Charis, an Arressan, took an instant dislike to Calder, due, no doubt, to the troubled history between Arressa and Pilalia. Calder did his best to seem harmless and took his assignment to help Cook in stride. No doubt his Luck was at play with this kitchen duty, even if all it meant was that he got to eat well.

Cook was like most cooks on ships; an older sailor who could no longer haul in the sheets or clamber up the rigging. It wasn't the first time Calder had peeled potatoes and chopped onions. He did it with a sense of the dramatic, keeping Cook entertained with embellished tales of adventures and helping him with a new seasoning for the fish stew.

All of which made him a friend of Cook and an enemy of Charis by the time the noon meal had been served.

Calder ignored the scowls Charis sent his way but he was curious why someone of the First Mate's rank would even care about a sailor who would be on board for such a short time. He wiped down the tables and scrubbed the pots, waiting until his Trait gave him some clues.

IT HAD ONLY taken Dag a few minutes to wander through the

town. Beside the tavern and inn, there was a store with a large warehouse attached and a few huts for woodworking or smoking fish. A cluster of small cabins looked neglected: no doubt they belonged to sailors who lived mostly at sea.

The only ship in the small harbour was the one she'd arrived on, but there were a dozen smaller boats; some were dinghies, used to fish or ferry sailors from ship to shore, but Dag had been surprised to see three of the smaller, sleeker sailboats that could be fitted with runners to skim across the ice in the winter.

Iceboats were mostly used to travel up the frozen rivers in winter, so she'd thought. What use would they be here in the middle of the Pale Sea? Although she supposed that a skilled sailor might be able to travel as far as Ostland in one during the summer months. There was little room for cargo so it would be used as a personal craft only.

When she'd wandered back to the store front, Dag had noticed a group of people waiting in line at a well.

"Is this the main source of fresh water?" she asked a woman with a bucket. Dressed in trousers, shirt, and vest, the woman's feet were bare.

"Only source that's public," the woman replied. "Tavern and inn have their own well, so I hear. And there's a spring up above." She gestured to the hill that rose steeply above the town. "I climbed up once. Not much to look at—the spring—but the view's nice on a clear day."

"Thanks," Dag said. She shaded her face to look at the hill. She thought there was a faint path so she headed towards it.

Dag climbed up the rock face, clutching at scraggly trees when the path became steeper. She grunted when her boot skidded and some loose dirt tumbled downslope. She grabbed a clump of grass and gingerly pulled on it, testing to make sure it would hold her weight before she hauled herself up another few inches. A few minutes later she was able to stand up on a flat rock. From here the path sloped up more gently. At the top was a small patch of green grass, and was that a cabin?

When she got closer, Dag realized that the cabin had been abandoned long ago. Wooden walls were splintered and half of the roof was missing. Past the cabin there were lush bushes and trees and a small stream trickled from between some rocks. The stream travelled a dozen feet before pooling in a small pond. Dag couldn't see where the water left the pond, and she assumed that it somehow drained to a well below.

She studied the stream and pond: small animal tracks had been left in the soft soil and the water in the pond wasn't in the least brackish. If this was the only source for fresh water for Strongrock, it would be very easy to divert it and deprive the town of water.

She walked over to the edge of the hill and looked down on the town. From here she could see that a well-worn path led past the tavern. She hiked along the edge of the hill until the tavern was directly below her. She could see the washing shed Inger had been standing in front of and beyond it there was a huddle of trees and a few more buildings. What was there? And what about the children Captain Ansdottir brought here? She hadn't seen any when she'd wandered around the small settlement. Were they kept somewhere else on the island?

Dag stared at the slope. It looked gentle enough for her to go down this way rather than returning by the path she'd climbed. She took a few steps down.

"*Skit!*" The clump of grass her foot was wedged against gave way, and she started sliding down the hill, her hands scrabbling at anything that might stop her. She'd seriously miscalculated the steepness of the slope.

A rock jabbed her in the hip, and she grunted with pain but at least it slowed her descent. A shower of pebbles and twigs followed her as she continued to slide downward, eventually stopping when the slope finally levelled out.

Dag sat up, wincing as she drew in a breath. She gingerly stood up and hobbled the rest of the way down the gentle slope until she stood behind the tavern. Now would be a good time to use the washing hut, she thought as she opened the door and stepped inside, and get rid of the dust she was covered in.

She stripped out of her dirty clothes and shoved them as far away from the overhead bucket as possible. They could use a wash too but she had to put them back on in order to return to Inger's room.

She touched her hip—she would have a bruise, but nothing seemed broken. She stepped under the bucket and pulled the rope. And sucked in a breath when the cold water hit her. Once she'd recovered from the initial shock, she rotated as the water sluiced over her.

It was sea water—she could taste the salt on her lips—and bracing. She let go of the lever and the water stopped. She had nothing to dry herself off with, so she struggled to get her dusty clothes back on. She'd change into clean clothes once she got back to the room.

Inger was there, sitting on her bed.

"You missed the noon meal," Inger said.

"Sorry," Dag replied. "We ate breakfast late so I should be fine for a while." She found her pack and dug out her other set of clothes. "That washing shed is great."

"It is, isn't it? The salt water isn't the best for the hair," Inger shook her blonde hair. "But I like it better than what we have at home."

At the Hall, they had their own indoor privy with a pump but the tub took a long time to fill. This was much faster.

"We should talk about home," Dag said. She pulled on a worn pair of trousers and a top that had once been white but now was a sort of washed-out grey. She still wasn't sure what she wanted to do about Joosep.

"I'm not going back," Inger said. "You can't make me."

Dag took a deep breath in order to force herself from responding immediately. Inger couldn't mean to stay here forever, could she? She sat on her bed and faced her twin.

"Can I ask why?" Dag asked.

"Don't try to talk me out of it," Inger responded.

"I'm not. But I'd like to understand."

"Oh, sure," Inger said. "That's fair." She pulled her knees up to her chin. "You've always been the special one; the one with the Trait people want. Me? I've been the one they tolerate because I'm your sister, and they know they won't get you without me."

"That's . . ." Dag was about to say it wasn't true but it was. Inger was at the Hall because Joosep recruited *her*, not Inger. "All right, it's true but you have a good life."

"No, I don't," Inger said. "I have a safe life, but I don't *do* anything. Here I can be useful. My *Trait* can be useful, even if no one here knows about it. And I love that." She paused. "At the Hall the only use they have for me is giving birth to more people like you."

Dag studied Inger's face. She'd always known that the Hall

didn't offer Inger as much as it offered her, but she'd thought it was enough. Why hadn't her Trait shown her that it wasn't?

Because it had and she'd ignored it. Dag wanted her life as an Intelligencer and she also wanted her sister with her. She didn't want to think about not having one of those things, or worse, having to choose between them.

"You're right," Dag said, and Inger relaxed. "But there might be more to it than that." She held up her hand when Inger would have interrupted. "I won't say anything or try to persuade you differently unless I find out that there is something hidden here that is a threat. You know how my Trait works; if there's a secret it won't be long before I know what it is."

Inger sighed. "What if I don't want to know? What if I just want to be happy and ignorant of anything that might be trouble?"

"Inger, you know that's not how life works," Dag said.

Inger nodded in agreement but she didn't seem happy about it. Dag wasn't happy either. If she found something that made life here unsafe for Inger, she'd have to tell her. But if she didn't find anything would she have to return to the Hall without her?

Calder looked up from the mound of potatoes he was peeling and grinned at Tepio.

"Come to make sure I'm staying out of trouble?" he asked the older sailor.

Tepio shook his head and looped his thumbs into his waistband. "I've never seen a man so happy to work in the galley."

"It's honest work," Calder said. "Nothing wrong with that. Besides, Cook is an appreciative audience. Not everyone is."

"I suppose," Tepio said. "I came to tell you that the First Mate is happy about the winds: he thinks we'll shave a half day off the time to get to Strongrock."

"Good to hear," Calder said, suppressing a smile. Would First Mate Charis like him better if he knew that his Trait was responsible for the winds? Probably not; he'd find another reason to hate a Pilalian. But half a day early meant only two nights spent on board. Should he be concerned that his Luck wanted him in Strongrock half a day early? Or on board this ship a half a day less?

"Heard from Cook that the potatoes was extra good on

account of you," Tepio said. "Gonna do them the same for dinner?"

"If Cook wants me to," Calder said. "It's his kitchen."

"Sure, right, I'll tell the lads." He grinned and rocked back on his heels. "Cook already said he'd have you do them the same."

"Don't worry." Calder leaned closer to Tepio. "I'm teaching him how."

Tepio laughed. "Lads'll be glad to hear that too. After dinner I'll show you your bunk." Tepio grinned and left.

Calder continued peeling potatoes. Yes, friends were always good to have, even if it was just for a few days. But he'd have to watch Charis. There was a man without friends. And Calder didn't think he'd appreciate Rahm the Pilalian having one when he had none.

Once the dinner was done and the pots and plates scrubbed and stacked, Tepio was as good as his word.

"This one's yours," Tepio said.

They were in the hold and hammocks stretched from every beam possible. The hammock Tepio had pointed to was above two others; always the least favoured since getting in and out could disturb anyone sleeping below. But Calder had slept in far worse than this. This hold was dry and clean and at least he had his own hammock and didn't have to share and sleep in shifts.

"Thanks," Calder said. "Potatoes always get me a good bunk."

"Hah," Tepio chortled. "If it were a longer trip we'd expect you to do magic with dried fish."

"Cod or herring?" Calder asked. "You need to treat them different."

"If you let Cook know in a nice way, I'll let you win the first hand," another sailor said as he joined them. "If you care to try your hand at ludus. I'm Steen."

"I could use a new vest, Steen." Calder patted his sharkskin covered stomach. "I've been saving to buy one made of whale but they cost a pretty penny." He'd played ludus many times and could count on one hand the number of times he'd lost.

"You think you're good, do you?" Steen said.

"I think I'm Lucky," Calder replied truthfully. He always warned them and they never believed him, but declining an invitation would make him more enemies than winning would. At least that's what he'd always found.

In the end there were five to play: him, Tepio, Steen, Jaak, and First Mate Charis. Calder's stomach lurched when the latter showed up. Charis already didn't like him; how would he feel when *Rahm* won all his coin? Calder couldn't make himself lose: he'd stopped trying to years ago, since it only made people angrier. It was bad enough to lose to a Lucky and smart player— it was worse when the player made stupid mistakes and still won.

The cards Steen dealt were old and had seen water more than once. Calder assumed that those used to playing with them could tell the cards apart by the water spots, but sadly for them it didn't help them against him.

"Sorry, lads," Calder said as he swept the coins towards him after the first hand. "Don't know myself if it's a knack or skill, but I did warn you."

There were a few grumbles but Calder's cheerfulness seemed to make losing a little more palatable. To everyone except Charis, that is, so he decided to try to win him over.

"So, First Mate Charis," Calder said. "A man doesn't get to your position just for trying. Did you study navigation in Arressa?" Arressa was known for its formal training for every major trade, including ship navigation.

"I did," Charis replied. He slid a card away from him and tapped the table. Tepio dealt him another card. "At the best schools on any sea."

"That's what I've always heard," Calder agreed.

"Do they teach you how to navigate through shoals?" Jaak asked. He was younger than the rest, with the blond hair and blue eyes of one of the Fair Seas Treaty Alliance countries. "Like the Teeth?"

"No one can navigate the Teeth," Steen scoffed. "Can't be done."

"I heard it has been done—and often," Jaak replied.

Calder felt his focus narrow and knew that this was relevant to his search for the Lund sisters.

"That's a tale," Steen said. "Nothing more than a story someone once told in a tavern to get a free drink."

"It could be done," Charis said. "With the right Captain and First Mate. And the right crew."

"How?" Tepio asked.

"Slowly," Charis replied. "And only on a calm day."

"Pirates do it, that's what I heard," Jaak said, his voice a low whisper. "That's how they escape the Fair Seas Treaty Alliance ships. They go through the Teeth."

"Privateers," Steen said. "They're privateers."

"What's the difference?" Tepio asked. "They board ships and steal cargo."

"It's a matter of who they work for," Charis said.

Calder kept quiet, although this too felt like information that he needed to know.

"Then who do they work for?" Tepio asked. "Aren't they neutral?"

"Strongrock is neutral," Charis said. "That's why we stop there." He paused to play a card. "But the ships that shelter there are not."

"They mostly take cargo from the Sapphire Seas anyway," Tepio said.

Calder played a card and won the hand. Charis glared at him but didn't say anything. Calder shrugged, pretending that the game was more interesting than the conversation.

"Why do you say that?" Jaak asked. "Did someone tell you?"

"My cousin," Tepio replied. "He works in the Fair Seas Treaty Alliance office. Most of the ships that are robbed belong to traders from the Sapphire Sea."

Tepio dealt another hand, and Calder tried not to let his annoyance show when he saw his cards: a winning hand straight from the deal. This would end the game. Was his Trait telling him he'd heard all he needed? The conversation had been interesting. He'd been sailing the Sapphire Sea for almost a decade, and he'd never thought about which ships the Pale Sea pirates stole from, but he'd never crewed on a Merchant Adventurer ship that had been pirated.

"So, why don't they stop them?" Steen asked. "If they know where they are, why don't they stop them?"

"It's just property, that's what my uncle says. And not even theirs. If it was their own ships and goods then the Fair Seas Treaty Alliance would root them out. But if Sapphire Sea traders are the ones losing then it should be up to them to stop them." Tepio tossed a card down. "At least that's what some of them say."

"And without consensus: without *all* the Clan Freeholders agreeing they take no action," Charis said. "Politicians can't make decisions. I prefer the chain of command on a ship. *Skit.*" He threw down his cards. "I'm out."

Calder put his cards on the table, grateful that Tepio had forced Charis out first.

"Again?" Tepio groaned. "You are the luckiest man I've ever played cards with."

"Sorry. I warned you," Calder said. He scooped up the coins from the middle of the table. He slid half of them across to Charis. "Here, this should be enough to buy every sailor an extra half-share of beer when they're allowed."

"You don't need to do that," Charis said.

"Sure I do. I made a deal with Jebris," Calder said, referencing the god of the sea. "He takes care of me and I do my part for those who believe in him. That's how I keep my Luck going." He grinned. "I'm sure some of the sailors on board believe in Jebris."

"More than a few," Charis said. He put the coins in his vest pocket. "I'll give this to the provisioner straight away so I don't get tempted to play more cards." Charis got up and headed off, trailed by Jaak.

"I'll just make sure they get there," Steen said and hurried after them.

"Well done," Tepio said. "It takes the sting out of losing, knowing that at least the men will benefit."

"It always seems like the right thing to do," Calder said. He stood up. "I'm for sleep." After a quick trip to the head, he found his hammock. No one was in the ones below so he scrambled up and settled in.

He heard a few men come in before he fell asleep.

DAG ROLLED OVER and punched the pillow. She'd been awake for an hour already. Her hip ached from her tumble down the hill yesterday: that was the excuse she'd given Inger for going to bed soon after dinner, but really, she'd been bored of hanging around the tavern while Inger worked.

And her sister had worked *hard*. Dag couldn't believe all the tasks required to get everything ready for the customers. Glasses needed to be cleaned, tables wiped, floors swept. Then the food and drink had to be stocked. Ursa had a cook but she herself picked the menu based on what she had in her cold room and what the day's catch was. Last night it had been crab: big ones that could each feed two people. And it had been delicious, but once Dag had eaten there hadn't been anything for her to do.

None of the other patrons were very interested in talking to her. Oh, they were polite and friendly because she was Inger's sister but when she'd try to steer the conversations to find out what was really going on, they evaded answering her. Usually her Trait helped her discover what people wanted to hide, but not last night. So, she'd given up and come up to bed. Now it was early and she was wide awake.

She looked over at Inger, who was still fast asleep, and probably would be for a few more hours.

Dag threw her covers off and got up. She'd use the bathing closet in the hopes it would ease the stiffness from her fall yesterday and then find her own breakfast.

The cold water did help her aches and pains, and it certainly woke her up but she hadn't been able to find breakfast at the tavern or anywhere else in the small settlement. There were a few fishermen up and about, and even if they were willing to sell her a fish, she had nowhere to cook it. It seemed that Ursa really did own every establishment that fed people. That meant Dag still had a couple of hours to wait before she could expect breakfast.

Not wanting to repeat yesterday's mistake of climbing above the town, Dag decided to explore along the coast. It wasn't a very large island, from what she could remember from her lessons; she could probably walk all the way around it in a day. She grabbed a quick drink from the well in the square and set off north.

Where the packed earth of the square ended, a path of sorts led through woods. After half an hour, the path veered back to the shoreline, and Dag stepped out onto a small, pebbled beach. Three seagulls skittered away from her, screeching at the intrusion. They took flight, landing on a craggy perch above the beach. Waves gently lapped at the shore, and for a moment, Dag wondered why no one lived over here.

Except there was no fresh water, and there was very little land between the sea and the rocks that sloped up towards the plateau.

At the far end of the beach, a rock face blocked the way. Dag studied it for a moment before grabbing a windswept tree. She hauled herself up onto the rock and edged along a narrow ledge.

Dag had been following the ledge for almost half an hour and was wondering if she should turn back when she heard something. Shouting, or crying; not the screeching of birds, at least not birds she'd heard before.

She reached a . . . not quite a cliff but the rock ended in a six-foot drop into the sea below. Past that there was another beach where a short pier jutted out into the water. A handful of children played on shore, dashing towards the sea and then rushing away to escape the encroaching waves.

Stunned, Dag sat down on a rock and stared. *This* was a secret. But was it the only one or just the first one? She'd found the children: hidden away from the pirate settlement. She counted over a dozen children of various ages. Were there more?

There were two wooden structures tucked into the trees farther up from the shore. One had a trail of smoke coming from a chimney, and the other was a long narrow building that looked like it could sleep dozens.

The second building had the same type of washing hut as the Broken Mast. This one wasn't fed by a cistern on top of the building; instead a wooden trough led from the rock face behind it. Another trough branched off towards the building with the chimney.

This beach had its own spring: why was it so sparsely populated? There was just a single boat tied up at the dock: one of the sailboats that could be converted to ice travel. Now the presence of the other, similar boats in the settlement made sense. They must be used to travel from one spot on the island to another, not from Strongrock to Ostland. This boat had probably brought the children from the ship here.

Dag decided that she'd found enough secrets for today. She was hungry and thirsty and had over an hour's trek to get back to the tavern. She stood up and took one last look at the beach before turning and heading back along the narrow rocky ledge. She'd come back another time. No one here was going anywhere, and she still wanted to make her way around the whole island. But not today.

If asked, she'd say that she made it to the first secluded beach and stopped there and napped or swam or did anything other than find a way past it. Tomorrow she'd head off in the other direction. If there were more secrets on Strongrock Island her Trait would find them. She needed to uncover all of them before she could decide what to do about any single one or understand how they affected Inger.

When she got back to the tavern, Dag was a little disappointed. No one had wondered where she'd been, no one had missed her. Inger was up and had breakfast ready when she returned to the room, but of course she believed Dag's simple explanation that she'd decided to explore.

After breakfast, Inger had the noon meal service to help prepare for so Dag headed down to the dock. The three small sailboats were still there. She walked over to take a closer look. They looked well kept—the woodwork gleamed as if it had been oiled recently and the sections of hulls that she could see were smooth and undamaged.

"Nice, aren't they?"

Dag turned to find a large, middle-aged woman with short, salt and pepper hair eyeing her. She was dressed in dark trousers and a pale grey shirt, with a leather vest.

"Very," Dag replied. She recognized this woman from the ship she'd travelled on. "I've never actually seen them on water before; only on ice."

"They be just as fast on the waves," the woman said. "You've the look of Inger about you. You her sister?"

"I am," Dag held out a hand. "Dagrun Lund."

"Margit Ansdottir," the woman said. She took Dag's hand and gripped it, hard. "Captain of the ship you stowed on to get here."

Dag tried to remove her hand from the captain's but the woman tightened her grip.

"You don't deny it?"

"Why would I?" Dag asked. Her hand was released and she resisted the urge to cradle it against her chest. "I was worried that someone had stolen my sister away and I didn't know who to trust." She fished her purse out. "I can pay passage if that's your concern."

Captain Margit's grey eyes stared at her, and then she blinked, slowly. "No. I heard you were willing to row ashore here and even though you were bad at it, I reckon you did work your passage off some. But when you want off this rock you'll need to barter with me."

"I'll look for you," Dag said. "Although my sister and I don't have immediate plans to leave."

"Your sister?" Captain Margit barked. "She's one of us, or I don't know people." She chuckled. "Inger's staying put."

"That may be her decision," Dag said. Were they being held prisoner? Would Captain Margit even *allow* her and Inger to leave Strongrock? It certainly sounded like she wouldn't be able to leave on her ship. "We really haven't had a chance to discuss it, what with her being so busy at the tavern."

"She's done well there," Captain Margit said. "For herself and Ursa. I'd hate to see either of them unhappy." She nodded. "That reminds me that I'm late for the noon day meal."

Dag watched her walk away toward the Broken Mast.

She'd just been threatened. That last comment about making Inger, and more important to Margit Ansdottir, Ursa, unhappy: that was the captain warning her not to do anything to cause trouble. Like try to leave Strongrock with Inger.

Since that was exactly what she was planning on doing, she'd need to find another way off this island; a way that didn't include stowing away on Captain Margit Ansdottir's ship.

She eyed the boats tied up at the dock. The dinghies would never make it as far as Ostland but the sailboats might. If she knew how to sail one.

CHAPTER 5

JOOSEP KNOCKED ON the door again and took a step back. He'd been irritated when Tarmo Holt had summoned him, but now that he was being kept waiting, he was becoming outraged.

He took a deep breath. He'd never tolerate one of his Intelligencers becoming this rattled so easily. Had he been sitting in an office too long? Maybe he should take an assignment himself to keep his skills sharp? But where could he go that would be of use and who could he leave in charge?

He couldn't be spared now anyway, not with a new Grand Freeholder due to be appointed in a few months.

But it would be good to remind himself of who he was and what skills he had. Especially considering how curious Holt was about Traits.

Finally, the door opened, and Holt's assistant Mykol stepped aside to let him in.

"The Grand Freeholder can see you now," Mykol said.

Joosep nodded coolly, as though of course waiting when he'd been summoned didn't bother him. But next time Holt requested his presence he might decline and force the Grand Freeholder to come to him. He was the one who would still be here in three months, not Holt.

Joosep silently blew out a breath. When had he let things

become about *him*? He'd always prided himself on not being political, on being able to work with and for whoever was Grand Freeholder. Holt was the fourth one he'd reported to, so why was he letting the man fluster him? Especially when he only had another three months of him?

"Master Intelligencer," Holt said from where he sat behind his desk. "Thank you for coming."

"You said it was urgent," Joosep said. He didn't wait to be invited to sit and simply took the chair in front of Holt's desk. He tried not to show that he'd been bothered by Holt making him wait.

"Yes," Holt said. "I've heard that the pirates are working under the protection of Ostland."

"Where did you hear that?" Joosep asked. "My Intelligencers report that Ostland has denied any relationship to the pirates." If they were working with pirates, it would violate their agreement with the Fair Seas Treaty Alliance.

"They are calling themselves privateers," Holt said. "That must mean they believe they are working with some sort of authority."

"I'm not aware that they have any legitimate authority." He'd trust Calder's word over whoever Holt was listening to. "They also call themselves the Fair Seas Seafarers and we both know that they are not working for any of the Fair Seas Treaty Alliance countries." He sat back in his chair. "If you tell me who you heard this from, I will try to verify it."

"I cannot disclose my source," Holt said. "It would put them in grave danger."

"Then I have to view this as nothing more than an unsubstantiated rumour," Joosep replied. What was Holt doing? Did he already have his own spy network? Is that what he meant when he said identifying his source would put them in danger? It was against the Treaty for any single country to have its own intelligence network. Holt knew that Joosep *had* to try to find his source now. "Is this what you felt was so important?"

"Yes," Holt replied. "But I can see that you do not. There is another matter, since you're here. What about the Lund sisters? Have they returned?"

"Not yet," Joosep said, "although I appreciate your concern."

"Of course," Holt said. "And the newest recruits? How are they getting on?"

"Just fine," Joosep said, confused. In the almost three years that Tarmo Holt had been Grand Freeholder he'd never asked about recruits. Or any Intelligencers other than Dagrun and her sister. Who were . . . "Are you asking about any specific recruits?" A set of twins *had* recently arrived from Langin, in Byholt. Was that what he was after? These twins?

"No," Holt said. "I just want to make sure everything is in order when I hand over this office to Swyford."

"I can assure you that everything to do with the recruitment and instruction of Intelligencers is as it should be," Joosep said. He stood up. "If there's nothing else, I do have other duties."

As he exited Tarmo Holt's office, Joosep wished that Dagrun was here; he'd have her find out why Holt was so interested in twins. He would have Calder look into what Holt had said about Ostland backing the pirates. And find out why Holt thought they were.

"Rahm, drop what you're doing and come with me."

Calder gave the porridge one last stir before letting the spoon rest against the side of the pot. First Mate Charis stood in front of him with Cook hovering at his back.

"Yes sir," Calder said. Had Charis somehow discovered that he'd lied about himself? "Cook? This can be served in another few minutes."

Because refusing would get him tossed in the brig or overboard, Calder had no choice but to follow Charis out of the mess hall. Sailors waiting for their breakfast stood aside to let them pass, and worryingly, none of them would meet his eyes.

Charis led them up on deck: it was a grey day and the water looked cold and choppy.

"I need you to work on deck today," Charis said. "A storm's coming in and one of my men is in the infirmary. Jaak!" he called.

Jaak came running. "Here, sir."

"Rahm's with you today," Charis said, and then he left.

"So, what's the task?" Calder asked.

"We're in the rigging," Jaak said. "And with this weather we could be in for a dance."

"I love to dance," Calder said, laughing. He didn't bother asking about the sailor he was replacing: riggers had lots of accidents. Except for him, of course. His Trait usually kept him from harm when he did dangerous tasks. Although there had been one time when a fall had put him in the infirmary beside a man with knowledge he needed. His Luck worked in unpredictable ways.

Jaak clambered up into the rigging and Calder followed.

They spent an hour making sure all the lines and sails were secured. They followed orders, that was all, and in this weather the captain, not the first mate, was the one giving them.

Calder hunched against the cold wind that blew in from the north. He was leaning against the mast, his bare feet on the spar that held up the mainsail. Jaak was one level above him. The boat surged and rolled in the rough sea, frothy waves spraying the deck below.

To starboard he could just make out a line of white: the Frozen North. An inhospitable land perpetually locked in ice and snow. They must be closing in on the Frozen Pass then, an often-treacherous gap between the North and Ostland Island.

Calder had been through the pass many times, even once in the dead of winter when the ice from the North crept so far out from land that they'd been forced to sail dangerously close to Ostland's rocky shores. It wasn't a trip he'd want to repeat, despite his Trait.

"Strike the royals!" came the call from below. Other voices echoed the order, relaying it all over the ship.

Calder looked down to see Captain Olmar on the bridge, staring intently ahead. Calder started to climb up the rigging, making sure his footing was secure before he reached for the next handhold.

By the time he reached the spar below the royal, Jaak was already out on one end. Calder carefully made his way along the spar below. Jaak waved and Calder quickly started untying the knots that lashed the sail to the bottom spar. Jaak reached down and pulled the sail in.

Calder moved past the mast to the other side, waiting until Jaak was above. Once he'd untied this side of the royal, Calder climbed up to Jaak's level and made sure the sail was completely secure.

An improperly tied sail could be dangerous if it came loose and caught the wind. The unexpected surge could throw a ship off course and send it into waiting rocks or force it broadside.

Once they had the royal in and tied off, they both made their way lower in the rigging, Calder once more on the spar below Jaak.

Cold rain needled him and Calder flexed his toes to keep them limber. He'd pretty much done every task on a ship—including being captain—so he knew exactly what should happen and when. So, when it didn't, he became concerned.

The ship was listing too much for the wind and current, and he was expecting Captain Olmar to call for the top gallant and top sails to be struck, leaving only the mainsail. But it was almost half an hour since they'd struck the royal and there were still no new orders.

Calder sidled up to Jaak. "Does the Captain usually take the Pass with this much sail?" Even in calm seas, the top two of the four sails were always taken down. Calder had never seen the Pass attempted with three sails up: you lost too much control over the ship.

"Dunno," Jaak said. "First time I've shipped with him. Been out with Charis before, though. Him I trust."

Calder looked down, trying to get a glimpse of who was on the bridge. There were three people but he couldn't tell who they were through the rain.

"I can't lie," Calder said, leaning close to Jaak. "We've too much sail for this. I've never been through the pass with three up, even on a clear day."

"Captain gets a bonus for every day he saves," Jaak said. "But Charis knows what he's doing."

"If you say so." His focus narrowed on Jaak's words, making Calder even more worried. Was his Trait telling him this was why he was in the rigging today? People with coin on the line could make stupid decisions and take excessive risks. He went back down to the lower spar but the feeling that this was going wrong wouldn't go away. Should he do something? He couldn't outright disobey the captain's orders, but there might be a way to force what he wanted to happen.

He waited another ten minutes before he felt like he had to act. Jaak's eyes were fixed ahead, so Calder was able to reach out and one-handed, untie one of the ropes keeping the top gallant anchored to the spar he stood on. He inched back to the mast, the rope in hand, before he finally let go. The line whipped away in the wind.

The ship lurched and rolled under them as the sail fluttered and flapped.

"Get that top gallant tied down!" Olmar shouted. The ship pitched again, throwing the captain into the wheel.

"I can't get hold of the line," Calder called up to Jaak. "Strike that sail."

Jaak nodded and started pulling the sail towards him while Calder skirted the mast and quickly undid the knot at the other corner. He then clambered up and pulled the sail in. He was trying the last knot when Jaak joined him.

"I should report you," Jaak said.

"Yes, it's my fault," Calder said. "I guess I didn't check that knot earlier." He met Jaak's gaze. "But look how much calmer things are. The captain would have wanted that sail in soon anyway."

And the ship was calmer. It still roiled and dipped with the sea but the drag from the sails was reduced and the ship had slowed.

Jaak shrugged. "Probably right about that." He crawled out along the spar holding the top sail and Calder stayed on the spar below.

He'd take whatever punishment would be meted out for not securing the knot—it was better than outright mutiny. It would be hard to prove it was deliberate, and every sailor on board would know that once the sail was loose, in this weather, the only practical thing was to strike it as soon as possible. Half a sail was worse than no sail.

Calder chanced a glance down and thought he saw two people staring up at him. So Olmar and Charis would be out for blood. He had to believe that he could pretend ignorance long enough to get to Strongrock.

Captain Olmar didn't have them strike any more sails. The rain suddenly stopped and the wind died. The rough seas calmed, and by the time they were through the Frozen Pass, the sun was shining.

A couple of sailors joined them and helped Calder and Jaak raise the two sails. Once that was done, Jaak and Calder headed down to the deck.

Captain Olmar and First Mate Charis were waiting for them.

"What in all the gods were you doing?" Olmar yelled. Calder saw Jaak bend his head, but he met the captain's gaze and stepped forward.

"It was my fault, sir," Calder said. "Jaak here trusted me to make sure that knot was tight enough and I . . . didn't do a good enough job. I am sorry."

"Why didn't you get that sail tied back down? I didn't call to strike it."

"That was my fault too, sir," Calder said. "I thought it would take me too much time to go catch the end; that it would leave you without control of the ship for too long." Calder shrugged. "It's been a while since I've been a rigger. I'm sorry I wasn't up to the task."

"At least we didn't lose much time. You're off at Strongrock?"

Calder nodded.

"First Mate," Olmar continued. "See that this man's duties are more in line with his abilities. I'll be below if needed."

Calder didn't move until Olmar was gone. He would have spoken to Jaak but the younger man had disappeared by the time he turned to look for him.

"I was wrong about you," Charis said. He stepped closer. "You did that deliberately in order to get that sail down and then you took the blame."

"I'm not sure what you mean," Calder replied.

"Sure you do. Captain Olmar wants me to assign you tasks more in line with your abilities. I have a feeling he doesn't realize that means his job." Charis shook his head. "I hate to say this, but no one else will. Thank you for saving this ship." He took a step back. "And report back to Cook."

"Yes sir." Calder did keep his eyes down as he turned and left. He hadn't expected anyone to realize what he'd done. Was it a good thing or a bad thing? As with anything to do with his Trait, it could be either. Or both.

DAG STARED OUT past the dock to the ship that was anchored in the small bay. It belonged to Captain Ansdottir, and right now it was the only way for her to get off Strongrock. She expected that if she decided to leave—without Inger—she'd be able to secure passage back to North Tarklee. But if *Inger* decided to leave with her, she wasn't confident they would be allowed to go. And Dag wasn't sure why.

Margit Ansdottir had said that Inger was "one of them". What did that mean? Was Inger privy to some information they wouldn't allow to leave the island?

Dag sighed. She'd find out. She had to, and soon. Her Trait worked best when she allowed it to uncover things, to naturally find things that were hidden. But she could force it to work for her.

All she needed was something specific—something that was being hidden—to focus on. But which hidden thing? She could practically sense other secrets on this island, and until she knew them all, she couldn't be sure she was focussing on the right ones.

What she could do was make sure she knew any potential ways off this island in case she and Inger needed to leave. There was a sailboat where the children were living, but there was no way to know if that boat would always be there. And she didn't know how to sail it.

She stepped off the dock onto the rocky shore and started walking south. The pathway was much easier to navigate than her trek north had been yesterday. Gentle waves lapped at the beach, and trees and grasses waved in the cool breeze. She rounded a point and stopped. There were two huts here, but rain barrels set against their weathered walls implied that there was no permanent source of fresh water. She didn't see anyone around and there was no dock or boat so after a quick look around she passed them.

She angled east at first and then the shoreline turned northward. Another hour of walking made her regret not stopping at the huts for a drink of water. She didn't have a water skin of her own, and she hadn't wanted to risk asking even Inger for one. She didn't want anyone to realize exactly what she was doing. It was one thing to explore just outside the edges of the town and a very different thing to search the whole island.

She stayed near the trees, where it was shady. The terrain was harder to navigate but it was a relief to be out of the sun.

She paused, contemplating turning back when something growled nearby. A bird screeched and shot into the air, and Dag nervously peered into the forest.

There was a path of some kind: had it been made by animals? She hesitated before stepping past a branch. Animals meant water, didn't they? But would there be something big enough to hurt her?

It was humid farther away from the shore and warmer. Without the sea breeze, insects buzzed about her, and she waved her hands, trying to shoo them away. She heard another low growl, and she stopped, trying to determine what direction the sound had come from.

It was a lynx, probably. At least she thought her instructor had mentioned that the cats lived on Strongrock. She wished she'd paid more attention to her lessons because she had no idea if a lynx would attack her.

She took a few steps deeper into the forest. The only sounds now were the buzzing of insects: even the birds were silent. Dag grabbed a fallen branch and raised it above her head, ready to strike if something attacked. She'd follow the path for a little while in the hopes of finding water but if she didn't find something soon she'd have to turn back. A forest at night with a lynx prowling around did not seem safe.

Despite the trail leading directly to it, if her foot hadn't sunk into the soggy loam, Dag wouldn't have noticed the small spring. It bubbled up from the ground and pooled under some fern leaves before saturating the ground. After checking to make sure nothing dangerous was nearby, she scooped some water up in her hands and drank.

It was refreshing despite its slight metallic taste. And the spring was so well-concealed that Dag wondered if anyone else had ever found it. Once she'd drunk her fill, she stood up and wiped her hands on her trousers.

She peered up through the trees at the sun. She'd been gone for three hours. Would it be better—take less time—to finish circling the island, or should she go back the way she'd come? She'd decide once she made it back to the shore.

She only had a small knife with her, but she did her best to mark trees as she walked back along the trail. If she needed to find this spring again, she liked to think that she could.

Once on the beach, Dag decided to push forward. She wasn't sure her sister would actually miss her for a few more hours, and if she turned back now she'd be late enough that even Inger would wonder what she'd been up to, which meant Ursa would as well.

After the captain's threat, she thought that neither Ansdottir nor Ursa would like Dag exploring the island. She might not get another chance to uncover some of the secrets that she felt Strongrock was hiding.

The sun was just starting to dip down below the tree line when she stepped onto another beach. At the far end there was a small, natural bay. A dinghy had been dragged up and overturned on the sand in front of rocks that rose sharply at the end of the bay.

Dag crept deeper under the trees. Was someone here, or had the boat been abandoned?

She watched for half an hour but nothing moved near the boat. Staying under the trees she paralleled the beach as she made her way toward it. She crossed a path that had been worn into the dirt of the forest: made with human feet, not animals, she thought. It led deeper into the woods and she felt the itch start between her shoulder blades. There was a secret at the end of this path: she took a last look at the boat before following it.

A rough structure stood in a clearing. The walls were made up of fallen trees lashed together into a square and set onto a layer of rocks. A weathered canvas cover was tied at the corners. The wind lifted the canvas and she saw a stack of wooden crates.

Dag circled the clearing but there was no one there, although she did see the old remains of a campfire.

She stepped into the clearing. The boat had no owner, not right now, so she should have time to find out what was hiding in the crates.

When she got to the structure, she realized that the canvas was a worn and patched sail, probably one no longer fit to use. The logs were as high as her waist, and there didn't look to be any door to allow a person to walk inside.

She untied one corner of the canvas and lifted it up.

Boxes and barrels of varying sizes were all stacked neatly inside. It looked like a warehouse of sorts, but why was it so far from the town?

There were words stamped on many of the crates. *Merja, Windswept, Stormrunner.* Were they the names of ships? She lifted the canvas higher. And there, in the middle, was that a cannon? She climbed up onto the logs and with the corner of the canvas in hand, walked across a few crates drawing back the cover as she went.

The cannon was a dull black and it rested heavily on a layer of rocks that kept it off the ground. *Diamanto* was embossed on one end.

She pried the lid off of a nearby crate: it was filled with long guns and pistols. The wind gusted and powder from the top of a barrel pelted her face. Her hand came away black when she wiped the grit from her forehead.

She looked out at the crates, wondering why the pirates were stockpiling weapons. Who were they for? She counted twenty-two crates, six barrels, and the cannon. Were there other weapons hidden in other parts of the island?

She walked back to the edge of the structure and jumped from the logs onto solid ground. She quickly retied the canvas at the corner and went to the edge of the clearing. Another secret uncovered but whose secret? What were the weapons for and why were they being kept here?

All questions she'd need answers to, if she was to uncover any risks to her sister. For now, she needed to go back to the beach and try to find a way past the rock face. She still wanted to circle the entire island: she had a feeling that there were more secrets to discover.

She was halfway back to the beach when she heard a shout. She scrambled off the path into the dense trees and underbrush and carefully made her way to the beach.

A ship was in the bay and a dinghy was being rowed towards shore. Someone in the stern was shouting and sailors pulled the oars in time to his commands. When the dinghy got close to the beach, two people jumped into the surf and dragged it towards shore. Half a dozen sailors swarmed over the sides and hurried over to the upturned dinghy. They righted it and had it in the water in minutes, heading out through the waves back to the ship.

The other dinghy had been pulled up onto the beach and crates were being handed from it into waiting hands. Sailors lifted them onto their shoulders and waded through the surf and dropped their burdens onto the sand.

Pirates—because who else could it be—unloaded another three crates. The second dinghy arrived back on shore with three crates and three barrels.

Once everything had been unloaded, teams of pirates—an even mix of men and women, from what Dag could see—hauled them up to the path. A couple of women stayed with the boats, either guarding them or making sure they weren't swept away by the waves.

Half an hour later the rest of the pirates returned, empty-handed. Some helped overturn one dinghy before they boarded the other one and rowed back out towards the ship.

It was dusk by the time the ship rounded the edge of the island and out of sight, heading towards the town of Strongrock.

Dag let out a big breath. It was already almost too dark for her to travel. She stared out at the jut of land the ship had disappeared behind. Now she knew for certain that Ansdottir's pirates were storing and hiding weapons. She didn't see how this *wasn't* a threat to Inger.

Her stomach rumbled, reminding her that she'd had nothing to eat since breakfast. She stood up and stepped out onto the beach. Already the footprints of the pirates were being swept away by the wind and the waves.

It was too late for her to reach Strongrock before dark. Her only option was to find a safe place to spend the night. And it wasn't going to be this beach; not when pirates had claimed it.

It wasn't until she stepped up on top of the rocks at the end of the beach that she saw the other, smaller inlet. There was no path down to it: just a drop into water from where she stood, but there was a tiny beach edged by a few trees. The beach ended at another sheer rock face on the far side of the inlet.

Dag stared down at the inlet. The water was clear enough that she could see the bottom. It looked sandy, but in the dusk, it was hard to tell exactly how deep the water was. There was a six- or seven-foot drop to the sea, but once she was in the water it looked like an easy swim or wade to the beach.

Concentrating on the water below her, using her Trait to see the Unseen, she walked out along the rock to a point where she *felt* that the water was deep enough. With a prayer to Jebris, God of the sea, she jumped, clutching her knees to her chest.

She bobbed to the surface and stood up to find herself in water that reached just past her waist. In only took a few minutes to wade to shore.

The sun didn't reach the narrow beach she stepped onto, and she shivered in the cool air beneath the trees. She pulled her wet boots off and left them where the beach met tall grass. It was dark now: too dark to travel any further tonight, so this protected beach would be where she slept. She sat down, her bare toes digging into the sand, as the stars started winking overhead.

It took her a while to realize that not all of the sounds of water were from waves. Underneath the rhythmic sound of waves there was a faint trickling. Her shoulder blades itched; her Trait had been triggered by something hidden.

Concentrating on the sound, Dag walked to the far end of the beach. She stopped and grinned. There was enough light for her to see that the rock wall glistened where a small trickle of water flowed down it. She dipped a finger in the water and raised it to her lips. Freshwater: the second hidden spring she'd found today.

She scooped water from the rock to her mouth, drinking her fill. By the time she was finished, a crescent moon had risen.

She stretched out on the beach with her bare feet to the water and a small clump of grass beneath her head. It didn't take long for her to fall asleep.

CHAPTER 6

CALDER DUMPED THE potato peelings into a separate pot and put it on the fire. Cook had welcomed him back with a grunt, but Calder was aware of the exact moment when the older man learned about his poor showing as a rigger.

Calder didn't care—in fact that was the response he'd expected: whispers and glares and sailors avoiding him. It was Charis' reaction that he hadn't expected. Or wanted.

"What are you doing with the scrap?" Cook asked. He sniffed the pot. "It should be in the slop bucket."

"A trick I learned on the Sapphire Sea," Calder said. "From a man who had cooked for the most powerful nobles. Boil up the scrap ends of everything to make the base for your next stew or soup." He leaned over the pot and waved a hand, bringing the steam towards his nose. "The flavour of everything is enhanced."

"Never heard of it," Cook said. "Seems a waste of time."

"You should try it," Calder said. "It makes even the plainest of ingredients taste better." It would be up to Cook to use this tomorrow. Calder would be leaving the ship as soon as it reached Strongrock.

"I would hate to waste the water you used up making it," Cook said. "Now leave my galley. Not sure the crew will be able to enjoy the meal with you standing in front of them."

"I understand." Calder grabbed a bowl of stew and a spoon and headed off down the corridor.

The hammocks were empty at this time of day. Everyone not on duty would be heading to the galley for dinner. He almost didn't expect to see his own hammock, or maybe to find it down on the deck but it was still strung up above two others. That didn't mean it hadn't been tampered with: he'd check to make sure it was secure before climbing into it. Falling on men below him was not something he was willing to risk.

Failing his duties as a rigger had demonstrated his incompetence, and some of his fellow crew members were angry. As far as they were concerned he'd put the whole ship at risk. But disciplining him for mistakes made on duty was the Captain's responsibility, not the crew's, and Calder didn't expect any of them to violate the chain of command.

But if he were to injure another sailor—say by falling out of his hammock—the crew would mete out his punishment. And they would be harsh.

"What are you doing here?"

Calder looked up to see Jaak glaring down at him from a second level hammock

"Eating." Calder sat down on the deck. "Cook thought my presence would turn the crew off their dinner," he said cheerfully.

"You think this is funny?" Jaak rolled over and out of the hammock, landing on his feet. "You got both of us in trouble."

Calder spooned some stew into his mouth and ate it, enjoying the flavours despite Jaak's glare. "I think that I'm the only one who's in trouble," he said when he finished chewing. "I took the blame and so Captain blamed me."

"Yeah? So what? I'm still getting sideways looks from the others."

"Sailors can look at people however they want," Calder said. "It doesn't mean they blame you."

"They do," Jaak said. "Especially First Mate Charis."

"I doubt it," Calder said. If Charis blamed Jaak for anything— and he shouldn't—it would be for *not* seeing what Calder had: that the ship was in danger if that sail had not been taken down. That blame lay with Captain Olmar.

Calder finished his stew and set the bowl down beside him. "You'll miss dinner."

"Not hungry," Jaak said. He paced the small area. "Everybody hates me already; this will just make it worse."

"Why would anyone hate you?" Calder asked, genuinely interested. He hadn't gotten that impression from anyone on board.

"Because I used to be one of *them*," Jaak said. "A privateer. No one trusts me."

Calder's focus narrowed at the word privateer. His Trait was activated.

"But you're not a privateer now," Calder said.

"That's not how they see it," Jaak replied. "Some of the crew have been boarded and stolen from. Think that's my fault. Not like I chose that life."

"Then it must have chosen you," Calder said. "And I'd think you'd be even more trustworthy since you obviously gave up that life." Although to be honest, Calder could think of very excellent reasons why the pirates would want spies on board other ships. But he would never choose someone like Jaak.

"I see it that way too," Jaak said. "Privateers picked me up from the streets of North Tarklee. I was starving after my brother went to jail. For stealing food to feed me! They took me to Strongrock; fed me; clothed me; taught me to fish and read. Then when I was big enough they put me on a ship with Captain Margit Ansdottir herself. The greatest captain on any sea." Jaak hung his head. "Not that I understood what they were about then. Stealing." He spat on the deck. "That's what done my brother in so I wanted no part of that."

"So that's when you left them?" Calder asked.

"Not right away, I'm ashamed to admit. I felt like I owed them, for saving me. But there was one ship we boarded where two people were killed." Jaak sighed. "I couldn't stomach that. Stealing is bad enough, but killing? I volunteered for the next trip to North Tarklee. As soon as my feet hit the dock, I was gone."

"Yet you stayed with the sea," Calder said.

"Been at sea for over five years," Jaak said. "Don't know anything else, really."

Calder sat silent for a few moments. There was something he was missing, something . . . "That's how you know the Teeth can be navigated through," he said. "You've gone through the Teeth yourself, with the privateers."

Jaak nodded. "No one believes me, not even the captain."

Calder wanted to say that was because the captain couldn't imagine anyone having such skills because his were so poor. Instead he said, "Charis does. The First Mate even said how he thought it could be done."

"Yeah," Jaak agreed. "The way he described it made me wonder if he'd been through them himself."

"Or maybe he's seen it done," Calder said. "From afar. He's seen a ship enter the Teeth and not founder."

"That could be," Jaak said. He scratched his head. "Maybe I will go get some dinner after all."

"Take this back with you." Calder held up his bowl. "Please."

Once Jaak had gone, Calder went to his hammock. He untied it to check the ropes. There; one had been cut almost through. He pulled out his knife, cut the rope completely and spent a few minutes splicing it back together. Once it was as good as new and he'd made sure nothing else had been tampered with, he strung the hammock up.

He'd take a quick turn around the deck; he had to visit the head anyway—and take note of who was here when he came back to climb into his hammock. It never hurt to know who your enemies were: at least the ones who wanted to really see you hurt.

"ARNOR," JOOSEP CALLED. "Arnor!" Where was his assistant?

"Sir?" Arnor stuck his head through the open door. He swallowed. "Sorry, I was just eating my dinner."

"Any news?" Joosep asked, ignoring Arnor's comment. He had yet to eat—and it was late—but a gnawing feeling in his gut was making him too uneasy to do anything but worry.

"About?"

"Calder or the Lund sisters," Joosep said. Then he took a deep breath. Arnor didn't have a Trait—he didn't know what it was like to *know* he should be able to grasp something and yet have it just out of reach.

"Sorry, I've had no word," Arnor said. "Is there anything else?"

"No," Joosep said. "Wait, yes. Have Gustav Gunnarson come see me after his meal."

"Yes, sir," Arnor said. He closed the door, leaving Joosep to brood alone.

Something was being hidden from him, he knew it. His weak

Trait was strong enough to tell him that. But what was being hidden and by whom? It had something to do with the Lund sisters, but he wasn't sure which one. And Tarmo Holt, of course.

There was knock on the door and Arnor opened it, a smile on his face.

"Gustav is here," Arnor turned and grinned at the young man who entered.

"Thank you, Arnor," Joosep said when Arnor made no move to close the door. He smiled at Gustav himself—he couldn't help it. It was the boy's Trait, after all.

Gustav took the chair in front of the desk. "Thanks!" he said to Arnor who beamed and finally closed the door.

"Gustav, how are you?" Joosep asked. He did his best to keep his voice level and serious, not an easy thing when Gustav's Trait—Charisma—seemed to seep out of him, infusing the air around him.

"Very good, Master Intelligencer. Thank you for asking."

"Good. I hear that you are doing well in your studies." Although after seeing the boy, Joosep had to wonder if there could ever be an impartial assessment of his progress. The lad was just so likeable. Even with his Unseen Trait he had a difficult time ignoring Gustav's Charisma.

"I am trying, sir."

"I'm sure you are. Do you feel up to working on an assignment?" Joosep asked.

"Already?" the boy seemed pleased. "After less than five years of study?"

"It's a small task, one that will not take you away from the Hall," Joosep said. "I need you to befriend someone. Get them to trust you."

"That sounds easy."

"It will be," Joosep said. "For you."

"And once I befriend them?" Gustav asked. "Then comes the real work?"

"Yes," Joosep replied. "Then you need to find out what they know about the dealings of a certain person. And no one can know you are doing this."

"Of course not, sir," Gustav grinned. "That's what we Intelligencers do. Keep secrets. Who is it?"

"Tarmo Holt," Joosep said. "I want you to get close to whoever is close to him and find out everything."

CALDER KNEW HE'D spent too much time on deck. Dinner was over and the next watch had already started. He'd been gone so long that he'd need to check his hammock again. And anyone he did that in front of was likely either waiting to see him fall or had sabotaged his hammock themselves. The precise situation he'd wanted to avoid by fixing his hammock early.

But he'd been trying to evade talking to First Mate Charis. The man had been standing between the bow, where Calder had been watching dark clouds scurry away, and the path to the hold. At one point he'd just need to leave.

"It looks like there's a storm heading north."

Calder turned and hid a sigh. "Yes, sir." Charis stopped beside him and stared up at the sky.

"Do you want me to say anything to the crew?" Charis asked.

"No, sir! I can take care of it." The last thing Calder wanted was the First Mate interfering. He did actually want to feel safe enough to sleep tonight.

"In that case," Charis said. "I was wondering why you are up here."

"I was making sure that whoever sabotaged my hammock had time to make it back below deck to see me not fall out of it," Calder said. "I prefer to know my enemies."

Charis grunted. "Let me know if there's anything I can do," he said.

"I'd appreciate it if I can be in the first boat heading to shore," Calder said. Once on land the crew would no longer care about him. Not enough to risk upsetting the authorities in a strategic port of call, anyway. That would bring the captain's wrath down on them.

Charis nodded and Calder slipped away.

He was halfway down the stairs when he heard footsteps behind him.

"What'd the First Mate want with you?" It was Steen, who'd lost to him at cards last night.

"Just reminding me that he wants me off this ship as soon as possible tomorrow," Calder said. He stepped off the last stair and into the corridor, Steen right behind him.

"I can make that happen tonight," Steen said.

Calder whirled on him, grabbed his arms, and twisted them behind his back. He shoved Steen into the wall of the narrow passageway.

"Discipline is the captain's job," Calder said into his ear. "Are you pretending you're the captain?" Impersonating the captain was such a serious offence that a man could be thrown overboard if found guilty.

"Didn't say that," Steen said.

Calder shoved him away, releasing him. He might be better to stay awake tonight after all. "I heard what you *did* say." He glared at the other sailor. "And I don't like threats. Keep away from me." Calder turned his back on Steen, wondering what his Trait would do if the man tried to knife him.

When he made it back to his hammock there was an ugly feel to the room. A few sailors sat around a table, cards laid out in front of them, but Calder was pretty sure none of them had made a move since they heard him coming this way.

He briskly went over to his locker; it didn't look like anything had been stolen but curious eyes were following his every move. Had something been done? Or had contraband been hidden? He inspected his belongings as he bundled them together and shoved them into his satchel.

His boots were still in the bag: if anyone thought it strange that a common sailor owned a pair of expensive and well-made boots they weren't saying anything. He'd brought them with him since he hadn't known what to expect: he still didn't know what to expect and he'd been in situations where lives were lost because of a lack of decent footwear.

He picked up his hat and brushed the feathers. They seemed more drab than dandy right now. Tucked inside the brim was a rope bracelet he didn't recognize. He left that hanging on a peg. No doubt someone had planned on accusing him of being a thief. He shoved his hat on his head, tucked his satchel under his arm, and without saying a word, left.

He went straight to the kitchen. It was the one place on the ship he was the most familiar with and it was Cook's domain: a place any sailor who wanted to eat wouldn't dare interfere with.

He knew he'd made the right decision when he found the door was unlocked: his Luck working for him. He went in and locked the door behind him. The only people on board with keys to this room were Cook and Captain Olmar.

With the door locked and a knife close by, he felt safe enough to sleep.

Seagulls cawing overhead woke her. Dag rubbed grit out of her eyes and sat up. She grabbed her boots—they were still too damp to put on—and made her way to the spring.

After she'd had enough to drink, she tied her boots together, slung them over one shoulder, and trudged back to the beach. The rising sun washed it with light and she peered in past the trees. A wooded area led up to a wall of rock.

Her stomach rumbled, but she ignored it. She'd missed meals before as part of her training, and she wasn't about to look for berries or mushrooms when she had no idea what might be edible. Hungry was always better than poisoned.

She headed under the tree canopy. Small birds twittered, and the bugs were out in full force. She kept her nose and mouth pressed into her elbow, trying to block the clouds of insects. The ground under her feet was spongy and her toes sank. Dag deliberately didn't look: one of the drawbacks of her Trait was that she uncovered things she'd prefer to remain hidden. As long as nothing bit her she didn't *want* to know what was underfoot.

With the rock face on her right, she walked for half an hour before stepping out onto another beach. Grateful, she walked into the surf to wash off whatever muck had collected on her feet.

In the distance, she could see the hazy outline of land. It could only be Ostland Island: she must be on the northern shore of Strongrock Island. The shoreline should turn south soon, towards the bay where the children lived.

Dag had already decided that she'd tell anyone she came across the truth: that she'd walked all the way around the island. No one needed to know why, other than that she was curious and bored because Inger was working so much. What she wasn't going to mention was the secrets she'd found or that she'd seen the ship and pirates.

Inger would believe every word Dag told her; then she'd repeat it until everyone in the Broken Mast believed it too. Inger couldn't lie and people seemed to sense that so they believed what she said.

Grinning, Dag headed along the beach. She'd found a way to

use Inger's Trait. Her smile slipped. But would Inger hate that her Trait was being used this way?

As an Intelligencer, Dag's own Trait was used, and she didn't mind: it was what she had agreed to. She was planning on using Inger's trait without her knowledge. But she couldn't ask her permission: Inger couldn't lie, and she needed her sister to believe what she told her so that others would believe it too.

An hour later, after navigating some treacherous shoreline, she was still thinking about Inger when she heard the shouts of children. She'd had such an early start that it was only mid-morning: had she reached the beach where they lived already?

Dag climbed down a pile of rocks and stepped onto the first beach she'd seen since the one she'd left at the north end of the island. Most of the shoreline in between had been rocky but passable, and she paused to enjoy the way the gentle surf washed up the white sand. She could see why the pirates had chosen it for the children.

The two buildings were at the far end, where she'd find the trail that led back to Strongrock. The small sailboat was still tied up beside the dock.

"Who are you?"

The voice had come from the direction of a stand of trees. It had been a young voice, and although Dag didn't see anyone, her shoulders itched and she had to force herself to not look up.

"Who's there?" she asked, hiding a smile. "I'm a bit lost, can you help me?"

Leaves rustled above her and then something dropped to the ground. A child—a girl of about ten—stepped out of the undergrowth.

"Lost from where?" the girl asked. She didn't look friendly.

"From Strongrock," Dag replied. "My name is Dagrun Lund. I was visiting my sister who is always working. I got bored and decided to walk around the island."

"Nobody can walk around the island," the girl said. "Teacher says it's impossible."

Dag shrugged. "I guess it's not." She looked up the beach. "Unless there's no way to get from here to Strongrock?" When she'd seen this beach from the far end, the path had ended at drop off into the sea. Was there no way to get up to that ledge? She had to believe that her Trait would find a way.

"Dunno," the girl said. "I'm going to get Teacher. You stay here." The girl ran off up the beach.

Instead of following the girl's orders, Dag walked slowly along the beach towards the buildings. When she was half way, she stopped and sat down to wait. She didn't want to threaten them, but she knew she had to get past them to get back to Strongrock.

After a few minutes, a large woman hurried towards her, a group of fifteen children following her.

"Who are you?" the woman asked. She stopped a few feet from Dag.

"Dagrun Lund," Dag said, still sitting. It made her less able to defend herself, but she wanted to look harmless. "I've been staying at The Broken Mast in Strongrock. My sister Inger works there."

"I've seen Inger," the woman said. She eyed Dag for a moment before she nodded, once. "And you do have the look of her. What are you doing here?"

Dag shrugged. "I was bored, and maybe a little mad at Inger. I came to visit her and all she does is work." Dag looked up and tried to look sheepish. "So, I thought I'd walk around the island. I thought I'd be back in time for dinner."

"Hah! Around the island in a few hours!" The woman stopped laughing. "Are you saying you walked all around this island?"

"I did have to swim in a spot or two," Dag said. She lifted her boots. "These may never be the same again."

"And what'd you do about food and water?"

"I found a couple of springs." Dag made a face. "Although the one might have been just a muddy puddle. But no food, so if you have a bite to spare I'd really appreciate it."

"Huh." The woman stared at Dag.

"You can have some of my lunch," a small girl said. She stepped out from behind the woman.

"Hush, Leja," the woman said.

"It's all right, Teacher," Leja replied. "I want to. I know what it's like to be hungry."

"Thank you," Dag said, her heart breaking. The girl couldn't be more than six. How much hunger had she endured in her short life? "I think I can make it back to Strongrock on my own. Just let me get past your . . . camp."

Teacher glared at her, then sighed. "Come up and have

something to eat." She looked down at Leja. "I reckon we all know what it's like to be hungry. And what it means when someone helps." She turned and strode off, most of the children running ahead of her. But the procession was eerily quiet, not like a normal group of happy children.

Leja and the girl she'd first spoken to remained behind the rest of them.

"Best get up," the older girl said. "Before Teacher changes her mind."

"Thank you." Dag got to her feet. Leja held out her hand and Dag took it, letting her lead the way. The other girl stepped in behind them and followed her as she walked along the beach.

"It's not much," Teacher said, handing a bowl to Dag when she was in front of one of the buildings. "Left over from breakfast, and cold."

"We don't throw out food," Leja said solemnly.

"Nor should anyone," Dag agreed. No spoon had been given to her so she dipped two fingers into the cold porridge and scooped it into her mouth. Cold, yes, but some flavourings she couldn't identify made it very tasty. Hopefully it wasn't anything that would harm her. She looked around at the circle of faces staring at her and scooped up more porridge. She didn't think Teacher would poison her in front of these children.

When she was finished, she handed the bowl back to the woman.

"Thank you." Dag wanted to ask where the children were from, but she didn't want to make Teacher angry. "You said that you've met my sister Inger?"

"I have," Teacher said. "I get back to Strongrock every few days. She's new at the Mast, isn't she?"

"Yes. I was away when she left home and I . . ." Dag looked out at the sea. "I was worried that something bad had happened to her." She looked back at Teacher. "Inger, she's smart and all but she just . . . trusts."

"Hah!" Teacher laughed. "She does at that. You're her big sister, then? Looking out for her? That's good."

Dag was about to disagree with her, but then she realized that although Inger was a few minutes older, Dag did feel responsible for her.

"I'll put this away, and if you think you can make it back by land, you go that way." Teacher pointed down the beach before she walked up towards the building.

"She's nice," Leja said. "Inger."

"You've met my sister?"

"In North Tarklee," Leja said and nodded. "She was nice to my little sister and me. We were cold and she let us borrow her coat. When we were on the ship to come here; the one with the lady captain."

"Captain Margit Ansdottir?" Dag asked.

"Captain Margit, yes." Leja looked down at her feet. "She got us from the lady in North Tarklee who saved us and brought us here, but I'm not sure she's nice." She looked back up at Dag. "Not like Inger."

Dag laughed. "Yes, Inger is nice. Much nicer than I am and that's the truth."

"I think you're nice," Leja said.

"All right, Leja, back to your studies." Teacher came back down to the beach. "Have you decided to walk? I could take you by boat but not until the end of the day. I got a schedule to keep these children on."

"I better go now," Dag said. "I'd rather not make Inger worry any longer than I already have."

"All right."

"Thank you for the hospitality," Dag said. She turned and started to walk down the beach. She looked back to see Leja, a smaller girl at her side, waving.

A six-year-old on the street caring for her even younger sister, Dag thought. How was that allowed to happen in North Tarklee? How was it that pirates were kinder to them than the community they were born into?

Another secret confirmed: the pirates really did take in children. She still didn't know why, unless it really was as simple as what Teacher had said: that they'd all known hunger. But could there be another—hidden—reason?

She looked up at the sky. It was less than an hour's walk to get back to Strongrock so she'd be there in time for the noon meal.

CHAPTER 7

Calder hefted his satchel, tucked his hat under his arm, and found an out of the way place to stand on deck.

He hadn't had to explain his presence to Cook this morning. The man had simply grunted when he'd walked into the kitchen, partly because Calder already had most of the work of making breakfast done. Cook was able to relax with his first tea of the morning: a treat he'd probably enjoyed only a handful of times since becoming the ship's cook. Besides, this was the last time he'd see Calder on board this ship: what did he care that the man apparently broke into his galley to work?

Once he'd eaten his own breakfast, Calder had left to wander the deck and do his best to stay out of everyone's way. He'd been subjected to more than a few glares but other than that, the crew ignored him. Once he was off the *Bright Breeze* he'd be as good as dead to them. Oh, there was always a chance they'd run into him in some distant port, but he could be ignored there too.

The ship rounded the tip of the island and the Strongrock harbour came into view. A group of buildings stretched along the dock and the land sloped up to the plateau.

A lone ship was anchored in the sheltered bay. As they got closer, Calder recognized it: the *Vassan*, a pirate ship captained by Margit Ansdottir. He'd heard that she was a formidable sailor, although he'd never met her. She kept to the waters around the Pale Sea while most of his missions had been spent farther afield.

Charis called out for the dinghy to be readied and Calder headed to it. He didn't try to help—he hadn't been assigned deck duties and his kitchen work was finished with breakfast—but he'd asked the First Mate to get him into the dinghy for the first trip ashore, and he wanted to be easily found.

"Rahm, get in," Charis said. "Passenger only. I can't wait to get you off this ship."

Calder nodded, grateful. He understood that the First Mate was trying to avoid complaints from the crew about him getting preferential treatment. Calder didn't care what reasons Charis gave, he wanted off this ship too. He shrugged. Charis' problems with his crew—or his captain—were not his concern. Getting off this ship and safely to Strongrock was.

Once the boat had been lowered and the rowers were in and seated, Calder swung his legs over the gunwale and stepped down onto the rope ladder. Or at least that was the plan. The ladder bucked away from his right foot. He looked over his shoulder; the Third Mate stared up at him before he deliberately let go of the rope ladder, spitting over the side of the dinghy.

Calder tried again, setting his foot on the ladder, wondering if someone else would try to dislodge him from it and dump him in the bay. He put his other foot on the next rung. The ladder bucked once.

"*Skit!*" someone bellowed from below.

Calder craned his neck: a sailor huddled on the seat closest to the ladder, his hand cradled in his lap. Even from here he could see that the thumb was dislocated. While everyone else was staring at the sailor, Calder scrambled down the ladder.

He stepped into the boat and quickly sat down in the prow.

"Swap out, man," the Third Mate said. "You can't row now."

Calder stayed silent as the injured man headed up the ladder and a woman took his place.

The Third Mate glared at Calder before calling out to the rowers.

"Starboard, row." The dinghy veered away from the ship and started to turn in a circle. As soon as the bow was pointed towards land, he called, "Port, join in."

It took a few minutes to reach the dock, and as soon as the

Third Mate had grabbed hold of it, Calder climbed out and onto the dock. A few insults were shouted at him, but no one tried to stop him as he walked away from the dinghy toward the small village.

The Broken Mast was a little more weathered than it had been when he'd visited it years ago. The inn and tavern were separate buildings and the proprietor was outside when he approached the inn. He followed her into the inn and handed over some coin in exchange for a key. He told her his name was Rahm, in case the crew of the *Bright Breeze* came looking for him, and she told him that she was Ursa Ozlinch. She owned both the inn and the tavern, where he should go for his meals.

The room was plain, but there was a sturdy-looking lock on the door. The privacy and safety of his own room was worth the cost, especially since it was Joosep's coin he was spending.

He dropped his bag on the narrow bed and sat in the chair by the window, peering out as a few of his former crewmates headed into the tavern. He debated skipping the noon meal but instead decided to give the *Bright Breeze* crew time to eat but not enough time to get drunk before heading to the tavern.

Calder stretched out on the bed with his head pillowed against his pack. He'd learned long ago to be patient with his Trait. He'd also learned that it was wise to sleep when the opportunity presented itself. You never knew when you'd get your next chance.

DAG RAN A hand through her tangled hair as she stared at the washing closet. She was desperate to clean up, but she needed to let Inger know she was back. She pushed through the tavern door and paused, allowing her eyes to adjust to the dim light inside.

"Dag!" Inger set a tray on a nearby table, rushed over, and wrapped her arms around her. "Where have you been?"

Dag hugged her sister before taking a step back. "Your customers won't appreciate you smelling like me," she said. She sighed. "I'm sorry. For some reason I thought walking around the island was a good thing to do."

"You did what? Oh Dag, what a bad idea." Inger shook her head. "Sit down somewhere and I'll bring you something to eat."

Inger turned to go but Dag grabbed her arm. "I'll come back," she said. "When I'm clean."

"There might not be any lunch left," Inger said. "A ship just dropped anchor and we're busier than usual."

"I'll take my chances," Dag said. Inger nodded and went back to her tray. Dag left her sister to deal with her customers and headed out through the back and up the stairs to their room.

Five minutes later she was standing under the flowing water of the washing closet. She let the water run longer than she should have considering she wasn't the one who had to replenish it. Once dressed in cleaner clothes she felt so much better that she would have been willing to do whatever was required to get water, if someone told her how.

Dag bundled up the clothes she'd worn on her trek and shoved them in a corner. She was wearing the last of her clean clothes and would need to do laundry soon. With a longing look at the bed, she headed back to the tavern in search of something to eat.

Hanne was at her usual table in the back. She nodded as Dag took a seat across from her.

The tavern was almost full, and although Dag recognized many of the customers, there were new faces: mostly men, when the pirates were more evenly divided between men and women.

Inger was collecting empty mugs from a table of unfamiliar sailors when one of them reached out and caressed her ass. Dag was on her feet before the mugs Inger had been holding hit the floor. She was only halfway to her sister when half a dozen pirates pulled the offender from his chair.

There was a short scuffle while the man was dragged out the door. The sailor's tablemates seemed to reconsider defending him and sat back down.

"Are you all right?" Dag asked Inger. She took her arm and pulled her back a step. Inger nodded but she was shaking.

"You'll be paying for them broken mugs!" Ursa said. She strode over and looked down on the three remaining men. "And extra for the disrespect." Ursa looked over at Inger. "That fine with you?"

"I'm fine with them paying double," Inger said, and Dag realized that she'd been shaking from anger, not fear. Inger walked over to the men. "You can get it from your friend later but you're not leaving until you pay up."

Ursa stood over them while they fished around for coin. Eventually the tavern owner was satisfied and the three men left.

"It's all yours, Inger," Ursa said as she gave the handful of coins to Inger.

"You take enough to cover the food and drink," Inger said. She tried to give some of the money back but Ursa shook her heard.

"This happened while you were working for me," Ursa said. "It wouldn't be fair if I was the only one who didn't suffer."

"I'll buy a round for the table that stood up for me," Inger said. "It was nice of them."

"Hah," Ursa said. "Buy them a round, sure, but that's not why they stepped in. You're one of us and we take care of our own. Now you go and don't come back until dinner. I'll clean up the rest."

Inger led the way to the back hallway and up to their room. Dag flopped down on her bed. Her stomach rumbled: she'd missed the meal, but she'd missed them before. She stifled a chuckle. That's what she'd told herself yesterday.

"Are you all right?" she asked her sister.

Inger paced the narrow space between the beds. "I'm fine. I'm just really angry." She paused to stare out the small window. "I don't think I've ever been this mad before."

"Someone put his hand on you without your permission," Dag replied. She'd been this angry when she'd found out that Joosep—and Tarmo Holt—had targeted Inger while she was on assignment. "You've a right to be angry."

"I do, don't I?" Inger said. She sat down on her bed and faced Dag. "And the way everyone stood up for me? People don't just do that."

"They should," Dag replied. "But you're right, they don't." She paused. "What do you think Ursa meant when she said that you were one of them?"

"Oh, just that I work for her," Inger said, and as soon as the words were out of her mouth, Dag knew that was a lie. Inger's lies were *always* obvious but more so to Dag than to anyone else.

Dag sat up and faced her sister. "That's not it," she said. "That's not what she meant. What happened while I was gone?" And had whoever talked to Inger deliberately waited until Dag was absent? Had someone noticed her leave and then talked Inger into . . . whatever this was? Her Trait was honing in on a secret. How many did this small island have?

"Nothing," Inger rolled her eyes. "Ursa and I talked, is all, and if I'm not telling you what we talked about, it's because it's not your concern. And I know you're my sister and you care about me, but I get to make decisions about my life."

"Decisions you don't want to tell me about?" Dag asked. "Inger, you know that will only put my Trait on high alert."

"See? That's why I don't want to tell you," Inger replied. "It always comes down to your Trait. Why can't you just let this be? I've made a decision that doesn't concern you and I'm happy about it. I would hope that you would be happy for me too."

"Maybe I could be if I knew what your decision was," Dag said. Inger frowned and refused to meet her gaze. Dag sighed. "Listen, I need to eat, so I'm going to go beg Ursa for some bread and butter or whatever she's got left, and we can talk more about this later."

Dag rose and opened the door. She turned back to Inger but her twin was staring out the window, ignoring her. Without another word, Dag left the room and gently closed the door. She'd find out what Inger's decision was—they both knew that her Trait made that a certainty—so why was Inger refusing to tell her?

Hanne was the only customer still in the tavern and Ursa was wiping down the other tables.

"I'm sorry," Dag said to the tavern owner. "I don't want to be a bother, but in all the excitement I missed lunch. Is there anything . . . ?"

"Of course." Ursa tucked the cloth she was using into her waistband. "I'll see what I can find if you tell me Inger is all right."

"She's good," Dag said. "She's angry more than anything."

"She should be," Ursa headed to the kitchen. "I'll be just a minute."

Once Ursa was gone, Dag took a look around. Instead of sitting with Hanne, she chose a table close to the kitchen that she didn't think had been cleaned yet. No sense making Ursa do extra work; Dag had the sense the woman would remember even the tiniest of slights.

"Here," Ursa came back in and set a plate and a mug on the table. "No charge since the earlier events caused you to leave. The fish cakes are still warm but the potatoes might be a little cold."

"Thank you," Dag took a sip from the mug. "Cider? That's very nice of you."

"Inger said you liked it," Ursa said. "And I want her to be

happy here." Ursa nodded and moved off, and Dag picked up a fish cake.

The fish cakes were so good that it almost distracted Dag from Ursa's comment. But there was something there that she wasn't seeing. Ursa wanted Inger to be happy and that seemed like a good thing. Inger was well liked as a server, and that made Ursa more money, and on the surface that related to her comment about Inger being one of them. But her Trait was telling her that there was something more to it.

She finished the potatoes and gulped down the rest of her cider. She thought briefly about leaving some coin anyway, but decided that might make Ursa angry. Instead, she gave the woman a big "thank you" before she left through the door at the back, near the taps. She wouldn't go back to the room—she'd let Inger have the time and space to herself. Instead, she walked out behind the tavern and found a tree to sit under.

CALDER HELD HIS breath, but his Luck held and Dagrun Lund left by a door that led past the bar. He'd been about to enter the tavern but had realized just in time that Dagrun was sitting at a table. He needed to contact her, but he didn't want to surprise her in public.

As he turned to leave, his attention focused on the only patron in the place, an older woman with close-cropped hair. She got up from a table at the back and headed straight to Ursa Ozlinch, who was wiping up a spill.

"Want a report now?" the customer asked.

"Sure." Ursa sat down at the table Dag had just vacated and the other woman sat across from her. Now Calder's focus expanded to include Ursa Ozlinch. He placed his back against the door and tried to shrink into the shadow; he had to trust that no one would come through the door and find him eavesdropping.

"You want some cider, Hanne?" Ursa asked.

"Hah, good joke," the other woman, Hanne, said.

"One of these days I'll get you to take a drink."

"Then you'll ruin me as your tattle," Hanne replied. She didn't seem offended so Calder assumed this was a regular threat. "The *Bright Breeze* is the ship that came in."

"And the cargo?"

"If it's what you're looking for, the crew that was here don't know about it," Hanne said. She snorted. "And no one said as much but the captain is stupid. I'm not sure anyone would trust him to carry anything special."

"Stupid?" Ursa asked. "How stupid?"

"Stupid enough that half his crew won't survive him," Hanne said. "They were complaining about some sailor who messed up orders going through the Frozen Pass but it sounded to me like he did them a favour by keeping them off the rocks." Hanne paused. "Been years since I shipped out but I know you don't take the Pass with three sails. Since the ship is doomed anyway, it could be an opportunity." She laid a hand out flat and the tavern keeper dropped a coin in it.

"Thanks," Ursa said. "I'll let Margit know."

Hanne stood up and Calder carefully opened the door and squeezed through it. He was outside on the path when Hanne exited. She stumbled as she walked past him, pretending to be drunk.

Calder didn't change his pace as he strolled away from the tavern. A tattle, that's what the woman had called herself, and not only was she *not* a drunk, she wasn't even a drinker.

And she was astute if she'd picked up that the captain of the *Bright Breeze* was dangerous to his men: Calder had thought only First Mate Charis knew that.

And Margit could only be Margit Ansdottir. But what was the relationship between Hanne the tattler, Ursa Ozlinch, who owned the tavern and inn, and the leader of the pirates? And what specific cargo were they after?

The path led out to a rocky shoreline, and instead of going farther, he turned inland and walked past a couple of small huts. Fishing nets and wooden traps for crab and lobster were piled along the sides of the buildings. In back, Calder had to duck rows of nets drying on racks.

He headed back towards the tavern, walking on land that sloped steeply upwards to the plateau. A few trees and bushes dotted the ground but most of it was covered in tall grass.

Behind the tavern he stopped, surprised to see the shower. They were common in countries along the Sapphire Sea but he'd never seen one so far north. It wouldn't be much use in the winter, when even the rivers froze over, but someone had lived in the south long enough to want to build one here.

He heard a cough and twisted to look. He hadn't seen anyone for a while; was someone following him?

He scanned the surrounding area; he didn't see anyone . . . ah, there, under that tree there was a flash of yellow. Blonde, he amended as he headed towards the tree, blonde hair. He wasn't surprised when Dagrun Lund looked up at him.

"What?" She scrambled to sit up, dragging her hair off her face. She sighed. "Joosep sent you?"

"Yes." Calder grinned. "He was worried."

She rolled her eyes and frowned, which surprised him. Dagrun Lund didn't trust Joosep? When and why?

"He knew I was coming to find my sister," Dagrun said.

"Can we talk here?" Calder asked. She was angry at Joosep and he wanted to know why. Dagrun looked around and sighed again.

"Probably not." She got to her feet. "This way." She led him past the shower, through a small door, upstairs and along a corridor. She stopped at a door and knocked once before she pulled out a key and unlocked it.

"Inger?" Dagrun stuck her head inside before opening the door wide and stepping inside. Calder followed, shutting the door once he was through it.

It was a small room with two beds, a window along the far wall and a table by the door with a lamp sitting on it.

Dagrun sat on the tidy bed and gestured to the other one. He moved aside a bundle of clothes and sat down.

"Sorry, Inger isn't much for housekeeping." She pulled her knees up to her chest and stared at him.

Calder grinned. He liked that she didn't feel the need to fill the empty spaces with chatter. Her eyes narrowed at his grin and he shrugged.

"Joosep sent me," Calder said. "As you guessed." He stared at Dagrun. He knew her—or at least he had met her—but she'd been a student until recently and he'd spent years away on assignment. He had no idea what her Trait was, although it would be strong, since she was a twin. And Inger's Trait—equally strong—wasn't considered valuable. Otherwise she would have been trained as an Intelligencer too.

She met his gaze and her eyes narrowed. "You're not telling me something," she said.

"Probably," Calder agreed. "That's what we do, isn't it?"

"Luck," Dagrun said. Calder did his best to hide his surprise, but he knew he hadn't done a good enough job of it because Dagrun smiled.

"How do you know?" There was no point in pretending she hadn't just identified his Trait. But his was a tricky one to guess. Had Joosep told her?

"My Trait," Dagrun said. "But yours is strong for someone not a twin."

"Who said I wasn't a twin?" It came out before he could stop it—or the bitterness that always accompanied the reminder that he'd been the Lucky twin. Her eyes widened, and he knew she understood.

"Yes, the opposite of Lucky is Unlucky," he said. "My brother died at six, almost to the second when our Traits manifested." He didn't go into detail; he didn't explain how the brewer lost control of a wagon full of barrels and that his brother was crushed and somehow he was spared.

"I'm sorry," she said, and he thought she really was.

"What does Joosep want?" she asked after a pause.

"He wants you to come back," Calder replied. "Why haven't you gone home? Inger is safe." He gestured to the room. Dagrun wouldn't be sharing a room with her sister if she wasn't safe.

"What's the hurry for Joosep?" Dagrun countered.

Calder felt his focus narrow. This was an important question, one he hadn't spent much time on, although he had asked Joosep that same thing.

"Now I'm not sure," Calder said. "He told me that a Trait said you needed to be found."

"Whose?" Dagrun asked.

"He didn't say," Calder replied. His own Trait was still focused.

"Because no one has a Trait that works that way," Dagrun said. "Joosep lied about that."

"How do you know?"

"I told you; my Trait." She frowned. "But why did he lie? Did he mention Tarmo Holt?"

"No." Calder stopped. Dagrun already knew something about Tarmo Holt. Did she know he was collecting twins? Looking for those with Traits so he could harness their talents for himself?

"You have information about Holt," Dagrun said. "I'll tell you what I know if you tell me what you know."

"All right," Calder agreed. He didn't think his information was something he couldn't share. Especially with another Intelligencer.

DAGRUN WATCHED CALDER Rahmson, wondering why he'd agreed to her terms so easily. She didn't know much about him; did he have his own doubts about Joosep?

"Tarmo Holt was pressuring my sister to bear children for him," she said. "And Joosep helped him."

"How did he help him?"

Dag noticed that Calder didn't ask about children. Had he already found out about that?

"He waited until I was on assignment—my *first* assignment—then he told Inger that Holt wanted to speak to her." She was still angry about this. "When she stalled, Joosep kept pressing her to meet with him. When she finally did and then refused his request, Holt threatened to have Joosep send me into danger." She paused. How much could she say without exposing Inger's—and her own—Trait? "Inger believed him and ran away."

"Why didn't she stay and wait for . . ." Calder paused. "That was your first assignment as an Intelligencer?"

"Yes." She didn't mention that she thought Joosep might have created it in order to get her out of the way. Joosep knew she would have figured out what was really happening. But saying that could expose her Trait, and she wasn't sure she could trust Calder with that.

"Joosep would never put any Intelligencer at risk and especially not someone just out of training." He frowned. "You knew that but Inger didn't."

"She does now," Dag said. "But still, Joosep had her meet with Holt. Holt's up to something."

"He's looking for Traits," Calder said. "I saw him tell someone to find twins. Right after sending a pair away because they were too young."

"Traits," Dag repeated. And *her* Trait in particular, why else would he be interested in Inger's children? "Is it usual for the Master Intelligencer to tell the Grand Freeholder what Traits are at work on behalf of the Three?"

"No." Calder actually looked worried, so Dag was pretty sure he was telling the truth. And probably wondering if Holt knew what his own Trait was. "The Master Intelligencer never tells anyone about Traits—not even the instructors, although I think they figure some of them out."

"But not yours," Dag said. *Nor mine*, she thought but didn't say.

"No one has ever figured out mine." Calder gave her a long look. "Until you."

Dag shrugged. He might find out what her Trait was—he was Lucky, after all—but not from her. At least not right now.

There was a noise from the hallway and then the door opened.

"Hey, Dag . . ." Inger stopped talking when she saw Calder.

"Quick, get in here," Dag said. She hopped off her bed and pulled the still-surprised Inger into the room. "Quiet."

"Is that Calder?" Inger asked. "What's he doing here?"

"Shhh," Dag said. She sat back down on her bed and patted the spot beside her. "He came looking for me. I'm wanted back at the Hall."

Inger sat down and looked directly at Calder. "Joosep sent you?"

"Yes," Calder said.

"I've been telling him what happened," Dag said. "With Joosep and Tarmo Holt."

"I'm not going back," Inger said. She turned to Dag. "I told you already."

"I was only sent for Dagrun," Calder said.

"Of course, you were," Inger said with a sneer. "Joosep doesn't care about me. No one cares about me."

"Inger, that's not true." Dag was hurt—she'd come all this way for her sister and now she was saying that she didn't care?

"Well, not you, of course," Inger said. "You should know I didn't mean you. But Joosep forced me to meet with Tarmo Holt, who only wants to use me."

"Yes," Dag said. "And Calder shed some light on that. Like we thought, Holt is looking for twins with Traits."

"But twins run in some families," Calder said. "If they run in yours, does Joosep know?"

"Yes," Dag said. "To both of your questions. Our mother is a twin, although her twin did not survive birth. Joosep knows that."

"So, we have to assume Holt knows that too," Calder said. He turned to Inger. "I think you're right to stay away. Something is going on—Holt has something planned—but I don't know what."

"Don't worry," Inger said. "Dag will figure it out."

"Eventually," Dag said. She wanted to signal to Inger to not say anything more, but she knew Calder would catch that and then he'd know that Inger had said something important. Or was that how his Trait worked? People just said things they shouldn't in his presence?

"I'd appreciate it if you'd let me know when you do," Calder said, and Dag caught that he said *when* not *if*.

"Are you staying long?" Dag said. "I'm not ready to return to the Hall."

"I can't leave on the ship I came on," Calder said. "I told them I was heading to the Sapphire Sea. I need to wait for the next ship going west."

"Captain Ansdottir goes to North Tarklee every few weeks or so," Inger blurted out. "You might be able to travel with her."

"That's how both Inger and I got here," Dag said, not telling him that she stowed away. Or that Margit Ansdottir didn't like her much.

"Thanks," Calder said. "I'll look into that. In the meantime, we need to pretend that we don't know each other so I can keep up the story I gave when I shipped in here." He pulled out a handful of coins. "But I'll share Joosep's generosity with you if you need it."

Dag held out her hand but Inger slapped it away.

"I don't want anything from him," she said.

"All right," Calder got up. "Next time we meet, we're strangers." He nodded and left.

"What was that about?" Dag asked Inger. "Because I wouldn't mind taking Joosep's coin and spending it on figuring out what he's up to."

"Oh, sorry," Inger said. "I didn't think of that. When did you run into Calder Rahmson?"

"He found me," Dag said. "I was out behind the tavern. I don't think anyone saw him come in with me."

"Well, I wish he'd leave," Inger said. "I don't like that he came all this way to take you back."

"Neither do I," Dag replied, wondering how long Joosep had waited before sending Calder after her. Granted, she hadn't actually had permission to leave North Tarklee, but once he'd found out she *had* left he should have given her more than a day or two. What was so urgent and important that Joosep needed her back at the Hall?

"I have to get to work," Inger said. "Come by for some dinner later. Oh, I almost forgot. Ursa was really impressed that you walked around the island. She said she'd love the chance to ask you about it." Inger left and Dag listened to her footsteps fade.

Ursa Ozlinch wanted to know about her walk around the island. Dag would bet she was worried about what she'd found. She'd tell her the truth—about the walk and the children. She wouldn't mention the stored weapons in the forest, of course, or that she'd seen the pirates. But she would talk to her. Dag had a feeling Ursa knew all of Strongrock's secrets.

CHAPTER 8

CALDER WANDERED INTO the tavern—it was the only place for him to get a meal—just as it was opening for business. He was hungry: he'd missed lunch, so he was hoping for an early dinner.

Inger was there, along with Ursa Ozlinch.

"Ursa," he overheard Inger say to her. "Espen heard that the ship is still docked—and will be overnight, so are we . . ."

"The crew can eat but if the sailor who put his hand on you comes in, I'll deal with him," Ursa said. "And the ones that were with him? Charge them whatever you want. But tell them up front."

"Thanks," Inger said. She walked away with a smile, which faltered when she saw him. Thankfully, Ursa didn't seem to notice Inger's reaction to him.

Calder sat down at a table and Inger came over to him.

"What can I get you?"

"An ale and whatever stew you have tonight," Calder said, making sure his voice carried to Ursa. "And I came in on the *Bright Breeze*, but I hope you don't hold that against me. They took a dislike to me and me to them, although there are a few decent folk on that ship. In fact, I'm not welcome on board and have taken a room at the inn." He smiled over at Ursa, who acknowledged him with a nod.

"You weren't with the group who was in here earlier, so you're welcome to eat here," Inger said. "I'll just be a moment."

Calder leaned back in his chair as Inger left. The only other customer in the tavern—he suppressed a smile—was Hanne the tattle, who sat at a table near the back.

Ursa Ozlinch seemed to be counting mugs at the bar, but Calder knew she was watching him. He didn't know what had happened with some of his former crewmates; he could only hope it didn't adversely affect him.

Inger came back and set a mug and a bowl down in front of him. Calder thanked her before she moved off.

He spent the next few minutes eating. The stew was decent: it could have used more spices, but he thought that about most meals he hadn't cooked himself. The Pilalian side of him liked a meal with heat and flavour.

When Inger wandered by, he asked for a second bowl of stew, and when she'd gone to fetch it, a group of sailors from the *Bright Breeze* walked in. He recognized Steen—the one who had threatened him—and Nils.

"Look who it is," Steen said, pointing at Calder. "The sailor who can't follow simple orders."

"Shhh," Nils said. "We already had trouble in here, we don't need more."

"This is a place of business," Steen replied. He was loud and Calder wondered if he'd already been drinking. While in port many ships opened their casks on board, but they were usually strict about how much each sailor was allowed to drink. "And I have coin."

Inger came out from the kitchen with Calder's stew, and Steen stepped in front of her.

"Hello, lovely," Steen said. Inger tried to dodge him, but the sailor kept stepping in front of her.

Calder stood up. "If you have a problem with me, then talk to me about it," Calder said. "I'd be happy to discuss the issue with you outside." He took a step towards Steen, and Inger sent him a grateful look.

Ursa Ozlinch had already come out from behind the bar. An imposing woman, she was taller than either of the sailors and broader as well. The way she was brandishing a large knife demonstrated that she knew how to use it for more than carving a roast.

"Get out of my tavern," Ursa said. "And tell the rest of your crew that none of you are welcome."

"But I haven't eaten yet," Steen said. Nils was trying to pull him away.

Calder took a step closer. Steen was still trying to keep Inger from getting past him, and he didn't seem to understand the threat Ursa posed. If he could, Calder would stop it from reaching the point of bloodshed.

"I think you should heed the lady's warning, Steen," Calder said. "And go back to the *Bright Breeze*."

"Who asked you?" Steen finally pulled his attention away from Inger and focused it on him. But he was still ignoring Ursa. "You're just a *skit* sailor who almost got us killed."

"You've got that wrong."

Calder whipped his head around in time to see Charis close the tavern door. The First Mate walked slowly towards Nils and Steen.

"If Rahm here hadn't done what he'd done," Charis continued, "we'd all be on the rocks off Ostland. You'd understand that if you knew how to sail."

"You're wrong," Steen said. "I seen how angry the captain was."

"Yes, he was angry," Charis said. He was only a few steps from Steen now. Ursa had backed away and now stood protectively beside Inger.

"It doesn't change the fact that if Rahm had followed the captain's orders most of us would be dead." Charis stopped in front of Steen. He punched Steen, who hit the floor, clutching his jaw. "Get him out of here," Charis said to Nils, who grabbed Steen under his arms and dragged him away.

"Captain will hear of this," Steen managed to croak out.

"He won't care," Charis said. He met Calder's eyes and shrugged. "I spoke to Captain Olmar and he couldn't see the truth even when it was pointed out to him. So, I quit. I'm not interested in dying on the *Bright Breeze*."

"I can't blame you," Calder said. He gestured to an empty chair at his table. "Feel free to join me," he said. "We'll probably be seeing enough of each other. I'm waiting on a ship; you too now, I'd guess."

"I hadn't thought that far out," Charis replied, "but I suppose that's the case." He sat down, looked over at Ursa and blinked slowly. Calder wondered what that meant, but then Inger brought his second bowl of stew and took Charis' order.

"Was this your first voyage with Captain Olmar?" Calder asked.

"Third," Charis replied. "But the first travelling this far. The *Bright Breeze* isn't a log hauler but we've mostly been up and down the coast hauling timber to the shipbuilders on Lavais. I didn't realize Olmar had no idea how to sail past Ostland. The man would have scuttled us if you hadn't been there."

"Maybe not," Calder said despite knowing that there was a very good chance they would have. Something about Charis didn't ring true. "Did the *Bright Breeze* bring timber to Strongrock?" Even Hanne hadn't heard what the ship was hauling, but the First Mate would know.

"No," Charis said. "Ahh, here's my dinner."

Inger set a mug down alongside a plate of fried fish and fresh bread and butter. Charis started to eat and Calder wondered if he had deliberately ignored his question.

Calder pushed his empty stew bowl away and fished out some coin. "Well, that's it for me. Have a good evening, Charis," he said and stood up. His Trait would help him find the information he needed when he needed it. And he'd always found it better to look like he wasn't interested. Nobody trusted someone who was too curious.

Charis waved a forkful of fish at him as Calder headed out. A group of *Bright Breeze* crewmen were huddled together a few paces away from the tavern, and he heard Charis being cursed. Calder walked in the opposite direction, toward the inn and his room. It felt like a good time to stay away from the trouble he thought was brewing tonight.

A LOUD NOISE jerked him awake. Calder peered out the window of his room to see a group of people in the square that surrounded the well. The sun had set and half a dozen people held torches. Someone picked up a log and swung it at a small cabin on the other side of the square. It hit with a thud and a few enthusiastic shouts followed.

He briefly thought about staying in his room, but instead he shoved his boots on—this could be one of those times where bare feet could be hazardous—and left. What was happening might not have anything to do with his assignment, but it could still affect him.

After making sure the door to his room was locked, Calder strode out the front door of the inn.

Now that he was close he recognized some of the *Bright Breeze* crew. Steen stood in the middle of the crowd, waving a log above his head.

A dark figure split from the group and headed into the shadows, and curious, Calder followed them.

The path wasn't well used like those around the inn and the tavern, but it was travelled often enough that it wasn't overgrown. The path led directly to a small house, and even in the moonlight, Calder could see that it had been built to be defended: the windows on the front were mere slits, and the door was made of the same dressed logs as the rest of the house. If this house had its own access to a spring someone could hold out for days.

The shadowy figure knocked on the door, and when it opened, a large woman was outlined by the light that spilled out: over six feet tall and almost as wide as the doorway she filled, she stared at her visitor for a moment.

"Jaak, you scoundrel," the woman said. "I thought you were never going to darken my door again."

The visitor moved into the light from the doorway, and Calder recognized his fellow rigger.

"Don't mean to bother you, Captain," Jaak said. "But I thought I'd warn you. The crew from the *Bright Breeze* is looking to cause trouble."

So Jaak had come to see Captain Margit Ansdottir. Her size was legendary, but Calder had often wondered if it was an exaggeration. Now he knew that it was not.

"I appreciate that, Jaak," Ansdottir said. "Does this mean you're returning to us? I always hoped that you would."

"You know why I left," Jaak said. "No disrespect."

"There are risks in everything," Ansdottir said. "Whether you're a privateer or crew on a Freeholder's timber hauler." Ansdottir leaned closer to Jaak. "I hear your captain would have sent you into the rocks off Ostland if it wasn't for a single sailor. You know that no ship I captain will ever end up on the rocks."

"That's not true," Jaak said. "I mean, not about you, about Captain Olmar. Who would tell you such a thing?"

"The First Mate," Ansdottir said. "He told me himself a few hours ago. And now I'll tell you something, for your own sake. Don't get back on that ship when it hauls anchor tomorrow. The rocks off Ostland aren't the only dangers for this ship."

"You're taking the *Bright Breeze*?"

"Shhh," Ansdottir peered out past Jaak into the night. Calder closed his eyes in case they reflected the light from the open cabin door.

"My offer still stands," Ansdottir said.

Calder opened his eyes. The captain was staring intently at Jaak.

"A full share, like always," the captain continued. "Like you were never gone, on account of you growing up here and all." Ansdottir straightened. "And thanks for the warning. Now you get somewhere safe and stay there." She stepped back inside the cabin.

Calder ducked behind a tree as Jaak hurried past him back towards the square. If the pirates didn't take the *Bright Breeze*, it very well could end up on the rocks. He'd always assumed that all captaincies were awarded the way they were for the Merchant Adventurers: by merit. Clearly Captain Olmar hadn't followed that path. His very first impression looked closer to the truth: the man was a Clan Freeholder.

Once he was sure no one inside the cabin was watching, Calder followed Jaak back towards the town square.

DAG FINISHED HER meal and rose from her chair. The tavern was almost empty, and when she'd asked Inger about it, her sister had said that the crew of the ship in the harbour was banned because of the incident that afternoon.

Dag was relieved—the thought of Inger being accosted again had worried her. What if no one was around to help her? She caught a glimpse of Ursa at the bar. Not that she thought the tavern keeper would let anything happen to any of her staff.

Ursa beckoned her to a table near the bar, and Dag nodded and smiled as she headed over. She sat down and the older woman grabbed two mugs off the bar and set them down.

"It's quiet-like now, so I thought we could talk," Ursa said.

"Sure. Inger tells me the crew of the ship at anchor has been banned," Dag said. "Thank you. I hated the thought that they'd be back in here causing trouble for her."

"No need to thank me," Ursa said. She took a gulp of her drink. "But I appreciate that you did anyway. Inger's part of *my* crew and no one messes with me."

Dag took a small sip—cider again—before setting her mug back down. She had a feeling she'd need a clear head for this talk. "Inger said you're interested in my trip around the island," Dag said, shaking her head. "I have to admit I was not prepared."

"Not many people attempt it," Ursa replied. "Though there's a few places people go to by sea."

"Yes, I did come across a boat on a beach early in my walk. I wasn't worried enough about not making it on foot to use it." Dag shrugged. "Not that I'm very good at rowing a boat anyway. And thankfully this morning I came across where the children live. They and their teacher were kind enough to give me food and water." Dag rolled her eyes. "They must have thought me ridiculous, walking around the island without even a water skin."

"I heard you were pretty thirsty," Ursa said. "And a good thing that no harm came to you. Inger would have been devastated."

"As I would be if anything happened to her." As soon as she said the words, she felt an itch between her shoulder blades—her Trait was active. Ursa was hiding something, but not about the island. About Inger. She looked around the tavern, but she didn't see her sister. She didn't see anyone except Hanne.

"Staff's gone," Ursa said. "Like I said, quiet tonight."

"Where's Inger?" Dag asked. She knew something had happened—or was about to happen—to Inger.

"She's part of my crew," Ursa repeated her comment from earlier. "And after tonight she'll be a full crew member."

"A pirate?"

"A privateer," Ursa replied calmly. "With a full share, like every battle experienced crew member."

"Battle . . ." Dag stopped. "*Skit*! You have no idea what danger you're putting her in." Inger's Trait meant that she would be seen by everyone. "She's not had any formal training." Dag had learned as part of her studies and had sparred with Inger, but her sister had no weapons training. Maybe they would keep her out of the fighting?

"Been learning ever since she got here," Ursa said.

Skit, skit, skit, Dag thought. Every single sailor she fought wouldn't be able to ignore Inger. Because of her Trait she would be the most obvious target in any fight.

"Where is she?" Dag asked. She got to her feet and Ursa simply watched her. Dag looked down at her cider. She'd only had that one sip, but she felt a little unsteady.

"I think you'll just take a nice nap and miss all the excitement," Ursa said. "Hanne!"

The woman scrambled from her table in the back to Dag's side faster than a drunkard should be able to. She gripped Dag's arm and Dag let her. Whatever Ursa had put in her drink hadn't affected her as much as the other women thought, but she wouldn't be able to fight them both. Even sober she wasn't sure she could best Ursa. Hanne was another matter.

"Where are you taking me?" Dag purposely slurred her words as Hanne dragged her from the tavern.

"To a safe place," Hanne replied. She hauled Dag out into the hallway, but instead of heading towards Inger's room, Hanne pushed her in the opposite direction. She stopped in front of a door, and while she fished around for a key, Dag leaned against the wall of the corridor. But as soon as Hanne opened the door, Dag straightened and shoved the other woman through it. The key was still in the lock and she turned it.

In moments Dag was outside at the back of the tavern. She heard Hanne's yells and Ursa's bellowing reply as she ran around to the front of the building. There was a bright flickering light in the direction of the town square; Dag headed towards it. She *had* to keep Inger safe.

Dag rounded a corner and skidded to a stop. It was chaos in the square. A fire burned in the centre, consuming a pile of what looked like items from nearby cabins that the crew of the ship had pilfered. Half burnt chair legs scattered the ground in front of the fire, and while she watched, someone tossed a small table onto the flames.

A huddle of sailors that Dag thought might be drunk stood in front of the fire waving flaming sticks and logs at the group of pirates who were lined up in front of them, long guns pointed at the ground.

Dag spotted Inger's uncovered head near the front line and

blew out a breath. At least her sister was still in one piece. She pushed her way through the crowd until she was behind Inger.

"Inger," she said into her sister's ear. "Inger!"

Inger looked over her shoulder, the feverish grin on her face turning into a frown when she saw Dag. "Go away before you get hurt," Inger said. "This isn't your fight."

"It's not yours either," Dag said. She swayed a little from the aftereffects of whatever Ursa had put in her cider and grabbed her sister's arm.

"It is," Inger said. "I'm making it mine. Just like I'm making these *my* people."

"I'm your people," Dag said. "And think about what will happen in a fight." She leaned closer. "Your Trait."

"My Trait," Inger said. "It's never about *my* Trait. It's always about *yours*. I'm tired of everything in my life being about you." She looked around. "These people appreciate *me*. Not my Trait and not my sister, *me*."

Dag took advantage of Inger's anger to pull her a few steps back from the edge of the crowd. They were still close enough to feel the heat of the fire but it was quieter. She looked around at the men and women pirates; they stood at the ready, not yelling, barely even talking. All of the shouting and cursing was coming from the other sailors.

"You can't trust them," Dag said, leaning in towards Inger. "Ursa drugged me."

"She wouldn't," Inger said, but she looked a little less sure. "She was just supposed to keep you safe."

"She was trying to," Dag said. "By drugging me. Hanne was going to lock me into a room, but I got away from her."

"Hanne's a drunk," Inger said. "Now I know you're lying."

"Hanne's just pretending to be a drunk," Dag said. "And Ursa drugged me to keep me from coming here and talking you out of this."

"You can't . . ."

Up front the shouting suddenly became more heated. The pirates beside Dag and Inger silently shuffled closer together. Dag pulled a protesting Inger farther back, away from the fire and the sailors.

"Ready!" a voice called out, and guns were raised to shoulders.

Dag craned her neck to see . . . Margit Ansdottir, a stern look on her face, at the rear of the pirates. Ursa stood beside her, her head above the shorter people near her.

Inger tried to raise her gun too, but Dag grabbed it and kept it pointed at the ground.

"What are you doing?" Inger asked. "Let go."

"No," Dag said. "Are you really going to kill these sailors? No one has even tried to reason with them. Is that fair?"

"But Ursa said they were going to attack us," Inger said. "We have to strike first."

"Look!" Dag pointed towards the sailors, who seemed to have finally realized the trouble they were in and had backed up closer to the fire. "They're not a danger right now."

"I guess not," Inger said. "But Ursa—"

"Ursa drugged me!" Dag said.

"Inger!" It was Ursa. She'd spotted them—well, she'd spotted Inger. If she'd noticed Dag, Ursa might have raised an alarm. "Come here."

"You can't," Dag said when Inger tried to move towards the tavern keeper. "Who knows what she'll do to me." The pirates around them were starting to look at them in a way that worried Dag. But it was also as though they hadn't really noticed them before, which seemed impossible given Inger's Trait. Unless for some reason her Trait had cancelled out Inger's?

"Come on," Dag said. She pulled Inger through the crowd until they were at the front. Both the pirates and the sailors eyed them warily but neither side tried to stop them.

"Tell the privateers they've already won," Dag said to Inger. "Keep their attention on you." She took a few steps away from her sister. Inger shot her a look full of disgust before turning to the crowd.

"Privateers," Inger called out. "It's done. These unruly sailors have been stopped by you; by all of *us*. I was harassed while doing my work by one of them, and I can't tell you how grateful I am to you; how much it means to me that you are willing to defend me."

Trusting her sister's Trait to keep the focus on Inger and her own Trait to keep the focus off her, Dag sidled into the centre of the sailors.

"You need to give up," Dag said. "And do whatever they want you to do."

"Why?" asked one, and Dag recognized the man who'd put his

hands on Inger.

"Don't be stupid," another sailor said. "They aim to kill us and take the ship. I say let them have the ship and leave us alive."

"Me too," a third sailor said. "What do I care about some Freeholder's ship?"

"You gonna become a pirate?" the first man sneered. "They aren't going to shoot any of us. And I for one won't be captained by a woman."

"Then you could very well be killed by one," Dag said. If even one sailor wasn't compliant, the pirates might kill them all. And what would they do to her and Inger? She glanced over at her sister, who was still keeping the attention of the pirates.

"Shut up, Steen." The sailor who spoke turned to Dag. "We'll keep him quiet. What do you want us to do?"

"Here," Dag said. "Tie yourselves up." She handed them rope and returned to Inger's side.

"They're your prisoners," she said to Inger, who nodded. Dag slunk away towards some bushes, hoping that what she'd done was enough to keep everyone alive. And keep Inger from becoming a killer.

"That was interesting," a voice whispered, and Dag froze.

She wasn't used to being noticed, especially when she was actually hiding. She looked over to see Calder Rahmson crouched in the bushes beside her. Why hadn't she seen him when she'd chosen this place to hide?

"A Lucky spot," he said with a shrug. "What you just did was dangerous. Why?"

Dag turned back to see the pirates walking past the fire towards the sailors. Dag didn't relax until it was clear that the prisoners weren't being shot; at least not this minute.

"I don't want Inger to become a killer," Dag said. "It doesn't look like she's in trouble." She blew out a breath. "And no one ever notices me."

"Yeah, well, someone did." She followed his gaze to where Ursa and her companion were. They had their heads bent together and the conversation seemed heated; every once in a while, one or the other shook their head or waved a hand.

"Captain Margit Ansdottir," Calder continued, "kept her eyes on you the whole time. That's partly why I did. She is not happy about this, but I don't think Ursa wants anyone dying on her island."

"It would ruin her fiction of being neutral," Dag said. "When the truth is that she is aiding enemies of the Fair Seas Treaty Alliance."

"Which now includes you and your sister," Calder said. Startled, Dag met his eyes. "Since you both helped capture a Freeholder crew."

Dag blew out a big breath. Calder was right: she and Inger would both be considered enemies of the Three. But she thought that she'd be able to explain to Joosep that it was the least bad outcome: if she trusted Joosep enough to talk to him.

Was she willing to trust him with her and Inger's lives? Her eyes strayed to her twin, who was helping the pirates secure their prisoners. Inger had been willing to kill for her new friends. Why? What hold did the pirates—and Ursa—have over her?

And who said the chance for bloodshed was over even now? The ship was still anchored in the harbour. She didn't think the captain would be allowed to just sail away.

JOOSEP LOOKED UP at the knock on his door. He frowned when the door opened without his permission. Arnor poked his head in.

"Gustav is here to see you, Master Intelligencer." Arnor's smile was wide as he stepped out of Gustav's path to allow the youth to enter his office.

"Thank you, Arnor." His assistant quietly closed the door. Joosep knew he should be angry with Arnor, but his lack of protocol was a reaction to Gustav's Trait, so how could he be?

Joosep indicated the chair in front of the desk and Gustav sat down.

"You have something to report?" Joosep asked. He had to consciously stop himself from smiling at the youth.

"Yes, sir," Gustav said. He looked around nervously. "Sorry, should I write it down? I'm not sure how . . ."

"Ah, my apologies, you have not been taught what's expected in a debrief," Joosep said. "Why don't you just tell me what's happened?"

"Yes, sir." Gustav sat up straight. "So, after we spoke I went around to see . . . well, to see if Tarmo Holt's assistant Mykol would be the person I needed to . . . befriend." Gustav leaned closer. "Well, he wasn't. He's not totally immune to my Trait, but I think he's either too focused or too afraid to say anything about Grand Freeholder Holt. But as I was leaving, I happened to meet his daughter Saulia. The Grand Freeholder's daughter, I mean, not Mykol's. Saulia was visiting her father: it seems he'd promised to take her to buy a new dress but he'd forgotten. She said he does that all the time, forgets to meet her and her mother. Who is lovely, by the way; Asla, but I didn't meet her right then. I mean, Saulia invited me to have lunch at their home, and since I was on assignment I thought it all right to accept. It means I missed lunch in the Hall, with my training group, so I'll be marked absent. Was that all right?"

"Yes," Joosep replied. "Your instructor was notified that there may be absences while you are doing this for me." Even though he was smiling, Joosep was becoming concerned about the nervous way Gustav was talking. Did he talk this way to the Holt's? Had he accidentally told them anything he shouldn't have?

"Did either of the Holt women mention the Grand Freeholder?" Joosep asked.

"Either of the . . . ? Oh, you mean Saulia and her mother," Gustav said. "Well, neither of them said anything directly, just that the Grand Freeholder was always being delayed and dinner plans often had to be changed." Gustav paused. "Oh, and Saulia likes to spy on her father. She swears that pirates were at their house late one night."

"Pirates? Are you sure?"

"*She* was," Gustav said. "And when I asked their housekeeper Maeve, she shushed me but then confirmed it. Two pirates came one night. Maeve let them in, but she didn't give me a very good description: just that they were big and brawny." Gustav paused. "That was my first visit to their apartment. I've been invited back to eat dinner with the whole family, including the Grand Freeholder."

"Well done," Joosep said. "And what have you told them about yourself?"

"They haven't asked much," Gustav said. "So, I told them the truth, or at least as much as I needed to. Of course, I didn't tell them I'm an Intelligencer. I said I was sent here by my family for schooling before heading back to Lavais Island, where I'm to follow my Da into shipbuilding. Which would be the truth if you hadn't found me."

"Good, keep to that story. It's simple and believable," Joosep said. "I'll look for another report after you dine with the Holt family."

"Of course, sir," Gustav stood up. "And thank you for trusting me with this."

"There's no one better," Joosep said. And he meant it. In a few days the boy had uncovered a secret Holt had been hiding for who knew how long.

Gustav left his office, but Joosep could hear Arnor fussing over him in the outer office.

As long as Gustav didn't give away his own secrets. Joosep had to admit he was still concerned: the boy seemed to have no guile, but he *had* already found a way into the Holt household.

And pirates! Why was the Grand Freeholder meeting in secret with pirates?

Chapter 9

Calder shook Dagrun: she'd fallen asleep when he needed her awake and alert.

"Shhh," he said when she blinked at him. "I think someone is still out there. Can you see?"

He'd had some time to think about Dagrun and Inger's Traits: and especially the way they'd used them to diffuse the situation in the night. He didn't know how they defined them but he was pretty sure that Inger was the one who was noticed and Dagrun went unnoticed. He was hoping it meant she would be able to see anyone who was hiding.

Dagrun rolled over and peered through the bushes. After a few moments she turned to him.

"There's someone in that cabin." She pointed to a small cabin to the left of the still-smouldering fire. "I'm not sure if they're sailors or pirates."

"We'll give them a chance to come out," Calder said. He looked at Dagrun. "You fell asleep." They were not safe: certainly not safe enough to sleep. Instead of looking embarrassed, anger clouded Dagrun's face.

"Ursa Ozlinch drugged me," she said. "To keep me away from Inger and whatever they were planning to do."

"It didn't work," Calder said, wondering if Dagrun had a little bit of Luck. But that would mean Inger had Bad Luck and she was still alive.

"No," Dagrun said. "She tried to have her pretend drunk lock me up. But I got away."

"Hanne," Calder said. Dagrun gave him a surprised look and he shrugged. "She's Ursa's spy. Which means she's Margit Ansdottir's spy."

"I came here on her ship," Dagrun said. "She sailed us right through the Teeth."

"So, she's the one," Calder said. Jaak had told him he'd seen it done. "Someone's moving."

The door to the cabin was easing open. He could only see the top half of the door and no one was in view, so he had to assume that whoever had opened it was staying close to the ground.

"Jaak, what in Nyorden are you doing?"

Calder turned his head in the direction of the voice, thanking Luck that neither he nor Dagrun had moved from their hiding place. Margit Ansdottir stepped out of a copse of trees to stand, hands on her hips, staring at the cabin. Calder followed her gaze in time to see a sheepish Jaak stand up.

"Just trying to keep out of the way, Captain," Jaak said. "Like you told me to. Didn't mean no disrespect."

"You're not boarding that ship," Ansdottir said sternly. "I told you that too."

"No, Captain," Jaak said. He took a few steps past the fire pit to stand looking up at her. "I heed your advice."

"Except when it comes to rejoining us," Ansdottir replied. "You've not heeded that advice no matter how many times I've given it."

"I'm sorry, Captain," Jaak said, and he really did sound sorry. "You know I can't be party to the killing."

"Why, Jaak, no one's been killed here," Ansdottir said.

"Not yet. But what about them who're on the *Bright Breeze*? What about Captain Olmar?" Jaak shook his head. "You saying that none of them'll be killed?"

"Most of them will die whether we take the ship or not," Ansdottir said. "Maybe not the next time they try to sail past Ostland, but it will be one time after that. Olmar is no real captain. And First Mate Charis? He's joining me. You could crew for him, if you'd rather."

"On the *Bright Breeze*?"

"Well, we won't be calling it that," Ansdottir said. "What do you say, Jaak? Are you ready to come home?"

"It's a very tempting offer, Captain," Jaak said. "Can I take a day to think it over?"

"One day, Jaak. Let me know at dawn tomorrow." Margit Ansdottir turned and walked away, and Jaak sank to the ground.

"How did I miss her?" Dagrun said beside him. "She should have been obvious to me."

"Not if she has the same Trait as you," Calder said. "Not being noticed or whatever you call it." She glared at him, which told him he was right. "I figured it out after seeing you and your sister last night. All eyes were on her. Except," he frowned, "Ansdottir watched you the whole time. She even pointed you out to Ursa."

"She must have my Trait," Dagrun said. "Nothing else makes sense. It would explain how she can navigate through the Teeth. Unseen. I can remain unseen and see things hidden."

"And Inger is the opposite," Calder said. "Seen." He nodded to himself. That's why she held everyone's attention even while Dagrun was walking the sailors out from under their noses.

"Where is she?" Dagrun asked. "Inger?"

"Are you worried?"

"Not that they'd hurt her," Dagrun said. "But she takes everything at face value. Oh *skit*. I told her Ursa had drugged me. I have to find her."

"Is she in danger?" Calder asked. He didn't see how knowing that would be a threat to Inger.

"You don't understand," Dagrun said. "Inger will probably ask Ursa about it. And she'll believe whatever lie Ursa comes up with, but . . ."

"Ursa might not trust her after that." Calder nodded. "All right. You stay here. I'll try to find her." He'd go for a meal at the Broken Mast; he hadn't been seen during the night so no one should question him.

"No." Dagrun put a hand on his arm. "I have to go."

"You can't. Margit Ansdottir was here looking for you." He shrugged. "No one is looking for me. I'll make sure Inger is safe and tell her not to say anything to Ursa and then come back here."

"All right," Dagrun said, but Calder knew she didn't like it.

THE BROKEN MAST was so quiet that Calder wondered if they were even open for business. But as usual, Hanne was at the back table. He took a seat at a table near the bar, assuming that since Hanne was there, someone would be serving something. A few moments later, Ursa came in from the kitchen.

"Not much choice after all the excitement last night," Ursa said.

"Anything you have will be welcome," Calder replied. "I ate an early supper and then fell straight asleep. Did something happen last night that I need to know about?"

"Nah." Ursa left and a minute later emerged with a bowl. She sat it down in front of him.

He leaned over to look. Porridge: not his favourite but it looked edible. He looked up. "Is there a spoon?"

"You're from the *Bright Breeze*," Ursa said flatly. "What are you doing still in town? That ship's due to pull up anchor soon."

"I came in with them," Calder said. "But I didn't exactly see eye to eye with the captain or the crew."

"You're the one who saved the ship."

"I'm not sure I'd say that, exactly," Calder said carefully. He'd heard Captain Ansdottir say that Charis had talked about him. Had Ursa heard this from Ansdottir? "It's not wise to disrespect your captain even if you're not crewing for them anymore."

"Fair enough." Ursa set a spoon on the table. She gave him a long look before heading back to the bar.

Calder picked up the spoon and ate his porridge. More salt would have helped, but he wasn't about to ask for anything, not when Ursa had barely decided to tolerate him. It wasn't until he pushed his empty bowl away that he remembered that Ursa had drugged Dagrun. She wouldn't do that to him, would she? He sat back in his chair and sighed. He had to trust his Luck: if he *had* been drugged it was because it would lead him to knowledge he needed and couldn't get any other way.

He didn't feel as though he'd been given anything other than porridge. Ursa had disappeared from behind the bar, so he paid— he deliberately chose a Pilalian coin—and left. He still needed to find Inger.

Calder wandered towards the inn and his room. He really should have gone there first: obviously not to look for Inger but in case someone had sent him a message. The door to his room was still locked, and when he entered, nothing seemed out of place.

He grabbed his fresh set of clothes and headed to the shower. Dagrun might not appreciate him taking the time to clean up but he needed to act as though he wasn't even aware of the events of last night. Besides, his Luck had to find him, not the other way around.

Because of the salt water the shower wasn't quite as refreshing as the ones he was used to, but he was able to wash off most of the grime. And dressed in clean clothes, he felt the way he was trying to look; as though he knew nothing and was affected by nothing the pirates or the *Bright Breeze* crew were doing.

And of course, as soon as he stepped out of the shower he literally bumped into Inger.

"I am sorry," Calder said loudly. "I didn't see you. Hey, I recognize you from the tavern. You work there, don't you?"

"Um, yeah," Inger said, clearly surprised to see him. "I'm just here to wash up before work."

"Another apology, then," Calder said. "I didn't realize I was making anyone wait." He stepped away from Inger, who still looked surprised. "Oh," he said. "Maybe I'm not even allowed to use the shower?" He lowered his voice to a whisper. "Dagrun says not to talk to Ursa about what she told you." And then, more loudly, "I'm just over at the inn so I assumed . . ."

"I'm . . . uh," Inger stammered. "Sure, it's fine." She ducked her head in an awkward nod and entered the shower.

Calder headed back to his room. He'd drop off his dirty clothes and then get back to Dagrun to tell her that her sister was fine and that he'd delivered the message.

"There you are," someone said as soon as he entered his room. Calder, key still in his hand, turned to find Charis sitting in the chair by the window.

"You didn't come back last night and now here you are acting as though nothing happened," Charis said. "What are you up to?"

"Me?" Calder forced himself to relax as he walked over and dumped his dirty clothes beside Charis' feet. "I just got back from using the shower." He sat on the bed and faced Charis. "Why?"

"You may have used the shower," Charis said. "But we both know you didn't sleep here last night. I wonder where you were."

"Keeping out of trouble," Calder replied. Had Charis been

spying on him? "Which I hope keeps me alive."

"You are good at that," Charis said. "And smart about it, too. Which is why I'm here talking to you instead of putting you with the rest of the *Bright Breeze* crew."

"I'm not crew," Calder said. "Not any more than you are."

"Exactly," Charis said. "Which is why I think I can trust you." He leaned forward. "I'm going to be captain of my own ship very soon and I'm looking for good sailors. I can't give you First Mate, but I could give you Second. Then you can prove yourself and work your way up."

"That's generous," Calder said. "But I'm not sure I'm up to the task." It was the *Bright Breeze* that Charis was going to be given, that was the only ship it could be. He was being asked to become a pirate.

"Rahm, we both know you've captained a ship or two. If you don't want it, say so."

"I'm on my way to Pilalia," Calder said. "That's the truth. Otherwise I'd seriously consider your offer. I think I've sailed with much worse captains than you and the lifestyle," he paused; he didn't want to insult him, "of a privateer isn't something I haven't lived before."

"I knew it," Charis crowed. "I told them you were one of us."

Calder had to revise his opinion of Charis: he hadn't mutinied. He'd been on board the *Bright Breeze* exactly for this reason. Charis already *was* a pirate.

"But it doesn't change the fact that I'm needed in Pilalia," Calder finished. Would that be a good enough explanation? Sides were being chosen and he'd prefer to be neutral.

"I'll have to discuss it with . . . others," Charis said. "But think about my offer." He got up to leave but turned around at the door. "In the meantime, don't go anywhere."

Calder joined in when Charis laughed but the laughter died as soon as the other man left. *Don't go anywhere* was a threat when it came from the only people with a way to get anywhere else.

He sighed and stood up. He still had to tell Dagrun that her sister was safe.

She was asleep, right where he'd left her. Calder felt bad that he hadn't been able to bring her anything to eat—it had been all he could do to get a meal himself—but he had brought her a water skin.

He shook Dagrun awake and leaned close to her ear.

"Inger's safe," he said.

"Thank Nyorden." Dagrun dragged a hand through her hair, dislodging a few leaves. She sat up and took the water skin he offered and drank deeply. "She was at the tavern?"

He shook his head. "She was waiting for me to finish with the shower. We didn't really talk."

"But she's safe," Dagrun repeated.

"Yes." He sat back, wondering how much he should tell her. "But she is one of them."

"I know. She told me she was joining them last night. That's when I," she paused. "That's when I had her use her Trait to keep their attention."

"While you used yours to get the *Bright Breeze* crew out of the line of fire," Calder finished. He'd thought as much: opposite Traits at work.

"She was willing to shoot them," Dagrun said. "I couldn't let her."

"No, I suppose not," Calder replied. He didn't think the crew would live very long anyway. The *Bright Breeze* was going to be captained by Charis, which did not bode well for the crew.

"I won't let my sister become a killer!" Dagrun looked away, and when she looked back at him, there was pain and worry in her eyes. "She'll never be able to come back if she does that. Not just to me, or North Tarklee and Nordmere, but to herself. Once she's killed, I'm afraid . . ." Dagrun trailed off and looked away again.

"That she'll like it," Calder nodded. He'd killed two men: both had been trying to kill him and he hoped he never had to do it again. But there were people who felt empowered by killing, who became addicted to the dominance they felt when dealing death.

"Yes," Dagrun said. "And that she'll get caught. Inger can't do much without being noticed."

"Her Trait," Calder agreed. "Do you think that's why the pirates seem so eager to have her join them? That they have a use for her Trait?"

"Oh skit, I never even thought of it that way but probably," Dagrun said. She blew out a big breath. "Inger thinks it's because they like her—that *Ursa* likes her."

"They do," Calder said. "But they probably want her Trait,

too."

"She always hated that her Trait wasn't useful," Dagrun said. "I don't think the pirates will use it for good, and she won't like it being used that way." She shook her head. "At least in the past she wouldn't have liked it, but now? I'm not so certain. They have some kind of hold over her that I don't yet understand. Do you think it's safe for me to go back to the tavern?"

Calder frowned. "I don't think anyone is safe, including me, although at the moment you should be fine. But we should choose a better rendezvous point, in case we get separated."

"There's a beach about an hour walk along the shoreline," Dagrun said. "With a dinghy pulled up on it. We can meet there. I'm going to talk to my sister." Without waiting for him to answer, she got up and strode away.

Calder stayed hidden for another half hour, wondering how Dagrun Lund knew about a dinghy on a beach: and who owned it. Eventually he headed back to his room. He would stay inside—except for meals—and try to stay out of trouble.

Dag didn't see anyone on her way to the tavern. Had Margit Ansdottir decided she wasn't a problem?

She'd spent the night in the bushes and she looked it, so she planned on slipping into Inger's room for fresh clothes and then having a shower, before showing up at the tavern.

"Where have you been?"

Dag looked up and saw Inger, her hands on her hips, glaring at her from beside the tavern.

"You look terrible," Inger continued. "Are you all right?" Now she looked worried, and Dag had a moment of smugness—but then she thought about how worried she would be—*had been* about Inger, when she'd disappeared.

"I'm fine," Dagrun said. She lowered her voice to a whisper. "I can't talk here. And I need a shower."

"You sure do need a shower," Inger said loudly with a grin. Dag rolled her eyes, and her sister silently giggled, which made Dag roll her eyes again. It wasn't anything to laugh about, fearing that your conversations were being listened to.

Dag headed around the corner of the tavern to the rear door, Inger trailing her. Once in Inger's room, Dag rummaged around for something clean to wear—at least cleaner than what she had on—and tossed a shirt and trousers onto her bed. Inger sat on the other bed and watched her.

"What do you know about Hanne?" Dag asked. She'd been thinking about who would be able to listen to them and Hanne was always in the tavern. Ursa's spy, Calder had said. Who else could it be?

"Hanne? Drunk Hanne?"

"Except she wasn't drunk when she tried to lock me up last night," Dag said. "Does anyone else sit with her?"

"She's always alone," Inger said. "At that back table. And she is a drunk. I take her drinks constantly."

"But poured by Ursa," Inger said. She sighed. "I told you that Ursa drugged me last night. Have you spoken to her?"

"No," Inger said. "I thought . . . well, after Calder told me not to say anything I didn't want to see her until I spoke to you."

Dag relaxed. "Good. I think I'll just do the obvious and you should too."

"I have a choice?" Inger said, and Dag actually grinned.

"Ursa told me I would be taking a nap," Dag said. "That's pretty clear that she had drugged me. So, you should be mad at her for that."

"I won't need to pretend that."

"And me, I went to watch what was happening, and then whatever she put in my drink finally kicked in and I passed out in some bushes." It was close enough to the truth. Margit Ansdottir had noticed what she'd done, but Dag didn't think the captain would personally question her about it. "You haven't been to the tavern yet today because you were worried about me and angry at Ursa."

"I *am* angry with Ursa," Inger agreed.

"Then go tell her. I'll shower and clean up and then come to the tavern. We'll see what Ursa does then."

"Should I say anything about Hanne?" Inger asked.

"No. I think that's a secret Ursa even keeps from the privateers." And that could be the thing Ursa would most want to keep quiet. Would the rest of the pirates be understanding if they knew that they were being spied on? That their conversations were being monitored and reported? Dag didn't think so. "Just try to treat Hanne the same as always."

Dag's shower was fast—she didn't know what danger either

she or Inger were in so she wanted to get into the tavern as soon as possible. There were half a dozen pirates sitting at tables. Her Trait meant that no one really noticed her when she entered, but a few people glanced her way once she sat down. As far from Hanne as possible. She'd thought about glaring at the woman, but if Hanne was a secret Ursa couldn't afford to have known, it wasn't safe to acknowledge her.

Ursa sidled out from behind the bar and came over.

"I'm not sure what lies you've been telling your sister, but I didn't do anything to you last night."

Dag had been looking at Inger, who was dealing with a customer, so it took her a moment to realize what Ursa had said. She looked up at the other woman's thunderous expression.

"What did Inger say?" Dag asked, trying to buy time. She knew the truth and so did Ursa, but would she and Inger be in danger if she pushed the tavern owner to admit it?

"That I drugged you," Ursa sneered. She raised one eyebrow, and Dag felt the challenge in that one small movement. "And that you passed out from it."

"I did!" Dag said. "Pass out, that is. From what you served me, although it was my own fault for drinking too much."

Ursa's expression changed from threatening to triumphant, and Dag suppressed a sigh of relief. But she wasn't completely relieved: the immediate danger might be over, but she and Inger were still at Ursa's mercy.

"See that your sister knows that," Ursa said. "And I want you gone. There's a ship due to go out today. You should be on it."

"I'll talk to Inger," Dag said. And she would, but right now she knew that she couldn't trust her with the truth. What hold did Ursa have over Inger? Was there a Trait at work that she hadn't yet discovered? She might leave the tavern, but she wasn't going to leave the island, not until she knew Inger was safe. And right now, she didn't think anyone was safe.

Inger headed her way. She slammed a mug down on the table, cider sloshing over the lip and onto the scarred wood.

"Why did you lie to me about Ursa?" Inger said.

Dag met her sister's angry gaze and shrugged. "I felt stupid that I drank so much." Convincing Inger of the truth again was only going to hurt her when Ursa could so easily talk her out of believing it. It would be better to have Inger trust Ursa's version until Dag could figure out how to permanently convince Inger that Ursa couldn't be trusted.

Inger glared at her but left. A moment later she put a plate of fried fish and potatoes in front of her.

"Ursa wants me gone," Dag said, grabbing her sister's hand. Inger shook it off.

"So do I." She stomped back to the bar where Ursa was filling some mugs.

Once Inger had filled her tray and walked away, Ursa caught Dag's eye and smirked. It took all of Dag's willpower to ignore it. Ursa might have won this battle, but Dag was not going to let her ruin her sister's life. But for now, all she could do was pretend that Ursa had won: she'd eat her meal and pack up her things and leave the tavern, but she was not boarding that ship.

Inger didn't come to her table again, so when she'd finished eating, Dag simply left payment and returned to Inger's room. She didn't have much to pack, but she bundled it all together and left. She needed travel rations, but since Ursa owned everything, she couldn't buy it herself. She'd ask Calder to do that. Seeing him was a risk, but he was the only person she trusted right now, and that included her sister.

CHAPTER 10

CALDER SAT BESIDE the small window, staring out through a sliver of space between the curtain and the frame. He didn't have a wide view of the area in front of the inn, but he could see an edge of the square. There had been a flurry of activity earlier: he assumed that someone from the *Bright Breeze* had come looking for their missing crew members. In the past hour or so only a single person had come to the well to get water.

He didn't plan on leaving his room today: there was too much he didn't understand about what was happening. He wished he had a Trait that he could force to work, but this situation was far too volatile for him to try to change how he used Luck now.

A knock on the door startled him. Had he been concentrating on what was out front so much that he'd ignored possible threats from inside the inn? What if it was Charis back for his answer? Could Calder afford to say no?

He crossed to the door and leaned against it. "Who's there?" he asked softly.

"It's me," a woman replied. "Let me in." He recognized Dagrun Lund: at least he assumed it was her and not Inger.

He opened the door, and Dagrun squeezed through it.

"I don't think anyone noticed me coming here," she said, looking over the small room, taking in the narrow bed pushed against the wall and the single chair perched beside the covered window. She stepped over and, without touching the curtain, looked out.

"At least I'm not being paranoid," Dagrun said, "if you're anxious too." She turned back to him and dropped a bundle on the bed. "Ursa told me to leave on the ship that's at anchor."

"She wants you dead," Calder said, surprised. "Why?"

"Dead? I thought she just wanted me gone."

"The *Bright Breeze* will be allowed to sail away from Strongrock," Calder said. "But my guess is that the pirates will take her before she makes it to the Frozen Pass. I think very few of the crew will survive."

"*Skit*! Ursa wants me gone forever!" Dagrun looked more angry than scared, and Calder wasn't sure if that was good or bad. "How do you know?"

He took a seat on the bed and gestured to the chair. "I was offered the position of Second Mate on the *Bright Breeze*," he said. "Although they'll change the name and probably make some other adjustments to hide its origin." He paused. "But why does she want you dead?"

"It's about Inger," Dagrun said and frowned. "It has to be. Whatever use they have for her and her Trait, I'm in the way." She met his gaze. "My Trait uncovers secrets—that's what it does—so why isn't it working now? Why can't I figure out why they want her?"

Calder shrugged. "I only know how my Trait works. But you knew enough not to get on the ship."

"Sure, because I'm not letting Ursa have Inger." She peeked out the window before turning back to him. "She's got . . . some kind of hold—or Trait—that she's using on Inger. I told Inger that Ursa drugged me and then half an hour later, Inger's mad at *me* because I've been telling lies about Ursa. She's mad at *me*!" She shook her head. "Whatever Ursa's plan is for Inger, she's not getting her while I'm alive."

"I think it's pretty clear that she knows that," Calder said. Dagrun's head came up and she stared at him. "Why do you think she wanted you on the *Bright Breeze*? Once you boarded that ship she could make sure someone killed you." He paused. "Although why would the innkeeper and tavern owner, a woman whose livelihood depends on being neutral, align herself so blatantly with the pirates?"

"Ursa knows all the secrets on Strongrock," Dagrun said. She grinned. "But I know quite a few of them too. I told you about the beach with the boat? What I didn't tell you is that there's something hidden there. I saw a ship anchor near the beach and pirates bring crates from the ship to the shore. They took them through the forest and added them to others in some kind of warehouse. Full of weapons."

"Weapons? How do you know?" Calder felt his focus narrow. This was important.

"I looked," Dagrun said. "After they left. I lifted up the tarp and counted the crates. And I saw a cannon. It said *Diamanto* on it."

"*Diamanto*!" Calder was more surprised at the name than the fact that there was a cannon. "The *Diamanto* was lost last year. It went through the Frozen Pass too late in the year, I heard. Thirty crew lost, including the captain and first mate." He'd been in the Sapphire Sea at the time, but he'd known men and women who'd died on that ship. "I seem to remember that there was very little of the ship left."

"Well, the cannon didn't look like it had been pulled from the sea," Dagrun said. "And some of the crates had other names: *Merja*, *Windswept*, and *Stormrunner*."

Calder closed his eyes. All ships that had been reported missing at sea and presumed lost with all hands. Had every single ship been pirated? Had all of the crew been killed? He opened his eyes. "I think Joosep has been sending me on the wrong assignments. These ships have all been reported as lost at sea."

"And the one at anchor here?" Dagrun said. "The *Bright Breeze*? You think that one will be next."

"Yes," Calder said. "And any weapons they were carrying will be added to the ones you found." He stood up and started pacing. "We need to tell Joosep about this."

"You think he doesn't already know?"

Dagrun's question stopped him cold. What if Joosep did know? "You think Joosep deliberately sent me on assignments away from the Pale Sea?"

"He forced Inger to talk to Tarmo Holt, who then threatened me," Dagrun said. "I'm not sure I trust Joosep." She looked away. "I'm not sure I trust you, but I don't have any other allies."

"But you have a plan. What can I do?" Calder asked. He wasn't sure he could trust Dagrun either: he had a feeling her loyalty would always be to her sister even if Inger became a pirate.

"I need food," Dagrun said. "Ideally travel rations for a few days—maybe a week."

"I'll do my best." Could he get some from Charis? "And I assume water."

"Not water. I found a couple of springs, and I have a water skin I'll fill before I go. And something to fish with?"

"Do you even know how to—" There was a knock on the door and Calder stopped mid-sentence. Another visitor? Dagrun was already on the floor and sliding under the bed. He grabbed her pack and set it down beside her. Once it too had disappeared, he went to the door.

"Who's there?" he called out.

"It's me, Jaak. I need to talk to you."

Calder opened the door to let in an agitated Jaak. He didn't even look at Calder: he simply started pacing the length of the room.

"Jaak, calm down," Calder said. He sat on the bed, partly to get out of Jaak's way, and partly to make sure Jaak didn't sit on it and discover Dagrun. Right now, Jaak didn't look like a man who could keep that kind of secret.

"I can't calm down," Jaak said. He stopped in front of him. "First Mate Charis told me, but I need to warn you, tell you that you can't! They're gonna force me back into this life, but you! You need to get away, Rahm. Far away from here."

"Charis told you what?" Calder asked. "Because I'll tell you the truth, he asked me to join him, and I haven't yet given him an answer."

"Oh, thank Jebris," Jaak said. He was visibly relieved. "Then you'll tell him no."

"What's wrong with telling him yes?" Calder asked. "I've done a voyage or two as a privateer," he said truthfully. "As long as the share is fair, what's the harm?"

Jaak's face clouded with anger. "It's stealing, which I don't like," he said. "But with this crew, there's murder. Now Captain Ansdottir, she don't make anyone kill who don't want to, but there's plenty who are all right with that, and the other ship's crew is dead all the same."

"Are you sure?" This must be the real reason why Jaak left the pirates before, not stealing, like he'd said.

"I've been through it once," Jaak said. "A couple of years ago. Don't want to do it again." The look he gave Calder was haunted. "Bad enough when we were just stealing, but the killing? I still hear them begging and pleading. Better if they had scuttled on the rocks and died clean."

Calder didn't have a reply to that. He had until the morning to answer Charis, and by then the *Bright Breeze* would already be in the hands of the pirates and the crew would be dead. But although he didn't have the power to stop it, he might be able to stop future attacks if he could explain what was happening to Joosep. As long as Joosep wasn't already a party to it.

"If I want to say no to Charis, would he let me leave Strongrock?" Calder asked. "Could you?"

"They won't let me leave," Jaak said. "Captain won't let me leave."

"Why not? She let you leave once."

"I slipped away," Jaak replied. "Even I didn't know I was going to do it until I did it. I shipped out as crew on another vessel within hours so's they couldn't find me and take me back. No, she won't let me leave."

"I still don't understand why not," Calder said.

"Because she don't like to lose!" Jaak said. "Not people, not ships, not fights. What's hers stays hers. Even if she has no use for you. Even if you *hate* her. What's hers stays hers."

"And you're hers how?" Calder asked.

"She picked me up off the streets. I was starving and freezing and my brother had just been jailed for stealing food to feed me." Jaak shook his head. "She kept me from dying, and at first I was so grateful. But now I know she owns me. Wish I'd died when I was a child; wish she'd never found me."

Calder sat back, startled by the despair and bitterness in Jaak's voice. When he'd met him, he'd thought him a happy-go-lucky man.

"Would they still let me leave? I don't belong to the captain." At least as far as he knew he didn't, but Charis had been a pirate all this time. Who knew what he'd said to Ansdottir?

"You might and not know it," Jaak said. "Captain said you saved the ship, so she knows about you." He sighed. "And it might not matter. There's no way off Strongrock that the captain doesn't control."

"Don't other ships anchor here?"

"Not any that make to the next anchor," Jaak said. He looked resigned and more than a little sad. "Well, that's all I came to say. Maybe it would have been better if I hadn't, but I thought you should know what you're agreeing to." He opened the door and then turned back to Calder. "They sure didn't explain any of that to me." He left and closed the door.

Calder got off the bed, and Dagrun slid out from under it.

"Whew." She brushed dust off her hair and clothes. "No one cleans under there." She dropped her bag on the bed. "He's wrong, you know. Your friend Jaak. There is another way off the island. Do you know how to sail?"

CALDER STARED AT her for a moment before he answered.

"I'm going to pretend you didn't just ask me that," he said. "And I would advise you not to ask any other sailor that same question. It's a serious insult."

"Oh, sure." She didn't really think of Calder as a sailor: to her he was an Intelligencer. "It's just that I know where to find a boat—a sailboat—that can take us off the island. It might even be a day or so before the pirates know it's missing." At least she hoped it would be there. Ursa had known about her visit with the children because Teacher had sailed that small boat back here and told her. Had Teacher sailed it back to the children's beach? That must be where this Jaak had lived too, if he'd been taken from the streets of Tarklee and brought here. Did all of the children become pirates?

"But someone owns it," Calder said. "Someone will miss it."

"Yeah, but it's a bit of a walk," she said.

"Near the weapons cache?"

"Yeah," Dag lied. "Close to that beach." She didn't completely trust Calder—not yet—partly because she didn't trust Joosep and he did. But she had to admit that he was right about one thing: it seemed that Ursa wanted her dead.

"All right." Calder stood up. "I need to see about rations." He shrugged. "And fishing gear. If I'm not back in an hour, I'll meet you at the beach near the weapons. If it comes to that, and we have to run, we'll be grateful for the chance to arm ourselves."

"You think it will come to that?" Dag asked. She knew Inger was in trouble—as was she—but was Calder really not safe? He hadn't given Jaak that impression at all. He could be lying to her. Her Trait hadn't been triggered, so she didn't think he was hiding anything, but what if his Trait was interfering with hers?

"I'm not sure," Calder replied. "There are far too many things I don't know. But the pirates? They have dangerous secrets, and they will kill to keep people from knowing them."

Calder left and Dag watched him from the window. He wandered to the square. When he went behind a building she lost track of him.

She grabbed her pack and headed to the door. Another reason why she didn't fully trust Calder—once he knew where to find the sailboat, there was nothing to stop him from leaving by himself and stranding her here. She'd be tempted to leave him behind, if she knew how to and could convince Inger to leave. She had to assume he would do the same thing to her.

The square was empty when she reached it. Where had he gone? She tried to keep to the shadows of the few buildings that ringed the square, but soon enough she was forced out into the open. And there was still no sign of Calder.

"What are you doing?"

Dag whirled to find Ursa glaring at her.

"Why aren't you on that ship?" Ursa asked. "I told you I wanted you gone!"

"I missed it," Dag lied. "I wanted to talk to my sister. To say a real goodbye."

Ursa looked her over, and after a moment, she shrugged. "Let's go find her." She turned and started walking towards the tavern.

Suddenly unsure, Dag followed a few steps behind. She took one look back and saw Calder, a fishing pole in one hand and nets over his shoulder. He made the Intelligencer hand motion for a question, and she signalled back that she might need his help.

Ursa stepped through the door to the tavern, and Dag followed, pausing to let her eyes adjust to the dark room.

Someone slammed into her, and she dropped her pack as she was pushed against the wall.

"Got her," a voice at her ear said. Her arms were wrenched behind her back, and she was shoved to the ground.

"Inger!" Dag called. Then a hand covered her mouth. Dag bit down *hard* and the person holding her howled in pain.

"You pile of skit!"

Dag's head slammed against the floor, and she tasted blood as she bit the inside of her cheek. She rolled over, and her attacker rolled off her. Then Ursa bent down, grabbed her left arm, and hauled her up, pushing her up against the wall. She leaned against the closed front door, blocking it.

"Inger!" Dag called again.

Ursa sneered at her. "She's not here. Hanne and I have plenty of time to finish what we started last night." She looked over Dag's head. "Get the rope from behind the bar." Dag looked over her shoulder to see a dishevelled Hanne limp away towards the kitchen.

"Hello?" The door jiggled, and Ursa frowned. Someone pounded on the door, and Ursa slid along the wall. "Hey, is someone here?"

Ursa glared at Dag and took a step away from the door. It opened, and Calder poked his head in.

"Oh good, you are here," he said. "I was hoping for some food that I can take with me. I'm going fishing and I don't want to have to count on my skills for a midday meal." He smiled and his gaze swept past Dag to Hanne, who was leaning against the bar before coming to rest on Ursa.

"You're the one Charis been talking about, aren't you?" Ursa said.

"That depends on whether he's been saying good things or bad," Calder replied. Dag noticed that he kept his eyes on Ursa, not even glancing her way.

"Good," Ursa said. "You're joining his crew, right?"

"Second Mate," Calder said. "That's what he told me."

"Not afraid of being a privateer?" Ursa asked, and Dag could hear the menace in the question.

"I've been at sea most of my life, so I think I've done most things at one time or another." Calder held up a fishing pole. "I'm planning on doing some fishing but wanted a guaranteed lunch. Can I get something?"

Dag thought Ursa was going to refuse him, but in the end, she gestured to him. "Hanne knows her way around well enough to find you something. I have something else I have to take care of."

"Sure, thanks," Calder said. He stepped past Ursa and gestured to Dag to be compliant.

Ursa pulled Dag out the door and dragged her around to the back of the building.

"You stay quiet until he's gone or I'll hurt Inger." Ursa opened a small door and shoved Dag through it.

Dag stumbled to the ground, and by the time she turned around, the door was shut. She heard the sound of a lock clicking into place, and then it was quiet.

She grabbed the door handle and pulled and twisted: the lock rattled, but the door didn't budge. She turned to investigate her prison. It was a storage room; burlap sacks were folded by the far end, but it wasn't storing anything at the moment. Except her. It had been built against the side of the tavern and the dirt floor had been dug down a foot. There was a tiny gap along one wall, but she had nothing to use to try to pry the planks away or dig the earth out from under the wall.

She crawled to the far end and felt among the sacks, but they were all empty. There was a loose strand of burlap: she started pulling it, unravelling it until she had a fairly long strand. Using her teeth, she separated it from the sack and started unravelling another length of fibre. Once she had a few strands, she twisted them together to make a thin rope. It wasn't a great weapon, but it was better than nothing.

Voices were coming close, and instead of waiting by the small door, Dag huddled at the far end. She didn't think Ursa would try to squeeze into this small space to get her, so that left Hanne, who she might be able to best with her thin rope.

She'd still need to get past Ursa, who wanted her dead. But Dag wasn't giving up without a fight.

The lock rattled, and then the door was opened. Ursa peered in.

"That's not going to help you," she said. "Sitting at the back like that."

"Where's Inger?" Dag asked. "What have you done to my sister?"

"What have I done to her besides give her a home and work and a chance to be part of my family?" Ursa asked.

"She already has a family."

"You? You're just her blood." Ursa stood up, and all Dag could see was her sturdy legs. "Hanne! Get out here."

"Oh hey," it was Calder again. "Hanne said to come and ask you if I could borrow this knife. I thought I might want to clean any fish I caught."

Ursa's legs left the doorway, and Dag scrambled over to it and peeked out.

"Where is Hanne?" Ursa asked.

Ursa took a couple of steps away from the door. Dag looked up to see Calder waving a kitchen knife in the air while Ursa stood staring at him with her hands on her hips. Dag launched herself at Ursa's legs. She caught her right on the back of the knees, and with a yelp, the tavern keeper fell over backwards.

"Hanne! Get her!" Ursa called even as Dag clambered to her feet. She stepped past Calder, who still brandished the knife.

"Sorry, Hanne's tied up," Calder said. "And you need to get in there." With the knife, he gestured to the storage shed.

"Make me," Ursa said.

"All right." The casual way Calder replied must have unnerved the tavern keeper because she moved towards the small door.

"I did tell you I've done most things at one time or another," Calder said. Once Ursa was inside the shed, he toed the door closed. Dag grabbed the lock and looped it through the rings and snapped it shut. For good measure, she tied the twine around it too.

"Thanks," Dag said to Calder.

He wrapped the knife in a cloth and tucked it into the netting that was slung over his shoulder. "Sure," he replied. "Now, let's go."

They took the path that led away from the inn in silence. It wasn't until they'd walked past the two forlorn huts that Dag broke the silence.

"Ursa said Inger wasn't there. Did you see her?"

"No," Calder replied. "I think she went with the crew to get the *Bright Breeze*."

Dag stopped and caught his arm. "Her Trait puts her at risk. She'll be the first target in any fight. Why would they do that?"

"To make her one of them," Calder said. "If she's part of their secret, then it's harder for her to leave and tell someone what they're up to."

"Because she'll be blamed too," Dagrun said. She turned to

look at him. "I'm pretty sure Ursa was going to kill me. I thought she wanted me on the ship?"

"She did," Calder replied. "I think her preference was to have Inger see you die in a fight. That way she can't be blamed and Inger knows that you're dead."

"That's horrible!" Dag couldn't imagine much worse than seeing her sister die. "And then Ursa could console her." She followed Calder from the beach into the trees.

"Yeah. It's a pretty hideous thing to plan."

"I'm not leaving without my sister," Dag said.

"That's what I thought."

"How much farther?" Calder asked. He swatted his sleeve, and a cloud of insects flew into the air.

"Another half an hour or so," Dag replied. "Here." She passed him the water skin, and he took a sip before handing it back to her.

He shifted the nets and sighed; his skin was itchy where the rope touched it. At least he was wearing his boots. This journey would have been so much worse in bare feet.

Forest lined a beach that led to a rocky outcrop. From this vantage he couldn't tell if there was a way around the rocks, but he knew that Dagrun had found a way past this point recently.

The beach ahead was empty, but when he scanned the sea in front of it, he saw something off in the distance. He crouched down, signalling Dagrun to do the same.

"There's a sailboat offshore," he said quietly. The small boat was still quite far from shore and hard to spot for anyone not accustomed to distinguishing whitecaps from sails.

"Are they looking for us?" Dagrun asked in his ear.

"Probably," Calder agreed. "Although it's possible they are simply heading to the weapons themselves." He shaded his eyes and stared out at the small sailboat. Unless this *was* the boat from the beach near the weapons: the boat they were planning on using to get off this island. It was coming in towards shore, and now he recognized Jaak. Even from here Calder could tell the younger man wasn't happy.

"Inger's there," Dagrun breathed. "No wonder you were able to spot it."

"There are too many crew for us to overpower them and take

the boat," Calder said even though he was calculating whether he could count on Jaak's help to subdue the other four sailors. But even if Jaak helped, he wasn't sure Inger would. Dagrun was convinced her sister was doing this against her will, but he wasn't so sure.

The sailboat suddenly changed direction and skimmed past them, heading back towards the town of Strongrock. Calder didn't relax until it was out of sight. Dagrun stood, and he pulled her back down.

"We should wait a while longer," he said. "If we disturbed a flock of birds they might turn back to investigate." He settled his back against a tree and dug the wrapped package out from the nets. "Have something to eat." He tore a chunk of cheese off for her and a second one for him. He hadn't been able to get much off Hanne—he'd been too concerned for Dagrun's safety—so there was just a small block of cheese, a strip of dried pork, and some hard journey bread.

They ate all of the cheese, saving the least perishable food for later. Calder rose and brushed sand and twigs off him as Dagrun did the same.

There were just a few seagulls floating lazily on air currents over the beach: he guessed they wouldn't cause a large enough disturbance to be noticed by those in the sailboat. Besides, enough time had passed that the sailboat should be back at the settlement.

"Let's go," he said and stepped off the grass and onto the beach.

They were a little more than halfway to the rocks when the seagulls started screeching. Calder looked over his shoulder to see a ship rounding the point behind them, two of the small sailboats flanking it.

"Run!" he called. He sprinted along the beach, dropping the fishing pole. It caught on the bundle containing the rest of the food which spilled out onto the sand. Calder ignored the loss and concentrated on reaching the rocks. Dagrun was right behind him as he climbed over the rocks and ducked under the cover of trees. It only took them a few minutes, but it was still too long. He heard shouts from behind as they charged into the forest.

"This way," Dagrun said as she edged past him. Instead of following the faint trail, she plunged into a thicket of ferns, pushing fronds out of the way. He waved away a cloud of insects and followed as she took them deeper into the forest.

Suddenly, Dagrun stopped and signalled for him to duck. They crouched in the soft dirt, and he concentrated on keeping his breathing steady and silent. He didn't hear anything, so he was surprised when Dagrun rose and scurried left.

Ten minutes later they were beside a wall of rock.

"We can hide up there," Dagrun said. She pointed, and he looked up but didn't see anything other than a fairly sheer rock face. "Trust me," she said. "My Trait."

She started clambering up, using hand and footholds he would never have noticed. She swung over a ledge and disappeared. He took a couple of steps back. Even from this angle there was no trace of Dagrun.

He stepped back to the wall of rock and reached a hand up. Following Dagrun's path, using the same hand and footholds, scrambling up the rock was easy enough for someone used to climbing rigging.

He heaved himself up and over a rocky lip and then slid down into a shallow bowl that was partially filled with dirt and tufts of dry grass. Dagrun was already flat on her stomach and inching towards the edge. Calder looked out over the tops of the trees to the sea. The ship had anchored near the beach where they'd been spotted, but the forest hid the two smaller boats.

He eased away from the edge onto the softer earth that filled the depression. There could be over a dozen searchers combing the forest for them.

Dagrun shimmied down to join him, shielding her eyes from the glare of the sun.

"Well, that's my Trait," she said. "Finding us a place to hide. Let's hope yours comes through as well."

"Let's hope," he agreed. At times his Trait worked in strange ways. And would his Luck extend to anyone he was with?

With his eyes closed against the sun, he strained to listen for sounds of the searchers: they were sailors, so he wasn't expecting them to have the best skills on land. It was quiet, though, too quiet.

There was a sudden flurry of wings as birds—disturbed by something in the woods—took flight. Calder turned and met Dagrun's wide gaze. He didn't need to see her finger to her lips to understand they needed to be quiet.

The silence was punctuated by a yelp, followed by a curse.

"Santu, shut up," someone hissed. *Charis*, Calder thought. He grinned—his chance to be Second Mate was gone.

"I don't see a way up," the first man, Santu, said. "Think they went that way?"

"You can't even climb rigging," someone else, a woman, said. "I'm not surprised you don't think you can climb that."

"I can rig with the best—"

"Shut up!" Charis, again. "I don't see a way up, even for someone who can rig as well as Rahm. We split up: Santu, you and Enni go east, and we'll go west. Shout if you see any sign of them."

Calder closed his eyes in relief as the searchers left.

He must have drifted off. The sun had moved, and his head felt hot. He squinted and looked over to see Dagrun, the water skin draped over her face, staring over at him, grinning.

"You slept," she said. "Luckily no one came back this way."

"Luckily," he repeated. "I am sorry. How long was I asleep?" He sat up slightly and rolled over, inching up to the edge of the rock. He hadn't meant to fall asleep. Did it mean he subconsciously trusted Dagrun?

"An hour," Dagrun replied. "The ship is still out there. Here." She handed him the water skin.

He took a sip. The water skin was less than half full. They'd need to find a spring soon. "What now?" He handed the water back to her.

"We go that way," Dagrun said, gesturing past her. "This ledge continues north, where it goes higher. There's flatter land up top."

"Your Trait?" he asked.

She shrugged. "I looked. Don't worry, I was careful."

"So, we go that way," Calder agreed. She'd left him sleeping and neither of them had been discovered. Could that be both Luck and Unseen working together? Could they somehow be complementing each other? He had to wonder why Joosep had never assigned more than one Intelligencer—had never combined Traits—for any assignment.

He looked out at the ship—it was Ansdottir's *Vassan* and not the *Bright Breeze*. Had the *Bright Breeze* already been taken?

There was no activity on the *Vassan*: no sails being unfurled, nothing to show that the ship was leaving any time soon.

"Let's go," he said. If Ansdottir wasn't going to leave, then they had to.

Dagrun nodded, got up into a crouch, and led the way along the ridge.

CHAPTER 11

THE HALL WAS quiet at this time of night, so only a few people saw Joosep as he walked towards the infirmary.

He'd received word this morning that Gustav had taken ill, and the timing was suspicious. The lad had become Saulia Holt's favourite in a very short time, and Joosep worried that Tarmo Holt had discovered that he was an Intelligencer student and poisoned him. Not to kill, thankfully, but to keep him away for a while.

Now Joosep had to contend with the worst aspects of being the Spymaster: he'd sent one of his people on assignment and they had been hurt, and could have been killed. And even more guilt inducing; Gustav wasn't fully trained.

"Gustav," Joosep said when he was ushered to the boy's bedside. "How are you?" As always, the minute Gustav's eyes met his he felt a jolt of pleasure. How was it possible that anyone was even able to poison him? Had it been someone with an opposite Trait, perhaps?

"Master Intelligencer," Gustav said, sitting up. "I am sorry I'm ill."

"It's not your fault," Joosep said, because it was his. "But I am curious to know if the Holt family had any plans that you are now not well enough to attend." Gustav swung a leg out from under the covers and Joosep stopped him. "I didn't mean that you needed to go and find out right now. But I am told you are recovering and could have visitors, if any would like to come."

"Yes, sir," Gustav said. "I will send a message directly to Saulia. She's already sent word that she wants to see me."

"I'm sure she does," Joosep said and smiled a genuine smile. It was very hard not to like this lad, even for him, even knowing it was because of Gustav's Trait. "I'll visit again in a few days."

He made his way back to his office lost in thought. He'd heard nothing from either Calder or Dagrun, and he had no one else with an appropriate Trait to send after them.

If Calder's Luck couldn't find Dagrun, then he doubted that someone with the standard non-Trait Intelligencer skills could. He wished he'd given Calder a time limit because really, if Dagrun Lund wanted to run away with her sister and remain Unseen, no one would be able to find her. Now he was left without his most experienced and talented Intelligencer and the knowledge that Tarmo Holt was meeting with pirates.

"Arnor," he said when he reached his office. "Make some discreet enquiries about Tarmo Holt's staff, both at his office and in his home. See if there is anyone that everyone despises: someone no one else can understand why they are employed there." If Gustav was universally loved then his opposite would be universally hated. And capable of recognizing the lad's Trait and poisoning him.

Tarmo Holt knew about Traits; had he already recruited people with them? Was Joosep putting Gustav in too much danger?

Dag stared down the slope. It was steeper than the one she'd slid down her first day at Strongrock, and no matter how hard she looked, she didn't see a good—hidden—way down. They were already pretty far inland: if they were forced to stay on this plateau they'd never find the weapons.

It might make more sense to simply cross the island to where the sailboat was and sail away. Or sail back here, if they were able to steal the boat without being seen. But that meant the possibility of leaving Inger behind, which she wasn't willing to do. She'd rather stay on this side of the island, collect some weapons, and then go back for her sister.

"It looks dangerous," Calder said from beside her.

"It does," Dag said. "Getting down alive doesn't mean one of us won't be hurt." She meant her, of course; she assumed that Calder's Luck would keep him safe.

"I'll go first," Calder said. He took the fishing net off and started shaking it out. "I'll set this out and hopefully we can use it to climb down part of the way. Once I'm at the bottom of the hill, I'll try to make a soft landing spot for you."

Dag sighed. "All right. Let me know when you're ready for me."

Calder searched for a few moments before tying one corner of the net to a rock. He tossed the opposite end downhill: it reached just over half way.

Sitting down, he slid onto the net. Half sliding, half crawling, he made his way to the end of the net. Gripping the net with one hand, he rolled onto one side as he searched for a foothold. When he found one, he let go of the net, his hands flat on the hillside as he slipped downhill a few inches before finding a handhold. He repeated his search for a toehold and slid further downslope.

Dag took note of Calder's path as he painstakingly made his way down the incline. He was careful to keep a steady pace, at times going sideways so he could wedge a boot against a rock, at other times hanging from a handhold. Finally, he was at the bottom.

Calder piled greenery along a six-foot-wide area before waving up at her. Dag took a deep breath before scrabbling down to the corner of the net.

With a firm grip, she reached with her foot to try to find Calder's foothold. But he was a few inches taller than she was so her boot couldn't reach it. She rolled sideways, hoping to find something not as far down. Suddenly, she slid down two feet, and a shower of gravel swept past her. Dag was still clinging to the net even as it slid downhill with her.

She let go of the net to free both hands to claw at the earth. On her stomach now, she tried to keep her feet pointed downhill and her face off the rocks as she picked up speed.

"Left, left, left," Calder called from below. She spared a glance at him and tried to send her feet in the direction he was pointing. Her already bruised hip hit a protruding rock, and she grunted with pain. Her left hand grabbed a tuft of grass, and she slowed a little before the plant slipped through her fingers. Then she felt arms around her: Calder had climbed up a few feet to catch her. He rolled over until she was half on top of him, and then they hit the wall of greenery. The net slid to a stop against them.

She wiped a fern from her mouth and groaned.

"Thanks," she said as she tried to untangle herself from Calder and the net. "Are you all right?"

"Never better," Calder said. He gently rolled her off him before he sat up. "Let's see what the damage is."

He stood up, pulling her with him, helping her get clear of the tangled fishing net. Holding his arm, she took a tentative step— her left foot seemed fine—another step—and her right foot was also good.

"I can travel," she said, letting go of Calder. Her hip was sore: bruised but no broken bones, so it shouldn't stop her from walking.

"Good," he replied. He bent down and picked up the net. "I wasn't expecting to get this back, but it might come in handy again." He grinned as he shook it out. A few minutes later the net—dustier than before—was once again looped over his shoulder.

Dag peered into the darkening woods. They'd come down from the plateau an hour ago, and the sun was starting to sink below the treeline. It was hot and humid under the tree canopy, and the insects seemed to be swarming more intensely than before. She thought they were close to the weapons, which meant they could be close to the pirates.

Ferns rustled and she froze. Then something small ran away from her; a rodent, maybe, or something else that a lynx would eat, but probably not the lynx.

From her side, Calder blew out a breath, and Dag realized she'd been holding hers as well.

"It has to be this way," she said. "But nothing looks familiar." She raised the water skin. It was empty, and she found that frustrating. She *knew* where to find water; just past the beach where the pirates landed and kept the dinghy—but they had to find it first.

"We'll get there," Calder said.

"Then we keep going," Dag said. She was grateful for Calder's confidence. He was self-assured and calm, and he understood things about their situation without being told.

She was used to Inger, who, no matter how much time Dag spent explaining things to, often just did not understand. She'd never realized how exhausting that was.

And it was probably equally exhausting for her sister. What was it like to be constantly told that you didn't understand, that the way you felt and what you thought was true was based on incorrect information, that there were things happening that you just didn't comprehend—and never would, because of your Trait?

She owed Inger an apology, but she wasn't sure she could do anything different in the future. Was she supposed to let Inger become a pirate just because she believed what they told her? Because making her see the truth was a constant, exhausting struggle? Because as draining as it was for both of them, Dag really *did* know better.

But Calder's presence was comforting. She didn't trust him, not completely, and she was certain he didn't trust her either, but she *did* trust his abilities.

She stopped and crouched, signalling Calder to do the same. He crept up beside her.

"I think we found the trail," Dag said. She pushed aside the leaves of a plant to expose a path worn into the earth. There was a noise from their left, and she dropped to the ground. Calder's shoulder hit her sore hip when he did the same, and she bit her lip against the pain.

A bird screeched, and she wondered if that was what she'd heard. She was about to look through to the trail when she felt Calder's hand on her arm. She turned to see him shaking his head.

Ah, there it was. Someone grunted, and then she heard the sounds of footsteps. She thought half a dozen people walked past, and then it was quiet. Calder's hand was on her arm again, this time pulling her away from the trail.

"Why were they so quiet?" she asked in a whisper. They were about thirty feet from the path: as far away as they could get without going through some very dense bushes and making a lot of noise.

"They know there's a chance we're out here," he whispered back. "They're listening for us."

"I need to see if Inger is with them," Dag said. "We'll be able to spy on them at the weapons cache. I can get there from here now that we're sure we're in the right place."

Calder stared at her for a moment before nodding, and she tried to hide her relief. She needed to find Inger: she'd do it by herself, but she'd prefer Calder's help. And his Trait.

It took them the better part of an hour to wind their way through the forest—too long in Dag's mind, Inger could have left the clearing already—but they had to circle around thickets of small trees and clumps of bushes that were too dense to go through.

Eventually they looked out past a hummock of grass onto the clearing. As she'd feared, the area was empty.

"Should we get some weapons?" she asked.

"Not yet," Calder replied. He glanced up at the sky. "It's too early to know if they're finished for today. If they come back, they might notice things missing."

"You are very patient," Dag said. Even she wasn't sure if she meant it as a compliment, but Calder just shrugged.

"That's how my Trait works," he said. "Luck can't be forced." He spread the net out and laid down, resting his head on it.

"Are you going to sleep?"

"No," he replied. "Just getting comfortable for what might be a long wait."

HE TRIED TO shift, but his arm was pinned down by something. Calder opened his eyes to find Dagrun's head on his outstretched arm. He hadn't meant to fall asleep, but the heat had sapped his strength.

He was about to gently move Dagrun's head off his arm when his focus narrowed on the tops of the trees. His Trait was triggered: that may even have been what woke him up.

He stared up at the sky: it was dusk, so he'd been asleep for a few hours. He gently pulled his arm out from under Dagrun's head. Her eyes opened, and she quietly rolled onto her stomach. He felt chilled where their bodies had been pressed together.

Soft footfalls sounded along the path, and he held his breath as three men stepped out into the clearing. Their dark skin barely reflected the light from the moon, which was probably why Pilalians had been assigned whatever task this was. Unlike the earlier group, no one carried any burdens, although they all held long guns, and the one at the rear had a pistol tucked into his belt. Calder's focus narrowed on the one with the pistol—his Trait telling him to pay attention to this man.

He turned to Dagrun, held a finger to his lips, and motioned that she should stay here while he investigated. The men were being quiet, but that didn't mean they weren't whispering to each other. He wanted to hear anything that was being talked about: any plans the pirates had.

Dagrun shook her head, and he frowned and shook his own head emphatically. He was the best choice for this. Like all Intelligencers, Dagrun would have studied other languages, but Pilalian was his father's language; there was no way she would speak it with his fluency.

She finally seemed resigned to staying behind, and despite glaring at him, she settled deeper into the grass.

Calder shrugged: he didn't care if she was angry with him, only that she didn't put them at risk. He peered out at the clearing. The men had flipped the tarp off the stored goods, and two of them were sorting through the boxes and barrels.

They didn't seem to be expecting anyone else, so Calder circled to the end of the clearing farthest from the trail. It took time, but luckily the men were having trouble finding what they were looking for. Eventually, Calder found a place to hide that was close enough to hear their whispers.

"We don't have all night," the one standing watch said in Pilalian.

"It's not here," one of the searchers said. "Charis said it was near the cannon, but it's not."

"Someone moved it, that's all."

"Or someone stole it," the third man said.

"Who would steal it?" the watcher replied. "And don't say spirits. They don't exist."

"They do, especially angry spirits: ghosts of murdered men," the third man said. "I've seen them with my own eyes."

"Shut up about spirits," the second man said. "We'll be pretending to be them soon enough." He stood up with a wide plank in his hand. "I found it. Let's get back to the ship."

The two who had been searching jumped off the stacked goods. The plank was handed off, and they started to pull the canvas back over the crates. The man in charge shifted, and

Calder saw what he was holding: an engraved and painted name plate from a ship. And he recognized the name: *Diamanto*.

They had the nameplate of a ship reported lost at sea. He tried to remember what type of ship the *Diamanto* had been. Were they going to disguise the *Bright Breeze* as the lost ship? Sailors were a superstitious lot: what would a crew do when they saw a lost ship bearing down on them? Especially at night and crewed by silent, almost invisible Pilalians.

He waited half an hour after they left before creeping back to Dagrun.

"Dagrun," he called when he thought he was where he'd left her. "Dagrun!" He tripped over something—the fishing net—but Dagrun was gone.

He couldn't stay here. If she was caught, they'd know he was close. If she wasn't caught, he still needed to find the sailboat.

With a silent curse, he picked up the net and looped it over his shoulder before setting off through the forest.

DAG'S SHOULDER BLADES itched: they'd been itching ever since the three men had walked out of the clearing and back onto the path. She'd waited for Calder as long as she could stand to before she'd stepped onto the trail and followed the men back here, to the beach.

She tucked herself under a huge fern and worried that Calder would never find her in the dark. She crouched down to watch.

A dozen sailors sat around a big fire: she recognized the three she'd followed from the clearing. A second dinghy was pulled up onto the beach. Beyond the fire, waves rolled up along the sand, their frothy tips glowing in the firelight.

"I thought we'd be sleeping on board," one of the men she'd followed said over the sound of the waves.

"Captain wants us on shore tonight," another sailor said. "So, we can start searching again at first light. She figures they're out of food and water by now." He looked at each sailor as though daring them to disobey him.

"Water," a woman said. "I'm missing rum! I bet the crew is getting a full measure tonight." Others grumbled about that, but the one in charge shushed them.

"You all volunteered, so stop whining," he said. "Plenty of sailors would trade places with you for the opportunity of extra shares."

"Only get extra shares if we catch 'em," the woman said. She frowned, but didn't say anything else.

"Who's coming now?" someone else asked.

Dag looked out past the group around the fire to see another dinghy being rowed towards shore. Three people were in the dinghy, but only one was manning the oars. And there was Inger! She was in the back, gripping the sides of the boat as it rose and fell with the waves. And up in front, riding the powerful swells with ease was Captain Margit Ansdottir. What was Inger doing with her?

The man who seemed to be in charge rushed into the surf, grabbed the rope that Ansdottir tossed his way, and towed the dinghy in to shore. Ansdottir jumped out and waded up to the beach and the group at the fire. The rower stowed the oars and followed the captain before Inger climbed over the gunwales and waded ashore.

Ansdottir was already sitting on a log recently vacated by one of the sailors by the time Inger joined her at the fire.

"Charis, did you get it?" she asked.

The man in charge nodded and grabbed a long plank. "The *Diamanto*," he said, holding the board up. "We can get a copy made for the other side. The ship is already getting new paint."

"Good," Ansdottir said. "I just received word about a meeting I need to attend in Strongrock." Dagrun caught the way she looked over at Inger. "With one of our backers. Pack up here. We'll worry about the . . . loose ends later." She stood up and walked back into the surf while the sailors on the beach hurried to get the dinghy afloat. A few minutes later and Ansdottir was on her way back to her ship, Inger sitting in the prow.

Dag slipped back into the forest. The itch between her shoulder blades had subsided, but it wasn't completely gone. Who was Ansdottir meeting with, and what did she mean by calling them a backer? And what did the pirate captain want with Inger? All Dag wanted was to save her sister, but could she if Inger had become some kind of mascot for Ansdottir?

In less than half an hour the pirates had doused the fire and loaded themselves into their own dinghy and rowed away from the beach.

It was too dark for Dag to see very far, but she didn't need to.

She knew where the spring was, and it was time to fill up the water skin. She felt a twinge of guilt at leaving Calder to fend for himself, but he'd followed his Trait, just as she'd done.

"There's no sailboat on this beach."

She'd been about to jump from the rock into the small, hidden bay. She turned to face Calder, who wasn't angry. At least he didn't seem angry.

"No," she agreed. "There never was. I do know where one is. Or where one was, when I passed it. And that's the truth."

"Are you heading there now?" Calder asked.

"No." She held up the water skin. "There's a spring just off a small beach over there." She pointed towards it. "You can't see it from here, but I found it last time I was here." She stepped off the rock and plunged the few feet into the shallow water. "It's just soft sand," she called over her shoulder.

She barely got the words out before Calder splashed down beside her.

"I'm not letting you out of my sight again," he said. "Until I know where the sailboat is."

"All right." She hadn't been trying to get away from him, but she could see how it looked that way.

They waded up onto the beach. Calder sat down and pulled off his boots, and Dag did the same, hoping they weren't ruined after getting soaked in seawater yet again.

She led the way to the spring. She cupped her hand and took a drink, stepping back so Calder could drink as well. Neither of them spoke as they took turns at the spring: she hadn't realized how dehydrated she'd become, and it took a few turns before she felt sated.

When Calder finally stepped away from the spring, she filled the water skin. She headed back to the beach and sat down, expecting Calder to follow her. Instead, he waded out into the water, uncoiling the net from around his shoulder. He came back a few minutes later.

"I'm not sure what fish are here, but it's a good time of night to catch something." He sat down on the beach beside her. "Now tell me why you left me in the forest."

"My Trait," she said simply. "I get itchy, back here," she reached a hand to her back. "All I need to do to find out what's hidden is follow whatever made me itch."

"Huh," he sounded surprised. "My attention focusses on one thing: it could be a word, a sound, or an action." He paused and stretched his legs out. "Or a person. And what hidden thing did you uncover?"

"Margit Ansdottir has a meeting in Strongrock with someone she called a *backer*."

"How do you know?"

"She came ashore," Dag said. "Wanted to know if . . . Charit—"

"Charis," he corrected her.

"If Charis had found whatever those men were looking for. He showed her a piece of wood and she said she had this meeting. Then . . ." she paused. "Then she looked at Inger, and I don't know how to explain it, but *that* was important. That look was important—there's a hidden meaning, or reason—for Inger to be there, with her. Inger didn't row the dinghy, and she didn't say anything, but there must be a reason why she was there."

"Inger came with Ansdottir?" Calder asked in a strained voice. "In the same boat as the captain, but didn't do or say anything?"

"Yes. I was surprised to see her. Are you all right?"

"I hope so," Calder said. "Because I just had that same feeling when you told me Inger was with Ansdottir—my Trait was activated."

Dag blew out a breath and tried to stay calm. Calder's reaction to Inger being with the captain of the pirates scared her more than anything else had.

"We need to find out who Ansdottir is meeting with," Calder continued.

"Yes," Dag replied, grateful that he wanted what she did despite her leaving him behind. "I was expecting you to resist more or be angry that I left or mad about lying about the sailboat."

"None of that matters," he said, "because both of our Traits are telling us that Inger's involved." He looked at her. "And I don't think either of us thinks that's a good thing."

CALDER GOT UP partly to check the net—he'd secured it as well as he could in the dark, but that didn't mean it was secure—and partly because he needed to think about what Dagrun had learned.

Someone was backing the pirates: he had to assume that

person was why they were stealing and hording weapons. But what did that have to do with Inger Lund?

Usually he waited for his Trait to work—waited until Luck gave him a piece of information he needed to get an answer. This time he was worried that he *couldn't* wait. But even if he thought he could force Luck, he had no idea how to do it.

He reached into the water, found the net, and started pulling it in. A few fish flashed in the moonlight, promising that at least they could eat. Suddenly worried, he patted his pockets. Ah, he had the flint and the knife from the tavern, so he could cook. He'd been at sea long enough that he knew how to prepare and eat fish raw, but it wasn't his preference. And Dagrun might not even try it: they both needed to be rested and fed and ready for anything.

With the fish cradled in the folded net, he waded back to the beach.

"We'll have something for breakfast," he said to Dagrun, who sat staring out at the water. He dug a hole in the sand close enough for the tide to fill it with water, but not so close that the waves would destroy it. He put the fish into the hole and covered it with the net. He looked over at Dagrun, who was now looking at him.

"We'll take the dinghy," he said. "It will be faster than going through the forest."

"What do you think Ansdottir wants with my sister?"

"I don't know," Calder replied. "But they know there's something special about her." He sat down in the sand beside her. "And we know she has a Trait."

Dagrun looked out at the sea. "Yes. If Ansdottir does have the Unseen Trait, then Inger would be impossible for her to miss. And I think the captain is smart enough to understand what that means."

"You think that's why she has Inger?" Calder asked. "Because she knows she has an opposite Trait?"

"Yes. Inger is so obvious to me, but I always thought it was because she was my sister." She paused. "My twin." She turned to him. "Have you ever crossed paths with someone with the Bad Luck Trait?"

"Yes. Years ago, I saw a boy on the streets of Pilalia." He smiled. "He reminded me so much of my own brother. I only saw him for a few minutes, but in that time, he was knocked into and spilled half of the cooking oil he was carrying and was stung by a wasp." His smile slipped. "Only later did I realize he had Bad Luck. And that I recognized that and equated it with my brother."

"I think Ansdottir recognizes that in Inger," Dagrun said. "She may or may not know what it is, but it's the opposite of her."

"But what does she want with her?" Calder asked. He sighed. That answer was for another day. "I need to get some sleep while I can. I'll be rowing tomorrow," he said, "and after, with Luck, I'll be sailing." He checked to make sure the fish were secure before looking up at the sky. It was a few hours until dawn. He rose and headed towards the trees. Once the sun came up it would be too hot to sleep without shade.

Dagrun was still watching the waves when he lay down.

CHAPTER 12

Something crawled across his face, and he swiped at it. He heard the sound of surf nearby, and he opened his eyes and rolled over. It was early—the sun had just come up—so he hadn't slept more than a couple of hours, and he felt like it. Dagrun lay a few feet away from him, her head pillowed on her arm and her knees pulled up to her chest.

He stretched, wondering at her Trait. She and her sister were identical, and when they were apart, he could almost mistake one for the other. But when they were together he'd swear they looked completely different. He shook his head; maybe that was the nature of Traits.

After a quick trip deeper into the forest to relieve his bladder, he walked down to collect the fish. Herring, as he suspected, but a few were a decent size. He spent a few minutes gutting and cleaning them before putting the filets back into the water-filled hole.

He found some rocks that were large enough for what he needed, and he put them in a circle before heading back into the trees for firewood. When he returned, he dropped a few dead branches beside the rocks. He stood up and stared at Dagrun, but she didn't stir. He shrugged and walked into the gentle surf.

Climbing back up the rock face was much harder than

jumping off of it had been last night, even without his boots on. He grinned: he hadn't hesitated when Dagrun had jumped; he'd just found her and hadn't been willing to let her get away again. He still needed to know where the sailboat was, although who knew if it would even still be where she'd seen it.

The dinghy was still hauled up on the beach. He picked through the remains of the pirate's fire: this wood was already dry, as long as he could get it back to the other beach that way.

He followed the path through the forest, pausing just before the clearing where the weapons were kept to make sure no one was there. He'd watched them all leave last night, but double-checking was always a good habit, he'd found.

He pulled the tarp completely off—he'd need a way to carry whatever he took with him—and hopped up onto one of the crates. He read off the names of ships Dagrun had told him: *Stormrunner*, *Windswept*, *Diamanto*, and *Merja*. And a new name: *Bright Breeze*. There were four crates with that label. He pried one open: long guns, about fifty of them. He would bet that very few crew members knew they'd been carrying these.

He sighed. And probably only the ones who had known, except for the captain, were still alive today. He hadn't been on board long enough to make real friends, and he had made a few enemies, but most of the men—like Cook—had simply been making their way in the world. It wasn't fair for them to die so pirates could get their hands on a few crates of guns.

He sorted through the crates and took what he wanted: some long guns, a few pistols, powder and shot for them all, and a couple of wicked-looking Pilalian short swords. Not many people knew how to use them, but they were extremely effective at close quarters. He'd use a bit of the tarp and ropes to fashion a hilt for one or both of them.

Once he'd chosen his weapons and rolled them into a piece of tarp, he lifted the lids on every single crate and punched holes in each keg of powder except for one. That one, along with a small cask of shot and a few more guns, he took into the woods. He placed a couple of flatter rocks under a bush and put his selected items on top of them before cutting a section from the tarp. Once the small cache was covered, he pulled the branches of the bush in front of everything.

When the pirates returned and found the weapons

disturbed—or ruined if it rained—he didn't expect them to bother counting the crates to see if anything was missing. And he and Dagrun would have extra weapons if they needed them.

He hefted the rolled-up tarp over his shoulder and headed back to the beach. He stopped to add the dried wood to his bundle before walking up to the edge of the rock that overlooked the smaller bay.

Dagrun was standing in the waist-deep water looking up at him.

"Good," Calder said before she could react. "Take this." He lowered the bundle down to her, and she grabbed it, shifting it onto her shoulder. Calder waited until she'd moved out of the way before jumping down. He waded over to her and took the bundle.

"I thought I'd let you sleep," he said as he headed towards the small beach. "In case we don't have another chance for a while." He dumped the tarp on the sand and rolled it out, displaying what he'd brought.

"The pirates are really gone?" Dagrun asked. "I was worried they'd come back."

"There was no sign of them," Calder replied, "so I went to the weapons cache and made some adjustments to the way weapons were being stored. I didn't mean to take so long: I originally went looking for dry firewood so that we can eat." He grabbed the charred wood and placed it in the centre of the circle of rocks, then dug his flint from his pocket.

A few minutes later he had the fire lit. Dagrun came and stood beside him.

"I thought we were using the dinghy," she said. "Why didn't you just row everything over here?"

He looked up and met her eyes. "If they decide to come back today they'll see that the dinghy is missing before they even land. That gives them the advantage. If they don't find out we've been here until they've gone all the way to the weapons cache, we have the advantage."

"All right," she crouched down beside him. "What did you do to the rest of the weapons?"

"Uncovered them, mostly," he said. "If it rains they'll be ruined."

"Good. What should I do?"

"Find us something to eat off?" he said. "Once the stones are hot, cooking the fish on them won't take long." He pulled the filets from the water and placed them on the stones while Dagrun headed into the woods.

She was back with some large fern leaves, which she rinsed in the surf before bringing them over to him. He put half the fish on each fern and handed her one.

It cooled quickly, and he ate with his fingers, picking through the odd bone he'd missed while cleaning them. It could have used some salt, but they were fresh so the flavour was excellent. All in all, he'd eaten far worse in better circumstances.

Dagrun tossed the skins from her fish into the fire and they sizzled.

"We leave at dusk?" Dagrun asked.

"No arguments?"

Dagrun shrugged. "Whatever else is going on, so far Inger is safe," she said. "She might be even safer if Ansdottir *does* know about her Trait."

"If Inger has value to Ansdottir she'll make sure she's safe." He had to admit that he was surprised that Joosep had chosen not to train Inger along with her sister. Any Trait could be put to use, couldn't it? Except maybe Bad Luck.

"Besides," Dagrun continued. "I'm a very poor rower, so I'm on your schedule."

"You are," Calder replied. That's why she needed him in the first place. She didn't know how to sail. "And you'll tell me where the sailboat is."

She ignored him and kicked sand on the fire.

"Dagrun," he said. "I'm not taking you with me until you tell me where you saw the boat."

She looked over at him. "I thought you didn't try to force things," she said. "I thought your Trait meant that you'd just learn things when you needed to."

"That doesn't mean I'm deliberately stupid," he said, and she smiled at that. "So Dagrun Lund, you need to tell me where the boat is."

"It's Dag," she said.

"What?"

"Call me Dag. And the sailboat is on the other side of the island. About an hour's walk north of the Strongrock settlement. Where the children live."

"What children?" Calder asked. "I haven't seen any."

"The ones they take from the streets of North Tarklee," Dagrun . . . *Dag*, said to him. "That's why I noticed Ansdottir in the first place. Children were being loaded onto a dinghy and taken to a ship. I followed."

"That's what Jaak meant," he said, "when he came to my room while you were hiding under the bed. He's the sailor who used to be a pirate. The one who told me to get out; that it was too late for him because they'd found him starving on the streets when he was young and kept him warm and fed." He didn't remind her that Jaak had said he wished he'd died back then instead of being forced to do things he didn't want to do. Not when this could be Inger's fate. Although Inger might not realize that she was being coerced.

"Starving," Dag said. "That's what I was told. Children like Jaak, who have been left to fend for themselves in the city, are brought to Strongrock Island. They live in a separate encampment. That's where I saw a sailboat."

"How long ago was that?"

"Three days, maybe four?"

As soon as she said it, Dag was shocked that it had only been three or four days. So much had happened that it seemed like she'd been at the children's beach so much longer ago.

"It's possible the boat is no longer there," Calder said.

"It's possible," Dag agreed, although she thought the pirates had their habits: like the dinghy they kept here. It was a sign that something went on at this beach, and to anyone taking notice it was a sign that the pirates were confident . . . and perhaps, complacent. "What do you think they're planning?" she asked. "With all the weapons?"

"They're getting ready for a fight," Calder said. "My guess is that they'll try to control the Frozen Pass. The pass is already treacherous to get through, and keeping it open and neutral is the reason the Fair Seas Treaty Alliance exists."

"For trade," Dag said. "The treaty is to keep the pass open for trade."

"Yes. Most of the wealth of the Fair Seas Alliance countries is dependent on it."

Dag's shoulder blades twitched—there was something

hidden—something important—in what Calder had just said. "So, all of the richest people in the Three are dependent on the pass being open? What about those who are not so rich?"

"They depend on it too," Calder said. "Timber from the Woodlea Forest is shipped through the pass to the Sapphire Sea. Ships built by Swyford are used to take everything through the pass. If they can't get through, neither timber nor ships will be needed."

"And people will be out of work," she said. "But we won't starve. We may not get fine wine, but we ship plenty of smoked, pickled, and dried fish."

"Sure, but the people don't own that food. They need coin . . ."

"And for that they need jobs," Dag finished. She shrugged but the itch between her shoulder blades didn't subside. "If ships are lost, won't more be needed? Won't there be a greater demand for shipbuilding?"

"Yes." Calder got up and started pacing. "That's part of the puzzle. The shipbuilders. That's always been one of Swyford's main industries."

"On Lavais Island." She knew quite a lot about whose territory it was. "It's controlled by Clan Freeholder Timonis. The next Grand Freeholder." She shrugged. "My assignment was in his household."

"The next Grand Freeholder," Calder repeated. "Except new ships won't be commissioned until they realize that the others have been lost: until they know that ships are not returning through the Frozen Pass. That could take months."

"There's something there," Dag said. "But I don't yet have enough information to know exactly what." She sighed. "Right now, it's too hot out here. I'm going to find a shady spot and take a nap. If the bugs will let me." She stood up and brushed the sand off her trousers and headed up to the edge of the forest. Calder stayed where he was, staring out to sea. He was still standing there when she lay down and turned her face away.

She puzzled over the secret—at what she felt was hidden— regarding the next Grand Freeholder.

Joosep had sent her on that assignment. She'd worried that he'd done it only to get her out of the way so that Tarmo Holt could convince—or coerce—Inger into doing something he knew Dag wouldn't approve of. But what if Joosep had legitimate concerns about the next Grand Freeholder that he hadn't shared with her? Or he simply needed to know more about the man who would be the next Grand Freeholder?

Joosep knew a lot more of the little pieces than she did: it was possible that his Unseen Trait had been just unsettled enough that he sent her there to find out more. Which meant her assignment hadn't been created to get her out of the way in order for Tarmo Holt to approach Inger.

But that didn't mean it hadn't been a secondary reason. She still wasn't sure she could trust Joosep.

INSECTS BUZZING IN her ear woke her up. She waved a hand to shoo them away and rolled over and sat up. The sun was starting to set; she was surprised she'd slept that long.

It took a moment before she spotted Calder: he was sitting with his back against a tree a little farther into the forest.

"Do you have the water skin?" she called out.

He reached behind him, picked it up, and tossed it her way. It landed a few yards from where she sat, and she crawled over to retrieve it.

She took a swig: the water was warm. "I'll refill it." She emptied the water onto the sand and headed over to the spring.

She'd had a drink and was filling the water skin when Calder joined her. She moved out of the way, and he cupped his hand against the rock to collect water.

"I didn't catch any fish," he said when he'd finished drinking.

"So, we should go," Dag said. Now that they were leaving, she was nervous. What if the meeting had already happened? What if trying to stay safe had made them miss the opportunity to find out who the pirate's backer was? She tucked the water skin into her waistband.

She'd have to trust Calder's Luck that they would find what they needed, which she hated. She didn't think he was hiding anything from her—her Trait hadn't been triggered—but she didn't like trusting him: she didn't like trusting anyone. In her experience, most people had secrets. Her Trait meant that she eventually knew what they were: which often led to her being disappointed.

Besides, Calder said his Trait would lead him to what he needed to know. And that was different from what she *wanted* to know: which was how to get Inger out from Ursa and Margit Ansdottir's influence.

She tied her boots together and slung them around her neck. Calder boosted her up the rock, and she climbed up and over the edge, staying low in case pirates were on the larger beach.

No one was in sight, so she scurried over to hunch behind the upside-down dinghy and peer out to sea. No ships were anchored off shore; no smaller boats bobbed on the water.

She returned and looked over the edge of the rock at Calder, who was staring up at her. He handed the bundled tarp to her: she grabbed it and set it down beside her, turning back to help Calder. But before she could offer him a hand he'd scrambled up the rock and was standing beside her.

"I'm used to climbing up and down rigging," he explained. He leaned down and picked up the bundle and headed towards the dinghy.

It took only a few minutes to get the boat righted and into the surf. Two sets of oars had been stored underneath it, and Calder held the boat steady while Dag loaded one set of oars. She dropped her boots into the bottom of the boat and climbed in. Calder shoved the boat away from the beach and hopped in.

"You sit here," he pointed to the prow. "And keep watch."

She nodded: because of her Trait, she'd be able to see any hidden dangers before Calder did. She half-crawled past him and perched on the seat, facing the sea, while he settled the oars into place. Soon the small craft was heading away from the beach.

Dag lurched in time to the choppy motion of the dinghy as Calder rowed them along the shore line. It was faster than walking, but even though there was no sign of anyone on either land or sea, she felt exposed. They rounded a small point of land, and she studied the beach. The cabins here had seemed abandoned both times she'd passed them, and they were counting on that remaining the case. There was still no sign of life: no smoke from a fire; no people about; nothing seemed to have been disturbed since she'd last seen the cabins.

She turned and tapped Calder on the shoulder. He stopped rowing and twisted his head to meet her gaze.

"I think we can go ashore here," she said quietly.

Calder nodded and glanced over his shoulder, looking past her to the beach. A few minutes later she heard the bottom of the boat scrape the sand. Calder pulled the oars in and then jumped out into the surf.

Dag followed, stepping out into water that came up just past her knees. She helped Calder drag the boat right up onto the beach. He grabbed the bundle of weapons, and she picked up both sets of boots and followed him to one of the cabins.

"We might need these now," he said. He unrolled the tarp to expose the guns. He handed her a pistol—she'd been trained in their use, the same as every Intelligencer—and took one for himself, along with a couple of curved knives.

It took them a few moments to load shot and powder into the guns. While Calder contended with the tarp, trying to fashion a harness for the knives, Dag pulled her boots on: they were stiff after being in salt water again, but she was able to get her feet into them.

"Do we leave the dinghy here?" she asked. "Or send it out to sea?"

"Leave it in case we can't make it north," Calder replied, "and have to come back this way. At least we won't be forced to stay on land."

"All right," Dag said. If they had to come back this way, that meant they'd been spotted. She wasn't sure how fast Calder could row, but she was certain one of the sailboats would be faster. So that made it easy: they couldn't be seen. "I'll lead."

"I'll . . ." Calder stopped mid-sentence. "You lead."

"Let's go." She set off along the path. They were close to the settlement: she'd known that, but it seemed like she'd taken only a few steps before she was looking out at the tavern. The lights were blazing, which she hoped meant that they were in time for Ansdottir's meeting. She signalled to Calder that she was going to scout ahead, and without waiting for his response, she stepped into the shadow of the tavern.

She made her way to the back past the storage room where Hanne had tried to lock her up. The door was ajar and she peered in: it was empty, as she'd expected. A broken lock lay on the ground, and she suppressed a grin. She liked the thought of Hanne waiting for someone to rescue her.

The door that led to the living quarters was closed, and for a moment Dag was tempted to enter and see if Inger was in her room. But her sister would be with Ansdottir, she was sure of it.

Her Trait indicated that the captain had a secret that involved Inger, so she probably wouldn't want her to be too far away.

The kitchen door opened and light spilled out, along with someone's shadow. Probably Espen the cook, enjoying a cool breeze after supper was finished. The shadow receded, but the door remained open. Dag peered in—Espen's back was to her, so she darted past.

There was only one more door: the one that led to the tap room. It allowed easy access for the barrels of ale and cider that were delivered to the bar. She eased the door open a crack and crouched low to the ground as she peered in.

Dag didn't see anyone although she could hear the low-level hum of multiple voices. She hesitated, wondering if she should go in.

"Get another jug, would you, Inger?" a voice said from nearby. Dag tried to make herself smaller as her sister walked into view.

"The apple or the pear?" Inger asked. She put an empty pitcher on the bar.

"Pear," Ursa replied, stepping into view. "It's Margit's favourite. Did you get the plate Espen made up for your supper?"

"Yes, thanks," Inger replied. "You seem happy, so I assume the meeting went well?"

"It did," Ursa replied, and Dag could hear the satisfaction in her voice. "You will have a special part to play, in the future. Margit was very sorry that you couldn't be allowed to meet our guest, but you will. Soon."

"I just want to help," Inger said. She walked past the bar and back out into the tavern, followed by Ursa.

Dag closed the door and edged away from it. The meeting was over—they'd known it was a risk that they'd miss it—and it looked like even Inger didn't know who the backer was. She should return to Calder and let him know. They still had to get past all of the buildings of the small settlement to reach the path that led south to the sailboat.

"Watcha doing?"

She'd been seen! Dag covered up her shock at her Trait not keeping her hidden and slowly stood up and turned around. It was a sailor she'd never seen before. He didn't look very old, and she wondered if he'd been taken in by the pirates as a child.

"Just tying my bootlace," she said. "I didn't want to trip out here in the dark. What are you doing?" She edged away from the door, wanting to keep their conversation from drifting inside.

"I was told there was a shower contraption out here," the sailor said. "Never seen one myself."

"I can show you," Dag said. "This way." He wasn't a pirate then: the children had their own shower. She walked towards the open kitchen door, horrified to see Espen standing in the doorway.

"Thanks for the plate, Espen," Dag said. "My friend here is curious about the bathing closet."

"You already thanked me," Espen said. He frowned, but Dag smiled brightly and led the sailor past him. She pointed at the shower, expecting to hear Espen call for help, but if he realized that she wasn't Inger, he didn't call anyone to chase her down.

She babbled a few things about the shower to the sailor, wondering how she could get rid of him. He stepped into the shower and came out shaking his head.

"Hear they have these in Pilalia," he said.

"In every home." Calder stepped out of the shadows. "But with freshwater, not seawater like this one."

"You've been to Pilalia?" the sailor asked, peering at Calder.

Calder signalled for Dag to come to him, so she wandered his way.

"He promised to take me there," she said when she reached his side. Calder looped an arm over her shoulder. "Unless he's been lying to me."

"Never," Calder said. "Now come on, you know my time ashore is limited." He spun the two of them around, and they started to head away. Calder turned his head to the sailor. "You understand, right?" The sailor guffawed as she and Calder walked away. Once they were around the side of the tavern, Dag slid out from under his arm.

"Thanks. The meeting is over, and we need to get going."

"What about Inger?"

"She's in the tavern with Ansdottir and Ursa." She shook her head. "There's no way to talk to her alone. She's safe enough for now. Ursa said they have a part for her to play." She looked around. "But someone saw me. I pretended to be Inger, and I think they believed me but if they didn't . . ." She didn't have to tell him that every sailor in the settlement would be looking for them if Ansdottir realized they were here.

"Then let's get through the square," Calder said.

Dag nodded and stepped back into shadows. The sailor was gone: apparently his curiosity about the shower had been satisfied, and the door to the kitchen was closed now. She led Calder past the kitchen and the door to the taproom. At the corner of the building, she paused. A shaft of moonlight bathed the patch of ground between the tavern and the inn. She peered out at the square: a couple of lights flickered. Torches, but whose?

She ducked back into the shadow, her shoulder touching Calder's.

"I think someone is in the square," she said. "And I don't remember there being a lot of hiding places."

"It's time to trust my Trait," Calder said. "Keep your head down and pretend you're so drunk that you can hardly stand." He put an arm over her shoulder, and she tucked her head against his chest.

Weaving, Calder steered them out into the open. He pulled at her just enough that she legitimately had trouble walking in a straight line. Calder started to sing in what she recognized as Arressan, his voice loud and off-key. Dag shifted her head enough to see that they were just on the edge of the square. A group of people were across from them, stacking boxes and crates by the light of a couple of torches. She saw a few barrels of what could be ale or cider.

"Heya," one of the men called. "You Arressan?"

"Who's asking?" Calder replied, his speech slurred.

"I recognized the song is all," the other person replied. Dag stumbled into Calder who laughed as they both almost fell.

"Oops," Calder said. "My woman might have had a bit too much to drink. And I haven't had enough!" he laughed loudly at his own joke. "What ship are you with?" Calder asked.

"Why do you want to know?"

"Just curious," Calder said. "Crewed on my share of hulks on the Pale Sea's all." Calder weaved a little before heading them across the square.

"It's the Neas," the sailor called out after them. "Out of North Tarklee. Since you're curious."

Dag felt Calder suck in a breath and pause for just a second. "Ah, I never shipped out on that one, but I hear she's fast."

"You heard right," the sailor said.

They took a few more steps, and Calder started singing again. Someone laughed—possibly the sailor who had spoken—and joined in. A few moments later Calder steered them off the stones of the square and onto the dirt path she'd taken a few days ago. Once they were out of view of the square, Calder stopped singing.

"What's the Neas?" Dag asked. She stepped out in front of him. "Why did that name surprise you?"

"It's a ship that belongs to Tarmo Holt," Calder replied.

"*Skit!*" Dag swore. "Everything seems to come back to Tarmo Holt. Do you think he's the one backing the pirates?"

"Maybe. Or it could be someone who works for him."

"Which means it would be him, whether he's here or not." She sighed. "Couldn't that ship have legitimate business here? It looked like they were unloading kegs for the tavern."

"What does your Trait tell you?" Calder asked.

"The best way to hide is in plain sight. I have to get Inger." She started to turn back the way they'd come, but Calder caught her. "Let me go! Holt is after Inger: I won't let him have her!"

"No. You'll be caught."

"What do you care? The sailboat is that way. It should take about an hour for you to reach it, and then you can sail away and report to Joosep. I need to get Inger."

"No," Calder said. He tightened his grip. "We need both of our Traits to escape."

"I don't care! I heard Ursa tell my sister that she has a special task, and Tarmo Holt is here! They're going to give her to him, I know it."

"They might be planning that," Calder agreed. "But talking to her didn't help before and it won't help now. You know that."

"*Skit*," Dag repeated. She blew her breath out, feeling deflated. "I *do* know that." She stopped struggling, and Calder relaxed his grip on her. She could run from him now, but he was right: Inger wouldn't listen to her—not fast enough for them both to escape. The only result of her going after Inger now would be that she'd be caught and locked up. And they wouldn't leave that to Hanne. No, Ansdottir or Ursa would lock her up, and she had a feeling that would mean no chance of escape.

"We stick to our plan," Calder said. "Get the sailboat and leave."

"You're right." Dag hated saying it, but it was true. "This way." The trees seemed to close in on her as she stepped under their branches and onto the path. Just enough moonlight filtered down for her to see the path. She was concentrating so hard on her footing that she didn't immediately identify the sounds as shouts.

"I think we're being followed," Calder said. "We need to move faster."

Dag looked up and cocked her head. More calls came from behind them. "I'll go as fast as I think is safe for you in this light," she said, hoping it would be fast enough.

CHAPTER 13

CALDER FOLLOWED DAG as closely as he could, watching as she identified hazards on the path. She pointed down with her left hand, and he slowed to navigate around a tree root. They'd been half-running for about fifteen minutes and whoever was chasing them had gained on them. He was pretty sure Dag could travel faster in the dark without him, but they needed to stay together.

He heard someone cry out in pain: proof that despite the torches their pursuers carried, they were still having trouble seeing all of the obstacles on the path.

Dag's hand pointed to the right. "Watch your step," she whispered over her shoulder. She leaped over a rock, and Calder copied her foot placement. A minute later he heard a thud and a muffled groan from behind them: *someone* hadn't seen the rock.

Suddenly, the trees thinned out and the path ended at a beach. Dag broke into a sprint and he followed, the Pilalian short swords slapping against his legs as he ran. The beach ended at a large rock, but even though he slowed, Dag didn't pause. She jumped up and clutched at a scraggly tree, using it to help her scramble to the top of the rock. Calder leaped up, grabbing the tree and pulling himself up after her.

Dag had slowed to edge along a narrow ledge that clung to the side of the rock, and Calder followed her onto the exposed path.

There were no trees to hide them from view, but there was enough moonlight for him to see where to put his feet. He glanced back along the beach as a torch burst through the trees, the shadowy shapes of their pursuers crowding behind it.

"Hurry," Dag called.

He shuffled after her along a path that curved behind an outcrop, effectively hiding them from their pursuers. Would the pirates find their way up the rock to follow them? He wouldn't have seen the way up if Dag hadn't gone first, especially not at night, but the pirates knew this island, and they knew he and Dag had gone *somewhere*.

Dag was ahead of him, and he followed as fast as he could while making sure his footing was stable. He paused and glanced toward the sea: and froze.

"Dag," he called out softly. "Stop."

She looked back at him. When he pointed she looked out across the water and crouched down. Calder crept over to her, being careful to keep his swords covered. Even with the moonlight someone using a telescope wouldn't be able to see much more than movement this far away, but anything shiny that caught the light would be visible.

"It's the Neas," he said.

"Is it a coincidence?" Dag asked. "They unloaded their goods and just happened to be leaving now?"

"No. They're too close to the island: this isn't the safest sea route to anywhere. They're looking for us."

"We have to keep going."

"Yes," he agreed. There wasn't a choice, not really. "We can't stay here. Whoever is following us will figure out where we went. How long until we reach the sailboat?" The Neas was far enough away that even if it spotted them it would take time to sail close enough to launch a dinghy.

"Less than twenty minutes," Dag said.

"That should give us enough time to get to the sailboat and get the sails up before they get here," he said. They also had the pistols if they needed to defend themselves.

"Remember my Trait," Dag said. "They could be looking right at me and not notice me."

"But they can see me," Calder said. As always, he couldn't trust Luck to do what he wanted. If Dag knew how to sail he'd send her ahead to get the boat. But if she knew how to sail, she wouldn't have needed *him* in the first place.

"I think it's wide enough here for us to go side by side," Dag said. "I'll stay between you and the ship. It should work."

"All right, *should* work is better than *will never* work," Calder said. "Maybe my Luck will help too."

"I hope so," Dag replied. She carefully stood up. Once Calder edged close enough, she wrapped her arm around his waist. "I've seen the sailboat twice: I'm counting on Luck that it's there now."

They moved slowly: more because the path was narrow and rocky and a fall would send them plunging into the sea than because they were worried about being seen. Dag kept their feet on the path, and Calder tried to figure out if they'd been spotted by the Neas or their pursuers had found the trail.

Every time he turned his head he unconsciously pulled her closer to him. As an Intelligencer he'd always worked alone—they *all* worked alone—but it was nice to have someone else he could depend on. And he thought it nice that Dag was depending on him. Even though he didn't think she trusted him. He grinned for a moment, but then the grin slipped away when he looked out at the Neas. He'd meant it earlier when he'd said it would take both their Traits to make it to safety. He'd spent ten years as an Intelligencer, and he'd never been hunted like this before.

"I think we're getting close," Dag said. "I have to warn you that there's a drop off into the sea right before the beach where the children are."

"Do we have to jump?" Calder asked.

"Probably," Dag replied. "There is a trail through the woods that I used to get here from the beach, but that will take much longer."

"And the pirates following us could catch up," Calder said. "So we jump."

In order to inch around a spot where the path had crumbled into the sea, they had to separate. Once the path widened out enough, Calder linked arms with Dag. He automatically glanced out to sea.

"*Skit!*" He sighed. "They saw me; when we separated, someone saw me."

"How do you know?" Dag asked although she didn't stop moving along the path.

"They're signalling." He glanced out at the ship. A single lamp swung back and forth from the stern, and suddenly lights appeared mid-ship. "They're getting a dinghy or two in the water in a couple of minutes."

"Then it's a good thing we're here," Dag said as she stopped, keeping a steadying hand on his arm.

Calder peered out past her. The beach was dark, but he could see two structures tucked in close to the forest. A small pier jutted out into the sea. And tied to it, bobbing on the waves, was a sailboat—as promised.

"The sailboat's there," Dag said. "I'm going to thank your Luck."

"I'll take it," Calder replied. He looked over the edge. There was a fifteen-foot drop into the sea: not a huge plunge, but they had no way of knowing what was under the water there. He knelt down to try to get a better look.

"There are rocks there," Dag pointed at a spot a few feet inland. "But nothing this way."

"You can see them?"

Dag shrugged. "My Trait knows where they are. Hidden, remember?"

He nodded. "All right. We stay away from those areas. Anything else?" Dag shook her head. "I'll go first."

He untied the tarp that held the swords, dropped them to the ground and unfolded the cloth. He placed his pistol in the centre of it. He held out his hand for Dag's pistol and put that in as well. He wrapped the tarp up as tight as he could, hoping to make it water tight.

"It won't keep them dry if it's submerged for too long," he said.

"But we might get Lucky," Dag finished.

"Let's hope," he said, not sure what he was hoping for. That the pistols were usable or that they never needed to use them? He handed the bundle to Dag. "You toss them to me once I'm down."

He stepped over to the edge to a spot where he would land far from where Dag said rocks were submerged. He jumped, pulling his knees into his chest.

He hit the water with a splash and went under. It was too deep to stand, so he kicked, propelling himself up. When his head surfaced, he took a deep breath before waving up at Dag.

"Drop the bundle, and then I'll get out of your way."

She leaned over and let go of the bundle. He grabbed it and started swimming towards the beach, awkwardly trying to keep it above his head. He turned when he heard a splash. A moment later Dag's head broke the surface, and she started swimming towards him.

"Is it dry?" she asked when she reached him.

"I think so." After a few more strokes he was able to stand. It was slower wading through the water, but it would keep the contents of the tarp as dry as possible.

"We woke someone up," Dag said. She was closer to shore and stood up, water dripping from her.

Calder pushed to catch up to her. "You take this," he said, handing the tarp bundle to her. "I'll make for the boat and make sure the sails are there."

"You mean they might not be?"

"If they're not we may need to negotiate," he said. "We still have some time before the dinghy from the Neas gets here. Besides, the people who live on this beach may not give the Neas crew a warm welcome. It's possible that not everyone will feel comfortable with Ansdottir's arrangement with Holt. Or that Holt even knows about the children who live here."

He dove towards the pier and the boat, swimming under water for as long as he could. When he surfaced, a figure on the beach was holding a lamp, looking out towards Dag. But not once did they swing the lamp to look in his direction. Was Dag somehow being seen on purpose, or was his Trait making her more visible? It didn't matter as long as Dag was keeping their attention.

The pier was just ahead: the sailboat looked lonely tied up to something that could accommodate a dozen boats the same size. What else had this cove been used for, before being used to raise children? Pirate business, probably.

He swam under the pier and then eased between the wet wood and the side of the boat. Hands on the gunwale, he hauled himself on board.

Calder opened a hatch and breathed out in relief: the sails were there, neatly packed away. He quickly untied the boat and pushed off from the dock. In a few minutes he had the sail up. Once wind puffed out the canvas, he sat down at the tiller.

There were more lights and figures on the beach now, most of them small. Dag was in the water in front of the group on the beach, but he thought she was too far away for their lights to reach her.

It was a little tricky getting close enough for Dag to toss the bundle into the boat. He threw her the painter, and she grabbed it and pulled herself towards the sailboat.

As soon as she had hold of the gunwale, he stepped back to man the tiller and set course for the open sea.

"We made it," he said to Dag as she joined him in the stern. Soaking wet, she dropped to the bottom of the boat.

"So we did," she replied and blew out a big breath.

DAG SAT IN the bow, peering at the dark sea ahead of them. She pointed out a submerged rock, and Calder steered the boat around it.

The ship—Holt's ship—was almost straight ahead of them, cutting off the way north to the Frozen Pass. She could see one dinghy in the water, and she assumed that the activity on board meant that another was being readied. As long as the wind held she and Calder should be able to outrun the dinghies. As long as the wind held.

When the rocks near the shoreline were no longer a threat, she turned to scan the beach behind them. A cluster of dark figures stood on the white sand, but the lamp had been doused.

Was Calder right that not all of Ansdottir's people knew about the captain's relationship with Tarmo Holt? The Neas' presence here might worry Teacher and the children. And no matter what Teacher thought about someone landing on their beach and stealing their sailboat, the threat posed by a ship could be greater.

"Hang on," Calder called out softly, and Dag tightened her grip on the gunwales.

The boat bucked over a wave, and seawater splashed up over the prow. She blew out, trying to move the wet strand of hair from her eyes, but she didn't dare reach a hand up. If she lost her grip and went overboard, Calder might not be able to come back for her even if he wanted to; not unless he was willing to risk almost certain capture.

There was a smooth patch of sea, and the sailboat picked up speed, heading straight for a gap between the Neas and the rocky cliff they'd just walked along. Dag craned her neck to look but didn't see any figures clinging to the trail: either their pursuers hadn't made it that far or they'd gone back to Strongrock for reinforcements.

The boat crested a wave and slid down the trough, and Dag was flung forward into the wedge of the prow. She dug her fingernails into the wet wood and knelt lower. The part of the boat that she was in was bearing the brunt of the waves, but there could be hidden dangers ahead that she needed to warn Calder about.

They were almost even with the Neas: men were scrambling into the now-lowered second dinghy. The first dinghy was heading towards them, someone calling a steady pace, urging the rowers on.

Then they were past the ship, flying over the dark, choppy sea. The moon highlighted the swells as Calder steered them directly away from the island.

Dag glanced back at Calder, who had one hand on the tiller while the other was flipping a rope back and forth, constantly adjusting the angle of sail. He was dripping wet, and she wondered how he'd managed to stay in the boat with nothing but the tiller to hold onto when a wave smashed into them, throwing him to one side, and she saw the rope around his waist, tying him in.

She looked ahead, trying to see what he was steering them toward. The sky was starting to lighten, but that didn't help her see what might be out there.

The Neas was far behind them now: her dinghies, having given up the chase, were back in the shadow of the ship. Would they simply go home, or would they try to catch them on the open water?

After another half hour the grey sky was light enough for her to see that they'd left Strongrock Island behind them. The swells were now larger but less violent, and she took a chance to rub her hands together, trying to warm them up.

"Are we heading to Ostland?" she asked, turning to Calder.

"No," he replied. "We're heading due west, but I'll turn north in a while and then go east to Ostland. We should be able to find a ship heading to Tarklee." He tucked the tiller under his arm and blew into his fisted hand. "Joosep needs to know about Tarmo Holt's involvement with the pirates."

"You're still assuming that he doesn't already know," Dag

replied. "I don't think we should tell him anything until we're sure he's not part of this." Joosep was why Inger had left North Tarklee, and now somehow, she'd been manipulated by the pirates. Dag didn't like that both Margit Ansdottir and Tarmo Holt had taken an interest in her sister, and Joosep bore some responsibility for that too.

"What if you're wrong?" Calder asked. "What if delaying giving him this information means he misses the only opportunity to confront—and stop—Holt?"

"Even if he can be trusted Joosep won't do anything," Dag said. "He'll wait until Tarmo Holt's term as Grand Freeholder is over and assume that Holt can't do anything for another six years."

"*Skit*," Calder swore. "You're right—Joosep *won't* act. He prefers to gather intelligence and give it to others so *they* can act." He met her gaze. "Is your Trait telling you that Joosep is working with Holt?"

"No," Dag replied. "But I think it's too much of a coincidence that we've found out that Holt is backing the pirates in some way. *That* seems like it was uncovered by a Trait—mine, yours, maybe both."

"We still should return to Nordmere," Calder said. "And find out what Holt is planning."

"I guess," Dag said, but she didn't like leaving Inger behind. She'd be all right, wouldn't she? Whatever plans they had for her wouldn't happen right away, and even more importantly, they required Inger to be alive. Dag shivered. She'd been trying not to think about just how much danger Inger could be in because then she would have to go back and find her. At least her Trait hadn't been triggered by a *hidden* danger. The obvious danger was quite enough.

Dag sat in silence, looking out across the Pale Sea. She felt it when Calder changed course and headed north, but she didn't say anything. She'd agreed to head back to North Tarklee, but it didn't feel right, leaving Inger behind. Even though there was no chance to find her sister and talk to her in private; to make Inger understand what was really happening with the pirates. And even if she could convince her, Ursa or Margit Ansdottir had some hold on her: some Trait that made Inger doubt her own sister.

She was puzzling how a Trait like that could work when Calder swore.

"*Skit!*" Calder said. He jumped up and grabbed the sail and ducked. "Watch your head."

Dag dropped to the bottom of the boat as Calder pulled at the sail until it was lined up with the prow. Once it caught the wind, he flattened himself in the bottom of the boat and reached out with one hand to grip the tiller. In a few moments they were speeding in the opposite direction.

"They saw us," Calder said. He shifted back to the seat at the stern. Dag lifted her head and looked past him.

A ship bore down on them from between a narrow pass.

"Is it the Neas?"

"Yeah," Calder said. "They can outrun us, so check the guns to see if they're dry enough to fire. It won't hurt to let them know we have a bite of our own."

"They'll catch us?"

"Not if I can help it," Calder said. He shoved the tiller over to one side, and the boat lurched, throwing Dag into the gunwale. "Sorry," Calder said. "I need to make us too difficult a target for them to hit with a cannon."

"Cannon?" Dag was too startled to be afraid. She found the rolled-up tarp and started undoing it. The pistols didn't have a very good range—the ship would have to get very close—closer than she wanted to think about—if they were to be effective. "What other weapons will they have?"

"Same as us: what you found on the beach is pretty standard for a ship like the Neas: pistols, long guns, and shot and powder."

Dag had the tarp unrolled. She picked up a pistol, but groaned when she saw the bag of powder. It was soaking wet.

"What happened to your Luck?" she asked Calder.

"It works in unpredictable ways," he replied. "I take it the guns didn't survive."

"Guns yes, powder no." Dag picked up a long gun and laid it across her knee. She'd wave it around and hope the crew from the Neas noticed it. It might gain them a few seconds or minutes, and that could be the difference between capture and escape.

They were travelling against the wind, and Calder continued to position the sail to keep them heading south. Dag kept her eyes on the Neas. It was gaining on them: now she could see the crew as they scrambled amongst the sails. They had the same problem:

they were also heading into the wind, but she thought it was more complicated to keep a multi-sailed ship heading straight than for Calder to do it in this small boat.

"They're turning," she said suddenly. She peered past Calder, who had twisted in his seat to stare behind them. "They're giving up, Calder, they're heading back north." And they were! As she watched, the ship made a wide turn. The sails filled with wind, and then it skimmed away from them.

"Huh," Calder said. He turned back and met her eyes. "Keep watch ahead."

"But they gave up!"

"Or they pushed us into a trap. Like I said, keep watch up ahead."

"Should we go to Ostland now?" Dag asked. Would the pirates have had time to get their ship this far from Strongrock? "We could wait until the Neas has gone through the pass and find a safe place to hide?"

"All right," Calder agreed. "It's a good a plan as any." He looked past her and frowned. "Sorry, it's too late for that."

Dag swivelled in her seat. "*Skit*." Two small sailboats were heading towards them, their sails puffed out with wind. "Can we outrun them?"

"And go where?" Calder asked. "The Neas is north and east leads to the Sapphire Sea. This little boat won't make it that far." He shifted in his seat. "Keep your head down. I'm going to go right up the middle and split them."

Dag lay down on the bottom of the boat. She didn't have to tell Calder that his plan was ridiculous, but she didn't have a better option. She peered over the gunwale. The boats were close enough that she recognized Margit Ansdottir in the one on her right. She stood with one hand on the tiller and the other one holding a pistol: aimed at them.

But she didn't shoot.

"Stop," Ansdottir called out in a booming voice. "You have no place to go."

Calder did something and their boat swerved towards Ansdottir's. The pirate captain tucked the pistol into her waistband and wrenched the tiller with both hands until they were no longer on a crash course.

"Charis said you were good," Ansdottir said, and then she

laughed. "I can always use a good sailor."

"I want my sister!" Dag called.

"She's mine now," Ansdottir said. "There's nothing you can do about that. But I can make her hurt herself if you don't stop this."

"No!" Dag wasn't sure if Ansdottir was telling the truth, but it had only taken Ursa a few minutes to convince Inger that she—her twin—had lied to her. She couldn't take a chance that Ansdottir could do what she said she could.

The two boats were close now. Calder was purposely heading directly at Ansdottir. The pirate in the second boat was giving them all a wide berth. Without thinking, Dag stood and launched herself into the sea. She thought she heard Calder's shout of dismay, and then she hit the water.

It was cold, much colder than the sea had been near the beach. Her head went under, and then she was struggling to reach the surface. Her hands felt like ice, then like lead, weighing her down. A large hand gripped her arm, and she was pulled up and over a gunwale. As she lay gasping for breath on the bottom of a boat, a figure loomed over her. She looked up at Margit Ansdottir.

"I didn't expect that," Ansdottir said. Then she laughed. "I like being surprised." She looked away from Dag. "Leave him," Ansdottir called out. "We got what we came for." Still chuckling, Ansdottir headed back to the stern. She grabbed the tiller and pushed it away from her. Dag felt the boat slow as it turned, the wind no longer filling the sail. She wanted to look to make sure Calder had escaped, but a fit of shivering struck her and she couldn't move. By the time the shivering passed and she had the energy to lift her head, the boat had rounded a point and was heading into the bay at Strongrock; Calder was nowhere to be seen.

CHAPTER 14

JOOSEP TURNED THE corner and skidded to a stop. Gustav was waiting in front of his office door, a frown on his usually smiling face.

"Inside," Joosep said as he quickly unlocked his door. He peered around, worried that someone had seen Gustav waiting for him.

He hadn't felt the need to lock his office until the day he'd found Tarmo Holt inside: was that something Holt had done on purpose? Had he wanted to ensure that Joosep locked his office door so that his spies could see who waited outside it? Had he put Gustav in even more danger? All he could do was hope that it was early enough that no one had noticed the youth.

Joosep sat at his desk and gestured to a chair, but Gustav didn't sit. Instead, he paced in front of it.

"Report," Joosep said, hoping that his terseness would somehow calm the lad down. He had to admit that seeing the genial Gustav worried rattled him.

"I know who poisoned me," Gustav said. He paused to shrug. "I feel so stupid. It was Asla Holt. She didn't want me seeing her daughter, and Saulia wouldn't listen to her."

"The wife," Joosep said. "Do you think Tarmo Holt knew?" And did Asla Holt have a Trait? Joosep didn't see how anyone without one could try to harm Gustav.

"No, neither did Saulia. She was furious with her mother." Gustav finally sat down. "Saulia threatened to tell her father, and Asla did *not* want that."

"But she didn't tell him," Joosep said. "At least, I haven't heard that Holt reported a poisoning."

"He's not here," Gustav said. "He's due back in a few days."

"What?" This was news. As Grand Freeholder, Tarmo Holt had a duty to inform the people who reported to him when he would be unavailable. "Are you sure?"

"Saulia was," Gustav replied. "And her mother seemed to agree. They argued about this in front of me. I don't think I'll be getting any more invitations to dine with the Holts." Gustav grinned. "Although now that Saulia knows her mother poisoned me I think it would be safe."

"You will not accept an invitation if it comes," Joosep said. "Your assignment is complete. But this is interesting information." What it meant, exactly, he didn't know.

"Don't you want to know where Tarmo Holt is?" Gustav asked. "You know?"

"Well, he might not be there right this minute," Gustav said, "but he was on his ship, and it was heading to Strongrock."

"Why would he be going there?" Joosep asked. The island wasn't part of the treaty—it claimed to be neutral—so what business did the Grand Freeholder of the Fair Seas Treaty Alliance have on Strongrock?

"Holt's wife and daughter wondered the same thing," Gustav said. "And they were angry because he'd been there just over a month ago. Holt expects them to lie and pretend he's at home. I heard Asla tell someone that her husband was ill in bed."

"Thank you, Gustav," Joosep said. "That's very helpful."

"Is my assignment still completed?" Gustav asked. He stood up but fidgeted and didn't make a move to leave. "I was worried that you'd say that because I don't want it to be."

Joosep met Gustav's eyes, trying with all his might not to smile. It was hard to be objective with the youth: he had to make sure he never forgot that.

"I don't want you in their house," Joosep said, giving in. "For your own safety you will only meet Saulia in public." Joosep sighed. "And please don't stand around outside my office again.

It's too conspicuous."

Gustav nodded and left, and Joosep had to hope he hadn't made a mistake. The youth wasn't quite half-trained, and he hated to put him in more danger, but the information he'd gathered was far too valuable for him to ignore. Joosep *knew* that Holt was planning something, and having a spy so close to him was critical to finding out what that was. But he had to wonder if he was agreeing to this because he'd fallen under the spell of Gustav's Charisma.

CALDER SCANNED THE sea on all four compass points before pulling the sail back over him. It was almost noon, and the sun was high in the sky. So far it was still bearable under the canvas, but that wouldn't last. He licked his parched lips, tasting salt from the air. He'd need water before the end of the day, otherwise he might become too light-headed to navigate.

He'd been so startled when Dag jumped overboard that it had taken him ten minutes to get the sailboat turned around. By that time Ansdottir had already plucked Dag from the sea. He'd watched them head back towards Strongrock knowing that he had no way to catch up to them, let alone rescue her.

What had she been thinking? Ansdottir had said something to Dag, and because his attention had been focused on sailing, he hadn't heard it. A threat to Inger, was what he thought, but why had Dag believed the pirate captain? Ursa had said that they had plans for Inger. What had changed?

He sighed. He'd have to go after her, of course. He wasn't sure she expected him to: *he* hadn't expected to make this choice. But there it was. He was going to risk his life for Dagrun Lund and her sister, if she'd come with them. And if Inger said no, he'd *make* Dag leave her behind, even if it meant she hated him for it. Because somehow Dag had become incredibly important to him, and not just to help stop whatever Tarmo Holt and the pirates were planning. He shook his head. She didn't even trust him.

He lifted the canvas off his face and took another look around. No ships, no gulls, no one to see which direction he headed.

It took only a few minutes to raise the sail and point the little boat southward. An hour later he reached the shoreline. Dead trees cascaded down rocky cliffs as though even they were trying to escape the Blighted Woods. Keeping well away from the rocks,

Calder turned east.

It was mid-afternoon by the time the Teeth were in sight. Keeping the Teeth to starboard, he steered north.

It was the long route back to Strongrock Island, but it was the best way to be sure—without any other way to navigate—that he wouldn't sail directly into the pirate settlement.

On this side of the Teeth the only ships he would cross paths with would belong to the pirates, so Calder constantly scanned for sails. He saw nothing on the horizon and began to hope that he would be able to return to Strongrock undetected.

The sun was setting by the time he finally reached Strongrock Island. He sailed west, hugging the coast, until he recognized the large beach where the pirates landed. In a few minutes he was in the small cove.

He pulled the sail down, hopped into the surf, and dragged the boat up onto the beach before heading to the spring.

He drank slowly, so it took a few minutes to slake his thirst. His lips were still cracked, but he was already recovering his energy. He slapped some water on his head and his neck, enjoying the way the breeze cooled his skin.

With a sigh, he turned to his tasks.

He pulled the little sailboat higher up onto the beach to make it safe from the surf but also easy to relaunch quickly, if he had to. He tied the sail between two trees to dry before unpacking the guns to retrieve the fishing net. He placed the net in the same spot as last time and sat down under a tree to wait and hope he was lucky enough to catch dinner.

HE WOKE TO darkness. Stars twinkled overhead, and the waning moon illuminated the quiet, deserted beach.

He hadn't meant to sleep so long: it was a testament to just how draining the day had been. He waded out to the net, half expecting it to be gone. Instead, his Luck held. Not only was the net there, but three fish were tangled up in it.

Not willing to chance a fire, Calder cleaned and gutted the fish by moonlight and after washing them in the sea, ate the fish raw.

He drank more water before lying down to get more sleep. His last thought was that in the morning he'd follow the path to the weapons and find the small cache he'd hidden there. And then he'd figure out how to rescue Dag.

WATER DRIPPED ONTO her lips and reflexively she sucked the drops into her mouth. She couldn't move her arms, but she was so warm—finally—that she didn't care. After a few weak struggles she gave up and just lay there, sucking water droplets into her mouth.

"Are you awake?" Inger asked, her voice said close to her ear. "Dag, are you awake?"

"Yes, awake," Dag mumbled. "Water, more water." Someone sighed loudly, and her head was tilted and a cool mug was pressed against her lips. She drew in a big gulp and sputtered.

"Slow down," Inger said, and this time it registered that her sister was with her

Dag looked up to see her sister's worried face hovering over hers. She tried to talk, but she coughed instead, and water trailed down her chin.

"Shhh," Inger said. "Take it easy. You scared me, Dag. Captain Ansdottir said you might never wake up. Another minute in the water and you might not have."

Dag struggled, but her arms were pinned at her side.

"Here." Inger did something, and Dag was able to free her arms. She shoved a blanket lower and sat up, leaning her head against a wooden wall behind her.

"Where are we?" Dag croaked. She wrapped her arms around her midsection and shivered. Inger pulled the blanket up around her chin.

"We're in Strongrock," Inger said. "At the inn. Captain brought you here straight away."

"Why?" Dag asked, when what she meant was, *why was she still alive*? Ursa wanted her dead, so if another minute would have accomplished that, why wasn't she?

"The inn is closer to the dock than my room," Inger said, as usual answering the obvious question. "Captain Ansdottir saved you, Dag, she *saved* you."

That's why, Dag thought. Ansdottir had Inger's gratitude. What would Inger agree to do in order to pay off this debt? What would Ansdottir expect to do with Inger's co-operation?

"I need to leave," Dag said. She struggled to move her legs, but a spasm of shivering left her weak. She closed her eyes. She wouldn't have thought a few minutes in cold water could sap her strength so completely, but there it was. She wasn't going anywhere for at least a day.

"No," Inger said. "You need to stay! With me!" She pushed Dag over a little and sat beside her on the bed. "I told the captain that you'd changed your mind, that you realized that you didn't want to leave your twin." Inger sounded very pleased with herself. "And that we'd only argued because I wanted to live my life, not yours."

"Did she believe it?" Dag asked. Ansdottir had a bit of the Unseen Trait, but Inger wasn't trying to fool her—Inger could never try to fool anyone.

"Why wouldn't she?" Inger asked. "It's the truth. I told you I was tired of living in your shadow, and next thing I know, you jump out of a boat so you can stay here, with me."

"Sure," Dag said. Would this give her enough time to recover? She hadn't changed her mind, but right now she didn't have the energy to explain to Inger that she'd jumped because Captain Ansdottir had threatened *her*. "Can I have some more water?" she asked. "And maybe something to eat?" She'd concentrate on regaining her strength and worry about how to get both her and Inger off Strongrock later.

"Oh, sure," Inger jumped off the bed and grabbed the glass from a small side table. "Here's the water, can you hold it yourself?" She handed the glass to Dag, who took a sip and balanced the glass on her chest. "Ursa said there's soup. I'll go get you some." She smiled and left the room.

Dag took another sip of water before setting the glass on the table. She was pleased that she'd only spilled a few drops. She leaned her head back against the wall and closed her eyes. As she drifted back to sleep she heard the door open.

Inger was back with soup, and it took all of Dag's energy just to eat it. Her sister was still talking when Dag fell asleep again.

SOMETHING UNDERNEATH HIM was cold. Calder opened his eyes to the underside of the tarp that he'd pulled over him before he'd gone to sleep. Rain drops splatted against it. He rolled over, away from the cold rivulet that had seeped under him, and yawned. It was too late for the sail, it would already be wet and . . . he sat up and pushed the tarp off his face. He ignored the rain as he looked around.

At least an hour, that's how long he thought it had been raining. His boots were wet and possibly ruined, but he pulled them on anyway, not willing to leave them behind.

If he was Lucky his little weapons cache would still be dry. He rolled the tarp up and tucked it under a tree before heading out into the gentle surf.

Climbing up the rock, his boots gave him more trouble than the rain did, but soon he was at the top, surveying the larger beach.

The dinghy was missing because he and Dag had used it to get to Strongrock and no one had replaced it. Did that mean the pirates hadn't been back here? He didn't see any ships or sailboats out at sea.

He skirted the beach and headed towards the path in the forest. Soaked trees dripped onto him and muddy puddles dotted the path.

When he reached the clearing, he took some satisfaction that the rain had drenched all of the crates: these weapons would need a lot of work before they were usable.

At his own little stockpile, so far the tarp was keeping the rain off, but the ground was becoming saturated. It looked like he'd come just in time to save everything. It was all coming with him now anyway.

So he didn't have to make two trips, Calder bundled everything into the tarp and dragged it behind him back to the beach. It would leave signs that *something* had passed this way, but it would erase his footprints.

He looked down at the shallow cove, wondering how to keep everything dry while transferring it to the smaller beach. It was raining harder now, and the bundle he was holding was already becoming slippery.

He'd need two trips for this, rather than risk ruining everything he had with one slip.

He found a dry spot under some trees, toed a couple of rocks into place, and set the crate of guns down on them. He propped the crate against the trunk of the tree and covered it with half of the tarp. He covered the powder cask with the other piece of tarp and carried it back to the rock ledge that led to the smaller beach.

It wasn't graceful, but he was able to get the cask down safe and dry. He waded ashore and, after laying down some rocks to keep everything off the ground, set the cask down under the tree, added the rest of his goods, and tucked the tarp around it all. Now he just needed the crate of guns.

Calder waded back out into the surf and climbed the rock once again. His head down against the rain, he stepped onto the beach.

There was a shout and he looked up: three pirates were on shore, heading towards him, and he cursed himself for his carelessness.

There wasn't enough time to get back to the beach and get the sails up on the sailboat before they caught up to him: if he lost the sailboat he lost his way off the island. For him and for Dag.

Instead, he ran into the densest part of the forest. He crossed the path that led to the clearing but kept going. Among the dense trees and bushes his boots gave him the advantage over the barefoot sailors.

He could hear at least two people following him. He angled away from the clearing, trying to be careful about where he put his feet; he couldn't afford to hurt himself, not if he wanted to escape.

Just past a large tree, he stopped. A marsh lay ahead, its reeds and tall grass crowding a hillock on the far side of a pool of brackish water. The rain had stopped and insects clouded around him. He gingerly stepped into the water. Strongrock was too far north for snakes, but he expected that something called this pond home. He only hoped it wasn't dangerous to him.

He took another careful step, putting his other foot into the same muck. The swamp sucked at his boot when he removed it, squelching as mud and decomposing leafy matter clung to the leather. One more long step and his foot found solid ground on a small clump of grass.

At the sound of bushes thrashing behind him he launched himself into a thicket, pulling reeds and grass together to hide him. He crouched low, his feet sinking into the soft earth as water seeped over the tops of his boots.

"Any sign of him?" someone asked from just inside the trees.

"Phew!" a woman stepped out of the brush. "This stinks." She peered at the ground, lifting one bare foot up and staring at the sole of her foot. "I'm not going in there."

"You will if he did," a man said as he joined her. "Don't see any footprints, though." He looked towards Calder's hiding spot.

"Skit, bugs!" He swatted at his face and bare arms.

"He's not here," the woman said as she waved a hand in front of her face. "If he was he'd be screaming about the bugs. Let's go. Even if he is here we'll smell him a mile away if he comes near us." She turned and headed back into the woods.

"What'll we tell the captain?" the man asked as he followed her. Any answer was lost as the two crashed through the brush, away from Calder.

Calder waited an agonizing ten minutes before he rose from his hiding spot. Any exposed flesh was covered in insect bites, and he resisted the urge to run. Instead, he carefully returned the way he'd come, watching for the sailors. He reached the path that led towards the clearing and followed it. Once he recognized the terrain, he circled around and found a place to hide. The sailors were already at the storage cache, and from their voices, they were not happy.

"I don't care," the woman said. "I'm not tellin' the captain that we let him get away. I'd rather say the wind blew harder over here and tore the tarp off."

"Captain'll know if we lie to her," a man said. He had a thick Yedrissian accent but from where he hid, Calder couldn't see if he had the dark skin of one. He couldn't see the third sailor—the one who'd chased him with the woman—at all.

"Then you talk," the woman said. "Whatever you want to say, I'll back you, but I don't want to be the one who tells her the goods are ruined and the skit who did this escaped."

Suddenly, Calder was pushed to the ground. "He didn't escape," a man said from above him. "Got him right here." A foot pressed hard on his back, and Calder struggled to suck in a breath. "Bring some rope over, wouldya?"

DAG ROLLED OVER and opened her eyes. Startled, she sat up.

"I didn't know anyone was here," she said.

"Yeah, well," Margit Ansdottir said. "Surprisingly, I'm overlooked a lot for someone my size." She leaned back in the chair and put a bare foot on the bed.

"I hear I owe you thanks for saving my life," Dag said. She had to pry her eyes from the captain's bare foot. It was heavily callused, but the sole was clean.

"Yep," Ansdottir agreed. "But it's not your thanks that I want to collect."

"I expected as much," Dag said, then she stopped talking. She'd let Margit Ansdottir tell her what she wanted. That way she could use the woman's own words when she tried to convince Inger not to agree to whatever it was she—or Tarmo Holt—wanted her sister for.

The two of them sat staring at each other for a few seconds, and then Ansdottir laughed. She pulled her foot off the bed and leaned toward Dag.

"We have much in common, Dagrun Lund, Intelligencer." She sat back, waiting for Dag's response.

"We do," Dag agreed, keeping her face as passive as she could. "My sister's well-being, for one." Had Ansdottir learned that she was an Intelligencer from Tarmo Holt? Or had Inger told her?

"Ah yes, your twin." Ansdottir smiled. "I never wanted a sister, but now I find out it might have been good to have a twin. My knack—what you call a Trait—would have been so much stronger."

"Or you could have had the opposite Trait," Dag said. "And you might not have made it out of childhood." *Like Calder's brother,* she thought. Even Inger didn't realize that she'd always been protected by Dag.

"Not that any of that matters," Ansdottir said. "The only thing that matters is what are you going to do?"

"About what?" Dag said. She spread her arms. "I'm recovering from my swim and am hardly in a position to do anything." She smiled sweetly. "Except thank you for rescuing me."

Ansdottir snorted. "That might work with Inger but not with me. We both know you didn't jump in the sea to rejoin her. But you didn't tell her the real reason, and that makes me wonder why."

"What have you promised Tarmo Holt?" Dag asked, suddenly tired of not talking about what was really important. Her Trait was stronger than Ansdottir's, but that didn't mean it wouldn't take hours to find out what she was planning.

"What do you know about Holt?" Ansdottir asked, her voice full of suspicion. "That your Trait at work?"

"Yes," Dag lied. Or maybe it wasn't a lie. "Does Holt know that you have a Trait?"

"No," Ansdottir replied. "*I* didn't know I had a Trait, just a knack, until he started talking about Intelligencers. Wants some of his own."

"I know," Dag said. "But he's not allowed. No one's allowed."

"Allowed?" Ansdottir guffawed. "Now you're just being funny. No such thing as *not allowed* when you're Tarmo Holt, Grand Freeholder for the Fair Seas Treaty Alliance." Still laughing, Ansdottir got to her feet. "We'll talk again, Intelligencer. For now, you let your sister nurse you to health. And think of ways that you can repay me for saving your life." She opened the door and paused. "'Cause I gotta tell you, Ursa is not happy that you're still breathing, and I need you to make having her mad at me worth my while."

Ansdottir left: Dag heard her heavy footsteps fade as she headed down the hall. A moment later Inger squeezed through the door.

"Isn't she great?" Inger asked. "I'm in awe of Captain Margit. She's an extremely skilled sailor, and her crew adores her. I get a little tongue tied around her, but you thanked her, didn't you? For saving your life, you thanked her?" Inger sat on the bed and grasped Dag's hands.

"I thanked her," Dag agreed. "More than once."

Inger squeezed her hands. "I knew you would," she said. "I told Ursa you were so grateful and that you'd tell Captain Margit that you were."

"I'm sorry, Inger. I'm a little tired." Dag lay down. "It's been a very . . . trying day for me. I think I just need to rest."

"Oh, of course," Inger said. "Sure, thanking someone for saving your life isn't something you do every day." She stood up. "I'll just see if Ursa has any more soup. Would you like that?"

Dag nodded, and Inger quietly left the room. Dag rolled onto her side and stared at the wooden wall. How was she going to make Inger understand that these people were threatening her? How was she going to convince her that they needed to escape?

CHAPTER 15

CALDER'S HANDS AND feet were bound, so he rubbed his face against the wooden hull of the sailboat, trying to relieve the itching.

"Bugs gotcha, huh?" the woman said. "Serves ya right." She scratched her own arm. "I got bit chasin' ya." She gripped the gunwale as the boat dipped over a wave. "Captain'll make you wish the bugs had finished you off."

Calder ignored her: she was a low-level sailor, not anyone who had real information. A wave hit the bow and seawater sprayed him: the salt burned his itchy skin. He winced. The sun was high in the sky now, and even out on the water, the air was thick and humid after the rain.

The Yedrissian was manning the tiller: he seemed to be the one in charge of this small group.

Calder took a deep, slow breath and blew it out even more slowly. He had to believe that this was due to his Trait; that his Luck was working to get him information that he needed, or get him somewhere he needed to be.

At least his sailboat and two caches of weapons had not been discovered. Not one of his three captors had wondered what he was doing on the beach or how he'd gotten there. All they had been concerned with was that he'd run when they'd spotted him, and then he'd shown up at the site of the destroyed and damaged weapons.

He was certain that once he was delivered to Captain Margit Ansdottir those questions would be asked. Would she send someone out to find the answers? The weapons might remain hidden, but the sailboat would probably be found. He still needed it in order to get off the island.

The wind picked up, and the crew fell silent.

"So, what happened to that, what do you call it, storehouse?" Calder asked. "Was there a storm?"

"There wasn't a storm and you know it," the man not steering said. "You did that."

"Why would I?" Calder asked. "I don't even know what was there. Was there food? I'm pretty hungry, so I wish I'd known about it earlier."

"You know exactly what was there," the woman said. "And you didn't want us to have them weapons. That's why you came back; to make sure we didn't take them."

"If I knew there were weapons then why didn't I have any with me?" Calder reasoned that any little doubt he could cast couldn't hurt. He didn't expect it to fool Captain Ansdottir, but it might be enough to delay his interrogation. And maybe he could find out if Dag was alive?

"You have your reasons," the male sailor near him said.

"Shut up, Benil," the Yedrissian said. "The captain will figure him out soon enough."

"All right," Benil said. "But he's why Satu and I are so itchy."

"Leave me out of it," the woman, Satu, said. "I don't want no trouble with the captain." She toed Calder. "Especially if he wasn't the one who removed the tarp," she muttered softly, and Calder grinned.

The crew was quiet for the next few minutes, and then the Yedrissian called out. "Strongrock ahead, mates. Look smart."

The other two sailors sat up, their backs straight. Calder, from where he lay on the bottom of the boat, could only see sky, but he felt the sailboat turn, and then Benil untied the sail and started pulling it in. He folded it loosely and placed it on the seat beside him. Satu stood in the prow, painter in hand. The small boat rocked when she jumped from it. There was a thud as she landed on a dock, and then the boat was tugged close.

"Get up," the command came in Yedrissian as the man pulled at Calder's arm, forcing him to his knees. "I said, get up!" he repeated in Nordmerian.

"I didn't understand you," Calder lied. "And my legs are tied together." He could have responded in Yedrissian, but he was hoping that if he didn't think his captive knew his language, he might give away a secret. The Yedrissian leaned over and cut the rope at his ankles. Calder lurched to his feet and stepped over the gunwale and onto the dock.

There were half a dozen sailors watching as he was marched along the dock to the inn. He briefly wondered if he was going to be put into his old room, but they pushed him down a hallway and into a cold storeroom. About five feet high, the room had been dug down into the earth. The underside of wooden floorboards stretched above him, and a small lamp illuminated one corner. A bundle of cloth had been tossed into the middle of the floor.

"Don't light anything on fire," a man said as he tossed a water skin at him. "No one will rescue you, and it's a bad way to die."

"It is, that," Calder said. His hands were still tied behind him, so the water skin dropped to the floor. When he knelt down to pick it up, he heard the door slam shut and what sounded like a lock clicking into place. He dropped the water skin on top of the cloth and hunched over, heading for the lamp. It took him a few minutes, and he scorched his wrists a little, but eventually he was able to burn through the rope and free his hands. Rubbing his wrists, he sipped water, trying to decide if he should simply wait for his Trait to work or try to escape and find out where Dag was.

Just in case, he tried opening the door, but it was locked tight.

JOOSEP FOLLOWED THE woman as she left the Hall. Kaja, a student who was part of Gustav's training group, had warned him that someone had been seen loitering near their class, and an instructor for a different group reported catching a woman rummaging through his desk.

She'd said that she was cleaning it, but the Hall only had two caretakers; a wife and husband who had been there for years. Someone was spying on the spies, and Joosep was going to find out who and why.

Once out in the street, the woman removed the kerchief that

she'd wrapped her hair in and tucked it into the waistband of her skirt.

"It's a lovely day, isn't it?" Joosep said as he caught up to her. He placed a hand on her arm and tightened his grip when she tried to get away.

"I'll scream," the woman said.

"No, you won't. If you were going to, you would have already." Joosep smiled into her furious face. "Do you know who I am?" He steered her around the corner and down a narrow alley.

"Should I?"

"You have been nosing around my territory for the past few days," he said. "So, I thought you might know who you were spying on." She flinched at the word *spying*. So she did know what was being taught. He turned her down another alley, this one even less busy than the last. Finally, she seemed to wonder where he was taking her and tried to pull away from him.

"It's too late to scream now, I'm afraid." Joosep stopped beside a small door and rapped on it once. Arnor poked his head out.

"There you are," Arnor said. He stepped back, and Joosep pushed the now visibly frightened woman inside.

"I'm not going to hurt you," Joosep said when the woman struggled to get away. "But you are going to give me answers." He pulled her along the narrow corridor, around a corner, and through a small door. Arnor followed them into his office, shut the door, and pulled the wall hanging over it to hide it.

"Sit down." Joosep had to push her into the chair. "See that we're not disturbed," he said to Arnor, who nodded and left the room.

He hovered over her, making sure she didn't try to bolt from the room.

"I don't really care who you are," he said. "I'm sure I can find out easily enough. Nor do I want to punish you, although I could do that as well. I need to know who you are working for and what you're looking for."

"He'll kill me," the woman said, fear in her voice. "Or my family, if he decides he wants me to suffer."

Joosep sighed. At least she hadn't wasted his time pretending she was innocent. But under threat of death? That was despicable even for Holt.

"What does Tarmo Holt want in exchange for the safety of you and your family?"

"You know?" she whispered. "How can you know and let him get away with it?"

"I suspect," Joosep replied. "I need much more than that in order to stop him. What are you supposed to do for him?"

"Find twins," she said. "I'm supposed to find twins. But none of the ones I've found have been right, so I thought I'd look at the ones who are right."

"The ones under my care," Joosep said. "How do you know they are *right*?"

"He said so. He said they had the talents he needed."

"He told you to try to take them from me? Even Holt knows that's impossible."

"No, he didn't tell me." The woman was terrified now. "Don't tell him what I did, please. It's just . . . I know twins run in families so I thought." She dropped her head into her hands. "I thought if I knew what families were right I could find more twins from the same families."

"I already do that," Joosep said and sighed. "But you didn't know that." He stood up. "Arnor!" His assistant opened the door and peered in. "Show my guest out, please. And make sure she can't get back in."

"Thank you," the woman said, visibly relieved. "I won't come back, I promise."

"You will," Joosep said. "When and if you find another set of right twins. You will come back and tell me before you tell Tarmo Holt. Is that clear?" She said, "yes," but Joosep doubted she would. He'd never hurt her family even if she didn't do as he asked, and she was convinced Tarmo Holt would. Joosep thought he would too.

But what was the rush? If he found twins they would need years of training—more than the six years until Tarmo Holt could become Grand Freeholder again. Although he himself had been putting Gustav to work, and he'd only been at the Hall for five years.

But why now? Why the sudden interest in Traits and twins who might have them? Did Holt think it would allow him to stay on as Grand Freeholder? But that was impossible. Or was he trying to set himself up as *his* rival, with his own Intelligencer team? But that, too, would take years.

Joosep frowned. Where in Nyorden were Calder and Dagrun? They were the ones with the skills—and good sense—to help him find out what Holt was after. All he was left with were the half-trained recruits and a few Intelligencers with not very useful Traits: Eevi was a Good Shot, and Jarri and Janni could Make and Unmake anything he asked them to. None of them had a Trait that would help uncover Holt's plans.

Except for him and his weak Unseen Trait. Was that enough to get past whatever defences Holt had surrounded himself with? He had to hope it was.

"I'VE BROUGHT YOUR dinner," Inger said, as she shouldered the door closed. She set a tray on the table beside the bed. "You look flushed. Are you all right?" Inger held the back of her hand against Dag's forehead. "You're warm." She poured a glass of water and handed it to Dag.

Dag sipped the water and placed it against her head. She'd been awake: she had actually just gotten back into bed a few minutes before Inger arrived. And she was warm because she'd been doing exercises: push-ups and squats to try to regain her strength. But having Inger think she was still very ill would work to her advantage. The longer everyone thought she continued to be weak and was still recovering, the more time she had to figure out what to do about Ansdottir and her threat against Inger.

"The water helps," Dag said. "And dinner should too." She picked the bowl of soup off the tray. The downside of pretending to be ill was that she wouldn't be given anything substantial to eat. She sipped the thin soup.

Inger sat down on the bed. "Ursa said I can give you anything Espen cooks for any meal at no extra charge," she said, beaming. "She really hopes you get better soon."

"Does she?" Dag asked. "Because Captain Ansdottir said something different." She put her empty soup bowl back on the tray and crossed her arms.

"You misunderstood," Inger said. "Ursa wants you to get better. She told me."

"The captain's exact words were *Ursa is not happy you're still breathing*," Dag said. "It's hard to misunderstand that."

"She didn't mean it," Inger said. "She couldn't have."

"You know how your Trait works, Inger. People can lie to you, and you don't realize it."

"She wouldn't lie to me!" Inger said. "She wouldn't!"

"Then Captain Ansdottir lied to me," Dag said. "But you know how *my* Trait works."

Inger stood up and started pacing. "Why would she lie to me? Why would Ursa say one thing to me and the captain say another thing to you?" She stopped and met Dag's eyes. "You tried to tell me not to trust them. You said they drugged you. They really did, didn't they? Hanne and Ursa?"

"Yes," Dag agreed. "They drugged me and tried to lock me up." She sighed. Inger seemed ready to believe her; she had to tell her the rest and hope that Ursa didn't convince her that Dag was telling her lies. "Do you want to know why I jumped into the sea?"

"To . . ." Inger paused. "It wasn't because you changed your mind, was it?" She slapped the side of her head. "I'm so stupid. Stupid, stupid skit!"

"Hey, stop that," Dag said. She reached up and grabbed Inger's hand and pulled her back down onto the bed. "Never say that about yourself. It's how your Trait works, that's all."

Inger took a deep breath and nodded. "I hate my Trait." She frowned. "So why did you jump?"

"Ansdottir threatened you," Dag said. She wasn't going to mention that the captain had said she'd have Inger hurt *herself*—Inger didn't need to worry about that. "She has a Trait, and I think Ursa does too. I think that's why Ursa can get you to trust her. There's a student like that at the Hall: Vilis." She didn't think Vilis' Trustworthiness Trait worked exactly like Ursa's, but the end result was the same.

"Vilis," Inger said. "I've met him a few times and really liked him. *Skit!* The same way I like and trust Ursa."

"Similar, I think," Dag said. She was relieved that Inger was willing to believe her, but would she still once Ursa had a chance to use her Trait against her? "You know you can always trust me, right?"

"You're my sister, of course I trust you."

"Just remember that," Dag said. "*Always* remember that."

"I will," Inger said. "I promise." She sighed and her shoulders slumped. "I just wish I wasn't so useless, or worse, a burden."

"Don't think that," Dag said. "Joosep was wrong not to train you along with me." Training might have given Inger more confidence in the abilities she did have.

"Do you really think so?" Inger said.

"Yes. Joosep never bothered to figure out how to use your Trait, but we already have."

"We have?" Inger asked.

"Yes. The night we stopped the sailors from that ship from being shot," Dag said. "You were able to hold everyone's attention while I got them to stand down."

"I did do that, didn't I?" Inger grinned. "Maybe my Trait can be useful?"

Dag didn't mention that the sailors were all dead by now since they were aboard the *Bright Breeze* when it was taken by the pirates. She hoped that none of them had been killed by Inger. "You did. I'm sure that there are other ways to use it; we just have to figure out how. But we will. Together, we will." She wasn't going to tell her that she'd already been using Inger's Trait: that convincing Inger meant that others believed her. She couldn't risk her twin telling Ursa or Ansdottir.

Inger leaned over and hugged her. "Thanks, Dag. I need to get this tray back to the kitchen and then get back to work." She stood up. "Next time I'll try to sneak you something more solid."

"I'd appreciate that," Dag said. Inger left and Dag could only hope that Ursa wouldn't realize she'd switched her allegiance again. That would make the tavern owner even more furious that Dag was still breathing. Would Ansdottir feel the need to remedy that?

THE DOOR OPENED out to darkness. The small lamp in the corner threw shadows onto the figure who stood in the doorway.

"Charis," Calder said. "I suppose I shouldn't be surprised." He took it as a good sign that he was being dealt with by someone who respected him as a sailor. Not that Calder thought Charis was here to set him free.

"The captain wants to see you," Charis said. "Don't try anything." He pointed a pistol at Calder, who shrugged and headed to the door.

"I wouldn't dream of it," Calder said truthfully. He'd wait for his Luck to make an appearance, rather than try to force it. Although this was one of those times when he wished he could make his own Luck.

He stepped outside and waited while Charis closed the door, then with the pistol shoved against his back, he was directed out into the yard to the small door that led into the taproom. When he entered the tavern, Inger Lund paused as she picked up a tray, her mouth an O, before she turned and left the bar.

"This way," Charis said, pointing to a small door. "Captain's in there. Be nice or you'll be dead."

"Should I open it?" Calder asked, gesturing to the door. Charis reached past him, knocked on the door, and then stepped back while Calder opened it.

Captain Margit Ansdottir sat at the head of a long table. She was flanked by Ursa Ozlinch on one side and the Yedrissian from that afternoon on the other.

Ansdottir lifted a mug and took a gulp before slamming the mug down on the scarred wooden tabletop.

"Is this the one who ruined our supplies?" Ansdottir asked.

"Aye, Captain," the Yedrissian said. "We caught him in the act."

Calder shrugged at the man's blatant lie, but he didn't say anything. It was never a good idea to interrupt people who were holding you captive. Besides, he wasn't sure Ansdottir even cared about his perspective. His Luck had already shown Inger that he was here. That might be the only positive thing he got from this meeting. He rocked back on his heels, waiting for whatever was going to happen to happen.

"What, no rebuttal?" Ansdottir asked him. "No declaration of innocence? No complaint about how you were in the wrong place at the wrong time? Speak up!"

"Well, not to overstate the obvious," Calder said. "But I wouldn't be here if I hadn't been in the wrong place at the wrong time. And that's whether I did what I'm being accused of or not."

"Hah!" Ansdottir pointed a finger at him. "Charis likes you. I can see why. Did you do it?"

"Does it matter?" Calder asked. "From what I understand, you had something stored out in the forest and now it's ruined. I'm not sure you care who caused the damage."

"No, you're right," Ansdottir replied.

Something in her tone of voice made Calder think that someone was in danger. Was it him? He didn't think so, at least not right now.

"What's done is done," Ansdottir continued. "But lying about it? That I can't abide." She turned to the Yedrissian. "Is there anything about what you've told me that you care to amend? Like saying that you caught him in the act?"

It was a double-edged sword, that question, and Calder thought the Yedrissian knew it. Tell the truth and admit that you lied to your captain, or stick to the lie and hope she believed you. Except he knew that Ansdottir had the Unseen Trait: she already *knew* it was a lie.

The Yedrissian's eyes widened and his hands started to shake, but he didn't say a word.

"That's what I thought," Ansdottir said. "Charis, make him an example. My crew doesn't lie to me, ever."

The Yedrissian preceded Charis out of the room, who closed the door, leaving Calder with the two women.

"Aren't you afraid to be alone with me now that Charis has left and taken the pistol?" He grinned. He knew that it was a ridiculous question. Each woman had at least fifty pounds on him, and he doubted he could best either one alone, let alone both of them together.

Ansdottir and Ursa looked at each other before bursting into laughter.

"Rahm, I'm going to hate killing you, but you have to die," Ansdottir said, and he thought there was real regret in her voice.

"Can I at least have one last decent breakfast?" he asked. "It's my favourite meal, and I would hate to think my last meal in this life was that slop I was fed this evening."

"That would be a shame," Ansdottir said. "Ursa? It's your kitchen." Ursa nodded. "That's settled; one last breakfast before you die in the morning," Ansdottir continued. "And I rather like not having to reduce the impact of the example Charis is setting for me tonight. Too many hangings in a row produce only fear, and the crew misses the important lessons I'm trying to teach them."

"I can see how that would be a problem," Calder replied, and Ansdottir laughed again. She looked at him and squinted.

"What were you doing in the boat with the Lund girl?" she asked.

"Trying to leave Strongrock," Calder said. "As you can see, it didn't work for either of us. At least I assume she's here as well."

"She didn't survive," Ursa said. "Water that cold? You know how little time a person has."

Calder closed his eyes. "That's too bad." It might be true, but only if they'd kept Dag's death from Inger. Because when he'd seen her, Inger had not had the look of someone grieving for her twin. As someone who grieved for his twin regularly, he was certain he'd recognize that in someone else.

"You knew her well, did you?" Ansdottir asked. "From being Intelligencers?"

Calder opened his eyes to find Margit Ansdottir staring at him. "My days as a spy are over anyway," he said. "So, there's no harm admitting that you have the truth of it."

"I really like you," Ansdottir said almost wistfully. "And according to Charis, you're a very accomplished sailor. It makes me sad that you have to die."

"Not as sad as it makes me," Calder said. "And I'm a decent sailor, but I don't possess the right qualities to sail through the Teeth. That I would like to see."

"Ah, you know about my knack," Ansdottir said. "My Trait."

"And Ursa Ozlinch has at least one of her own," Calder said. Ansdottir looked at Ursa, who raised her eyebrows and shrugged. Ah, that surprised them both. "I'm not sure what it is yet, but I'll figure it out if I need to know."

"What's your Trait?" Ursa asked.

"And you were both being so polite up until now," Calder replied. "Even Intelligencers don't tell each other their Traits."

"So, who knows?" Ursa asked. "Someone must?"

"The man in charge knows," Calder replied. "He's the only one who does, as far as I know." He smiled again. "So Tarmo Holt will be left trying to figure it all out on his own. I heard the Neas was here, in case you're wondering how I know about Holt."

"You recognized it as his? And yet I don't think you even sail the Pale Sea." Ansdottir shook her head again. "I am really, really sad that you have to die."

There was knock on the door and Charis entered. "It's done," he said. "In the square."

"Thank you, Charis," Ansdottir said. "You can take our guest back to his quarters. He's negotiated a breakfast in the morning, so see that he gets it, before." Charis nodded and prodded Calder with his pistol.

"Oh," Ansdottir said. "Make sure the other one is removed before you end our friend here. He doesn't deserve to be tainted by the lying piece of skit."

"What was that about?" Charis asked once he closed the door to the room.

"Oh, you know," Calder replied. "Just making friends." As he was pushed through the taproom, he spotted Inger Lund again, serving drinks to tavern patrons. She blinked slowly and then scowled at him, and he deliberately looked away from her. And his eyes fell on Ursa Ozlinch's tattle, Hanne. Her eyes flicked from him to Inger and then back to him, and a slow smile spread across her face. Then he was pushed out the door and into the night. He let himself be guided back to the small cellar. Once Charis had locked him in, he tested the lock. But Luck didn't make it easy on him and leave the door open. He sat on the cloth and leaned back against the wall. He'd have to wait—and hope—that his Luck worked.

CHAPTER 16

DAG SAT UP, her hands already clutching whoever had grabbed her.

"Shhh, it's me," Inger whispered.

"What time is it?" Dag had been fast asleep: she rubbed her eyes. "What's wrong?"

"Calder's here," Inger said.

"Where? Is he all right?" Had he come to rescue them? She pushed the covers off and started to get up.

"He's being held prisoner," Inger said. "I saw him earlier, but I couldn't just leave. I had customers to serve. I would have been missed."

"Prisoner?" Dag sat back down on the bed. "Where?"

"In the cold cellar here in the inn," Inger said. "He's to be executed right after breakfast."

"Skit, skit, skit." Dag ran a hand through her hair. So much for Calder rescuing her; she'd have to rescue him. "How long until breakfast?"

"A few hours," Inger said.

"Skit," Dag said again and sighed. "Where exactly is this cellar?"

"I'm coming with you," Inger said. "I feel responsible. Neither one of you would even be on Strongrock if I hadn't run away, so

I'm going to help get you—both of you—off this island."

"Yes," Dag said. "And you'll leave with us." She stood up and started dressing. She'd come to take Inger home, and that was still her plan. She tied her boots and hung them over one shoulder. She might need them later, but she'd be much quieter in bare feet. "Show me where he is."

As quietly as possible they crept down the hall to the back of the inn. Dag had only been in the inn once when she'd visited Calder and now, in the middle of the night, she found the layout disorienting. Thankfully, her twin knew the way, and soon they were standing in the hallway that led, Inger said, to the cellar.

Dag held a hand up for Inger to stay silent as she peered into the gloom. She didn't think they would leave Calder unguarded, but where was the guard? There was only one way to approach this room. She felt a chill run down her spine just before she heard a floorboard squeak. From behind them.

"Who do we have here?"

Dag ducked down to hide in the shadow. Her Trait should be enough to keep her from being seen, she hoped, but Inger's meant that she had no chance of escaping notice.

"Hanne, what are you doing here?" Inger asked. The shadow that was Inger shuffled into the middle of the hallway. Dag took the opportunity to shift a little closer to the cellar door. Her Trait might not be enough to hide her from Hanne forever, but combined with Inger's there should be enough time for her to unlock the door.

"I'm supposed to be here," Hanne replied. "And you're not."

"I was curious," Inger said. "There was talk in the tavern about a prisoner. A Yedrissian? I've never seen a Yedrissian, and since I heard he was going to be executed in the morning I thought . . ." Inger paused. Dag had been about to reach out to the lock so she stopped too, her hand in the air.

"I thought," Inger continued. "I'd come take a look while he was sleeping."

"It's too late for that," Hanne said with a sneer. "The Yedrissian was hanged tonight. You can still see him in the square, though."

"Dead!" Inger exclaimed, and Dag flicked the lock open before retreating to the shadowed corner. "I don't think I want to see him dead."

"Well, that's the only way you'll see a Yedrissian tonight," Hanne said and cackled with laughter. "Go away before I fetch Ursa. She won't like hearing that you listen to talk while serving her customers."

"Please don't tell her," Inger said. "I'll just go up and check on my sister, and then I'll head to my room." She looked at Hanne. "Please?"

"Get going then," Hanne said. "But remember, I can tell Ursa you spy on her customers whenever I want."

"I'm leaving," Inger said. She headed down the hallway, slipping past Hanne, who turned to watch her go. Dag lifted her boots from her shoulder and threw them. One hit Hanne in the temple, and she dropped to the ground with a yell. By then Dag was on top of her, using her body to keep the other woman on the floor. Dag clamped a hand over Hanne's mouth and pushed her chin into the floor so she couldn't bite her hand.

"I hate this one," Calder said from her side. He looped a piece of cloth around Hanne's head, allowing Dag to remove her hand as he tightened the cloth between the other woman's teeth. He tied a knot at the back of Hanne's head. "Thanks, by the way."

"Sure," Dag said. "You have her under control?" She barely waited for Calder's nod before she sprinted down the hall.

"Inger?" she called softly. "Inger?"

"I just saw Hanne," Inger said loudly.

Dag peered around a corner. Inger was talking to a man in the hallway.

"Charis." Dag turned to find Calder at her shoulder. That was the second time he'd been able to sneak up on her: was something going on with her Trait? And Inger's? Her sister had lied tonight and been believed, and now she was trying to do it again. She'd never been able to lie before: she *shouldn't* be able to lie and now here she was doing it twice in one night.

"Hanne told me to leave," Inger was explaining to Charis. "She said the Yedrissian was already dead."

"What's he to you?" Charis asked.

"Nothing," Inger stammered. "I've just never seen one before. I hear they cover themselves in tattoos."

"Yeah? I hear they breathe out smoke, but that's not true," Charis said. "There's nothing special about them, especially this one. Oh, except he's dead on the captain's orders."

"I'm sure she had a good reason," Inger said. "Well, I guess I'm to bed. I have to work in the morning, you know, over at the tavern." Inger started walking away, but Charis didn't move. "Could you walk me back?" Inger asked. "Now that I know there are so many dangerous people on Strongrock, I'm a little nervous to be out when it's so late."

Dag had to suppress a snort when Inger said that. Inger had lied—again—and Charis must have believed her because he followed her out the door.

"Let's go," Calder said. He led the way along the hall, but when they got to the doorway, he paused to let Dag leave first.

Once outside, she flattened her body against the side of the building. She could see the square from where she was. A gallows had been set up and a body swung from it. Calder joined her at the side of the building.

"I did say thank you, didn't I?" Calder asked again.

"Yes," Dag replied. "Let's go get Inger." She wasn't leaving without her sister, and Calder must have realized that because he didn't protest. "Is Charis on patrol or something?" she asked him. "Would he still be around after walking Inger to the tavern?"

"I don't know," Calder replied. "I haven't noticed the pirates patrolling before, but they've never had a hanging either. Maybe Charis' conscience won't let him sleep. On the way here, I probably saved his life, and his orders are to hang me in the morning." Calder shrugged. "Can you get past him?"

Dag looked across to the tavern. There was an empty area to cross, and it was lit by moonlight. She looked up: there were a few clouds overhead.

"Probably," she said. "I'll wait for cloud cover."

"All right. I'll meet you at the abandoned cabins." Calder met her gaze. "I'm pretty sure they didn't find the sailboat. It's at the hidden beach."

"Pretty sure?" Dag asked. If the sailboat wasn't there, they'd be stranded.

"I'm feeling Lucky tonight," Calder replied. "I did just escape hanging."

"You did," Dag said. Although she thought it more because of her than his Luck. And Inger, of course. Whose Trait didn't seem to be behaving as usual. Was that Calder's Luck at work? Could another person's Trait—a Trait not related to yours—affect yours?

"Ready?" she asked him. A cloud obscured the moon, and without waiting for his reply she sprinted across the clearing to huddle beside the tavern wall, Calder a step behind her. She paused for a few moments, and when she didn't hear or see anything, she started edging along the back wall, keeping in the shadows.

She stopped beside the closed door that led to the taproom. She could get to Inger's room through here. She waved Calder on: he gripped her shoulder and looked her in the eyes, and then he was past her. She waited until he was beyond the tavern before she reached up and carefully opened the door to the taproom.

FROM THE PATH, Calder peered out at the tavern. He didn't like leaving Dag behind, but he would be more of a hindrance to her than a help for this. And she would hate it if he implied that in any way she wasn't capable. Besides, if she and Inger were in a hurry it would be a better use of his skills to make sure no one was either on the path they had to take or at the huts.

With one last look at the tavern, he turned to follow the trail that led away from the tavern. Roots and rocks threatened to trip him or turn an ankle, so he had to go slow. It was very different from Dag leading him, guiding him past every hazard.

He heard a noise from up ahead and ducked off the path. As soon as he stopped moving, insects converged on him. He did his best to ignore them, not daring to risk disturbing the foliage around him to wave his hands to keep them away from his face.

He peered through the vegetation: there was a light up ahead, and it was stationary. If it wasn't someone walking along the path, then who was it and what were they doing?

Calder frowned. He had to clear whoever it was off the path: Dag and Inger could come running this way at any time, chased by pirates. He wasn't about to let them run into whoever was here.

As carefully and silently as he could, he crawled through the underbrush parallel to the path. Luckily, the wind picked up; rustling through the trees and hiding the noise of his movements as he moved closer to the light.

A lamp had been hung from a branch, and three sailors huddled in the middle of the path. Calder recognized two of them:

Benil and Satu, the pirates who had captured him along with the now-dead Yedrissian.

"I says we keep our mouths shut," Satu whispered loudly. "Unless you want to end up like Kagiso?"

"But he's dead because he lied to the captain," Benil said. "We need to tell her the truth while we still have the chance."

"I agree with Satu," the third man said. "You never lied. Nobody asked you anything, so you've had no chance to lie. Captain, she don't like liars, but she don't like sailors wasting her time neither."

Calder had to agree with this man: he wouldn't offer up anything to Margit Ansdottir unless asked. But none of that mattered to him. All he cared about was getting these three off the path. He picked up a rock and threw it further into the forest.

"What was that?" Benil said. "Were we followed?"

"Probably just an animal," the unknown man said. "We're in a forest."

Satu slapped at her neck. "Wish it was something that liked to eat insects. Miss that about being on the sea: winds that blow the bugs away."

"What kind of animal?" Benil sounded afraid. "I hear there are lynx out here. Are we in danger?"

Calder reached around for another rock. His plan had been to lure one of the sailors into the forest and take them prisoner, but scaring them all into leaving would be even better. He threw the rock in the same direction he'd thrown the last one, but it hit a tree and bounced back to land on the path right in front of him. He swore under his breath and slunk further away from the path.

"It's getting closer!" Benil said.

"I'll scare it away," the unnamed man said. Branches rustled, and then there was a crack as a limb was torn off a tree. Calder heard a footfall on the path near him.

"I'll—" A bell clanged in the distance.

"Skit!" Benil said. "Do you think it's for us?"

"I hope not," Satu said. "It's roll call. We gotta go."

One of them grabbed the lamp and led the way down the path, the other two following him back towards Strongrock.

Calder waited a few minutes to make sure they really were gone before he stood up and stepped onto the trail. He looked back towards the settlement, hoping to hear the sound of running feet, hoping to see Dag and Inger rushing out of the forest towards him.

But there was nothing except the ringing bells. They would continue to ring until every sailor had been accounted for or they knew who was missing.

Had his disappearance been discovered? Or had Dag and Inger been caught? Would roll call be rung for either of those situations?

He hesitated, tempted to head back to find the two women, but it wasn't the plan he'd agreed to with Dag. He had to sail the boat: he couldn't allow himself to be captured, not if any of them were going to get off this island.

With a sigh, he headed away from the tavern, away from the ringing bells, away from whatever danger might have found the Lund sisters.

DAG WAS JUST outside of Inger's room when the bells started ringing. She grabbed the door handle: it was unlocked, and she breathed a sigh of relief as she ducked into the room, closing the door behind her. Her mouth was open, expecting to have to calm Inger down, but her sister wasn't there.

"*Skit!*" she muttered under her breath. Where was Inger? She heard the sound of running feet out in the hall, and she rose to the balls of her feet, ready to tackle anyone who opened the door. But the door remained shut, and no one called Inger's name, looking for her.

At first Dag was relieved, and then she got worried. What if no one had come for Inger because they already had her? What if the ringing bells were *because* they had her?

She danced from foot to foot, wondering what to do, wondering where her sister was. And the bells kept ringing. She blew out a breath. She needed to find Inger.

The hall was silent now. The whole tavern felt empty, although she knew she couldn't actually know that for sure.

Dag slipped out into the hallway and down the stairs. The back hallway was empty too, and she went through a half-opened door and into the corridor that led to the kitchen. Would Espen be there starting his work for breakfast, or had the bells interrupted him? The door to the kitchen was open, but she didn't hear any noises from inside the room.

She crept along the hall and peered into the kitchen. It was empty, but the fire was lit: and untended. She hurried to the door that led outside and left the tavern to the sound of ringing bells.

She huddled against the side of the tavern in almost the same place she'd been when Calder had left her to head to the huts. What had he done when the bells started ringing? Had he given up waiting or . . . she felt cold all over.

Did the bells have nothing to do with Inger and everything to do with Calder? Had he been caught? Were they hanging him right now? Her heart constricted: no! She had to stop it! She had to save him!

She ran towards the square, dashed across the clearing between the tavern and the inn and stopped, pressing herself up against the wall of the inn. She leaned out around the corner of the building for a better look.

Torches lit up the line of pirates. They were quiet except for a few coughs and the sounds of shuffling feet. A figure swung from the gallows, and Dag's heart clenched in fear.

Not Calder. She let out a shaky breath. This man's skin was so dark that it looked black: too dark for Calder's nut-brown skin. It was the Yedrissian who had been hung in the night.

Her relief evaporated when two people cut the man down. Were they getting the gallows ready for Calder?

Suddenly, the bells stopped. Margit Ansdottir stepped forward, and every sailor snapped to attention. And there was Inger, standing between Ursa and Hanne, who looked frightened.

"There has been an escape," Ansdottir said, her booming voice carrying to Dag. "The man known as Rahm escaped in the night. I want to know if any of you helped him!"

The sailors shuffled, but no one spoke. Ansdottir walked past them, staring at them one at a time. Dag looked at Inger again, only to find her sister looking right at her! Her twin tilted her head from side to side and then looked down. Dag followed Inger's gaze to her clenched hands. She unclenched her right hand once, then again before Dag's eyes rose to find Ursa frowning at Inger. Who blinked and scratched her nose, ignoring the tavern keeper.

Dag pulled her head back behind the inn wall. Inger's signal had told her to leave. But how could she leave without her?

But how could she save her?

It would be hours before Inger would be alone. She heard her sister's name and looked out again.

"Inger's sister is missing as well," Ansdottir said. "Who saw them? Rahm and Dagrun Lund. Someone must have seen them; someone must have helped them get away."

Ansdottir paced in front of the assembled pirates before stopping in front of Hanne. "You, it's your fault they escaped!" She stared at the older woman, who sent a frightened look towards Ursa. Ansdottir nodded her head and two men grabbed Hanne and pulled her, struggling, towards the gallows.

"Margit," Ursa said. "She's mine."

"Now, she's mine," Ansdottir replied. "The prisoner escaped from one of *your* people. I am holding you—and them— responsible. But I will give you a choice. Either lose this one or the other one." She gestured to Inger, and Dag had to grab the wall of the inn in order to stay on her feet. No, they couldn't mean to hang Inger! She *would* try to save her, or die trying. Anything would be better than watching her sister die.

Ursa and Margit Ansdottir continued to face each other. Dag could feel the tension from where she hid; she couldn't imagine what Inger was feeling, with her life in the balance.

Finally, Ursa shook her head and looked away. Hanne cried out, and the men took her up the stairs to the gallows. Dag didn't stay to watch; while all eyes were on poor Hanne, she ran across to the back of the tavern. A few moments later she was on the path to the beach with the abandoned huts. And Calder, she hoped.

THE FERN WAVED, stirred by a gentle breeze. Calder pushed a frond aside just enough to let him watch the place where the path spilled out onto the sandy beach. He absently scratched at an insect bite.

The bells had stopped ringing a few minutes before he'd reached the beach. What did that mean for Dag and Inger? Had they been able to get away?

He froze at the sound of running feet. Someone ran past and was halfway to the first hut. Dag! He blew out a breath in relief.

He waited to see if she'd been followed, but he didn't hear anyone else behind her: not even Inger.

"Dag!" He rose from his hiding place. He'd only taken two

steps towards her when she launched herself on him.

"I was so worried," she said, her chest heaving as she wrapped her arms around him. "I thought . . . I thought they'd hung you. But it was someone else on the gallows."

"The Yedrissian," Calder said. He'd automatically pulled Dag into his embrace, but now he felt awkward so he dropped his arms and stepped back. "Where's Inger?"

Dag ran a hand through her hair. "She's . . . they hung Hanne. Because you and I escaped, they hung Hanne."

"And Inger?' Calder repeated, confused. Hanne wasn't Ansdottir's crew; she was a spy for Ursa. Did that mean Ursa and the captain were on bad terms?

"She's not safe," Dag said. "But I couldn't get to her. Ansdottir gave Ursa a choice: Hanne or Inger. She chose to let Hanne hang. But Inger could be next, if Ansdottir doesn't trust her."

"It wasn't about Inger," Calder said. "Or Hanne." He didn't say that hanging either one would have served Ansdottir's purpose. "It was about power: who holds the power on Strongrock. By hanging one of her people, Ansdottir let Ursa know that she rules Strongrock." He looked back at the path. "Were you followed?"

"No."

"Then we should leave," he said. "If you're sure we can't get to Inger."

"Not for hours," Dag replied. "Days, even. Ursa isn't going to trust her for a very long time. If ever."

"Then we'll have to come back for her," Calder said.

"If she survives." Dag didn't sound hopeful but she started walking towards the far end of the beach.

Calder followed her. The dinghy was where they'd left it. They would be exposed on the sea, but it would be faster than walking along the trail.

"It wasn't personal," Calder said, catching up to Dag. "For Ursa, yes, but not for the captain. And Ansdottir still has plans for Inger: for her Trait. Inger should be safe as long as she does what Ansdottir asks."

"How do you know?" Dag stopped and met his eyes. Hers were grief-stricken, and all Calder wanted to do was make her feel better. But not by lying.

"The captain lives by the rules of the sea," Calder said. "She made an example of Hanne, and as I said, it was a show of power to Ursa and all of the pirates. That's why they rang the bells for roll call: so that everyone could witness Ansdottir's rule. At sea the captain is the law and now Ansdottir needs to be the same on land, where *Ursa* has always ruled. Nothing shows who has the power more than the ability to remove—even kill—your adversary's people." He bent down and grabbed an edge of the dinghy and pulled up, flipping it over. Dag dug around in the sand and found the oars.

"This was a power struggle?" Dag asked. "Ursa and Ansdottir? I thought they were tight allies?"

"So did I," Calder agreed. He pushed the boat into the surf and held it while Dag climbed in. She had the oars in place by the time he'd waded out up to his knees. He gave one big shove and then hopped into the boat, scrambled to get seated behind the oars, and started rowing away from the beach.

"My guess," Calder continued, "is that Ansdottir received instructions from Tarmo Holt to make sure Strongrock is under her control."

"Why wouldn't she trust Ursa?" Dag asked. "Why hang one of her loyal accomplices?"

"That is a very good question," Calder said. They were rounding a point now and he had to combat cross-currents. "But I think Inger is safe, at least for now."

"I hope so," Dag said.

For the next few minutes Calder rowed in silence. It was almost dawn, and they had one more point to round and then they would be at the beach where the pirates landed their weapons.

"There's a ship," Dag said suddenly.

Calder swung his head around. A ship: the *Vassan*—Ansdottir's ship, was coming up fast from the south. They must have stayed far out to sea so they couldn't be spotted from the island. Calder redoubled his efforts. He had to get them to the beach: the pirates were already launching the dinghies.

"Get ready to run," he said to Dag. He checked behind him: two small boats were in the water. Wait, make that three, there was a sailboat, too. He and Dag didn't have as much time as he'd hoped.

The surf tossed their dinghy closer to shore.

"Get out now," Calder called. As soon as Dag was out of the

boat, he pulled the oars in and stepped to the prow. When Dag was halfway to the beach, he dove towards her and surfaced just in front of her. Waist-deep water tugged at him. He turned to see a wave starting to form behind them. He grabbed Dag's hand and, when the wave hit, pulled her off her feet. They were pushed towards the beach, and when he stood this time, the water was only knee high.

Dag gasped in a breath as he pulled her with him onto dry sand.

"I'll meet you in the small bay," he said. She nodded and headed towards the rocky ledge while he dashed into the trees.

The small cache of guns was where he'd left it and he grabbed the crate and ran to the ledge. Dag was already on the beach, struggling to drag the sailboat into the water. Calder jumped, doing his best to keep the guns above his head. His feet hit sand and his knees buckled. A wave crashed into him, spraying water onto his burden. He raised the crate above his head and waded to the beach as fast as he could.

The sail, thank Nyorden, was still tied between two trees. It was dry and fluttering in the wind, which he thought a good sign. He quickly untied the sail and joined Dag at the boat.

"There's a cask of powder and some shot," he said pointing. "There in the trees."

Dag nodded and raced away, leaving him to deal with hoisting the sail. She was back in a few moments and heaved her bundles into the bottom of the boat before leaning against the stern and pushing the boat along the sand.

Calder tied one last knot before jumping out to help Dag. He put his shoulder to the hull and pushed the boat into the surf. As soon as the boat was afloat, he jumped in and set the tiller into place.

Dag hauled herself over the side as he tilted the sail. The wind caught it immediately, and the boat skimmed over the waves. A rock scraped along the keel as he headed out past the point. The *Vassan* was just ahead: he maneuvered around it, but he didn't see the two dinghies or the sailboat. Someone on the *Vassan* shouted, and then a bell rang out. With no other direction offering escape, Calder headed east, steering the sailboat past the ship.

"Can they catch us?" Dag asked as she crawled to his side.

"Not if my Trait keeps the wind in our sail," Calder said. "And yours can get us through the Teeth."

CHAPTER 17

DAG STARED BEHIND them while Calder did something with the sails. The boat surged ahead when the sail filled with wind. To their stern, a sailboat rounded the point.

"A boat is following us," Dag said, and Calder turned his head to look. "I think it's Ansdottir."

"I doubt she's better at sailing small craft than me," Calder said. He grinned at her. "And I should have Luck on my side."

"Let's hope," Dag said. She didn't mention that Luck would have let them escape without being spotted. She stayed low in the prow, trying to keep out of Calder's way while still watching both the path ahead and their pursuer.

Calder had pointed them east, she thought, although the wind was coming at them, in almost the opposite direction. Calder continuously shifted the sail, making multiple zigzags across the waves to keep the little boat heading generally into the wind.

Dag kept an eye on Ansdottir, who was doing the same back and forth zigzag but not as seamlessly as Calder, and so was falling behind, little by little.

Movement behind Ansdottir caught her eye: the ship sailed into view, now out from behind the island. A moment later it had caught up to Ansdottir.

"How much farther to the Teeth?" Dag asked. "We have more

company."

"Who?" Calder turned his head. "*Skit*. Hang on." He pushed on the tiller, and the boat swung south. Calder grabbed the bottom of the sail and held it out. He let go as the wind caught it, puffing it out alongside them. The boat bucked, and they were skimming directly across the path of the ship.

Dag looked up: she could see pirates scrambling in the sails as the ship tried to turn around. Then they were past it, and Ansdottir's small sailboat changed course, still following them.

"I'll need you to watch the way ahead," Calder called. "We'll be at the Teeth soon and you'll need to navigate us through it."

"All right." Dag huddled in the bow, facing forward. When she looked back past Calder, the ship had turned and rejoined the sailboat in pursuit of them.

Satisfied that Calder was keeping them in the lead, she peered out at the sea in front of them.

Straight ahead and to their east a forest of jagged rocks jutted up from the sea. The Serpent's Teeth: although Dag didn't see how any ship the size of Ansdottir's could have navigated them. Had they been this close together when she'd gone through them while Dag was on board? She wasn't sure even this small boat would be able to make it through.

Calder untied some ropes and rolled the sail down until only a small square of fabric was left. The boat slowed just as they passed the first rocky spear.

"Right," Dag said, pointing her arm to the right. The boat responded to Calder's hand on the tiller, and it slipped past another rock.

Dag inched forward along the gunwale until her head was over the water. They passed another sliver of white rock, its thin length reaching down into the sea farther than she could see.

She concentrated on the path in front of them, ignoring the feeling of urgency from being pursued.

"Left." She pointed her arm. "Right." They glided past more rocky spikes, the boat edging alongside a submerged one. They were barely moving now. Calder grabbed a corner of the sail as the wind fluttered against the canvas.

Dag chanced a look behind them. The ship had veered away and was heading farther from them, but Ansdottir—in the other small sailboat—had followed them into the Teeth.

Dag swung her head back to the path ahead. She called a few directions, and the boat squeezed through a narrow gap before Calder made a sharp right. A moment later, she heard a scraping sound from behind them.

Ansdottir's boat was listing to one side, and two figures sat huddled in the back, staring at the sea around them. A third person—Margit Ansdottir—was busy rolling up the sail, which she then tied off.

"They've run aground," Calder said. "They might even be taking on water."

Dag was about to say good, when she realized that one of the huddled figures was Inger.

"Inger's on that boat," she said. "We can't let them sink." Just as she hadn't been willing to stand by and let Inger die by the noose, she wasn't going sit by and let her sister drown.

Calder met her eyes, frowned, but then he nodded. "We'll make sure they don't drown. We have to turn around in order to reach them."

Dag nodded in relief. She knew she was putting them both at risk; just because she didn't want the other boat to sink didn't mean the people in it would appreciate their efforts. But she was grateful that Calder hadn't argued. It took a few minutes of delicate maneuvering before they were able to get the small boat turned around.

Once they were a dozen yards from the other boat, Dag called out, "Inger! Are you all right?"

"Are we supposed to swim to you?" Ansdottir called back. "You think my crew won't come to rescue me?"

"If you're taking on water," Calder replied. "Your crew might not make it in time. But Inger is welcome to join us now."

"How generous," Ansdottir said. "Once we're off this rock, I will catch you. And you won't like what I do then."

Dag rummaged around in the boat. She grabbed a pistol and armed it with powder and shot. She handed it to Calder and readied another one for herself.

She stood up and pointed the pistol at Ansdottir. "We could just shoot you and your friend and come get Inger," she said.

"That's actually a good plan," Calder said. "Tell me why we shouldn't? It's not like you haven't ordered the deaths of whole crews just to take their ship."

Inger stepped in front of Ansdottir. "Because you'll have to shoot me first. And I know Dag won't do that, will you?"

"Inger, what are you doing?" Dag asked. "Get away from her; we can end this right now."

"No," Inger said. "I told you I'd made my choice. Why won't you believe me?" She scowled, and Dag wondered how Ansdottir had again convinced her sister to side against her twin. Then she saw Inger's right hand: her sister was using an Intelligencer signal to tell Dag to leave. But why wouldn't she come with them?

"Inger, we talked about this," Dag said. "You know how we both are."

"You can talk about your Traits," Ansdottir said. "I know all about them. Enough to know that Inger can't lie. So, when she says she's chosen to be part of my crew, I know I can trust her."

Inger signalled again, disagreeing with what Ansdottir had said. Was Inger lying to Ansdottir or to Dag? And how could she when she shouldn't be able to lie to either of them? Yet just as she had back on Strongrock, she was lying.

"Dag," Calder said. "We need to turn around now or when Ansdottir's crew gets here we won't be able to escape."

"All right." Dag kept the pistol with her as she called directions to Calder. When she could, she stared at Inger and Ansdottir. What was her sister doing?

Once the bow was pointed east, Calder looped a rope around an outcrop of rock to keep them in place.

"That was interesting," Ansdottir drawled. "The two of you have useful skills. Too bad you can't be trusted."

"Neither can you," Dag said. "As Ursa probably realizes now. You're the reason she's lost Hanne," Dag continued. "And it looks like Inger as well. Ursa didn't strike me as very understanding."

"Ursa and I go way back," Ansdottir said. "She'll get over it."

"Dag," Calder whispered. "We need to go. They are not taking on water and Inger . . ." He paused. "I'm sorry, but Inger isn't willing to come with us."

"You're right," Dag said. "Inger," she called. "One last chance. Come with me back to North Tarklee."

"How many times do I have to tell you that I've made my choice," Inger said. "Just go."

Dag met her sister's eyes, and then Inger looked away. She sighed. Whatever Inger thought she was doing, by staying here

Dag was probably making it harder.

"Let's go," Dag said. She scrambled to the prow of the boat, leaving Calder alone at the tiller. As she directed them through the Teeth, she tried to ignore the fact that she was leaving her twin behind.

It was half an hour before she looked back; by that time her sister was hidden behind multiple jagged spikes. She bit her lip and tried to fight her tears, wondering if she would ever see Inger again.

JOOSEP HAD LISTENED outside the door for a few moments before easing it open. It was early, too early for the warehouse to have more than a single guard patrolling it. That man was now gagged and tied up behind a stack of crates. Since nothing in the warehouse had seemed out of place, Joosep was going to investigate any documents that might be kept in this small office.

Once through the door, he crossed to the battered desk. The single drawer held a few sheets of blank paper and a dried-up bottle of ink: nothing to indicate that this was used as a place of business. So where was Tarmo Holt keeping his records?

Joosep had already searched the man's official office; that was where he'd found this address. A warehouse in a less than desirable part of South Tarklee. What was the Grand Freeholder—who was also Clan Freeholder for Nordmere—doing with *any* property in South Tarklee, Swyford?

He reached a hand under the desktop to feel if anything had been concealed there, but he didn't find anything. He stood up and sighed, staring around the small space. He had to admit that Holt might not have ever set foot in this office. He'd need to try his main office again. He must have missed something there. Or perhaps he kept his sensitive information in his home? Would he have to retract his order for Gustav to stay away from Holt's home and send the lad there to search?

He circled the room, checking corners and tapping walls as he searched out any secret compartments, but once again, he found nothing.

He opened the door and stepped out into the warehouse, cursing his feeble Trait. And was slammed to the floor. Someone pressed down on his back, hard, and he struggled to draw in a breath.

"We don't want him dead," a woman said. "But he doesn't need to be conscious, either."

Joosep tried to roll away, but the person on top of him sat on his legs and pinned his arms to the ground. A rope painfully bound his wrists together, and hands encircled his neck. He struggled to breathe before he felt his consciousness slip away.

HE WAS LYING on his side. Joosep gulped in a big breath and felt his throat burn. When he tried to move his arm, he realized that his hands were tied together in front of him. He rolled over onto his back and stared at the ceiling: undressed wooden planks spanned the small, dirty room. He moved his head to one side, feeling packed earth underneath his cheek, layered with dust. The walls were also rough wood. And permeating everything was the smell of old urine.

It had the look of a stable, although one that hadn't seen horses in years. He was alone and tied up.

Joosep rolled his shoulders. He didn't seem hurt, other than a sore throat and hands that were numb from being tied together.

How much time had passed, and when would anyone notice that he was missing? That's when Joosep realized that whoever had taken him knew who he was. No one had asked him his name; no one had asked him anything. Just that single comment about needing him alive.

Which meant that Tarmo Holt had taken him prisoner. He closed his eyes, cursing his stupidity. He'd been an administrator far too long to simply start spying again. He must have made mistakes that Tarmo Holt had noticed.

And yet another mistake: he hadn't even told anyone what he was doing or where he was going. There would be no rescue even when he was missed. And who knew how long that would be? A week? A month? When would Arnor become worried? And what would he do when he did?

Mentally, Joosep went through where his Intelligencers were. No one was expecting new assignments; no one was due back in to report. Dagrun and Calder were still missing, and there was no way to know when either of them would return. If Calder did come back to North Tarklee, how long would it be before he realized Joosep was missing? Would Luck show him where to look?

The door to the room rattled and then opened. Joosep lifted his head to see Tarmo Holt enter, followed by a middle-aged woman and a solidly built younger man.

"My good friend Joosep Sepp," Holt said. He walked over to him and toed his leg. "It seems you were caught trespassing. Terribly inept of you, don't you agree?"

"I was just thinking that myself," Joosep agreed. "My skills are not what they once were."

"Quite right," Holt said. "But it's a self-revelation that is bad for you and good for me." He gestured to the woman, who stepped out of the room. "Because you've put me into an entirely self-reflective mood, I'll tell you that I have no intention of killing you."

"Should I thank you?" Joosep asked. Holt might not kill him right now, but he couldn't afford to let him go.

"Gratitude would be appreciated," Holt said. "But it won't change what my plans for you are. Not after you stepped right into them." He chuckled.

The door opened, and the woman returned with a crude mug, a wrapped bundle, and a bucket. She set them all down in the middle of the floor and backed away

"Some food and drink," Holt said. "And a promise that I'll be back to see you, eventually." He smiled and left. The woman stood and stared while the man placed a boot on Joosep's chest as he untied his wrists.

"We'll be guarding you," the woman said. "So don't go thinking you can escape. This," she nodded at the items, "is all you get. Each day we'll bring you new and collect the old." She headed out the door, and the man followed her. Joosep heard a lock turning.

He rubbed his arms, ignoring the pain as circulation returned. He was Holt's prisoner, and it sounded like it would be for a long time. At least it gave him hope that he might survive this. But if he couldn't count on being rescued, he'd have to try to escape. It looked like he had time on his side. Maybe that was the only thing he could count on.

He crawled over to the bundles: a mug of water, a slab of cheese, half a loaf of old bread, and a bucket, to use for slops. Not what he was used to, but better than many citizens had each day.

CALDER HADN'T WANTED to distract Dag from the challenging task of navigating through the Teeth, so except for her terse directions, they spent the morning in silence. But he knew she was devastated at leaving Inger behind, and he wished that somehow he could ease her pain.

"Left and then straight for two boat lengths," Dag said. She looked over her shoulder. "We're getting close. The path is widening out."

"Good," Calder said as he pointed the tiller with one hand and adjusted the sail with the other. "We should be able to make it to Lavais Island by late day. Hopefully from there we can board a ship for North Tarklee. If not, then we'll have to chance this little boat."

"You don't want to sail this one there?" Dag asked.

"A boat this size isn't meant for long distances," Calder replied. "As it is we'll need good winds and calm seas to make it to Lavais today." He looked up at the sky. The sun was beating down on them, but would it be the same tomorrow? "North Tarklee is more than a few days away, and being out at night in a boat this small is going to be very uncomfortable." It would also be very dangerous in bad weather.

"Left then a quick right," Dag said. "Then go straight for . . ." She paused and stared ahead. "A long time. We're not out completely, but there's a big gap."

Once Calder had gotten them past the turns, he stood up and stretched. And grimaced in pain. He'd been leaning between the tiller and the sail for so long that his muscles had tightened up.

"Are you all right?" Dag asked. She had left her perch in the bow to grab the water skin. She took a drink and handed it to him.

"I will be," he said. "How about you?" He drank a few drops of warm water and handed the water skin back to her. Dag didn't meet his eyes, and he sighed. "I am sorry about Inger."

"I don't think I can talk about it," Dag said. "Not yet."

Calder reached out and drew her to him, and she leaned her head against his shoulder. "When you're ready," he said when what he *wanted* to say was that they'd get Inger back. But he didn't know that, and he wouldn't lie to Dag, or give her false hope.

"Thank you." Dag stepped out of his embrace and headed back to the prow. She sat on the seat and looked ahead before turning back to him. "I can't believe Ansdottir does this in a ship."

"She doesn't," Calder said. "At least, she doesn't do it here. The Teeth are farther apart in the north."

"So you took us to the most dangerous path through the Teeth?"

Calder shrugged. "They didn't give us much choice about which direction to take. Besides, Ansdottir on a ship can outrun this little boat, even in the Teeth," he said. "I didn't think she'd follow in the sailboat." He certainly hadn't expected her to have Inger with her.

"Why do you think she got stuck?" Dag asked. "When we didn't? It looked to me like she was following our path exactly."

"Luck," Calder replied. "What else?"

"I thought it might be my skill, actually," Dag replied.

"You mean your Trait?" Calder asked. "You consider it a skill?"

"Sure," Dag said. "At least how I use it is a skill." She paused. "Do you think Traits can change over time? Have you ever heard of that?"

"I guess it's possible," Calder said. "No one really knows much about them. Joosep is the first one to try to harness them, as far as I know. Why?"

"Because I think Inger's Trait changed. At least, she did something I never thought she could do."

"I saw her signalling," Calder said. "When she stepped in front of Ansdottir. She was using Intelligencer signals, wasn't she?"

"Yes," Dag said and sighed. "She used to help me practice. She was telling me that she was lying. Except Inger *can't* lie: it's always been impossible for her to lie and have people believe her. It's her Trait; it's being Seen and always being obvious. But she lied and Ansdottir believed her. I probably would have too, if she hadn't signalled."

"You're sure she was lying?"

"Yes, because it wasn't the first time she lied and was believed. So it wasn't a coincidence or a single, desperate act," Dag said. "Which means that somehow her Trait is changing." She met his eyes. "Which means that any of our Traits could change too."

"But we don't know why, so we can't guard against it," Calder replied.

"Or try to make it happen," Dag said.

"We should discuss this with Joosep when we get back to the

Hall," Calder said. "He might have seen it before." Dag frowned when he said Joosep's name. "We don't have to trust him in order to get information from him."

"I guess," Dag said. "But if anything happens to Inger I am holding Joosep responsible. It's his fault she left the Hall in the first place."

"I know." Calder still wasn't sure what Joosep's role in that was, but he'd known Joosep for most of his life. He didn't think the Master Intelligencer had intended for anything bad to happen to Inger. All he could do was hope that Inger stayed safe and came back home to Dag.

And if she didn't, if Inger got hurt, or was lost to the pirates forever, he might be forced to choose between Dag and Joosep. And right now, he wasn't sure which of them he'd side with.

It was mid-afternoon by the time they'd truly left the Teeth behind. Calder quickly raised the sail. There was a good breeze, but he wasn't sure it was good enough to get them to Lavais by nightfall.

"We should start making good time to Lavais now," he said to Dag, who was lying in the bottom of the boat with her hand over her eyes. She squinted up at him.

"How long?" she asked. "We're almost out of water."

"Five or six hours, if this wind keeps up." He looked overhead. The sun was shining, and a few high clouds dotted the sky. "Longer if the wind dies."

Dag sat up and looked out across the sea. "My eyes hurt," she said. "From looking for a path through the Teeth." She rubbed one eye with a fist. "Do you ever have consequences from using your Trait?"

"No," Calder replied. "But I don't try to *use* my Trait, at least not in the same way you use yours. I try to get myself into situations where my Trait can . . . manifest. I've always thought that Traits *couldn't* be forced, but you can focus yours when you want to. Unless you are always aware of the Unseen?" He was very curious. Intelligencers never discussed their Traits with anyone other than Joosep. Or siblings, he guessed. It would be hard not to talk to a twin, like Dag and Inger, when your Traits were opposite.

"I can focus it," Dag said. "But it's harder than if it just happens."

"Harder how?" He looked up at the sun, trying to gauge their position. He hadn't spent much time this far south in the Pale Sea. He was routing them a little west of Lavais, so he hoped. If they reached land, they could follow the coast until they spotted the island, and sailing close to shore—even the Blighted Woods—felt safer than the open sea.

"It takes more concentration," Dag said. "I have to really focus on something, and then my Trait will take over and let me see what's hidden. You've really never tried to force Luck?"

"I never thought it possible," Calder said. "Joosep never suggested I try, and unless it's changed, none of the teachers even discuss Traits."

"It's the same," Dag said. "It's been, what, ten years since you completed your training?"

"Yes." He made a slight turn to keep the sails filled. "Ah, look there." He pointed off to starboard. Intermittent plumes rose into the air. "Whales."

"Really? I've never seen them." Dag leaned out over the gunwale. "I see the back of one. They're huge!"

"These ones are smallish," Calder said. "They come through the Teeth farther north. Bigger whales don't make it this far into the Pale Sea." A whale surfaced close by. "They're what the Teeth are named for."

"Serpent's Teeth," Dag said. "I guess if you just saw their backs you might think whales were sea serpents."

In a few moments they'd left the whales behind. Dag lay back down in the boat, and Calder stared ahead. They should see land in about an hour, if his calculations were correct.

DAG RUBBED A knuckle against her eye. The sound of the sail flapping overhead almost lulled her back to sleep. Instead, she forced herself to sit up. Calder hadn't had any more rest than she had in the last day; it wasn't fair for her to sleep while he had to stay awake and sail them to safety.

"Are we getting close?" she asked. She had to shade her eyes to see him clearly. He smiled, and her heart skipped. When had Calder become so important to her?

"Yeah," he replied. "I'm following the coast now, so it might be another few hours."

Dag crawled closer to him. The sun was behind clouds, and

the wind was cool. Thick forest lined the land on the right, and she shivered. The Blighted Woods; forest so dense that it was impassable, except for the rivers that snaked through it. It was only safe to travel there in winter, when whatever creatures lurked there were blanketed by snow. Then boats like this one, fitted with skis, could glide up the frozen rivers.

"Have you ever been in the Wood?" Dag asked.

"No reason to," Calder replied. "Not even for Intelligencers."

"I guess not." There were no villages in the Blighted Wood; although, there were rumours that thieves hid there. A gust of wind whipped waves that splashed over the gunwale.

"Hold on," Calder said. "The weather's turning. It looks like we're in for rough seas." Dag followed his gaze overhead, where angry clouds seemed to grow darker by the minute.

She grabbed the gunwale with both hands as another wave crashed into them.

"Hold this steady," Calder said. She slid over and grabbed the tiller. It jumped and bucked in her hand, surprising her with its strength. Calder stepped over to the sail and started rolling it up. Once three quarters of the sail was rolled up, he sat back down and took over the tiller.

The wind changed direction, and the boat tilted towards the land. Dag grabbed the gunwale to keep from sliding to the other side. Calder pulled at the tiller, and the boat evened out again.

Then the rain hit: a cold, pelting rain that drenched her in seconds. She pushed her wet hair from her eyes and held on. Calder sat in the stern, both hands on the tiller, and she wondered how he could even see in this rain. Then she realized that he might not be able to.

She leaned over to him. "Do you want me to guide you again?"

Calder shook his head. "Not from the prow. I wouldn't be able to see if you'd gone overboard. Grab that rope."

She reached for the rope; it was wet and slippery, but she gripped it tight. Calder took a few minutes to tie a rope around each of them and secure the ropes to the boat.

"Just in case," he said.

Dag nodded and then started shivering uncontrollably. Calder pulled her close, and she settled into his warmth. She stared ahead, trying to see any obstacles through the sheets of rain. Water was starting to accumulate on the bottom of the boat, and for the first time, she was afraid.

"Should I bail?" she asked Calder. The only thing they had to bail with was the water skin. Which meant that what little water they had would be contaminated.

Calder shook his head. "Not yet. We can carry more water than this and stay afloat. It might even help stabilize us, although it's harder to steer."

A wave struck the side of the boat, and Dag was thrown into Calder. He steadied her with a hand before putting it back on the tiller. She sat back down and tried to get a firmer hold on the side of the boat. She peered into the rain. A dark shape loomed ahead.

"Calder!" she shouted. "Turn right!"

"Hang on." He stood and pushed the tiller left with both hands, and the boat veered right.

There was a scraping sound from underneath, and Dag clenched her teeth. A tree limb, dead leaves trailing on the water, leaned out over the sea. They skimmed past it, so close that for a moment branches caught in the sail.

She looked over at Calder, who was struggling to manage the tiller. She pointed to the mast.

"I'll sit there," she said. "And hopefully see things like that sooner." She crawled through a two-inch layer of water in the bottom of the boat. With her cold hands on the mast, she stood up. The rolled sail was at her shoulder. She looked back: she could just see Calder through the heavy rain. She waved and he waved back, confirming that he could see her. She ducked under the sail and stared out past the prow of the boat.

The rain continued to fall, and the wind whipped at her wet hair. Waves tossed the boat, and a couple of times she lost her footing, only staying on her feet because of her tight grip on the mast.

Something on the left again! She ducked under the mast and pointed right. Calder waved at her, and the boat turned. A wave slammed into them, and her feet went out from under her. Sea water washed over her, and she felt it tugging her with it. She scrabbled to hold onto something, anything, but her grip slipped on wet wood.

The air went out of her lungs when the rope around her waist went tight. She grabbed at the rope and pulled herself along it. Then Calder was hauling her over the side of the boat, and she realized that she'd been swept overboard.

"Are you all right?" Calder asked.

Dag nodded weakly. She coughed. She was cold, and her throat was sore. She sat miserably in the bottom of the boat, aware that Calder was fighting the stormy sea but without enough energy to help him.

Eventually, she realized that the rain had turned into a fine mist, and they were no longer being tossed around so violently. Shivering, she lifted her head to see Calder's grim face. She mustered up the energy to crawl over to him. His hand was cold in hers when she gripped it.

"Think we're out of it?" she asked.

"For now," Calder said, but he didn't look like he was happy about it. "I need to find a place to land." His face softened when he looked at her. "Do you think you can help me find one?"

"I'll try." Water sloshed in the bottom of the boat as she made her way to the mast. She leaned against it, shivering, as she scanned the sea. She could just make out forest on their right, so they hadn't wandered very far from the Blighted Wood. She was about to direct Calder there when something caught her eye on the left.

"Calder, land; an island, I think," she pointed. "Could it be Lavais?"

"Yes!" he replied. "It has to be. Between the Teeth and Lavais there are no other land masses."

"Oh good," Dag said, and then she slid down the mast until she was sitting on a boat rib, covered in cold water. She heard Calder exclaim, and she felt something warm against her cheek.

CHAPTER 18

CALDER HAULED DAG into his arms, lifting her part of the way out of the water that covered the bottom of the boat. She shivered so violently that he almost dropped her.

"We're almost there," he said even though he was certain she couldn't hear him.

A small harbour came into view: it was deserted, no doubt due to the storm. He used one hand to steer past the few boats that were anchored offshore and headed towards a dock that was attached to a warehouse. With his other hand he held Dag against him, hoping his body heat would help her stay warm.

He was coming into dock too fast and had to put Dag down, doing his best to prop her up so that her body stayed dry.

"Heya!" he called as he dragged the sail down. He bundled it up and shoved it under the bow seat, not caring how much work it would need to be seaworthy again. The boat slowed now that the sail was down and he balanced in the bow as they approached the dock

"Heya," he called again. As soon as he could he put a hand on the dock, slipping the painter around a piling. The rope jerked taut, and he almost lost his footing as the side of the boat scraped against wet wood.

Before the boat could bounce away from the dock, he leaned

over and picked Dag up, carrying her towards the bow.

"I gotcha," a woman said from the dock. A rough hand gripped the gunwale and pulled until the stern was close enough to the dock for him to climb onto it.

"Thanks," Calder said. "Is there someplace warm I can take her?"

"Caught in the storm, huh?" the woman said. She was dressed in an oiled coat and her head was bare. A salt and pepper braid draped down her back. "This way."

Calder followed her through a door and into the warehouse. A small fire burned in one corner, and he rushed Dag to it. He lowered her to a skin—seal, he thought—that lay in front of a rough hearth.

"Here," the woman said, handing him a woollen blanket. "Best get those wet clothes off her."

Calder and the woman stripped Dag: her skin was pale and she felt like ice, then they rolled her up in the blanket and lay her close to the fire. He took a smaller blanket, folded it, and put it under her head.

"I'll make sure no sparks catch," the woman said. "There's a spare set of worker's gear over there. You need to change too."

Calder nodded and headed where she'd indicated: a peg set in the middle of the wall that had clothing hanging off it. Even just a few feet from the fire he felt chilled. He quickly peeled off his clothes and donned the rough trousers and loose shirt. He brought his wet clothes back to the fire and spent a few minutes laying his and Dag's clothes out to dry.

"Your boat won't be there when you go back," the woman said. "In case you go looking for it."

Calder leaned over Dag: her breathing was steady, and she'd stopped shivering, but she hadn't woken up. He sat down beside her.

"Thank you," he said. "For the help and the fire. And I don't care about the boat unless it causes any damage."

"No worries there," the woman replied. "I didn't mean it would drift away." She sent him a sidelong glance. "On Lavais we don't like pirates, except to steal from."

"I see. Of course, you recognized the boat," Calder said.

"Boats be our business," she agreed.

"I'm not a pirate, I'm," Calder reached over to his wet trousers.

Ahh, it was still there in the waistband pocket. His coin flip had been right that he'd need it. He showed her his patch. "I'm with the Fair Seas Treaty Alliance. Calder Rahmson." He motioned to Dag. "Dagrun Lund. I'm pretty sure she has her patch here somewhere too."

"Well, that changes things," the woman said. "Happy to help. I'm Solvig Madsen. I'll get you some soup." She stood up and walked away from the fire.

Calder leaned over to watch Dag breathe in and out. He heard a door across the warehouse close. He had no reason to distrust Solvig Madsen.

Lavais Island's business was ships. He wasn't surprised they didn't like pirates, although he should have realized that even the smaller sailboats would have been built here. And then been stolen by the pirates.

Solvig would be even angrier if she knew that ships thought lost at sea were actually lost to pirates. Men from Lavais had likely died when the pirates took the ships.

Dag didn't move in the few minutes it took Solvig to return with a tray that held three steaming mugs. She hooked a foot around the leg of a table and dragged it closer to the fire before she set the tray down on it.

Calder pulled Dag into a sitting position with her head on his shoulder. She might not be awake, but he would still try to get something warm into her. He took a sip from one mug, a salty fish broth probably made from dried fish. It was a little too hot to give to Dag. He blew on it before taking another sip.

"Where'd you come from, in that boat stolen from pirates?" Solvig asked.

"Strongrock," Calder said.

"You saying you came through the Teeth? Never met anyone who did that."

"We were being chased," Calder said. "By the owners of the boat." The soup had cooled, so he lifted the mug to Dag's lips. She didn't wake up, not exactly, but she did open her lips, and when he tipped some soup into her mouth, she swallowed.

"Pirates," Solvig shook her head. "Hate 'em. Heard that captain of theirs can get through the Teeth on a ship. Any truth to that?"

"True," Calder said. "I know someone who was aboard when

Margit Ansdottir sailed through the Teeth." He didn't mention that it was Dag: he trusted Solvig to not betray them to the pirates, but even he didn't know who to trust in the Three.

After he gave Dag another sip of soup, she seemed to settle into a deeper sleep. He lay her down in front of the fire again and drained the soup. He put it on the table and picked up the other mug. He'd had no sleep and little to eat or drink all day; he needed that second mug of fish soup.

"Can we stay here for a few days?" he asked Solvig, who had been watching him silently since finishing her own soup. "And could you help keep our presence a secret? The less people who know we're here the better."

He was hoping to allow Dag at least a few days to recover. And he needed to try to get in touch with Joosep. Their patches meant they could get help, but Joosep had to send money to cover the costs of help as well as their trip back to North Tarklee.

"I just got the one bed," Solvig said. "But you're welcome to it. I spend most of my time here or on the dock anyway."

"Thank you." He sighed, relieved to have at least a few days. "Do you have something I can write on? I need to get a message to the Fair Seas Treaty Alliance offices."

Solvig went searching for writing materials, and Calder closed his eyes, just for a moment.

JOOSEP SAT UP at the sound of the door opening. Light stabbed at his eyes. It was always dark in the stable, and it took him a few seconds to realize that it wasn't the woman come to give him food and water.

"Where is the list of Intelligencers, students, and teachers?" Tarmo Holt asked.

"There isn't one," Joosep answered, truthfully. He was the only one who knew every single Intelligencer and student. The teachers, well they were paid by the Fair Seas Treaty Alliance, so there was a record, if Holt knew where to look.

"I want the names." Holt stepped closer and peered down at him. "All of them!"

Joosep sighed. "We both know that I'm not going to tell you," he said. "What kind of Master Intelligencer would I be?"

"A poor one, but I've always thought that," Holt replied with a smile. "Perhaps a few days without food and water would help you realize it's in your best interest to tell me. Besides, I already know some. Dagrun Lund, for example."

"And that's the only one you know," Joosep said. "Because Inger isn't an Intelligencer."

"But Dagrun can probably figure out the others," Holt said. "Isn't that her Trait? The Unseen? I know people who say they've both been quite helpful on Strongrock."

"So, you *are* friends with the pirates," Joosep said. "Dagrun was assigned to find out about your relationship with them," he lied. He only knew about Holt's alliance with pirates from Gustav. But what had he meant about the Lund sisters being helpful? What was Inger Lund's relationship to the pirates? Dagrun would never let her sister become an enemy of the Three, would she? Or was that why she hadn't returned? She hadn't been happy with Joosep's role in Inger's disappearance. Had he lost Dagrun's trust? Had she allied with Holt?

"I don't believe you," Holt said. "But I still need the names of the Intelligencers, the students, and their teachers. Now!"

Joosep tapped his head. "It's only up here. And if anything happens to my head, you'll never get the information."

"What about your assistant's head?" Holt asked. "Arnor? I'm sure he knows what you know. And if he's not willing to tell, it won't matter to me what happens to his head."

"He might know a few," Joosep said. Arnor didn't know everyone, but he knew enough to compromise the whole organization. But he was also smart enough to stay out of Holt's hands. Even though his boss hadn't been.

Holt smiled. "No doubt a few will lead to a few more. It will be a good place to start, then." He rapped on the door and it opened. "No food or drink for you today, I think," Holt said. "If Arnor gives me what I want, I may reconsider." He stepped out of the room, shutting the door behind him.

A lock clicked into place, and the room was dark again. Joosep stared in the direction of the door.

He had to believe that Arnor had already hidden. Or he'd been captured and hadn't spoken. In which case, he hadn't made things worse for his assistant. He also hoped he hadn't made life more dangerous for Dagrun and her sister. He didn't think Holt had spoken to them himself, but he might. He *was* Grand Freeholder: would Dagrun align with him and tell him what he wanted?

He sat up straighter. If both he *and* Arnor were missing, someone would realize something was wrong. Would they do anything? He was training spies—he had to assume one of them would suspect that something had happened. But would they know *what* to do, even if they suspected something was wrong?

He slid lower against the wall. Unfortunately, the ones out of training had Traits that wouldn't help find him. Which left Calder and Dagrun; but without knowing where they were or even if they were alive, he couldn't hope that one of them would return and realize that something was wrong.

He'd spent time trying to find a physical way out of this stable prison to no avail. But was there a way to use what he knew to get out? Not by telling Holt the truth: he would never betray his people or the Three. But there had to be another way.

Dag coughed and tried to roll over, but she could barely move her arms. Confused, she struggled to free them from the blanket she was cocooned in. She yawned, sat up, and pulled the blanket up over her bare breasts. She didn't remember undressing. Or coming in . . . here, wherever here was.

The last thing she did remember was being on the sailboat spotting land and then . . . She wasn't waking from a simple sleep.

Calder was stretched out beside her, and worried, she leaned over him. Asleep, that was all. They were both safe and warm and dry. She must have passed out, and Calder had somehow found safety.

She rubbed her hands against the dry and warm skin of her arms. He'd saved her life: his too, maybe, but hers for certain.

She spotted their clothes laid out nearby, so she wriggled out of the blanket and crawled over to them. Hers were still slightly damp, but since there wasn't another option, she put them on anyway.

Her boots sat close to a fire that was burning in the well-used fireplace. The warmth only reached a few feet into the large space she and Calder were in.

There was a table nearby with a chair pulled up to it, but she didn't see any other furniture. She stood on shaky legs, wondering if she should wake Calder but decided against it. He wouldn't have felt comfortable enough to fall asleep if it wasn't safe, and he needed his rest, after what she'd put him through. All she wanted was to relieve her bladder and then go back to sleep.

She padded out across a floor of hard-packed dirt to the small door that was set into the far wall. She was halfway there when the south wall opened. A lamp bobbed as someone entered the space. The wall slid closed and an indistinct figure carried the lamp towards the fire: and Calder.

All feelings of safety vanished, and Dag sprinted back to Calder and the fire.

"Who are you?" she asked.

The figure holding the lamp turned, and a middle-aged woman smiled at her.

"You're awake," she said. "Calder," she gestured to him, "wanted something to write on. Not something I keep around here, seeing as I can't write myself, so I had to go out for it. I'm Solvig Madsen, and this is my warehouse."

"Dagrun," Dag replied. "Thank you for lending us your warehouse and fire." She shivered. She wasn't sure what Calder had told this woman, but he obviously trusted her, at least a little. And she had more pressing needs. "I was looking for the privy."

"Sure," Solvig said, gesturing to the far corner Dag had been heading for. "There's a small room with a barrel set into the floor."

"Thanks." Dag hurried to the door that led into a small apartment. She barely glanced at the kitchen, instead opening a door in the narrow hall. The barrel was set into the floor, a clay pipe leading away from it. She heard the sound of waves and assumed that the pipe led to the sea.

She relieved herself and left, heading back into the warehouse. She didn't feel comfortable leaving Calder asleep and alone with Solvig for longer than she had to.

Calder was awake when she returned. She sat down and pulled her blanket across her back. Solvig had added more wood to the fire, but Dag still felt chilled.

"How long was I asleep?" Dag asked Calder quietly.

"A few hours," he replied. "You'd just spotted Lavais, and I sailed us in and found our host Solvig." He sat up, and she noticed he was wearing a rough shirt.

"I'll get more soup," Solvig said. She tossed one last piece of wood on the fire and then headed across the warehouse.

"Thank you," Calder called after her. "She's been very generous," he said to Dag.

"I appreciate it," Dag replied. "I see that you got clothing." She didn't really care that he'd seen her naked: he'd been saving her life.

"Solvig helped me get you in the blanket," Calder said. He stood up and shook out his blanket before folding it and laying it down beside her. He sat down on it and looked in the direction their host had taken. "We need to talk about what we do next."

"Solvig said she brought something to write on," Dag replied, then yawned. She was still bone-tired. "You have something in mind?"

"I think we should stay here for a few days. A rest will do us both good. Solvig recognized the sailboat. I had to show her my patch so she would know that we're not pirates." He stared at the fire. "I want to write to Joosep and ask him what I should do next." He turned and met her eyes. "His response will tell us whether we can trust him or not."

"Yes," Dag said. It was a sound plan. They both needed a rest, and she welcomed the chance for the Master Intelligencer to prove he could be trusted: or not. "I'll help with the note." She'd build in an Unseen test that Joosep's Trait would see to make sure *she* believed what he said.

"That would be great," Calder said. "Ahh, Solvig's on her way back."

"Here," Solvig said, setting a tray down on the small table. "Eat up."

"Thank you," Dag said. She took a mug from the table and sat back with it. She took a tentative sip. It was salty, and fishy, but hot. "And for everything else you've done for us—for me."

"You're welcome," Solvig replied. "But you can really thank me by catching the *skit* pirates. They steal from honest, hard-working Lavaisians, and it's not right."

"I said that we weren't pirates," Calder said. "Not that we were stopping them."

"You have patches. You can tell whoever needs to know that they must be stopped." Solvig sat down in the chair and glared at them.

"You're right," Dag said. "We can. But pirates want us dead."

She leaned past a surprised Calder to get closer to Solvig's ear. "So, you can't tell anyone what we're doing. Or even that we're here." Even though her Trait was Unseen, and her lies would be believed, she thought the truth was more powerful in this case. "And I am sorry. Our presence puts you in danger."

"I haven't told anyone," Solvig said. "Calder already asked me not to, so I won't. Although any Lavaisian would be willing to help you defeat the pirates."

"I'm sure they would," Calder said. "But we need secrecy. And a place to rest for a few days and wait for a reply to the message we want to send to North Tarklee."

Solvig leaned back in her chair and smiled. "Already told you, you can stay here. And I can take your message myself. My brother lives in North Tarklee. I haven't visited him in some time."

"Thank you," Calder said. "And the sailboat we came in?"

"It's already gone," Solvig said. "No one will see that craft for a season. It's probably already been fitted with skis for winter." She laughed. "No one will know you're here." She got to her feet. "I'll see if there's enough food for you. Weather's turned calm, so I'll be on my way as soon as you write that letter."

CALDER PULLED THE paper over to him along with the quill and ink well. He hoped that getting these unusual-for-her supplies hadn't raised suspicions for Solvig, but there wasn't anything he could do about it if it had.

"I'll tell him I haven't been able to convince you to come back," he said to Dag, who sat beside him, staring at the paper.

"Yes. Say that Inger found work on Strongrock and she loves it," Dag said. "And that I won't leave without her. It *was* the truth, a few days ago."

"He'll read more than what's written?" Calder asked. "Because of his Trait?"

"Yes. So, don't tell him where you're writing from. Just ask if he thinks you should stay a few more days." Dag yawned, her eyes drooping. "Would you normally ask for money?"

Calder grinned. "I have in the past. He always slips in a Pilalian baisa for me." He leaned over, dipped the quill into the ink and wrote a looping *J* at the top of the page, followed by a few sentences. "*Mission not yet completed,*" he read. "*As IL found work and won't leave, and DL will not leave without her. Need direction. Also coin since expenses are mounting. Please send reply with my messenger.*" He looked over at Dag. "Anything else?"

"Yes," Dag replied. "Ask him why he never trained Inger."

"All right," Calder replied. He wrote down the question. "I was wondering that myself. She has a strong Trait, why not figure out how to use it?"

"Joosep thinks Inger is stupid," Dag said, and Calder was surprised at the bitterness in her voice. "And not worth training since she can't understand anything not on the surface."

"He's wrong. She's very smart." He sighed. "No wonder she likes the pirates." He didn't sign the note—he never did—before folding it into a small square. He created a map to Joosep's door on a second piece of paper. Solvig didn't read, but she came from a boatbuilding and seafaring community: he was certain she'd understand the map. "I'll give this to Solvig."

"All right. I think I'm going to find that bed."

Calder watched Dag walk across the warehouse and pass through the small door on the far wall. He'd always admired Joosep, but not training a strong Trait like Inger Lund's just didn't make sense. But it did help explain Inger's need to find a place of her own. Even if it was with pirates.

He got up and slid the large warehouse door open just wide enough for him to see out. A few men were cleaning gear on boats tied up at the dock and Solvig was chatting with a fisherman. And as promised, there was no sign of the sailboat that had brought him and Dag here.

He waited just inside, out of sight. Solvig hadn't told him, but he assumed that once he opened the warehouse door, she'd see it. And he was right. She nodded to her companion and headed towards the warehouse.

Calder stepped farther into the space as Solvig slid the door open enough to squeeze inside.

"You're ready?" she asked.

"Yes." He gave her the note and the map. Her eyes widened when she traced the route.

"This leads to the heart of the city," Solvig said. "Will I be allowed to journey so far in?"

"You will with this." He handed her his patch. "Just bring it back, along with a response."

Solvig tucked the note and patch into a pocket, keeping the map separate. "Now I really believe that you can do what I need you to do," she smiled. "And make those in power understand that the pirates must be stopped."

"It's what I want them to understand as well," Calder said, wondering if Solvig would be so helpful if she knew that nothing in the note concerned pirates. But that discussion would have to wait until he and Dag were sure they could trust Joosep. Because Dag was right: if Tarmo Holt was conspiring with pirates, who was to say Joosep wasn't as well?

"Come, I'll show you my quarters," Solvig said. She led the way to the small door and Calder followed her into a narrow hallway.

"You'll need to stay in here," Solvig said. "With the door locked. It has to look like I am away."

They were in a small living area that had two chairs pulled up in front of a table that was littered with broken nets and fishing gear. A small oil burning stove sat against a wall and there was a pump with a bucket below it.

"Water is from a cistern on the roof," Solvig said. "With the storm you should have plenty. I have a couple of fish pies and a few carrots and an onion." She gave him an apologetic smile. "I can't get more fresh food without raising questions. But there is plenty of dried and salted fish." She opened the lid of a box: fillets of dried fish were stacked inside. "You'll hate it, but you'll eat."

"Any flavourings?" Calder asked. "You'd be surprised at how many different ways I can prepare salt fish."

"Huh," Solvig grunted. "You're in luck. I was paid in spices for a favour I did." She headed back down the hall to the warehouse.

Calder followed her to a low shelf a few feet from the doorway: he could already smell the rich aromas. Small pouches and boxes had been carefully placed on each shelf.

"Spices from every known country," Solvig said. "So I was told. Don't really know what to do with them myself, so they've been here for a few months. Take whatever you need."

"Thank you," Calder said. He certainly wasn't going to complain about salt fish; he was grateful to have any food, but the spices were a delightful bonus. "I'll make you something with them when you return," he said. "I assume we need to be careful with any fire."

"Yes." Solvig led the way back into her quarters. "The stove burns fish oil and it smells, but it doesn't smoke much." She headed to a small door. "The privy is here." She opened the door to a small room. A bucket was buried halfway into the floor. "Pipes lead away from here to the sea below the pier," Solvig said.

She closed the door and headed to the door at the end of the hall. She cracked it open. "Your friend is here already, I think."

Calder leaned past Solvig to see a narrow bed and a small side table. Dag's blonde head was at one end of the bed, and a blanket covered her.

"The trip here was hard on her," he said.

Solvig nodded and shut the door. She squeezed past Calder and headed back to the main living space.

"It's not much, but it should do you," she said.

"Thank you," Calder said. "I'm used to a hammock in a ship's hold. This amount of privacy is a real treat."

"Good. I should be back in a couple of days," Solvig said. "Get anything you need from beside the fire before I put it out and lock up."

It took Calder just a few minutes to gather his clothes and a few blankets from the warehouse. While Solvig made sure the fire was out he went back into her quarters.

A quick peek showed him that Dag was still sleeping, so he started clearing the main table. After a trip to grab the spices, he put his selections on the cleared spot on the table. It had been so long since he'd had such an array of spices to cook with that he was almost sorry that they had fish pies for today.

Solvig popped her head in to say goodbye, and after he heard the lock turn, quiet settled over the warehouse.

Calder sighed. As a sailor he never had much free time or privacy, and here he had both. They had two, maybe three days to wait until Solvig returned—and that was the best case. She could run into bad weather or have trouble getting in to see Joosep, despite the patch.

Calder filled a bowl with water and submerged some salt fish fillets. He might as well get started on tomorrow's meal. Once that was done, he looked around the small space.

What to do with his time? He sat down and pulled a tattered piece of rope towards him. Without thinking, he spliced it together, tossed it aside, and grabbed another piece.

Joosep blinked when the door opened. His lips were cracked and dry, and his throat felt scratchy; he'd lost track of how long it had been since he'd had a drink of water. Holt had threatened a day, but it felt longer.

A figure loomed over him.

"It's curious that no one seems to miss the Master Intelligencer and his assistant." It was Holt. He was holding a clay cup, and Joosep couldn't help staring at it. He licked his lips and Holt laughed.

"This water is yours if you tell me what I want to know," he said. "Students, teachers, and Intelligencers. I'll kill your assistant if you don't tell me."

Condensation dotted the outside of the cup, and Joosep couldn't take his eyes off it. But despite his preoccupation, his Trait could still tell that Holt was hiding something. "You don't have Arnor," Joosep croaked out. "You'd have brought him to me in pieces if you had."

"You're right," Holt replied. He tipped the cup, and water spilled out onto the dry dirt floor of the stall. He stopped pouring. "I still have half left. It's yours if you tell me what I want."

Joosep closed his eyes so that he didn't have to look at the cup. He tried to chuckle, but it came out as a croak that ended in a strangled cough. He took a deep, steadying breath before opening his eyes and meeting Holt's gaze.

"I swore an oath many years ago," Joosep said. "The same one you swore when you became Grand Freeholder: to put the Three above even my own life." He smiled. "I meant it."

"*Vardya!*" Holt said. He threw the cup at the wall.

It shattered, and shards of wet clay rained down on Joosep. He desperately wanted to pick up the pieces and lick the moisture off of them, but he wasn't going to do that in front of Holt. Instead, he smiled.

"You really don't have Arnor." His smile widened when Holt swore again, left the room, and slammed the door shut.

In the dark, Joosep hunted for shards of clay, picking them up and sucking them dry. Part of him knew that this small amount of water would simply delay the process of dying of thirst. But another part of him wasn't ready to give up.

He still had people out there, and Arnor was one of them:

Arnor, who knew almost as many secrets as he did. Joosep might not be saved from Tarmo Holt, but the Three—the Fair Seas Treaty Alliance countries—still could be.

DAG YAWNED AND stretched before pushing the blankets down to the foot of the bed. A sliver of light spilled in from around the cloth that covered the small window. Dusk, she thought, or could it be dawn? She wasn't sure how long she'd slept. She'd felt warm, finally, after the mad escape through the rain.

She stood up and stretched again. She was wearing her own shirt, but she'd laid her trousers out on the chair. She picked them up to find that they were finally dry, and she pulled them on.

The hallway that led to the living area was dark. She hadn't done more than pass through it, hunting for the bed, when she'd come in.

"You're awake," Calder said from the gloom. "Sorry, no lights allowed. Not until Solvig gets back."

Dag could see enough to find her way to a second chair. Something on the table in front of her smelled enticing and unfamiliar. "She's gone? Thanks for handling everything. I'm just so exhausted."

"Cold water steals all your energy," Calder said. "It happens."

"Not to you."

"I'm used to it," he replied. "Even on the trip to Strongrock I had to rig in the cold rain. I don't think you've ever had to. Not rig, I mean stay out and work in cold rain."

"My first assignment was as a housemaid," Dag said. "No cold rain."

"Housemaid," Calder said. "You said it was for the next Grand Freeholder." She paused, and he could almost hear him smile. "Joosep sent you there for a reason. It might help us figure out what Holt's plan is."

"You're right." She gave him the same report she'd given to Joosep: was it just over a week ago? How had so much happened in such a short period of time?

"So Timonis is next in line for Grand Freeholder," Calder said. "Holt obviously knows that. Nothing you found out could derail his appointment."

"Holt wouldn't be named his replacement anyway," Dag said.

"It's not Nordmere's turn."

"No, but could he benefit from a delay? You said he was trying to recruit Inger for some longer-term plan."

"But that would take years," Dag said. "He was looking to pair her with some unknown man so they could have children with Traits."

"Which means he must already be working with someone—a male—with a Trait," Calder said.

"Probably a young man," Dag said. "Inger would never have children with just anyone. I can't think who it might be, and I know everyone's Traits. I know even when they don't know it themselves."

"Really?" Calder asked. "You can spot Traits?"

"Sure. That's how Joosep finds us all too," she said. "We both have the same Trait, although mine's stronger." She paused. "I don't always know exactly what the Trait does. Take Ursa Ozlinch. The closest I can come to figuring out her Trait is that she's some kind of Keeper. She keeps a tavern and an inn and owns most of Strongrock. And she's been able to convince Inger into staying with her even after I've exposed her lies."

"Interesting," Calder said. "You heard what Jaak said when he came to my room. That what's Ansdottir's stays hers, including people. Jaak was talking about himself."

"It might be Ursa who is behind that."

"It's possible," Calder said. "That could be another reason why Ansdottir hung Ursa's spy. She knows Ursa is good at collecting people and wants to make sure she knows that anything that belongs to Ursa is Ansdottir's if she wants it."

"That's still part of a power struggle," Dag said, trying not to think about how close Inger had come to being hung, "and maybe Ansdottir didn't trust Hanne."

"Maybe she doesn't trust Ursa." Calder stood up. "We're not going to figure this out right now. Solvig left us a couple of fish pies. I'll put the stove on low to heat them."

Dag pushed her plate away. The pie was bland but edible. She yawned.

"Sorry," she said. "I think I need more sleep."

"All right. You take the bed, and I'll figure out something out here."

"No! Skit! I didn't mean it that way. It's tight, but we'll both fit in the bed." She hadn't even suspected that Calder would assume she should get the bed all to herself. "Inger and I have shared smaller, believe me." Not recently; they hadn't needed to in the Hall. "If anyone sleeps out here it'll be me. I've already had a chance at the bed, and you've been awake far longer than me."

"If you're sure," Calder said.

"Yes, absolutely."

Calder headed for the bedroom, but Dag didn't feel quite tired enough, not after sleeping so much of the day already. She peered out the window—it faced a dirt path that was lined with buildings. No lights were on in any of the ones she could see, so she assumed they were for work—shacks for curing fish or workshops for tasks related to shipbuilding.

After a half hour of watching nothing, she headed for bed. She squeezed in beside Calder and stared up at the ceiling. She was aware of Calder's breathing and his warmth, and she realized that sharing a bed with him wasn't anything like sharing with Inger. As tired as she was, it took her a long time to get to sleep.

CALDER WOKE SLOWLY. There was an unfamiliar weight on his shoulder, and when he turned his head, he felt Dag's hair on his face. He froze: his left arm lay under her, and his hand rested on her hip. He gently moved his hand off her, surprised that they'd both been comfortable enough to get so close in sleep. He didn't have a lot of experience sharing a bed: most of his time on the sea had been spent in hammocks strung in ship holds, and he'd never pursued a long-term romantic relationship. Between his work and his father's bad example, he'd always figured he was a poor bet. But he had to wonder what it would be like to wake up with Dag every day. Not that she was looking for anything from him.

Carefully, he pulled his arm out from under her. She stirred and rolled towards him, and in order to keep out of her way, he ended up pressed against the wall. He slid out from under the blanket and edged off the bed.

In the main room he looked out the window. A gentle rain fell, muddying the path that ran along the landward side of the building. He saw someone wearing wet-weather gear enter one of the cabins, but other than that, it was quiet.

He'd been to Lavais once before and knew that the ship

building took place in a larger bay that faced Swyford, rather than this smaller bay that seemed filled with fishermen and craftsmen and Solvig and her warehouse.

He drained the salt fish and refilled the bowl with fresh water, then filled a pot with fresh water and put it on the small stove. He lit the wick, keeping the flame low, put some tea in a mug, and waited for the water to boil.

There was enough light to work by, so he picked up a tangled and torn fishing net. He wasn't used to being idle. He was sipping his tea and working on the net when Dag entered.

"Do you want some tea?" he asked. "Fish stew is still a few hours away." He'd changed the water again but would need another fresh soak to leech more salt out of the fish.

"Tea would be great," she said. She grabbed a mug from a shelf while he lit the stove again.

"The tea's in the pot on the top shelf," Calder said. Dag pulled it down and shook some leaves into her mug.

"I hope Solvig forgives us for using up all of her supplies," Dag said. She put the tea away and sat down across from him. She picked up the net. "At least you're repaying her with repairs."

"It's more to keep busy," Calder said. He met her eyes and grinned. "I'm not even sure she'll thank me. The warehouse is almost empty, so this might be the only work she has to keep her occupied."

"Why is that?" Dag asked. "The warehouse, I mean. It *is* empty. Shouldn't it be full?"

The water was boiling, so Calder put down the net he was working on, turned off the stove, and tipped the water into Dag's mug.

"Trade's been interrupted," he said. "Because of the pirates. Remember the names of ships on the crates of weapons stored on Strongrock? Every single one of those ships was carrying something besides those weapons. Those trade goods would have been taken or lost when Ansdottir's people attacked: trade goods that would have otherwise ended up in this warehouse and other warehouses like it all around the Pale Sea."

"I guess I knew that damage was being done to the Fair Seas Treaty Alliance countries," Dag said. "But it seemed so hypothetical. This empty warehouse makes it seem more real."

"Trade affects everything. Before long there will be whole

industries that are no longer functioning."

"I still don't see why they wouldn't just build more ships." Dag said.

"They could eventually," Calder replied. "Once they know the ones they have are lost. But merchants are in business to make money, and losing a ship and its cargo is expensive. And that doesn't even consider the loss of sailors. Even if a merchant can recover from that, why would he risk sending a ship through the pass? And what crew would be willing to sail for regular pay?"

"Solvig is right," Dag said. "The pirates need to be stopped. But Joosep hadn't even assigned you to that. He might want this to happen."

"Maybe." Calder didn't want to believe Joosep was working against the Three but if he wasn't, then the Master Intelligencer had missed something huge. "I don't see how any of this benefits Tarmo Holt. He and the rest of the Freeholders stand to lose fortunes with trade disrupted."

"But lumber will be less expensive, won't it?" Dag asked. "If no one needs it?"

"I suppose. But who would want it, even if it was cheap?" It was time to change the water for the salt fish. When he was done, he sat back down. Dag was staring into her mug.

"There's something there," she said. She shook her head. "I just don't have enough information to uncover the answer." She looked up at him and sighed. "In the meantime, why don't you teach me how to fix this fishing net?"

"Sure."

Teaching Dag how to splice the rope and then tie the knots to fix the netting took most of the afternoon. The fish stew was simmering: along with the salt fish he'd added the carrots and onion and had been liberal with the spices.

It was almost dark by the time they ate. After two bowls each, Calder added more water to the pot and turned the flame on the stove as low as he could.

"More of the same for tomorrow," he said. He was still hungry and had to assume Dag was too, but they had to ration the food.

"It was good," Dag said. "Thanks. Where did you learn to cook?"

"My father. He's Pilalian, as you might have guessed." He laid his arm on the table beside hers. Even in the waning light the difference in skin tones was apparent. "Although my mother has your colouring." He felt heat where their arms touched. "Pilalians use a lot of spices when they cook." He pulled his arm away from Dag's, but his awareness of her only intensified. "Whenever I had the chance, I badgered my father into teaching me how to cook."

"You don't like boiled potatoes and cabbage?" Dag asked. She smiled and his heart stuttered. "Or pickled beets and herring?"

"I ate plenty of those," Calder said. "When I was at the Hall. My mother knows better than to feed me that when I visit. I cook for her."

"Then we make the perfect team," Dag said with a laugh. "I can't cook at all. Not even the traditional dishes." Their eyes met, and Calder couldn't look away. Something shifted between them, and Dag's smile faded.

"A perfect team," Calder repeated softly. He put his hand on the table palm up, and Dag laid her hand on his. He closed his hand, lacing his fingers with hers. His heart racing, he leaned over their hands.

She met him halfway—warm lips and hot breath mingled, and then soft skin met soft skin and he forgot to breathe. Her hand tightened on his as their lips—the only other place where their bodies met—melded together. He felt her smile against him, and he pulled away to stare into blue eyes that seemed to see right through him. And maybe they did.

And then she leaned across and kissed him again. He wasn't sure who moved first but they were both on their feet, arms wrapped around each other, and he felt heat all along his body where they touched. Their lips parted, and he took a shaky breath, inhaling her scent.

"I hadn't planned on that," Dag said, and he looked up in surprise. "I don't think you planned it either."

"We should stop," he said. Whatever this was, or could become, would it jeopardize their mission?

"Do you want to?" Dag asked. She leaned away from him but didn't let go.

"No, I don't want to stop."

"Me neither." She led the way to the bedroom.

Once there, he felt almost shy. He'd spent countless hours sailing shirtless yet when he took his off in front of Dag, he felt self-conscious. Until he felt her hands on his chest and the need surged for his skin to be against hers.

Clothing gone, he revelled in the feel of her against him. He pulled her onto the bed on top of him as he placed feverish kisses down her neck to her shoulders, stopping to suck one nipple into his mouth. Dag pushed into him—into his arousal—before she straddled him. With his mouth still on her nipple, he felt between her legs. She arched away from him, panting. Then he was in her.

He thrust up and she pushed back with her hips, leaning over him. Her hair trailed across his chest as her lips met his. Another thrust and another and then she tensed, clutching him, and he thrust one last time, stiffened, and held her tight as he shuddered into her.

Dag relaxed onto him, their bodies slick with sweat where they touched. He cradled her head against his shoulder as his heart rate slowed. He kissed her forehead and blew out a contented breath. Dag feathered one hand across his chest then she propped her head up and met his gaze. A slow smile spread across her lips, and he felt his own smile in response. She reached up to kiss him—a long slow kiss. He was still in her, and she raised her eyebrows at his arousal. He shifted until he was on top, her legs wrapped around his waist.

They lacked the urgency of the first time, but soon the gentle thrusts became stronger as the heat built up between them. Dag gasped, and he pushed into her one last time, straining at his release.

He rolled off her and lay on his side staring at her profile in the dim light that edged in around the curtain. She turned her head, and he gently tucked her hair behind her ear.

"I'm so glad we didn't stop," she said. He nodded—words were beyond him—and smiled, wondering if his Trait, his Luck, had anything to do with Dag being here in his arms, sharing her body and a bed with him.

He tightened his grip on her and she sighed. He watched her eyes droop closed and then her breathing evened out as she fell asleep. Leaving him staring at her profile as the room darkened.

CHAPTER 19

THE STABLE DOOR rattled, and Joosep covered his eyes against the expected glare of a lamp. He was past caring who was coming in, just as he was past expecting anyone to bring him water.

"Drink this."

He opened his eyes to see a clay mug held in front of him. It was shoved against his face and water spilled out onto his cheek. He grabbed the mug and sipped, careful not to drink it too fast, before squinting up at the woman.

"Go on, drink it all," she said. "Grand Freeholder says you need to be recovered, at least a little."

He took another sip. "Why?" he croaked. She didn't answer, not that he expected her to. But the last thing he wanted was to be useful to Tarmo Holt. To his shame, he wasn't strong enough to turn down the water.

Once he'd emptied the mug, he was handed a piece of hard cheese. He chewed on it, wondering what the woman would do if he refused. Holt needed him for something, so he had some value, at least. It had been a day since he'd been asked about Arnor. Did that mean his assistant had been found?

"On your feet," the woman said.

Joosep tried to stand up, but he was too weak so the woman grabbed his arm by the elbow and towed him out of the stable.

His eyes watered at the onslaught of light, although once he could see, he realized that there were only three lamps on a small wooden desk. Tarmo Holt stood on the far side of the desk, a pistol in his hand.

"Sit down," Holt said. He waved the gun at a chair that sat in front of the desk. "And sign that note."

Joosep sat down. A piece of paper was laid out on the desktop, a quill and ink pot beside it. "What am I signing?"

"A message to your Intelligencer," Holt said. "In response to a note that was delivered this evening. The woman is waiting for a reply." He leaned over the desk. "Since you're so reticent about naming your Intelligencers, you're going to tell this one to come back here so I can meet him or her myself."

Joosep scanned the note. It was for Calder. "All right," he said. The minute Calder saw that this wasn't Joosep's handwriting he'd know that something was wrong. He picked up the quill and dipped it into the ink. Holt was allowing him the chance to send a message after all.

"Wait!" Holt frowned. "Why are you agreeing to this so easily?"

Joosep put the quill down and simply stared at the paper in front of him. Without reading the original note, he couldn't be sure what Calder's plans were.

Holt paced in front of the desk, keeping the pistol pointed at Joosep. "He or she will know, won't they?" he said. "Because you didn't write the reply or because it should be in code?"

He stared at the note, ignoring Holt. Why the explanation about Inger Lund not being trained as an Intelligencer? Had the note Calder sent contained a message from Dagrun? Were she and Calder working together?

"Tell me!" Holt pounded the desk with one hand. "Why are you so willing to sign this?"

The truth wouldn't hurt him, he decided. "The note is not in my hand," Joosep said. "So it will not be trusted. Even with my signature."

"Skit!" Holt grabbed the note from the desk and crumpled it up. "Paper!" he called, and the woman scurried out the door. A few moments later, she returned with a few sheets of paper. She presented them to Holt, who pulled one piece and slapped it down on the desk.

"Write exactly what this said," he said. He put the crumpled note on the desk.

"All right," Joosep said. He smoothed out the original note and started copying it, word for word. He smudged a couple of letters, then signed it, before sitting back to let the ink dry.

Holt leaned forward and compared the old and new notes. He nodded. "Take him back," he said to the woman. "And give him one cup of water each day."

Joosep stood up and meekly followed the woman back to his cell. Sitting in the dark, he smiled. He'd been able to get a message out to Calder—and Dagrun if they were together. He might not live—he'd been prepared for that—but at least now he knew he wouldn't take this secret to the grave.

DAG TRAILED A hand along Calder's chest, heading under the covers. She touched him—he was already erect—and he sucked in a breath. It was morning, late morning, she guessed but they hadn't actually slept much the night before.

"When's Solvig due back?" she asked, even though she knew their host wasn't expected back until tomorrow midday at the earliest.

"Why? Do you have plans?"

"I certainly do." She gripped him before swinging a leg over his hips. "But they don't include Solvig."

"Are you going to tell me what your plans are?" He nuzzled her neck.

"How about I show you?" Dag seated herself on him, slowly sinking down until he was embedded in her. She leaned down and kissed him, her tongue dancing with his. "How do you like my plans so far?" she whispered in his ear.

"Brilliant," he said. "Feel free to include me in any future plans." Then he pushed up and she was lost to the passion.

DAG LAY HALF across Calder, her head on his shoulder. Her stomach growled, and he laughed, causing her head to bob up and down.

"We should eat," Calder said. He kissed her and shifted around until he was sitting.

"You know I can see right through you," she said. "My Trait tells me that keeping me fed is all part of some secret strategy."

Reluctantly, she sat up—she didn't want to leave the bed—didn't want to deal with any problems the real world had in store.

"Not so secret." Calder stood up and started searching the small room. He tossed her shirt and trousers at her—she didn't actually remember getting out of them last night—before he sat on the bed and pulled his own trousers on. She ran a hand down his back, enjoying the feel of his muscles under her hand.

He leaned over and kissed her. "I need to keep your strength up for later." He stood up. "I'll check the stew. It might need more water."

She watched him leave—he hadn't bothered with a shirt, and why should he, when she'd probably just take it off him soon enough.

She was tired, but deliciously so. It took her a few minutes to dress and make her way to the living area. Calder was stirring the stew when she stepped up behind him and wrapped her arms around him. She pressed her cheek into the bare skin of his back.

"Water is heating for tea," he said, turning around. "And stew will be ready in an hour."

"You are very domestic," she said. If it had been up to her, they'd have been gnawing on salt fish until Solvig returned. She sighed and left him to sit in a chair.

"I like to eat," Calder said. "The best way to make sure I do is to know how to cook. And it comes in handy." He sat down across from her and laid his hand on the table. She put her own in his, staring at the way their fingers—his dark and hers light—intermingled. "Nothing makes sailors appreciate you faster than making their meals taste better."

"Ah, so it's not all Luck?"

"No," he replied. "Since I've never tried to force my Trait, I've always relied on other things. Although even then Luck sometimes intervenes."

"How so?" She'd always had times when she'd forced her Trait to work; so not doing so seemed alien.

"The first time I cooked on a ship it was because the cook slipped and broke his arm," he said. "Him falling? That was Luck. I volunteered to be his hands because I knew that it was a job no one else wanted to do. But then—Luck—I found a selection of spices that the cook had no idea how to use. It made me everyone's favourite new sailor." He grinned. "And allowed me to be trusted enough to get the information Joosep had asked for."

"How old were you?"

"Sixteen. It was my second assignment."

"Sixteen!" She was shocked. She'd known Calder had arrived at the Hall young but that young? "You were six when you were recruited?"

He sighed. "I told you about my twin." She nodded. "Joosep heard about his death and my miraculous survival. He arrived a month or so later. I've asked him how he knew what my Trait was, but he never gave me a good answer."

"He wouldn't be able to," Dag said. "He knew because of his Trait. Can you describe how your Luck works?" He shook his head. "I don't think any of us know how or why Traits work. Not even Joosep."

"Hmm." Calder pulled his hand from hers, and for a moment she was worried that she'd offended him. But he simply made tea and brought it back to the table.

"Joosep doesn't talk about Traits to anyone," Calder said. "And since we all work alone, none of us talk about our Traits amongst ourselves."

"Until us," Dag said. "Inger and I talk, but it's more about how to manage her Trait so she doesn't get into trouble." She groaned. "That came out wrong, but that's probably how she sees it. All I want is for her to stay safe." She ran a hand through her hair. She'd failed in that, because now Inger was with the pirates.

"We'll find her," Calder said. He reached for her hand, but now his touch wasn't comforting, and she pulled her hand away.

The mood was broken, and no matter how much she told herself that she was allowed to have this time with Calder, that it didn't affect the search for Inger, she felt guilty about it. Her sister was with dangerous people who had almost hanged her. How could she possibly have forgotten that?

Calder sensed the change in her mood but didn't press her on it, instead allowing her to drink her tea and eat her stew in silence. After that, she headed to the bedroom. Ignoring the evidence of the past night's passion, she curled up and fell asleep.

"Dag, wake up."

Someone shook her shoulder—Inger? But no, Inger was still being held by the pirates.

"Calder?" She sat up. It was dark but some light filtered in from the hallway, outlining Calder. "What's wrong?"

"Solvig's back early. You need to come."

She slipped out of bed—she'd fallen asleep in her clothes—and padded out to the living area. Calder paced the small room—which frightened her—and Solvig sat at the table. Three lamps threw shadows on the walls.

"Did you get a note from Joosep?"

"Yes," Calder said. He pointed at a piece of paper that sat on the table. "Something's wrong, but I need you to confirm it."

"All right." She sat at the table and pulled the paper over to her. "*Where are you?*" she read out loud. "*Return to the Hall immediately. Have supplied coin. Bring DL with you.*" She looked over at Calder. "You're right, something's wrong. This note was written by Joosep, but it doesn't sound like him."

"Solvig never met with him," Calder said. "And the coin he sent didn't contain a Pilalian baisa. But that's not everything. Solvig saw something else."

Dag dragged her eyes off the note—there was something there that she just couldn't quite see.

"Ghost ship," Solvig said. "I saw a ghost ship and a ghost, so I thought."

"What ship?" Dag asked confused. "What ghost?"

"It was the *Diamanto*," Solvig said. "It was dark but I recognized it; that ship was built right here on Lavais."

"It's the *Bright Breeze*," Calder said. "Overhauled to look like the *Diamanto*. It has to be."

"And the ghost?" Dag asked even though her Trait already knew."

"It was you," Solvig replied. "I saw your ghost on the *Diamanto!*"

"Inger!" Dag said. "It has to be her. This was close? The ship was near here?"

"It was sailing into the main Lavais harbour," Solvig said. "In the middle of the night."

"We have to leave," Calder said. "I think the pirates are taking the island. We have to leave right now."

"But Inger is here," Dag said. "I don't even have to go find her, she found me." But the pirates wouldn't welcome her, and they certainly wouldn't welcome Calder.

"Dag, come on, we need to leave." Calder crouched beside her, and she heard the panic in his voice. "We might not have even an hour before they arrive. We can figure out where to go later, maybe even the Hall, like Joosep's note said."

"No!" And then she realized what was troubling her about the note. "Not the Hall." She pulled the note over. Yes, now she could see it. "Joosep sent a message. See where the ink has smudged? These letters? H, E, L, D, H, O, L, T. Held Holt. Tarmo Holt has Joosep. We can't go to the Hall." And just like that, she realized that she'd made her decision. Just as Inger had chosen the pirates over her twin, Dag was choosing Calder—and the Intelligencers—over hers.

CALDER SHOVED THE boat away from the dock and hoisted the sail. It wasn't the boat they'd arrived in—Solvig had always said they wouldn't see that one again. This one was smaller and would be much slower. But it would hug the coastline in a way that the pirates—sailing a ghost ship that they wouldn't want seen in daylight—wouldn't be able to.

Dag sat facing him, but she was looking past him, at Lavais, where her sister was.

He'd thought he'd lost her just as soon as they'd found each other. When she'd shouted *no*, he'd been certain she was going to try to find Inger, that he would have to leave her behind. But then she'd shown him Joosep's hidden message. And he'd been relieved that she was coming with him.

But now they had two people to save: Joosep and Inger. Along with the Fair Seas Treaty Alliance.

THE END

Dag and Calder's adventures continue in 2019 with *Traits and Traitors.*

ACKNOWLEDGEMENTS

Thanks to everyone at Tyche Books – especially my editor Karley Hauser and publisher Margaret Curelas.

Biography

Jane Glatt loves that along with creating original worlds, writing fantasy allows her to indulge her curiosity about an eclectic group of subjects. So far she's researched synaesthesia, medieval guilds, tidal rivers, cities atop bridges, pirates and privateers, plants used for healing and the history of spying. For that last one she blames a visit to the International Spy Museum (yes it's a real place), in Washington D.C.

For news on Jane's future releases visit her website http://janeglatt.com/index.html and sign up for her newsletter.

www.ingramcontent.com/pod-product-compliance
Lightning Source LLC
Chambersburg PA
CBHW032122180726
48284CB00002B/656